LIFE ON SANDPAPER

D0507202

LIFE ON SAND-PAPER

YORAM KANIUK

TRANSLATED BY ANTHONY BERRIS

Series Editor: Rachel S. Harris

DALKEY ARCHIVE PRESS
CHAMPAIGN AND LONDON

Originally published in Hebrew as *Chaim Al Neiar Zchuchit*
by Yedioth Aharonoth, Tel Aviv, 2003
Copyright © 2003 by Yoram Kaniuk
Published by arrangement with the Institute for the Translation of Hebrew Literature
First edition, 2011

Library of Congress Cataloging-in-Publication Data

Kaniuk, Yoram.
[Hayim 'al neyar zekhukhit. English]
Life on sandpaper / Yoram Kaniuk ; translated by Anthony Berris. -- 1st ed.
p. cm.
ISBN 978-1-56478-613-5 (pbk. : acid-free paper)
1. Kaniuk, Yoram. 2. Authors, Israeli--Biography. I. Berris, Anthony. II. Title.
PJ5054.K326H2313 2011
892.4'36--dc22
[B]
2010038344

Partially funded by the University of Illinois at Urbana-Champaign
and by a grant from the Illinois Arts Council, a state agency

The Hebrew Literature Series is published in collaboration with the
Institute for the Translation of Hebrew Literature and sponsored by the
Office of Cultural Affairs, Consulate General of Israel in New York

The publication of this book was sponsored by
the Oded Halahmy Foundation for the Arts, Inc.

www.dalkeyarchive.com

Cover: design and composition by Danielle Dutton
Printed on permanent/durable acid-free paper
and bound in the United States of America

Dedicated to

Lee Becker (Kaniuk) Theodore
Gabriel Solomon (Gandy) Brodie
Charlie (Bird) Parker
Alfred Thornton Baker III

Author's Note

It isn't entirely incorrect to call this book a work of fiction, despite its being an account of my memories from a certain period of my life, and despite the fact that many of its characters might also appear in history books concerning those same years.

As Aristotle said, "It is not the function of the poet to relate what has happened, but what may happen—what is possible. . . . The poet and the historian differ [in that] one relates what has happened, the other what may happen."

There had been a war and I was wounded. When I got back I was remote and detached from everything, didn't speak for days and would draw on the walls because I'd killed people before I'd kissed a girl. We were drinking at Café Piltz with Menashke Baharav who played "The Battle in the Negev Plains" and I went out to the old boardwalk by the sea. I stood there and sensed a living thing nearby. A pungent, sweet fragrance. And I sneaked a look and there was a woman's silhouette. We moved toward one another gradually. Finally, without a word, we kissed. My leg was in a cast and I dragged myself along with her up the London Garden to the Excelsior, a so-called hotel for soldiers. We went up to the room where there was a narrow single bed and a few rotting apples. In the window was the sea. And a full moon. She shouted in German and kissed my boot thinking I was a Gestapo agent. She was oh-so-good and showed me what to do. In the morning we looked at one another. We couldn't just ask what's your name, what's yours. We stood on Ben-Yehuda Street eating pretzels and she looked at me lovingly and I at her, and I didn't know what to say and started walking north from Bugrashov Street toward my parents' house and the street filled up with carts, buses, bicycles, a few cars. I realized then that I wanted her, and she watched me, pained, from afar, turned around and walked away, defeated in my new country. I recalled the tang of distant places that came from her, her clothes that gave off a foreign fragrance. I tried to follow her but I was limping and she vanished into the morning noise, her eyes withdrawn. I loved a girl who'd previously been another man's girlfriend and had stopped loving him before he'd managed to die but was obliged to sit with his family, mourning as if she was still his girl. We used to slip away to the park to be together. She felt guilty and ended up leaving me, but then fell in love with a friend of mine.

It takes a lot of nerve to bang your head against the wall. These are the things I leave behind. Simcha begat Sarah, Joseph, and Alexander. Mordechai begat Moshe and Bluma. His great-grandmother, a Jewish queen, rode naked on a horse through the town so that salvation would come. In 1970, H. said: Danny's dead, Bill's dead, once again our generation is starting to die. Sarah, my mother, said at the old cemetery, when she went to visit her friends, that she remembered how, in May 1921, they'd brought Brenner and his comrades to the high-school building. They had been torn apart, mutilated, there were twenty-two of them. She said: I covered their disfigured bodies with sheets. They were buried together since it was impossible to tell who was who. Forgive me that this is my legacy to you.

I worked on an immigrant ship and was made fun of when I went to the museum in Naples instead of to "69," the best brothel in town. Outside they were selling little girls for ten cigarettes each. A young woman holding a little girl by the hand said: My sister. Clean. Shaved. Young. I gave her some change and went to the museum. The young woman prayed to the Madonna, behind whom a barefooted priest who'd collect horse manure for heating had placed an oil lamp, so that it would look like the image was weeping. In the museum they had the Pompeian Frescoes. I was hungry. A thin man with a huge pot tied to his belly was selling spaghetti. I asked for some. With or without, he asked. With, I replied. He pulled two bottles from his pockets, took a swig from each, gargled the mixture in his mouth, and sprayed it onto the spaghetti. I walked a short distance so he wouldn't see and threw the stuff away. Hordes of children sprang up and devoured it, even the newspaper wrapping. I took an antiquated taxi to my friends at "69," who laughed: A socialist has come to the heart of capitalist decadence. There was a naked woman there spinning around on a piano stool, and made-up girls for sale sat around making faces. A friend brought over a gaunt, frightened girl. This one, he said, has only been here since Tuesday. I took her and bought her some trinkets she'd been staring at in a shop window and then some shoes and a coat. The dollar was worth at least five hundred lira and we felt rich. I took her to a restaurant in Santa Lucia, one of the dozens of empty restaurants waiting for customers who never came. I fed her. She ate like a tigress. The waiters with their stained sleeves made chewing motions and I invited them to eat too. The chef came over and I invited him and his assistant as well. And also the owner, who sat like a commanding officer supervising everything, and they were all scared of him, but he was hungry too, so I asked him to join us. We drank wine. Mount Vesuvius gleamed in the light coming from some ship. I took her for a walk. She said, My name is Angelina, and asked for shoelaces. I bought them for her. She tied them together into a long string that she then tied to my wrist and said, I'm your dog, don't leave me. The immigrants were already on board. We launched the *Pan York* and Angelina cried at the port. Grandmother died. Grandfathers and grandmothers died. My parents, Moshe and Sarah, died. Friends died. A year in Jerusalem on the roof of an old monastery school. A huge tree in the courtyard. They said that St. Hieronymus once sat under it.

Then came a year in Paris. We painted. Café Le Dôme. A few affairs and the story with Flora. Why, of all things, was it the movie version of *Guys and Dolls*, which I saw in May 2002 in a building that's a year older than me on Bilu Street, and in which they sing "Luck Be a Lady Tonight," why was it that particular movie that triggered this book, this journey. At the opening of my first exhibition in 1952 at the Feigel Gallery on Fifty-seventh Street, New York, New York, a woman named Beulah I didn't know then but with whom I later became very close bought a painting. I was thrilled because I'd made two hundred dollars. I realized that if I'd sold one painting at the opening I'd sell many more over the two weeks of the exhibition. At the end of the evening there were ten of us left, maybe more. We were drunk on the sweet wine that Feigel, who'd discovered Kokoschka in Prague, had served the guests. I invited them all to a Lebanese restaurant that was usually almost empty. The owner, Anton, would come to the table, recommend things from the menu, take our orders, write them down meticulously, stand at the hatch in the kitchen wall, shout out the entire order, go into the kitchen, prepare the food, call out all the orders from the kitchen, then come out, take the tray he'd placed on the window ledge from inside, serve, and quietly go back inside to wash the dishes and, before his customers left, wipe the table. After we'd eaten I bought everybody tickets to *Guys and Dolls*, which was then ending its Broadway run after many years. I spent all the money I'd received for the painting. Life as a musical: funny, human, illusory, and at eleven-thirty at night we walked to Forty-second Street where there was a movie theater that screened comedies. There were convex mirrors in the foyer that distorted everyone who walked in. We were drinking from a bottle of bourbon that Cyril Johnson, the drummer, had bought. There was a huge Wurlitzer there, spitting sparks and with revolving arrows at the top, making exploding sounds and laughing horribly, and Cyril told it, I'm from Mars, what's a nice girl like you doing in a place like this? I don't remember which movie we saw, two movies actually, and I can't remember the second one either. It was cold and started snowing. We went home. Not that we really had homes. We sang "Luck Be a Lady Tonight" and then I made it to bed with or without someone but I can't remember that bit either.

In the morning I went to the drugstore on the corner of Sixth Avenue and Eighth Street. I ate eggs over easy and thought, who in the world could have invented a more original name for the stuff. There was an old man sitting there, already drunk, I could see how he was making an effort and failing to find his mouth with his hand and introduce a roll into it. I fed him. He asked for a cigarette, I gave him one and lit it. The jukebox was playing "Moonlight in Vermont." The guy said I was probably an awful artist. I told him about what had happened the night before because I didn't have anybody else to tell, since whomever it was who'd been or not been with me, shared or not shared my bed, had disappeared early in the morning, assuming she'd spent the night, and we hadn't had the chance to talk. The guy did his best to enjoy the story and asked how much I'd gotten for the painting and I said two hundred bucks and remembered that three years earlier in Paris, Katya Granoff, for whom Soutine was a religion, had shown a few of my paintings at her gallery on Rue de Seine. An American had bought one. Back then everybody used to sit in the Café Le Dôme with a glass of water and two coffees. Out of the blue I had thirty thousand francs, which back then amounted to a whole month's salary behind a desk. I walked over to a taxi parked in the middle of Boulevard Montparnasse. I got in and told the driver, Drive! I said it like a bigshot. He was surprised and asked where to. All day, I said. We drove. I saw Paris through the eyes of an American millionaire. I bought wine and cheese for the driver. He sang to me. He had a rough voice and a questionable ear but he was nice and polite. Every few hours I gave him some more money. We drove to Maxim's and went inside. They tried to stop us because we didn't look like their sort of clientele but Paris was impoverished then, there was one traffic light in the whole city, at the Trocadero, and I gave the maitre d' a hundred and the driver and myself sat down and for a few thousand more ate the most sumptuous meal of my life. The driver was euphoric and shouted to the other drivers as they passed us, America, America! We drove over the bridges, stopped at the Café de l'Opera and had coffee and pastries. Finally it was evening, we got back to Le Dôme, the guys saw me get out of the taxi, the driver hugged and kissed me. I went into the café and discovered that I didn't have a sou left for a cup of coffee. The man who bought my painting was a wealthy American who'd brought the first Cadillac the French had ever seen over from New York to Paris. He brought his wife and daughter, the tall Yolanda, as well.

The next day, Yolanda came for her father's painting. She saw my squalid room and spoke to the concierge who shouted at her, I've told him, I've got no blankets for him, he can cover himself with girls. Yolanda went to the épicerie and brought wine and food. She saw me as some starving artist out of the movies and we spent a day and a night together. Her body language was soft but angry as well. Retroactive anger, maybe. I sketched her in charcoal. Her father didn't know. Her mother did. Her mother had a sharp face, a short nose, luxuriant hair, eyes like an owl's. It wasn't long before she too took me to bed. I carried on for a few days alternating between mother and daughter. I wasn't particularly proud of myself but my conscience then was, as it remained for many years to come, weaker than my need to be with a woman, any woman, single, widowed, young or old. In the end they met in my room and there was shouting and tears, but they still conspired against the father, he agreed to buy another painting and drove his Cadillac around, taking pleasure in seeing the French people he despised, ever since he'd served in the US Army in Paris, admiring his car, while he called them all collaborators. I looked up Yolanda in New York. Like most of my women she was tall. She refused to see me, but her mother wanted to. For her I was a pale boy, Jewish, but different from her. Deep sorrow and lust and recklessness were in me, she said. We met once in a while in hotels that she chose and we'd curse at one another. She hated me and I loved being with her and she bought me three beautiful shirts and a warm coat and one day she vanished. The daughter wouldn't talk to me on the phone. In Paris there was Flora. She looked and moved like Arletty in *Children of Paradise*.

Arletty, the beautiful actress, was no saint, and at her trial staged by French hypocrites she angrily defended her relations with the Germans: "My heart belongs to France, but my ass is international." I went to a bistro in Montparnasse. Anyone who wasn't sad was kicked out. Flora seemed blind to her own beauty. I looked at her and she at me. A few days later I already knew that her name was Flora. She had a shy smile, but also a mysterious coldness about her, making her face a mask. Her eyes reflected this strange melancholy, and there was an embarrassing awkwardness between us. After a clumsy attempt at courting her, she saved our story from falling flat by ensuring that we'd stand embracing by the Seine. Afterward, in my room. She'd come in the daytime. At night she disappeared. All the while a Rolls-Royce would be parked by the house, and in it a grim-faced older man in a fur coat. The chauffeur in his cap would get out, raise his head, look at my window, and get back into the car. She said that the man was her fiancé. I understood that because of something that had happened a long time ago she now had to marry him. Again and again she asked me to order her to stay with me. She said there were secrets, dark intrigues, she spoke of beatings, of death, she sang some anthem, maybe Ukrainian, declared that she wished she didn't love me. She said something about a place where there was shooting. About hounds and the man who'd bought her. I didn't understand love because back in the youth movement in Zionist-Socialist Israel I'd learned that love was just something you either discussed or sang about. I didn't understand, how could I give her orders? I didn't understand those secrets threaded through the sewer mazes of her sinister history. I said that I couldn't love her and certainly couldn't give her orders. She asked me to teach her how to say "Ze'evi" in Hebrew, wolflike, and she learned how to say, "Thou shalt not muzzle the ox when he treadeth out the corn."

In Paris, 1950, the Soviet Union was a sort of religion. "Chips fly when you chop down trees," they'd say each time they heard about another half million people slaughtered by Stalin. Thorez, the man who'd lead the revolution in France; Stalin, the dove of peace, progressive culture, socialist realism; while Flora's religion was the Zodiac. Fatally deceived by degenerate capitalism whose day was surely coming. She suddenly came in wearing heavy clothes, a fur coat, patent-leather pumps, she spoke of fate, wealth as liberty, revulsion at the masses, contempt for the shirkers, she carried the stench of decay. Fear of black cats. Fear of sitting on a suitcase. She'd repeat the word Ze'evi over and over and the sexy Biblical verse I'd taught her, "Thou shalt not muzzle the ox when he treadeth out the corn." She said she had to have an answer, stood in the small attic room and said this was the moment for me to command her. I said, Are you out of your mind? You want me to debase another human being? Man is the image of Creation. She looked anxious and her eyes sparked contempt and then she pulled away from me. She'd come wearing heavy clothing but it was hot. July. She went down to rue de Rennes and started walking. The Rolls-Royce drove after her and she threw the fur coat inside. On seeing her from above I had an epiphany. I recalled Bialik's saddest poem: "From the window, a potted flower / gazes all day down at the garden / There in the garden are all its friends / while up here all alone it stands." In the revelation I smelled onion mixed with roses and I saw a bridal veil. I realized that I loved her. That I did understand after all. I understood that she was an ox that shouldn't be muzzled in my corn. I quickly went downstairs but she had vanished. I ran as far as Saint-Germain, and just like with the refugee girl in Tel Aviv by the sea, and like in *Children of Paradise*, in the tragic and unforgettable final scene when Jean-Louis Barrault loses Arletty in the crowd, I saw her and I shouted at her. A big colorful procession appeared from the direction of Saint-Michel. It was the 14th of July. She didn't hear and disappeared. I searched for her all over Paris, remembering her divine scornful look. Just like Arletty's. She didn't touch things. There was always air between what she held and the object itself. She loved submissively, but with anger.

Afterward, things happened. I saw Mané-Katz painting a Rubens-esque model and she was white, glowing, fat, and wearing a crucifix on her chest, sitting with her ass on a Torah ark curtain. The little man explained that it had been saved from a burnt synagogue in Lodz. I'm not religious but I hit him. The model yelled. A big black man came over and threw me out. I went to the sculptress Hanna Orlov who lived close to the Académie de la Grande Chaumière and had modeled my head and later cast it in bronze, and I told her about this. She laughed. She showed me a sketch by Modigliani that he'd given her himself with a dedication in Hebrew. The winter was harsh and I passed out because of my war wound. I was told to go to New York because there they were waiting to see their first Hebrew soldier. I had an Ordinary Seaman's certificate from the time I'd worked on the illegal immigrant ship, the *Pan York*. I boarded an Italian ship that flew a Panamanian flag carrying German farmers to Alberta in Canada. The work was tough. The sea raged. There were maybe twenty passengers in cabins because it was a cargo ship. The herd of German cows and bulls weltered in the hold. The crew, mainly Italians, stood on the bridge and pissed on the Germans who lay huddled together drunk on the deck, shouting. In the cabin next to mine there was an American girl returning from Paris after some frustrated love story. She licked chocolates and we lay next to the porthole and the waves crashed against the glass and this turned her on. She wasn't pretty but was also not not-pretty, she had a tattoo on her ass. She was one of those girls it's good with but are quickly forgotten, and she said she was from Minot, North Dakota. The story of the name Minot, she said, was that there were nine knotholes in the walls of the first log cabin and there were ten pioneers and the Indians were shooting at the cabin and one man shouted where's my knothole, where's *mi not*. I didn't see her again, but once she read a review of an exhibition of mine in the paper and sent me a photo of her with a man and five kids, and for some reason I wasn't sure whether it was her family or if she'd hired them. Maybe I'd been cruel to her and I remembered how indispensable she was up against the waves that couldn't come through the porthole. I reached Newfoundland. I found a job on a fishing boat sailing to New York and we docked at Hoboken, New Jersey.

Gandy Brodie who I'd met in Paris was waiting for me. In Paris he'd taken me to a jazz club called Chez Inez. The owner, Inez, was a singer and married to a Dane. Gandy used to draw caricatures of people, most of whom claimed they looked nothing like his drawings and so he'd give them their money back, but there were always a few too embarrassed to complain, so he earned a little bit.

It was there that I made my acquaintance with jazz. Gandy played me a Billie Holiday record and said that her voice was like dried-up water. I didn't know what that meant, but I liked it. He'd sent me a letter in Paris and on the envelope wrote: To Yoram Kaniuk, An Israeli Citizen in Paris. Said I should come. When I arrived he asked me how much money I had. Eight dollars and forty cents, I replied. He seemed disappointed because although he was a Jew he was one of the ones who think that every Jew, apart from him, is wealthy. We took a bus to Manhattan and from there, somewhere around 100 and Something Street, we walked. The sun was shining. It was a beautiful fall day. A pleasant aroma of roasting coffee and flowers and in every store and restaurant the jukeboxes played two songs, "Somewhere Over the Rainbow" or "Stormy Weather," and I felt I'd come home. I fell in love—unrequited love—with the city I'd live in for ten years. Gandy wore a colored scarf around his neck. He was a young, handsome man with straggly hair, gestures that were heavy but at the same time lankily elegant. Solomon Gabriel Brodie was born in the Bronx at a time when his father would take a belt, chew on it, and give it to his family to chew on and then, said Gandy, the good times ended and the Depression began. He was wild. Daring. He knew every haunt in New York, especially places where you could eat cheaply. He had affairs with old women who helped him out because he was an artist, and he also had some kind of mysterious relationship whose nature I never fathomed with a Japanese man, with whom he'd hide out for a few days every now and then. His best friends were jazz musicians. Before we met in Paris they'd have parties for him where they passed the hat for him to go to Paris, which he wanted to reach so badly. But after the parties he'd squander the money and put off his trip until the next party. And one day he did go. He reached Paris wearing overalls and the moment he disembarked he wanted to go home. That's when I met him. He said that after New York, Paris was like summer camp. He was called Gandy because he did a gandy dance, like the Chinese immigrants working themselves to death laying the American railroad tracks, who according to one explanation I heard learned it from a traveling Indian with a dancing monkey. Nobody in New York could do that dance like he did. Like a Chasid crossbred with a Greek country bumpkin. For a while he'd danced with Martha Graham but she said he should give it up because he was too heavy. Since then he painted. He didn't know how to paint but his paintings were like his dance, like his enthralling personality, filled with difficulties, desire. He'd knead the paints into some soft chaos, but with a sure hand, and daubed sand on his paintings and painted layer upon layer. Gandy was open, but at the same time he kept secrets about his past and he wouldn't talk much about it. Rumor said that he'd been in a fight once, that somebody had tried to kill him. People said he was a panhandler and liked to invite people to have a coffee or whiskey with him. We grew close and liked one another. He was my guide to the human and economic sewers of New York, every hidden corner, to the Mafiosi of Little Italy who liked to watch him dance and would throw money at him. Once he decided that he had to meet Charlie Chaplin. He took a Greyhound bus to Los Angeles, walked down Sunset Boulevard and found Chaplin's home. He knocked at the door and said, I'm Gandy Brodie from New York, and the butler slammed the door in his face. He turned around and went into the yard, feeling dirty from his long walk in the sun, and gave himself a shower with a garden hose he found there, and when he started brushing his teeth he was found by the police who'd been called by a neighbor because on Sunset you don't walk on foot or brush your teeth in backyards. Gandy was arrested and he said he was surprised by his arrest because he'd been brushing his teeth and had wanted to tell Chaplin something and that he was Gandy Brodie from New York. He returned to New York happy. Walking down the street with him was like going into a bar in a hick town with a population of two hundred. Everybody knew him. Someone would say, Hi Gandy, and he'd ask, Have you got five bucks for me, I'm pretty deep in the hole, and sometimes they'd give it to him. He didn't believe in work and so except for once a month, for a single day, he never worked in his life. He lived off things I didn't understand, he knew how to demand things from people because he was an artist. Gandy took me to Greenwich Village and sat me down on a bench in Washington Square and said he had to go and he'd be back later today or tomorrow. I sat there alone with the sack with my stuff I'd brought from Paris and waited. I didn't know a living soul and evening fell. Apparently I wasn't concerned.

A small yelping poodle rubbed against my legs. I stroked it. A young woman, I don't remember whether she was good-looking or not, was tied to the dog and I think her name was Gloria. At first she regarded me with contempt because I looked like a vagrant. I didn't have a cent to my name. I said something, then she said something, then I said to her, "Taketh me to thy pad," because at Chez Inez in Paris I'd learned what was then known as bop talk and which later became widely used American slang, but at the time was the secret language of jazz musicians. I'd studied *Julius Caesar* in high school and now I joined the two lingos together. My sentence turned Gloria on and she asked what a pad was and I explained that it's an apartment, she hadn't heard the term before and seemed amused. We talked for a while, I petted the dog again. She took me to her apartment near the park on Fifth Avenue, building number one, twentieth floor. She fed me. I told her stories, that I was from the desert and my mother was a shepherdess and that I rode camels, because camels, or so I'd been given to understand by Gandy back in Paris, work wonders in New York. I told her about a girl I'd loved in Israel who'd dumped me. I told her that my family were farmers in the Jordan Valley and they'd known the Patriarchs Abraham, Isaac, and Jacob personally. We got into bed and did what you do in bed and she said, You could pull a knife now and kill me, and I agreed that objectively speaking that was true. She said, You don't know me subjectively, and I said neither did she. She got up and walked backward with her eyes closed and didn't bump into anything in the bedroom filled with all kinds of clothes, tennis balls, chairs, and her intimidating little dog, and there were lots of shoes spread all over the beautiful wooden floor. There was an iron there too. The telephone was on the floor. Again she walked backward with her eyes closed and kept saying, Look how marvelous I am! She fell asleep but I still couldn't drop off myself and so I looked at her. She slept like a soldier at roll call, disciplined and obedient, her arms at her sides. But on her face I saw an expression of hopeless anguish. It hurt me. I had enough of my own. I almost left, but this was a new type of loneliness on the twentieth or thirtieth or fifteenth floor of a fancy building, loneliness I hadn't yet encountered. And then the phone rang, she jumped up, answered, her eyes flashed with hatred, she pushed twenty dollars into my hand and threw me out. There was a drugstore by her house on the corner of Eighth Street and Fifth Avenue. I went in and had breakfast and went back to the park and sat down on the same bench. Gandy came and didn't apologize. He said he knew I'd be there.

After that I stayed for two or three days in a room somewhere around there, went to the Mount Sinai Hospital and told them something or other and gave them a letter I'd been given in Paris in order to get a resident's permit for America that wasn't easy. I was treated at the hospital. Doctors came to see the wonder: an Israeli soldier who'd established a state in the face of seven Arab armies. They gave me a private room, my own nurse, a transistor radio. In the door there was an oval window through which the doctors peeped at the first Zionist soldier they'd ever seen. They operated on me until my leg and eye got better. Gandy came and stole a few bouquets from different rooms and the radio too, which he later sold and then bought me a coat, because the one from Yolanda's mother had been stolen, but the hospital brought in a new radio right away. Gandy got a nurse into a closet with him and the closet door locked and the nurse yelled and they had to call the maintenance man to get them out. After two weeks they discharged me. They passed the hat in the dining room and the whole medical team collected four hundred dollars for what they called minor expenses, and four hundred dollars was a lot of money back then. Gandy took half and I was supposed to begin the rest of my life with the other half. I found a room on Eleventh Street between Fifth and Sixth Avenue. The women's prison was next door. The women would stroll on the fenced-off roof of the sixth floor while their pimps down below shouted filthy endearments up at them. Somebody brought me an easel. With the money I was given at the hospital I bought canvases and I left a little for food and rent, which came to five dollars a week. I bought paints and brushes and started painting. That evening there was a knock at the door. The landlady came in and sat down. She was fat and younger than I am today but pity is timeless and never looks in the mirror. She had the face of a bulldog. She laid out everything I needed to know. Girls were forbidden, but on the other hand she didn't really check and every so often she raised the rent by a dollar but sometimes she didn't and that all depended. On what? You should know! I wasn't allowed to make any noise but she was half deaf. If I didn't pay on Monday of every week, I'd be thrown out. Keep the room clean. The bathroom and a public telephone are in the hallway and are shared by everyone on the floor. She left, and in came six young guys who it turned out also lived in the building and they brought me blankets, sweaters, shoes that they told me to try on, and I did, a scarf, a suitcase for my travels in case I had to escape the landlady, a typewritten page documenting the landlady's daily movements, how she got up at eight A.M., how she couldn't hear, how she always opened a window at nine A.M., how she peeked out whenever she heard the toilet flush, how at ten A.M. she went from room to room after the lodgers had gone out and rifled through their belongings, how at night she tried to stay awake until nine and always fell asleep in her chair, how at one A.M. she always had to go to the bathroom and then put on her nightgown because the heating would have switched off and how she would then just lay in bed. So if I had to clear out, well, now I had a suitcase and it would be best if my clothes and other belongings were always ready to be packed up quickly, and also I should keep her daily schedule handy so I would know when it was the best time to leave. We drank wine and talked. I was surprised by this warm welcome. Next morning Gandy took me to a drugstore and explained a few basic facts of life. First, to make a phone call all I needed was a dime. If I called from a public phone, dialed zero, and said, Sorry, wrong number, I'd get my dime back in the coin-return slot and could dial again for free. Gandy taught me how to eat for free at bars and weddings. He took me to a bar on Fourteenth Street. Spread out on the counter there were plates of sardines, tiny sandwiches, tomatoes, pretzels. I tasted them all. The place was packed all the time. Hordes of anxious people who needed a drink. A tired, sullen, and impatient bartender hurried over and Gandy couldn't decide whether he wanted Beefeater with mocha or a whiskey sour but with Canadian whiskey, and all the while he was wolfing down huge amounts of sardines and hardboiled eggs and putting whatever other food he could lay hands on into a paper bag and saying I'm sorry, and the bartender finally lost his patience and went to serve somebody else and came back and Gandy still couldn't make up his mind if he wanted Bacardi on the rocks and then remembered that he actually was late for something and had to leave and the bartender lost his temper but there were more than forty guys sitting there shouting at him and he forgot. A few years later Gandy accused me of teaching some Israeli friends the trick with the dime and the wrong number because the phone company, instead of returning dimes, started to return nine one-cent stamps that came out of the coin return slot, but who wrote letters back then?

We began showing our paintings on Greenwich Avenue. Gandy would dance in front of the paintings to attract attention. I stood to one side. We sold a few sketches and we sometimes painted the young girls whose resolves were weakened by the anguish that Gandy expressed so picturesquely by rolling his eyes and raising his long lashes all the way up to his eyebrows. But that wasn't enough to make a living. I started using enamel paints because they were cheaper. I painted on the backs of used canvases. Before Christmas we painted greeting cards that we unsuccessfully displayed in Rosetta Reitz's legendary store on Greenwich Avenue. At Jewish weddings I learned how effective it was to say just a few words of Hebrew, which attracted warmhearted attention and when anybody asked me if I was from the bride's side I had to say I was from the groom's side, drink fast and eat fast and leave. I learned where to get cheap meatball-and-spaghetti meals in various, almost secret locations. New York was wonderful to me and to improve my English I read detective novels by Ellery Queen, Dashiell Hammett, and Rex Stout. I'd sit with a dictionary, try to make sense of the English, learn the words, practice. Gandy and I argued about painting.

Together with the painter Larry Rivers we were chosen to be the protégés of the critic Meyer Schapiro. Following numerous arguments I had with Rivers about abstract expressionism and for reasons of his own he stopped painting abstracts and began doing nude portraits of his ex-wife's mother. But Gandy didn't side with Rembrandt, Grünewald, and Hooper, Gandy favored Mondrian,

Motherwell, and Jackson Pollock. He took me to Hans Hoffman's school because it was only from that point that I'd be able to scale the lofty mountain of art. I hated that stuff. I said that Hoffman was a false guru. People made pilgrimages to see him. Hundreds of artists did what was known as action painting in his studio. Anybody who didn't paint that way was condemned. Even Larry Rivers who years later would become one of the truly great American artists. I brought some paintings I'd done in Paris. It was 1951. I entered the big room that was Hoffman's temple. There were hundreds of artists outside painting the exact same painting. They all seemed pretty agitated and daubed their canvases with controlled anger, rounding on and assaulting their canvases with passionate expressions on their faces, stamping on them, slashing them, spraying paint, they looked like a tribe of savages, and I was ushered into the temple. Hans Hoffman was sitting in a tall chair like a rabbi. He wore a huge turban. Spoke with a German accent. He looked at me aggressively, with some contempt, even pity. Gandy was trembling and began fiddling with his scarf and Hoffman looked at my paintings for a while and handed down his verdict: He's either too much of a painter or not a painter at all. I didn't really understand this but on our way out Gandy explained that it was a compliment, that what he meant to say and didn't was that I was a painter but in the wrong way.

Days passed. I painted. Gandy came and went. An Israeli woman came by and brought me money from her aunt who'd heard about me from one of her friends. I sat in the drugstore on the corner of Eighth Street and Sixth Avenue and next to me was a stern-faced man with deep-set eyes beneath beetling brows. He was drunk and looked at me and suddenly laughed. I asked what was funny and he said, America is drowning and you've come here to die with it, my name's James Agee, a writer! I didn't know who he was and the man went on for hours about America being a terrible, insidious civilization whose end was near. He tried to sing me a song, but was really just reciting it, about two airplanes in the sky that meet and the American pilot says I've destroyed the Eastern hemisphere and the Russian pilot says I've destroyed the Western hemisphere, and they chorus together: What will happen when the fuel runs out? I liked his loneliness. He was the most serious film critic in the United States. During the Depression he wrote a book about poverty in the South that was banned for a long time. He gave me a rare copy of *Let Us Now Praise Famous Men* with photographs by Walker Evans. Agee also wrote one of the most beautiful American novels, *A Death in the Family*, and from time to time we met on his regular corner after a night of drinking. There was a concentrated, melancholic seriousness to him and he would say things that weren't always connected to each other and then would laugh at what he'd said, get up and hop around the drugstore on one leg, describing America as Rome in its decline. He refused to look at paintings by someone like me, a colonialist from Palestine, he didn't remember my name but was happy when I showed up. I saw a firm but generous Calvinist sincerity in him. He was filled with enthusiasm but wasn't excited by his own enthusiasms. He spoke of his heroes, Mother Jones and Eugene V. Debs who organized the railroad workers. His words tasted of faraway torments. We used to walk the streets late at night and he would be awake and asleep at the same time. Behind all the bombastic rhetoric with which I was already familiar from my time in the youth movement he had a talent for awkward but precise storytelling and knew how to describe doorknobs, the features of policemen, the smashed face of a black child, and talked a lot about Africa, which he'd never visited and which in his view was the future of humankind, because humankind had begun there in the Garden of Eden until the white man destroyed it and trampled over the continent, and maybe that's why he later wrote the screenplay for *The African Queen*.

An apartment on Fifth Avenue and Tenth needed a painter. I went there and said I had housepainting experience from Paris. Following Gandy's instructions I said I'd painted the home of Baron de Rothschild, because in fact I'd seen, with a friend, the walls and the colors of the Rothschild palace and I'd thought about what Lincoln had said, that if the Lord had money, He'd surely live there. I painted the apartment. I tried my luck with the lady of the house and she said I was insolent and while she didn't actually punish me she rejected my advances and laughed a bitter selfish laugh whenever I looked at her. In the evenings Gandy and I would go to Birdland to hear some jazz. Jazz was never really popular in America. Years later George Shearing who wrote "Lullaby of Birdland" told me that he was flying someplace or other and the pilot recognized him. They landed for a short layover. The passengers got out for some fresh air. The pilot asked Shearing, who was blind, if there was anything he could do for him. Shearing sat down in the cockpit and asked the pilot to take his guide dog out for a short walk. The pilot took the dog and when the passengers came back they saw a blind man in the cockpit, and ran. I tried to fathom how Gandy managed to make a living but I couldn't and mentioned to him that my money was running out and he talked to somebody at Birdland and the guy, I no longer remember who he was, sent us to Minton's Playhouse in Harlem. I met Charlie Parker, I heard him play. He was the world's first black cowboy. Later I learned that he collected pistols of the kind you see in Westerns, Hopalong Cassidy was his hero. He made a religion of roasting chickens, loved model railroads, and dreamed of driving a gold-plated Cadillac. In the midst of all the filth around us I sensed a primeval shyness in him. He was a huge and intimidating sentimentalist and the first time I heard him I felt like I was seeing God die. When he played a song and his high forehead was covered with sweat, the music searched for itself between his hands playing the saxophone, and I heard the echo of Negro funerals from the place where jazz was born, rejoicing and laughing when another black man had died, and my grandfather's prayers as well. I told Charlie Parker about the Rabbi of Liadi. I explained that during Napoleon's siege of Moscow there was a violent debate among the Jews as to whether Napoleon's victory would be good or bad for their community. Rabbi Israel of Kozienice wanted Napoleon to win while the Rabbi of Liadi did not. It was decided that they both should go to the synagogue at the same time and whichever one of them was first to blow the shofar would be considered the winner of the argument. The Rabbi of Kozienice arrived at the same time as the Rabbi of Liadi but was the first to start blowing the shofar, so the Rabbi of Liadi snatched the notes from the Rabbi of Kozienice's shofar and thus, from a distance of nine hundred kilometers, decided Napoleon's fate in Moscow. Bird said that any jazz musician who doesn't go and turn jazz into some ice queen to be worshipped from afar like that Dave Brubeck guy ought to know how to snatch notes from a shofar. Outside everybody was playing the numbers and losing loads of money to the black pros all dressed to the nines in their flashy suits and magnificent ties. Bird liked to see Jimmy Slyde beating Napoleon in Moscow with his tap dancing.

One night some time later we were walking down Fifth Avenue. By the Olivetti store, on a concrete pedestal, was a typewriter. Opposite we could see big buildings with the lights on and hundreds of women's asses, bent over polishing the floors in the neon light. The avenue was empty. We put some paper into the machine and Bird dictated me a letter. A cop came and complained that there were no crimes committed around there. It had been like that every night for a year now, and his wife laughed at him because every other bastard at the station had a few crooks pinned like medals to his chest and their wives were teasing his wife because her husband had nothing. Minton's Playhouse was on 117th Street, between Lennox and Seventh Avenue, not far from the Savoy Ballroom and the Apollo. Late at night they let musicians whose licenses had been revoked because of drugs play there. A lot of people loved to come listen. Ordinary people off the street. Whites. Blacks. Hookers. Pimps. And police officers. I got a job washing dishes and waiting tables, taking orders from a black man named Andy. They liked having a white boy washing dishes for them. I was young and they dressed me in dark clothes so I'd look even whiter. They bought the clothes at the pawnshop on the corner and for two months I lived in a room just above the club. I had a half-Japanese half-black girlfriend who lived across the street and would make up little voodoo dolls. She'd lay me down on my stomach and walk barefoot over my back, bending her toes, and I felt ashamed at seeing her act like a kind of slave. She was beautiful, but like Flora she was just waiting for me to give her orders. Billie Holiday made up a song called "Yo" for me—that's what they called me—"Yo's Blues." But I don't want to talk about myself. Jazz flowed into me. The sad humor of the musicians. Billie Holiday reached for notes and sang them as if she were weaving a sad carpet and she'd take me on walks and I talked and she listened or maybe she didn't, and said she didn't understand that crap. We kissed. She said she'd had better kissers. I was there and she wanted to kiss somebody and I was nearest and I was talking and making a fool of myself. She was lost and looked like an abused bird. They told me they called her "Lady Day" because when she was a waitress she used to bend over to take people's money and they'd see her breasts and say: *Lady*. She was a vanquished queen who refused to relinquish her kingdom, even in the gutter. I met her years later at Tony Scott's, the clarinet player. She sang "Mein Yiddishe Mama" for me. Nobody could sing it like her. She published an autobiography that opened with the words: "Mom and Pop were just a couple of kids when they got married. He was eighteen, she was sixteen, and I was three."

Bird liked me and there was Max Roach and tap dancing, and there was Ben Webster who every week would pawn his sax and Bird and I made him reclaim it and then they'd play together. Crazy Bud Powell would join them. His head was fucked up from all the beatings he'd taken because of the color of his skin. He'd get up onto the piano and crow Cock-a-doodle-doo and then play and everybody would cry at the way his notes would hit you in the gut. Bertrand Tavernier's movie *'Round Midnight*, starring Dexter Gordon—who'd also join in sometimes—was partially based on the life of Bud Powell. Powell went to Europe, climbed trees, came back, went again, wanted love but there wasn't any. I remember dragging him home but I can't remember where.

Lady Day kissed me and hated me because I wasn't cruel and didn't hit her or shout or take her money, I was too innocent for her, too clean, not a pimp, I talked to her about Milton's poetry and other poets I liked and painting, she liked it but it didn't really interest her. She sang, Hush now, don't explain, you're my joy and pain, my life's yours love, don't explain; and that's how it is, she told me, a flower doesn't explain itself, fire doesn't explain itself, and love doesn't explain itself. She loved like she talked, thought I was really just trying to butter her up and wasn't interested myself in whatever it was I was saying about Rembrandt or Vermeer, back then I was trying to figure out where the light in Vermeer's paintings came from, what it was about that trick of his that made his work so appealing, and she didn't really have anything to say on the subject, she thought she was unworthy of talk like that. For her I was a phony from a world she wanted to live in, but she'd missed the boat. And sometimes at four or five in the morning we'd go to a small club, where a fat black man called Slim Gaillard played. Slim would wait for Bird and Lady and told me that I was white trash, but sweet. He played with his huge hands downside-up; he had fingers like frankfurters and his fingernails touched the keys and for an entire hour he sang a song that nobody has ever made sense of, "Cement Mixer (Puti Puti)," and I plunged headfirst into three or four ecstatic months of fast painting, new colors, I started mixing oils and enamels, I learned to paint jazz, think jazz, breathe jazz, feel the beat, the bebop. I'd think of a double bass and feel the rhythm coursing through me.

Minton's was one long party. People hardly ate there. They liked to laugh, cry, and drink. I'd mainly wash glasses. They wanted me to circulate between the tables so that the clients could see the white waiter from Jerusalem—Tel Aviv didn't mean anything to them. The hookers sat with their arms around each other and ordered Bacardi or scotch with milk and flirted with me. They said I was what was left for Bird between the notes. The cops were mostly drunk. The musicians went wild competing with each other. The whites in the audience sat mesmerized and everybody looked at them as if they were counts doing them the honor of visiting a Harlem whorehouse. I served them and when they thought of it they even paid me. Luckily an ancient black woman across the street made me a meal a day in exchange for my stories about Jerusalem and the Jordan River and there was a kind of a dull golden tinge to this deceit. The musicians gave themselves noble titles, they loved monarchy, pomp, dressing elegantly: Billie was Lady Day, Lester Young was Prez, Ellington was Duke, Basie was Count, and Nat Cole was King. They greeted each other the way they'd seen in movies about English royalty. I was a message sent out to the entire world: Here in the asshole of creation the real flowers bloom, and a white sack of shit from the Holy Land of Jesus, Moses, and Abraham—they've got him in their pocket. They are his intimate friends and he makes them beautiful. They complimented me. Their kindness was unconditional save for the fact that they decided I had to serve them drinks devotedly. They appreciated that more than I realized since I thought they were actually doing me a great honor. They didn't want to see my paintings and drawings, except for Bird who'd come up to see them. Gandy would show up, the hookers wanted me to be their baby, but while the music and the atmosphere were bewitching, the women weren't, even though they were melancholy. The Japanese voodoo lady found somebody else and left. After the girls stopped kidding around in the club they were dragged out by their pimps, and some time later crawled back inside, all black and blue. Then they would be called "queens" and had drinks on the house and only the cops and the tougher detectives would dare to mess with them. I used to eat with the musicians at Jimmy's Chicken Shack where we had chicken and coleslaw or a steak that they held with tongs and seared with a blowtorch and I said that one day I was going to write because painting was beneath contempt and Ben Webster asked me what I'd write and I said a book that would be called *The Future of God*, though I wasn't at all sure He had a future.

I had an evening off and went over to Minton's bar above the club. Ben Webster was there. A tall woman in a green baseball cap who'd arrived in a limo asked him questions about jazz. Her chauffeur was waiting for her in the limo, looking straight ahead though there was nothing to see straight ahead. Ben was drunk and flat broke and for every drink she bought him he answered a question, as if he was some kind of jazz historian. He dropped names like Jelly Roll Morton, Mezz Mezzrow, Fats Waller, King Oliver, he introduced me as a Doctor of Jazz, the youngest professor in Berlin. Then he told her that there was a jam session at the Five Spot and the woman asked Ben—who hadn't been sober since his baptism and probably not even then—she asked if you had to suffer in order to play jazz. Suddenly he seemed jovial. He looked at and said gleefully, Sure. Suffering's the only way. You have no idea how much. If you want to play you have to find suffering and use it. He asked her to write all this down because it was important, and she started writing and he said: The first thing you have to remember is that all this jazz stuff is shit. But you have to remember too that we're all suffering. Just suffering? We're lost, and you should make a donation so it'll be easier for us to suffer, because with money in our pockets and booze in our blood, suffering is much more pleasant. We all got into the limo and drove down to the Village. Waiting at the Five Spot were Dizzy and Max Roach and Miles Davis and Bird. Ben introduced the tall woman as an authority on jazz from Memphis, Tennessee. In the corner sat five Italians in yellow camel-hair coats with their guns bulging under their vests, and then the session began. The Italians cried and their tears were so big you could hear them splashing on the floor. They wept and wiped their eyes with handkerchiefs. Then they looked out the window and seemed upset. They went outside for a few minutes and burned the chauffeur's balls with a blowtorch because they thought he looked suspicious. Then they bought everyone roast chicken, French fries, coleslaw, and Cokes. Ben began playing. Bird admired him, he said, That's some sound! That's something! Dizzy charged from the side with his crooked trumpet. Bird said that Dizzy had the best phrasing in the business. Even Max Roach, who earlier had been staring into space, grabbed his sticks, threw them into the air, furrowed his brow, and started drumming. I could sense how they were building a complete and harmonious composition out of improvisation, variation, I could sense what the music was intending to become. Bird started playing opposite Ben Webster and then Miles Davis joined in. The audience was silent. The tall woman said, Jazz sounds like the night. As close as you can get to prayer. Everybody looked at her and she didn't dare open her mouth again. Dizzy, who Bird said was the architect of the style, stopped playing and so did Max Roach. Dizzy yelled: Now it's war! There were three saxes left, Bird, Miles, and Ben Webster: the Father, the Son and the Holy Spirit. The three of them started sweating and playing with screeching love. They began with "Cherokee" and "A Night in Tunisia" and moved on from there. The Italian gangsters wept, each musician tried to cut the other two but still wanted to be loved by his friends. A war for kisses. Three musicians trying to reach out and touch their own edges over the abyss of their incompetence like dogs sneaking out and risking their lives just in order to piss and mark their territory. This is love, yelled one of the Italians zealously and pulled out his gun and fired into the air and then he turned pale and shouted: Pure genius! And when there was a moment of silence Bird or Ben would take this silence and put it into their sound. Bird seemed angry and kissed Ben and took his notes from him. The tall woman sat there openmouthed and one of the Italians stuck a bottle of Coke into it and she drank up without touching the bottle with her hands and everyone looked at her and she whispered, I've got teeth of steel, and one of the gangsters yelled, Just don't suck my cock, and she laughed and the bottle fell to the floor and broke. Each of the three wanted to beat the others but also to lose the battle. Bird suddenly seemed to move apart from them, everything was forgotten, he hated everyone and their mothers too and he played a long solo until Ben and Miles laid down their musical weapons and seemed astounded and embarrassed and went over to kiss Bird but he pushed them away and went out in tears. There was a difficult silence. The woman got up and put a thousand dollars in Ben's hand and said, That's for everyone, thank you, and she drove away. I went outside, Bird was standing there crying. He played "Hava Nagila" for me and said, Miles will win in the end and I'm sorry for Ben, but I'm not sorry for myself.

For two years I continued going to Minton's even after I'd stopped working there. Gandy found us a club in the Village called the Village Vanguard owned by Max Gordon. It was there that many American performers got their first break. He owned another club uptown, the Blue Angel, and that's where the big money and the fame were. Art and beginnings and love were at the Village Vanguard. That's where you'd practice and get discovered. To get the audience warmed up, Gandy was tasked with bringing a few artists in every evening, we got a meal and a drink and a few dollars for applauding enthusiastically and getting the rest of the audience to join us. I moved into a room on Twelfth Street. I borrowed money, I don't remember from whom. On Saturdays I'd go up to Minton's and make a few extra bucks, and listen to Billie Holiday sing "Yo's Blues." Sometimes there were fights: people who ran out of white powder tried to steal money. Outside, cold and tough and merciless, stood the pushers. I felt at home in the Village and I realized that there were two New Yorks, one went up to Fourteenth Street and from there, with the exception of Harlem, lay America. Flannel suits. College students with crewcuts. All the Catchers in the Rye. The world. The system. The lie. The money. Down here, below the prime meridian of Fourteenth Street, there was anger. There was the future. People wore dungarees you could only buy at two Army & Navy stores, one on Twenty-third Street and the other on Thirty-fourth. Somebody bought me dungarees or Levi's, today they're called jeans. I had to sit in a hot bath for an hour just to get the pants soft enough to move and I spent another few days feeling like I was walking around in a suit of armor. The dancers were there, the painters, the writers, the poets, the bohemians, there was an Italian café on MacDougal Street, the only one in New York then, and there were Italian restaurants in Little Italy, in each of which sat a Don surrounded by hardened young toughs. If the Don liked you they'd feed you pasta for nothing. I became friendly with Robert De Niro Sr. who was a proud handsome gentleman and every now and then we'd walk together from Washington Square to West Broadway and Sullivan Street, sometimes with his little boy who later became an actor. He wasn't a successful or well-known painter. He was well liked but nobody understood the elegance of his paintings because he had found a way of incorporating the Italian Renaissance into modern art as though Picasso or Pollock had never happened. People refused to acknowledge him as an artist. I liked his paintings more than those by some of the bigger names. Unlike some of them, he wasn't a sham. He didn't paint wallpaper like Pollock. De Niro would never decorate his canvases with careless, soulful splashes, making simple decorations like Motherwell and the others. At the artists' club on University Place I came to blows with Franz Kline whose paintings I didn't like at all because he'd brutally criticized De Niro.

At night we continued applauding for Max Gordon and launched numerous performers on their careers. Later, maybe after a year, we'd already made a name for ourselves as claqueurs, and were invited to a show by Billy Strayhorn, the sweetest of men, who was Duke Ellington's arranger and wrote my favorite song, "Lush Life," and who was short and gay, and like Gandy had gone to Paris and come back right away. He was a composer and had a pained smile and died young, but was doing Ellington's arrangements then and writing songs like "Take the 'A' Train." He and Duke worked together at the Paramount Theatre on Times Square, appearing with his band during the intermission between two movies. Duke asked Strayhorn to bring us along because the career of Frank Sinatra who was performing with him then was taking a near-fatal nosedive. The audience hated him. He'd left his wife and people jeered at him because he'd been cheating on her with Ava Gardner. After taking a break, full of sorrow and fear, he was trying to make a comeback. We went to the theater. Backstage we saw Sinatra with a contemptuous but defeated expression on his face. He gave us shots of rye and a plate of spaghetti with meatballs and Duke played. Duke had about two hundred suits backstage that he would change every hour, and after he'd finished playing he introduced Sinatra and invited him to come on stage. We applauded and the audience got up and left the theater shouting, Get off, Frankie. Sinatra was shocked. He sat backstage and didn't talk to us. He knew we knew that Duke had done him a favor and he was ashamed. We were the most professional claque in town. Between acts Gandy took me to the Palace, he brought overalls, we put them on, went backstage where he found a wooden beam that we carried inside like we were stagehands and we saw a performance by Judy Garland. We went back to the Paramount and saw Sinatra working hard. Sweating. Hurting. Crushed. Trying not to give in. One night Sinatra was sitting with his head between his knees, swearing like a soldier. He'd arrived angry. Furious. He wanted to kill. His lips were clenched, his hands were trembling, he looked like a washed-up boxer. I could tell his mind was going back to the jungle he'd come from. The ghetto. I knew that this time he'd come to win. To wipe out the backstabbing sons of bitches who'd once respected him and now came just because of Duke and cursed at him for two-timing Nancy. He stood there. We clapped. He shot us a scornful look. By the second or third number we could see him getting back the killer instinct he'd had when he was a kid; hunched and thin as a beanpole, he suddenly straightened up and his eyes glowed with anger and disgust and he was filled with power. He fought like a matador. Sang like cowboys fight in the movies. He didn't sing, he fucked them senseless. He conquered them. And Duke, who was listening, turned pale, passed up his set, and stood wordless backstage. We stopped clapping, tears streamed down Sinatra's cheeks, he knew he'd won, the catcalls subsided, the people who'd got up to leave came back and sat down, he was like a boxer who'd been given one more chance to win or die in the attempt. He killed them. They started shouting and clapping. He finished his set and didn't wait for the applause, he shot one disparaging look at the audience, smiled a tiny smile, exited, and despite the applause did not come back. He didn't pay us that night. Or offer us a drink.

At the Village Vanguard I met a couple of Israeli artists, Ilka and Aviva, who'd made an impression on the New Yorkers. Ilka, who had a wooden leg, played the panpipes and had a beautiful bass voice like Chaliapin. Aviva played the tambourine and sang with him and they were extremely popular. They invited me to a party thrown by a friend of theirs who lived at Sammy's Bowery Follies, which was the Ziegfeld Follies for amputees, the obese, people with sixteen fingers, dwarfs, female vocalists who'd lost their voice. A big room under the Third Avenue El. The trains passed noisily overhead and rattled the windows. American folk singers like the Weavers and Martha Schlamme sang Hebrew songs as well as English and Ilka accompanied them on his pipes or with his bass voice lowered even more. In a corner sat the most fair-skinned naked girl I'd ever seen. Her skin was transparent. You could see the white flesh beneath it. She sat there examining her left big toe with exaggerated interest. Aviva saw me looking at her and said, That's Pat, a real character. I moved closer while she made a big effort not to notice me and once she did she asked if I thought her big toe was pretty or was it too thick, and added in a sweet Southern drawl, Ah want the truth now, Ah don't want y'all talking behind mah back. I said that, first of all, I could see her back through her transparent stomach, and furthermore I wasn't an expert on big toes, but relative to mine hers was pretty. She asked me to take off my left shoe. I did. She asked me to take off the sock. I did, and she looked at my big toe for a long time and said in a tear-choked voice that I was a liar and that my big toe was far prettier than hers and that this wasn't fair. Ilka sang, "So perish all Thine enemies, O Lord," and she joined in that bellicose song and to my surprise she knew the words, and then she asked me who I was and why. I explained that I was a painter and after about an hour I told Aviva in Hebrew that I was going to move in with this wonderful creature if only she'd put some clothes on, because I love it when women undress for me. Pat smiled and asked what I'd said and I translated and she said, I think that perhaps in light of the situation and the beauty of your left big toe, I'll take a chance. My apartment is no palace, though. Pat was tall, her face was pale and as though shrouded in a pinkish veil and her hair was golden, but there was a hint of asymmetry to her, maybe a spark of innocent yet mocking playfulness, which made her not a cover girl but more beautiful than she first seemed. More beautiful than dazzling. She got dressed and we slowly walked to her house on the corner of Division and Canal. An old, bleak building. Subway trains passed every few minutes shaking the sidewalk and, I later discovered, the building as well. It was clear that we'd be going upstairs together. She said it was important that I know that a month and a half earlier there'd been one unpleasant night with a guy whose body she'd wanted to hate, and he'd raped her and she got pregnant and as she'd already had three abortions she couldn't risk another one.

On the way to her railroad apartment that had four old interconnecting rooms, she told me I should know right off the bat that she'd sold her unborn baby to a company and every week a doctor who didn't speak but just examined her would come by and give her instructions, medicine, and vitamins, and that the company mailed her a regular surrogate fee. She spoke slowly, pulling the words from a mound of cotton wool, they dripped from her mouth and stuck together in a whispered incantation and remained suspended there between her and the listener for about a hundredth of a second and only then were heard. Her words were always a kind of a shroud being cut through with a delicate knife for dissecting butterfly wings. Her place was unheated. It was winter and cold. In the kitchen that was the train's caboose there was an old gas stove and she put on the kettle. All the rooms contained remnants left behind by previous tenants: wobbly stools, couches, on the window ledge an empty vase with a few withered flowers that disintegrated to dust when I touched them. A broken black piano and on it a pile of *Herald Tribune*s from the previous century. In one I found an article on the fastest ship in the world, which traveled from New York to San Francisco in only one hundred and eighty-three days, and I also found articles on the mills in Liverpool by Karl Marx. Somebody had left behind a faded ballet slipper. A small piece of cardboard with an old photograph of a soldier stuck to it and the inscription, "Waste Helps the Enemy." There were dried-up cacti, two naïve paintings of little girls that looked like sleeping dolls. Through one window you could see a wall of wooden planks plastered with a gigantic, flaking Alan Ladd movie poster, concealing behind it a derelict movie theater, and next to the poster someone had scrawled, "There is Life Before Death." From the window of the second room you could see the bridge arching over to Brooklyn and part of the road leading to it and in the distance you could see the bridge spilling onto the other bank. In the middle, under the bridge, was a small island bisected by it. As I looked out a man led by a huge dog passed below. Pat stood behind me and laughed at him through my hair. The dog peed on some shreds of the poster torn up by stray cats and the guy yelled, That'll show you, Alan, you big shot! and he looked up at the window and waited and Pat called to him in her flowery voice, See you tomorrow, honey. The man was pleased and stroked his dog lovingly and it growled happily at the window. The cold went right to our bones. Every few minutes the building shook as the A Train passed underneath. The apartment cost eighteen dollars a month because Pat wanted to save. The only possible place to be was in bed. We got into it and I didn't emerge until hunger got the better of me. I went downstairs, five floors, and found myself in front of stores selling tefillin and mezuzahs. *Taleisim Tefillin Mezuzahs Bar-mitzvah Sets. Mantelich für Torahs. Hebrew Books and Taleisim, Silk or Wool, 59 Cents. Prayer Books. Kosher Market.* And next to another movie poster featuring Myrna Loy, her eyes scratched out by cats, was a sign: God Bless America. In the small grocery the shopkeeper looked at me and said, Ah, you're the Jew from upstairs? And you're called *Yoiram*? Yoram, I replied. He said Yoiram and *shalom aleichem* and what would the princess from upstairs like? And I said he should give me whatever she usually bought and he did and asked, And Yiddish, you know? I said no. A *goy*, he said. Listen good, the first time and only the first time it's for free, but don't go getting any ideas. Apart from the usual stuff he also gave me some pickled herring wrapped in newspaper and an old woman came into the store with a small bunch of flowers and said, That's for the *goya*. She's sweet, eh? Not far from there stood the *Yiddish Forward* building, the tallest one around.

When I got back I found in a corner of the front hall, hidden in a semi-basement, a small Hebrew bookstore with a Hebrew sign. Outside there was a bookstand with Agnon's *Thus Far*; *The Travels of Dr. Yoffe in Eretz Israel, 1865*; *Moses Montefiore's Debates with*

Philanthropists, Warshawsky Press, Warsaw. Inside sat a man in a threadbare corduroy jacket. Gloomy and sullen he sat under a lamp covered with dead flies. I looked around. In an Ashkenazi dialect he said, The flies had a *milchumeh*, a battle against the flypaper, and the flypaper won. *Hörst du*? The Mayor wanted to clean up the filthy city. We cleaned up and the filth came back. The Mayor came and I told him, we're fighting but the dirt is winning, eh? You murderer of Hebrew. I asked why he called me that, and he smiled the most bitter smile I'd ever seen. It was two years since I'd seen Hebrew books and I wanted to buy one but he said that there were enough bookstores in Tel Aviv, and that the Sephardic Hebrew we spoke in Israel was a whore. I'm telling you that this is the last time I'm talking to you because you're Arabs. How do you know that's the way they spoke in the Bible? Barbarians, reading Bialik in Sephardic pronunciation as if that's really Bialik? And then, after he'd got over his outburst he said I could take a book from the stand outside because they were cheap ones he wouldn't sell me, but would give me as charity. He said, I've got a son who's married to an American in Chicago, a doctor, so what, can I go to Eretz Israel now? Great writers used to live here, would you care to know who? Leibush Kolodny who wrote wonderful feuilletons, who reads them today? Yechiel Rabi-nowitz, who wrote *The Golden Crown*, and the poems, oy, the po-ems, "From beneath the gray roofs of my heart . . ." I make a living from Talmuds and Torahs and siddurim, but I won't sell them Sim-chas Torah flags with the apple and the candle. *Goyim* . . . People had gathered at the entrance to his shop. One of them, who intro-duced himself as a hatter and had soft facial features, said that the bookseller was like all haters of Modern Hebrew and that's why he wouldn't sell me books. The hatter explained in Yiddish that the bookseller was shouting in English since he didn't want to waste any more honest Hebrew on me and added, Listen, everybody's got a country, every Zulu's got a country. Every *dreck* has got a country. The People of God don't have a country. We have the Messiah. We are the old people in the kindergarten of history, and if the Holy One, blessed is He, had wanted a Jewish state he would have established it long ago. I went upstairs, told the story to Pat, we got into bed, we ate in bed and I heard a toothpaste commercial on the radio. I got up shivering with cold and painted her with what remained of my oil paints. I went for a walk north to Eleventh Street and looked at the prison roof. Gandy came to have a chat because he'd heard about Pat and said he'd seen her from a distance and she was beautiful. I said thanks. A woman shouted because she thought I was somebody else, an old woman spat as she passed me, I can't remember where the time went or who I was in the story. Across from Pat's apartment on the same floor lived the author Morom Morom who was known as "The Great" and it was said that his real name was Kuty Hayerushalmi and perhaps he wrote Morom or Morom Morom wrote him. He saw time in reverse, told what would be in the past, and didn't always remember what was in the future. He lived with a young woman whom he taught Hebrew in Canaanite script and used to bring me milk because he thought I needed all my strength for a *goya* like Pat and he informed me in writing that he wanted to recruit me to the People's Salvation Army he had been working on setting up for twenty-two years. The building shook every few minutes and it took a while to get used to this. Without warning a new poster appeared on the wooden wall across the street: "Camel Cigarettes—More Doctors Smoke Camel—Top Quality Cigarettes," and then I received my draft papers. Not for the People's Salvation Army. I didn't have an American passport or a Green Card. I went to the recruiting office in Manhattan and was taken inside. They checked my papers and sent me for a medical. There were thirty young guys naked and shivering and a doctor examined us one after the other. He was escorted by a brawny sergeant major who refused to smile. The doctor reached me and looked at my leg and examined my left eye. What's this? he asked. I was wounded, I replied. Where? In the war, I said. Which one? In Israel, in 1948. Against the Arabs? Yes, I said. He ordered me to get dressed. I stood there fully dressed next to a line of naked scarecrows whose testicles hung shaking like jelly and the sergeant major said, This man's a military hero. This is how I want you in Korea. Not like dishrags. Look at him. He was badly wounded yet he's volunteering. I was embarrassed. I didn't want to tell him that I hadn't volunteered at all. The doctor was surprised and asked, Is this recent surgery? I told him I'd just been operated on again here in New York. The sergeant major saluted me and I was sent home with a 4-F form and Pat laughed and asked me to show her how it all went. It was cold and I stripped in front of the Southern doll who lay sprawled on one of the many armchairs. She watched and suddenly burst into tears. I asked, Why are you crying? If you'd been drafted and got killed in Korea I would have killed myself, she said. There was something primordial about Pat, as if she were linked directly to the beginnings of the world. I knew it didn't sound right, but when I told her as much, she wept to hear that stupid sentence of mine, overjoyed, and said she remembered being born and that she'd looked back at the place she'd emerged from and said, It's a pity I'm not going back in there. On the radio someone was singing "Hello young lovers, wherever you are." I'd walk down Delancey

Street and find everything I'd left behind and hadn't dreamed I'd ever leave in Tel Aviv's Carmel Market and nobody spoke English except the Irish cops. In a movie we watched on Second Avenue W. C. Fields said that any man who hated dogs and children couldn't be all bad. Pat disagreed but Gandy, who'd come for coffee, concurred and said that kids devour dogs and vice versa. I asked where and he said, You'll see, here it's dog-eat-dog. The whole country was mobilized against the Reds. They were constant warnings about an A-bomb dropping on the city. An evil bomb. Not like U.S. bombs. People were starving because they'd been kicked out of their jobs. There were flags everywhere and people in the street would stop just like that and sing "The Star Spangled Banner," and I read *One Lonely Night* by Mickey Spillane who was the most popular writer at the time. The legendary Mike Hammer said: "I killed more people tonight than I have fingers on my hands. I shot them in cold blood and enjoyed every minute of it . . . They were Commies . . . They were red sons of bitches who should have died long ago . . . They never thought that there were people like me in this country. They figured us all to be soft as horse manure and just as stupid." People built bomb shelters and every street held drills to prepare for the final blow.

Pat's story is Pat herself. She was born in Birmingham, Alabama where her father was the Ford Motor Company's head representative. Pat was destined to be a Southern belle. The scent of magnolias was infused into her blood along with needles of love. At seventeen she fell in love with a colored yard boy. They made love a few times. She brought him gifts she stole from the house. They were caught. His head was cut off with a grub hoe and Pat saw the head fly into the river. As she told this story her eyes filled with tears but she smiled too like someone recalling a terrible but beautiful memory. I ran to the river, she said, and the severed head had a sweet smell. They threw her out of the house. She traveled north and met a circus. Wearing a short skirt she worked with the elephants, then arrived in New York. She hadn't learned a thing in the South except for being beautiful and elegant so she could marry a Southern gentleman, and so she became what was known as a call girl. She made good money although she mostly talked dirty to her clients, most of whom were businessmen visiting New York, and in her soft whispery Southern drawl told about how they could fuck her and how she would suck them and how they'd screw her hard, and her soft, melodic, well-bred voice and her girl-next-door looks all made for a pleasant evening and her clients would get excited and come and be satisfied without ever penetrating her. One day her father showed up. He wasn't happy when he saw her. He went downstairs, bought a red coat, and gave it to her. Didn't say a word. He looked at her with passionate grief and slammed the door behind him. She wore that coat all the time. And even today, fifty years later, when I close my eyes and try to envision her, I still see the red coat set off against her white face and the impish smile of a mischievous, sad, but naïve virgin. She was chronically late and was well liked by the Jews on her street. Whenever a *minyan*, a quorum of ten men, was needed to say *Kaddish*, she'd go from store to store collecting hapless males and drag them to the house of the deceased. She liked taking me to the *Yiddish Forward* building. There was a big notice board at the entrance with obituaries. Old people, sometimes couples, men wearing berets and occasionally yarmulkes, would slowly falter up to read—purely by chance, of course—about friends who were gone, and they'd nod their heads: Ah, she's died too, and look, that funny Mishke's gone as well, he's not so funny now. Pat made friends with the woman who sat in the lobby; her face was almost crystalline, as though it had been molded from a mixture of wax and marble. She wore a black dress. Her nose was thin and a huge gold Star of David hung from a chain around her neck. She sat at a table with a big book and crossed out the names of the dead who appeared on the notice board from the *Forward*'s subscription list, since in any case the children would call tomorrow and cancel the subscriptions themselves. She took pride in beating them to the punch but was sad that subscribers had died. She said that if she wanted she could really tell those children off—in racy English spiced with Yiddish. She sat there, grim-faced, suffering like a suffocating fish as she bore witness to the sinister plague of Jewish mortality, and seemed both sad and proud. The number of readers was steadily dwindling. The Yiddish Theater on Second Avenue was already about to give up the ghost. Pat herself was a champion mourner for the dying Jews and she'd sometimes attend the funerals of people she'd never known and drag me along too. People loved her innocent beauty and the obscure fears she gave rise to; a kind of remorse for something they knew nothing about. Most of the Jews called her Ruth. For the owner of the Hebrew bookstore on the first floor, the death of every Yiddish reader was also—despite his pain at the death of another Jew—a personal victory. He liked to describe—not to me, because he wouldn't speak to me—but to Pat on my behalf, all those reporters with their rakish berets, their pencils tucked behind their ears, looking for scoops among the Jews who had in any case dropped dead thanks to Yiddish and that profane Sephardic Hebrew—they were all scandal-chasers and looked ridiculous. Before the Angel of Death had so much as twitched, he told her, it was Eretz Yisroel that killed them. He said that the women in the Yiddish newspaper building were knitting sweaters for the dead. I could see that the woman in black was silently outraged about this seeming epidemic, but whenever the old man looked at her she just smiled and measured him with her hands as if preparing him for his coffin. She said that when she saw somebody become bent and bowed and small, she always thought, He's measuring himself to fit the grave, and she had to smile affectionately at him. Once, the man's teeth fell out. Right onto the Book of the Dead. She kissed the book after she'd placed his teeth back in his mouth and continued burying her Jews in silent protest. Pat said that if Yiddish died in America, New York would become Calcutta. Pat introduced me to Herzl Jungerman who was said to be the oldest and best-known journalist on the paper. He'd come in every morning, enter his office, go over the paperwork, and write the obituaries. The dead had already been measured while alive, so it was no great effort. When Pat first introduced us I noticed he was measuring me too. Height. Eye color. Date of birth? he asked. Place of birth? Tel Aviv. Aha, they die over there too. His entire life he'd measured people for their obituaries, said Pat, and the people who passed him in the hall were scared of him and hid. You could see the Manhattan Bridge from her apartment too. From both sides of the river the Pepsi-Cola and Coca-Cola billboards were waging the war of the century right under our noses.

Pat had a handsome Chinese friend, a former dancer named Chao Li. Every two weeks she'd dress up in cheap evening clothes and go to see him. She never explained, but as she left she'd embrace me, frightened. She once said it was better I didn't ask so I wouldn't know. She'd come back with a flippant but irate smile and call me

Mr. Yoiram and shut herself up in her room. And after a while she'd snuggle against me and talk about her childhood, and I'd pamper her even though jealousy was gnawing away at me. She wanted me to touch the baby she said was dead in her heart and disgusted her. One evening Chao Li called. She begged him to change his mind, but he demanded that she come. I took her to him. He came down, sized me up mockingly and said, Wait here till I'm done. She threw me an unhappy glance, forced on a smile, and went up with him. There was a broken bench outside the building and I sat down and waited for her. I smoked. Next day I felt I was suffocating. I thought I'd swallowed a bone. I called AT&T and asked them to add my name to Pat's account as a joint subscriber. Pat went to sleep after she got back from Chao Li's. She said it was the last time and I listened to her voice but thought I was already dead. She went shopping and I called Information for my number and address. The operator gave me my address and number and so I knew I still existed. Pat left again and I was panicking. The house shook terribly and I switched on the radio, some woman on the phone was asking the show's host what she should feed to her sick goldfish and then two old ladies came on who'd been living together for fifty-five years in a house they had to vacate now and they had no place to go and who would take pity on them, and the host suddenly became animated and described these old ladies he'd never met in his life as frail, forlorn, and they cried, they really cried over the radio. I thought, there's somebody worse off than me. One night we came home from a movie about the South. I lectured on and on about the Scottsboro Boys and their dubious trials and recited the words of my instructors from the youth movement in Tel Aviv. Class. Capitalism. Workers. Racism. I said that perhaps justice was a cruel word. Listen,

Pat said, there's no absolute injustice either, you're a sweet idiot. But like everything else about her, offense took its time, and eventually her anger rose and became tangible and I'd never seen such rage in her before. She talked incessantly in her honeycomb voice and was appeased only when I kissed her left big toe that she still thought was not as beautiful as mine. I thought we'd settled the argument but next morning she was waiting for me in her red coat. She stood there firm and furious and said, You're coming with me. Where to, I asked. Come, she replied. I can't remember whether we took a bus or train. She was silent for hours and I was stifled and stiff as usual, and outside the scenery changed, getting more and more untamed. We reached Birmingham, Alabama, in the afternoon. We went into a diner and had something to eat. Some tough-looking guys, gray eyes, blond hair, were sitting there, bored and staring at us. One got up and moved over to Pat and fixed her with an evil glare. I got up to defend her, although judging by his appearance I knew that my combat experience establishing a Jewish state in a hostile region wouldn't do me any good this time. Pat whispered, Don't worry, honey. She turned to the guy and in her most cloying Southern accent told him, Fuck off! He came closer. She then delivered a sharp and wonderfully professional kick to his crotch, his friend came up and she whispered something, I didn't hear what, and he took to his heels as the first guy somehow managed to get up and do likewise. Yoiram, she said to me, here you can forget about your "Palmach." We went to the cemetery. We walked along a shady avenue of bougainvilleas leading to a small wooden church. Thick fragrances filled the air and I saw pink and red flowers and lilies and magnolias. Pat stopped by a grave against which leaned a skillfully decorated cardboard sign. I moved to stand in front of it and read:

Our Loveliest Girl, Pat. Born in Birmingham, Alabama, April 12th, 1928. Died February 5th, 1949. May God Bless Her Soul. I heard a sound behind me. I went back to Pat and she was staring transfixed at the approaching crowd. Alone. I no longer existed. A line of people was approaching. Pat said, There's Grandma, the one in the wheelchair. That's Mom and that's my Dad. There's my brother and my sister Virginia. That's my nanny who looked after me. The congregation stopped at the improvised grave and Pat's father spoke of his daughter, how lovely and delicate she looked at her debutante ball when she wore the white gown that had been made for her. Nobody saw her standing there. They looked but didn't see. Pat started crying and said, Grandma, Dad, Mom, Nanny, Virginia, John, Melinda . . . But nobody responded. As if she was talking to a wall with eyes, she said, I love you. Hug me. Touch me. Mom, Dad. And then in a faint voice, Have mercy on me. They didn't bat an eyelid. Turned to the headstone and talked about her some more and praised her and even laid down a wreath. Her nanny wept and her mother also cried and said it was a shame she'd died so young. They stood in silence for a while. Pat didn't say another word. A few minutes passed and the sun began to set and the headstone turned red and they began to leave. Pat said to their backs as they left, Forgive me. Where is your Christian forgiveness? They didn't look at her. After they disappeared down the path between the splendid gravestones, an old colored man appeared, glanced smilingly but not without sympathy at Pat, didn't say a word, it seemed that he wanted to speak but stopped himself and he took the sign and vanished. We walked along the flower-lined path between the gravestones and Pat said, Yoiram, never, you hear me, never ever come here from Israel to teach me about the South! She was silent on the way back. A few hours later she said, They're good people, Yoiram. They don't know any better. They love me and they live in a world you don't know and can't understand. We returned and I painted Pat nude in the red coat. I painted her as a modern Astarte, with a primeval expression. I worked for a few days, Pat walked around naked despite the cold. She said she should have stood naked in the cemetery too. The doctor came to examine her and told her that the day after tomorrow she'd be going to a hotel on Broadway for the final weeks of her pregnancy. I took her. We went up to the room. A guy calling himself a lawyer came in. He didn't say whose lawyer he was and he informed me that I could visit her a few more times but only between four and five in the afternoon and added that there was no point in arguing. Pat was now huge. Her face was gray. She asked me to make love to her one more time and it was difficult with the huge mountain she'd become but still it was good. She bad-mouthed men, they got out of it all so easily, with syphilis at the worst. We hardly spoke. She listened to the radio and looked out of the window. When her labor pains began I took her to the hospital in Harlem. A nurse was waiting for us. A young doctor arrived and asked me to leave. I called Ilka from a public phone and he came right away. A few hours later Pat gave birth. We didn't see the baby but Pat said she'd had a girl and would have her circumcised. I went home. Ilka called to say that something had happened and that I should come over immediately. I got to the hospital and Ilka said that some stupid nurse had allowed Pat to breastfeed the baby and now she'd changed her mind and wanted us to help her escape from the hospital. I scoured all the department's exits and hallways and Ilka found out from a doctor wearing a Star of David around his neck how things worked there and then he ordered a taxi to come to the back while Pat waited in bed dressed and holding the baby. We quietly climbed down the fire escape and reached the taxi. The driver got out to open the door just as five cars screeched to a halt. They surrounded us. A few unpleasant-looking guys jumped out and it was like an old movie, but it hurt for real. They beat the hell out of us. Ilka lay there in the parking lot with his wooden leg. Pat lay on the concrete. I was battered and flung into the bushes while the baby was swallowed up into a car where a woman was sitting with a scarf tied around her head. The cars took off and Pat never saw that baby again. We brought her back to the apartment. She was weak and threw up. Ilka called the doctor who ordered her to rest and prescribed some medicine. I went out to buy it. At the drugstore they didn't want to take my money. The Hebrew bookseller stood there pale and wanted to talk to me, but was unable to. The woman in black from the paper came and helped us take care of Pat. She tried calling the number of the contact man that she'd been given at the hotel but was told that the number had been changed. Pat lay in bed for five days and wept. The floor at the bedside turned into a lake. You're from the desert, she said, so take the tears and water it. Ilka sang "How Lovely are the Nights in Canaan" that my mother had loved to sing to me, and Pat stopped talking. When she started again, she said viciously that she hated me and refused to eat. She said we could have saved her. That I'd done it on purpose because I was jealous of the man she'd made love to. I didn't respond and we forced her to drink. She was weak and unsteady when she got up to go to the bathroom. Ilka left with Aviva and she said quietly, You could have saved me but you didn't. I woke up in the morning and she wasn't there. I looked for her but she hadn't left a trace. I called Chao Li whose number was scratched in the plaster over the gas stove and he sounded friendly and said he was sorry for me but it really was of no interest to him. I waited about a week and didn't hear from her. I went to the Waldorf Cafeteria on Fourteenth Street where the Yiddish and Hebrew writers sat at separate tables and asked one of the few customers of the Hebrew bookstore downstairs if he'd seen anything and he said he hadn't and he was sorry since the whole neighborhood had heard, and in Odessa even the worst gangsters wouldn't have been so hardhearted. Then he said there'd been another tragedy, their old waitress of the past twenty years had died and the writers needed a new intermediary. They were there every afternoon.

I saw that the tables were quite close to one another. The men were wearing berets or bohemian hats, colored neckties and cashmere scarves around their necks, and corduroy pants, except for one who was wearing flannel. Their expressions bore a sadness that they made into poetic sadness. Even the way they stirred sugar into their tea was poetic. Burning eyes, some kind of piety and purity. They drank their tea and every other minute a heartrending *oy vey* would ring out. They chain-smoked and the debates at the two tables, each of which refused to acknowledge the other's existence, concerned the life and death of words. A faulty line in a Hebrew poem would give rise to a bellow of pain or apprehension from the Hebraists and mocking snorts from the Yiddishists. They were noisy and the new waitress, who didn't know them, was unable to fill the shoes of the old one who'd died. They despised the new *goya* because she didn't know who liked milk in his tea, who took sugar, who drank coffee or seltzer, and how to translate their pain and mediate between the two tables because she knew neither Hebrew nor Yiddish. One of them told me that O. Henry had called

New York Baghdad-on-the-Subway, for us it's Warsaw-on-tea-and-
Zucker. They used teaspoons, forks, and teapots in their arguments
about the Korean War. They moved tanks and bombed armies using empty tumblers. The war on their tables was far more logical
than the one they read about in the *Forward* or from those turn-
coats at the *New York Times*. They thought up plans replete with
cunning tactics to outflank the enemy and designed surprise rear
attacks. There were no missiles back then but they had missiles as
well as airplanes that flew at the speed of light and rays that could
penetrate tanks. But their primary obsessive occupation was still
poetry and literature. Undying loyalty to their two languages. Slaves
to poetry. It was a bitter battle. They worshipped literature like the
loyal entourage of a cunning and unfaithful mistress. The number
of their readers dwindled daily. Sometimes a few of their surviving
admirers would come by, trembling with excitement as they peeked
at the writers through the cafeteria window. Shy and burning with
desire they'd beckon me with crooked fingers to come outside and
I'd go out and they'd ask me whether Chaim B. had recovered and
if H. had finished writing his long poem. They'd send messages of
love and encouragement via me and the poets and writers, as if by
chance, would glance out and wave limp hands as if they'd spent
all their lives onstage at Radio City Music Hall in front of applauding thousands. They, of course, wrote for posterity but they paid
me twenty dollars a day to act as mediator. They sat each at their
respective table—it had been that way for decades. Eternal hatred
permeated with mutual longing. The Yiddish table would call me
and somebody there, Bashevis Singer perhaps, would say in a voice
heard not only at the adjacent table but in the Bronx as well, that I
should be so kind as to tell, but gently, the poet G., who'd written a

not-too-bad poem in Lodz forty-five years ago, that his new poem in *Ha-Doar* or alternately in *Der Yidisher Kemfer* was so lightweight that the cupboard in which he'd put it had flown away, and he didn't know why the cupboard was flying away until he remembered that it held the poems of this esteemed and honorable poet. I said that Frischmann had written the same thing about I. L. Peretz and he said that he got it from the same source in Warsaw. Through me they passed brief, violent, passionate messages and they usually wouldn't refer to one another by name but would say, That fellow over there sitting to the right of A. with the black cap, or that sickly man with the purple beret who keeps looking for *maidelach* through the window. They spoke loudly because they didn't altogether trust me despite the twenty dollars a day and the two free cups of coffee, and when a Hebrew poet would shout to me and I would shout it on to his actual addressee that in his long poem there were *davka*—a word they loved to use and which does not exist in English, and they'd sigh excitedly as if by using it they were taking their revenge on that bitch of a language—that in his long poem there were *davka*—impossible to translate into English!—two good lines, even though they'd been written fifty years ago by Nachman Bulkovitz, there would be loud laughter from one table and bitter loathing grumbles from the other. But I loved seeing these poets and writers meet at funerals. They'd embrace and cry and shed tears on each other's shoulders. Funerals were cease-fires between Hebrew and Yiddish. Their wives, who'd been friends back in Warsaw or Odessa, would kiss. They'd tell stories about the childhood of the deceased whom they all knew well and their love for one another knew no bounds. But once they got back to their tables hostility reigned supreme. There they were the Yiddish bastards on one side of the ring and the saviors of Hebrew from its defilers in Eretz Yisroel at the other.

Every now and then I would check the emergency room at five different hospitals; somebody had told me that Pat had hired a private detective and that in order to pay him she'd gone back to the world's oldest profession. Years later she called. She asked me to come to the cemetery in Yonkers. I went. She was standing erect but sorrowful over a small headstone and said that her girl was buried there. She asked me to go to bed with her. It was already evening. There weren't many visitors. I couldn't refuse. And I didn't really want to refuse. She said she felt like a skeleton making love to a human being. We hardly spoke. She didn't tell me much. I went with her to her small room in the Chelsea Hotel and stayed with her all night. In the morning she stood there, dressed like a Park Avenue lady, magnificent and angry with me for having stayed. She said she'd put the doll that used to live with us in the Division Street apartment in the grave. So her darling girl could have both a mommy and a daddy. She still had the same disconsolate majesty. She tried to be the Southern lady her parents had wanted. But when she cried it seemed like she was shedding old tears. She asked where was the God of the Jews who allowed such a thing. Freddie the drummer who lived on Charles Street with his wife or girlfriend who turned tricks on the side, said that she saw her now and then and she always seemed angry.

Freddie's wife worked at the Wellington Hotel and bought him a new cashmere sweater every week. She liked the white stuff. Freddie was the first around to own a television set and his wife or girlfriend was a hooker and could see through walls. Freddie went to the bathroom to try and hide, but she saw everything. The white stuff was on the table. They sat across from each other with the stuff between them. He took a razor blade, arranged the stuff into a neat square, both of them were like hawks, ready to kill each other any minute, verifying that the square was precise, nudging it a bit to the right or a bit to the left until it was perfect. Sarah Vaughan on the phonograph. There they sit, their eyes glued to the white square like a couple of hungry tigers. He carefully positions the razor above it, slices down toward the center, tries to cut a precise diagonal, the phonograph stops playing, only the endless scratching of the needle in a dead groove, Freddie tries but she yells, Don't cheat, and he says, I didn't. She looks like a wild animal. She grabs his hand and then he slaps her and she slaps him. He's yelling and together they bring the blade slowly down to the powder and as his hand tries to make its final approach she screeches, No! A bit to the right! And then together and in absolute silence—I'm sitting in the corner afraid to breathe—they cut the white square into two equal parts. They take turns going to the bathroom. Tie a rag around their arms. Take a syringe of warm water and shoot up. A few minutes later they calm down and embrace. He makes me laugh with his impersonations of his imaginary friend, the English Lord Henry S. Tiepelhonf, who I would have seen had I stopped in London with my ship, and then she tells me about a john who wanted a kiss for two hundred dollars and she said her kisses were only for Freddie, and when he tried to force her she threw him naked into the hallway. Freddie says no, the john actually threw *him* out. Love becomes tangible in the room. He goes over to his drums and takes out his sticks. Charlie Grant comes along and joins in with his clarinet. Jerry Tallmer comes looking for me. Freddie's wife has got to get back to work and Freddie gets into bed with her. Afterward she gets up and he goes to the bathroom, she looks at the wall and says, What beautiful piss he's got. And somebody, maybe Jerry, says, That game of theirs with the diagonal is fucking scary.

I said my good-byes to the neighbors at Pat's building and moved to a new room opposite a small Russian restaurant. The restaurant was called Alex's Borscht Bowl and was owned by Alex and his wife Sonia. My landlady decided to smile at me because Gandy had told her that my father was some big shot at the UN and he could send her lots of diplomats with money dripping out of their pockets. A paper-thin woman passed by and laughed. She said I was Swiss. She asked for my father's address. She said you could see I didn't have a mother. She sang "My bonnie lies over the ocean, my bonnie lies over the sea," and the landlady kicked her out. She said she'd never eat at Alex the Communist's. Sonia, his tiny, charming wife, didn't like the pimps who'd come into the restaurant after they stood outside shouting to their girls on the roof of the neighboring women's prison, but Alex exclaimed with ideological, proletariat fervor that they were just girls who'd had bad luck and been corrupted by the capitalist system. Those poor girls and their pimps, he said, were innocent victims of imperialism, which was presently fighting against the world of tomorrow in Korea. In a socialist state there would be no whores. Sonia said there were death camps. Alex shouted, Stop killing Arabs in Wadi Hanin. Sonia said, I'm here, Alex, I'm with you. Alex was a dwarf and so was Sonia. She was about four foot six and he about four eight. Even though they were in their early sixties they looked like kids. She'd wind her braid around her head and look like Natasha from *War and Peace*, and when I said so Alex said that love is not, as they say in Russia, only a matter of chemistry between two people, and blushed. He flew the Red Flag behind the counter from time to time and hung a portrait of Lenin up and fought with his wife for most of the day. Luckily for us, Sonia—the most ardent Zionist I've ever met—won on certain points. When she'd see his Red Flag going up she'd conspire to get Alex outside for a moment and swap it for a Jewish National Fund donation box or an Israeli flag. Alex liked me despite my being a Zionist colonialist from Palestine. He was one of the bravest revolutionaries in the Village, which as we know was hardly empty of competition in this regard. He knew Plekhanov's *The Role of the Individual in History*, most of Lenin's writings, and *Das Kapital* by heart, and would recite Yesenin and Aleksandr Blok—*The Twelve* in particular—and Pablo Neruda too. Sonia, whose beauty was faded like an old photograph of herself as a girl, challenged him at every opportunity, but they still served the best beef stroganoff in town. That's what Gandy and I used to eat there with Freddie who Alex always hoped would come along with us because he was a Jew whose wife had been exploited by imperialism and instead of jailing that scumbag Truman they'd put her inside for two weeks. Freddie would stand outside Alex's restaurant and shout to his wife on the fenced-off roof of the prison and cry since he didn't have any new sweaters and then he'd eat something with us. Sometimes in the evening other communists would drop by. Sonia would sing "Carry a Flag to Zion" and "Hatikvah" and "Be Strong, All Our Brothers" and other Zionist songs to spite them. They would drink vodka and sing working-class songs that I knew in their Hebrew versions. Between rounds of cooking Alex sat and thought up strategic plans that he called "subterfuges" to overthrow American capitalism, and Sonia would counter by declaiming the number of kibbutzim in the Negev Desert and singing Hebrew pioneering songs that got on his nerves.

One day, Gandy, Freddie, and I were sitting there and Sonia lost her temper and tore up a photograph of Stalin and replaced it with one of the Labor Zionist leader A. D. Gordon. Alex was shaking with anger. But the ideological struggle that had persisted between them for forty years had taken its toll and finally exhausted them. They started yelling but fell asleep in the middle. When they dropped off, usually in the middle of fighting but also occasionally while cooking, they would sink onto the green couch under the photograph of Plekhanov, who, to Alex's sneering delight, Sonia didn't know was one of the revolution's greatest thinkers. On the couch they would embrace. She would curl up to him and with a sweet smile on their faces they'd fall asleep. As they were childless, due to what Sonia called the ideological struggle that had consumed them, they became their own children. They were fully aware of each other's weaknesses and laid semantic ambushes for one another. And practical ones too: the *Daily Worker* was replaced by *Ha-Doar*. Their prolonged battle was bitter indeed, since it's no easy thing to foment an international communist revolution from a small restaurant that only has ten tables on the ground floor of an old building facing the old Jewish-Portuguese cemetery, next door to the building where I lived then, just as it's no easy thing to conquer Umm Joni, irrigate the Negev, and strike back at communism from the other side of the same restaurant. Sonia had wonderful eyes, soft and kind, and Alex wasn't exactly Gary Cooper, but he beamed a stubborn authority and he really and truly burned with ardent conviction. Sonia said that Alex was far more of a Talmudist than a communist and at night when they were tired and before they fell asleep embracing on the couch, her head in his lap, he'd sing Hasidic songs in a voice full of yearning purity. At night, in the silence of the night, on the couch at the entrance to the restaurant that was all they had, America was no longer a branch of Chase Manhattan and Israel wasn't the world's enemy and what saved Zionism was Sonia's borscht which she only ever made on the condition that Alex left the kitchen because otherwise he'd steal her recipe.

I don't know where the urge came from, but that one time at Alex and Sonia's, maybe because of Pat, I went to the cemetery. Not the Jewish cemetery, one farther away. There was a young woman standing there by a gravestone. She stared at the stone and wiped her eyes. I came closer and said something and she said, Ah, my husband. When? I asked. Four years ago, she said, he died in an accident. He was devoted. He didn't love me but he was devoted. I come here to look for his love and forgive him. We went to her house. She lived on West Sixtieth Street in a brownstone that was all hers. Not far from there was an Automat I liked better than all the restaurants in New York because it was clean and had the best coffee in town and the food was simple and delicious. She sat with me. I don't remember her name. I told her about Alex and Sonia and their fifty-year long love and their ideological battles. She didn't know what Zionism was so I didn't explain it to her. She came from Albany, New York, and was a woman of means and didn't have to work, she said. It was nice, I said, to go out just like that once in a while and pick flowers at a cemetery. She looked at me and smiled. I remember a lovely smile. She said, Over a year ago a guy tried to hit on me by the grave, maybe it's an epidemic, but he disgusted me and you don't. Late in the morning I went down to a diner on Broadway with a huge appetite aroused by my marathon with the nice woman, and I had fried eggs with a double serving of hash browns and two Thomas' English muffins, one spread with tangy cheddar cheese and the other with marmalade. I drank two cups of coffee and went back to the Village and my room.

My landlady was standing in the doorway of the building wearing my mother's face and said sourly what she perhaps thought I didn't know myself, that she hadn't seen me in the house that night, and I told her that I'd been busy with a meeting at the UN with my father and the Secretary of State and she started trembling and her snorts of approval sprang directly from her thirst for my father's supposed gold, I hopped up the stairs and went into my room and fell asleep. Gandy came and woke me up. We argued over the concept of a painting not based on nature, as distorted as it might be in the final product, and had a lively discussion about Picasso's *Night Fishing at Antibes*, perhaps the only work I liked by that artist who started the revolution I detested so much, and which hung in the Museum of Modern Art. Gandy brought a Rex Stout detective thriller and a printed copy of a poem he said he'd heard last night after I'd disappeared, probably with a Belgian countess, a poem that e. e. cummings had recited at Sherry Abel's. Afterward I painted him. He took a canvas, hung it from a nail on the wall, and did one of his crucifixion paintings. On the radio Mahalia Jackson was singing gospel. I said she sang from where sighs come from. Gandy said I had to hear Sister Rosetta Tharpe. We went to Madison Square Garden. It was packed. Tens of thousands of black people. In the middle there was a small stage. On the stage stood a short fat singer with a few musicians behind her. She stood there facing that vast audience and got married right there to a little man who didn't dare utter a sound and the preacher blessed them and the audience clapped and she sang in a tremendous voice, without a microphone, to an audience of thirty thousand men and women, she sang like a thunder rolling through a valley. She sang, "It's so high, you can't get over it, It's so low, you can't get under it, It's so wide, you can't get around it, You must come in by the door," and the whole audience rose to its feet and clapping with the rhythm sang along with her and shouted and cried and conquered that song, they sang and swayed for a long time, in unison, thirty thousand people moving as one and singing. She descended to near silence and they went down to total silence, then she climbed up to part the sea and they parted the sea, and Gandy sang with them and I looked on enviously and said, If that doesn't open the gates of Heaven, then what will? And Gandy replied, No, it doesn't open anything. But suddenly on the way home on the subway he spoke emotionally of his childhood, his parents on the Lower East Side who lived not far from the building where I used to live with Pat. He'd never spoken about it before. Now he told me about the neighbors, the neighborhood gangsters who spoke Yiddish and how he didn't have enough money to study and how there was hardly enough to eat. We went outside, started walking, people loved to see how he walked. Like a dancing wolf, not a monkey. Slightly awkward and heavy and his gait was light, his legs supporting a good weight. Maybe a tired horse—precise, melodic, slow—but proud of his poverty.

In the lighted window of Alex's Borscht Bowl we could see Sonia and Alex asleep on the couch and in the fluorescent light they looked like a sculpture. I ran upstairs, brought down a sketchbook, and from the opposite side of the street did ten drawings of them in each other's arms on the couch, enfolded like a mother and her embryo, and then the landlady called me to the phone and an Israeli man with a 1920s accent said that he'd heard about me from Ya'akov Har-Perachim who I'd once met and asked if I could do a few illustrations for a poem by an important poet named Abraham Menachem Abramovitz. I didn't know the poet and asked what the poem was about. He said about life, love, death, envy, fear in the camps, the Nazis, you get it, right? I did a few illustrations and he came to collect them and said that it was just what he wanted and left me fifty dollars. I went to the Cedar Tavern, pushed my way through a sea of people, and drank Old Crow bourbon. Poets read from their work, drunk. Dylan Thomas, who used to spend a lot of time at the White Horse on Hudson, would come down to the Cedar Tavern and drink huge quantities and declaim and go down on all fours and piss on the floor and beg everyone's forgiveness and they all told him that they forgave him and he thanked them and read his poems again, he took to writing them on pad, and then the place burned down.

Maybe it burned down because Lyndon LaRouche was standing there. Laroche is a historical figure bordering on the pathological. He had many admirers. And followers. His Progressive Labor Party was then in style. The angst-ridden psychologist Reich was God and masses of people in the Village sat in "orgone boxes," because God was an orgasm and the boxes they sat in helped them achieve better ones, as did giving lots of blowjobs. Adele Schwartz, Gandy's close friend who modeled for Hans Hoffman and who herself painted and looked like a gypsy, came over and I was happy to see her. She sat at the Cedar Tavern every night. Her face was slightly coarse but her body was well sculpted. She grew up in a Jewish orphanage and in her childhood had wanted to be called Barak Ben-Avinoam. She was completely devoted to Reich. It was then that LaRouche left his followers and went looking for new ones and went to war against Reich who was already dead. Then he fought to get back his followers and declared that there was an international conspiracy that included the Queen of England, the President of the United States, and the Pope, all of whom were running the world's biggest drug operation—production, distribution, and sales. Hundreds of billions of dollars went into these three pockets while a few measly millions were spent on sporadic attempts at law-enforcement. Here and there some unfortunate drug dealer would be jailed and never know that the hand that had thrown him into prison was the same one that gave him his livelihood. LaRouche founded a whole new movement of paranoiacs and decided to run for President. Later he was convicted of tax fraud and spent a few years in prison. La-Rouche might have been crazy but he was intelligent, but the people who believed in him are long gone. One night he told me that he wanted me to deliver this message to Ben-Gurion: It is possible to understand pessimism and defeat using a particular balance of sweat and depression. He talked about pride and depression and Hitler and Jesus and God and the Pope and went on with a story about a girl who tried to drive him crazy, he said that Ben-Gurion would understand that—the girl used to wait for him wearing a pink 1930s slip, making rowing gestures with her hands. Her lips were parted and painted bright red, they looked like the mouth of a fish suffocating out of water and flapping as it neared death. Movements that were perhaps supposed to be somehow linked to sex because she thought they were reminiscent of how Rita Hayworth moved, Rita Hayworth who she thought she resembled. They had secretly implanted a network of cables in his brain. Love is something that happens everywhere. It needs to be honed. It sometimes enters evil minds. What do you do? You point a broom to heaven and then make it into a sundial and then the broom becomes just a stick. Then he calmed down and said that at Roosevelt High there was an argument between the kids as to what their parents had accomplished. One said, My father designed the Washington Bridge; another said, My father built the Empire State Building, and then a Jewish boy, who didn't have such an illustrious father, asked, Have you ever heard of the Dead Sea, and they all said, Yes! and then he said, Well, my father killed it! And then the Cedar Tavern burned down but was quickly rebuilt because hundreds of artists, writers, and poets were waiting for what they called their house of prayer to be returned to them. Dylan Thomas sat outside drunk writing a poem and I stopped there and he said, Are you really from Israel? I said, Yes. He said, two screwed-up peoples, the Irish and the Jews. Genius. Pathetic. Magnificent. The filthiest of the lot, they rise the highest and fall the lowest.

I had a few drinks and crawled over to my friend Sandy Sachs's place. She lived on Waverley Place not far from Washington Park on the other side of the Cedar Tavern and used to sit naked on the toilet. The bathroom door was always open. The apartment door was also never locked. Her face was daubed with white cream and resembled a mask, her head adorned in a knotted towel that gathered in her damp hair; she made extremely alarming statements in front of her guests who knew she'd be sitting on the toilet and so didn't bother to knock on the door. She said she'd seen two of my paintings and that I was a phony. She said I must paint the following: a young girl in the arms of an old man. The painting's character demanded that the girl be a child, but actually she isn't, she's an adolescent. The painting's size wasn't important and its style must be realistic. Expression depends of course on your talent, but at the same time on the feelings of the viewer. Eyes, say the Chinese, have no tongue. The position of the two figures is most important; this painting is a painted dream. The girl is clearly clutching at the old man. Her face is buried in his chest in innocent desperation. The old man's arms are around the girl's shoulders in what appears to be a protective gesture. But it seems that it's the man who needs the embrace most. Misery must be apparent on the old man's face and he's taller and wider than the girl. He's not really looking at her. His gaze is fixed in space. In his eyes there isn't even a glimmer of the warmth that might demonstrate some compassion. The moment freezes the old man's face at the height of a slight nod. His pain is hidden. Were the painting to have a different character, you would put an opaque wash in place of his painted features to symbolize the inwardness of his pain. That's why it's impossible to compare the girl's desperation with the old man's pain. And yet one can say that the man seems as though he's waking up to something familiar, like someone who hasn't lost any of his strength, while the girl is stunned by a sudden blow that you, as her painter, cannot remember having seen delivered. In contrast to the figures the light is soft and limpid. You can add the aura of a summer's afternoon, the contours must be almost as strong as those in a Rouault painting or the stained glass of a church. The shadows are faint; the corners are sharp. Everything is very lucid or very dark. The white paint becomes grayish as it touches the man's hair and bluish as it touches the sky. She was perhaps hallucinating. Afterward Sandy told me, rumbling like a madwoman, about a play she was writing. She got off the toilet and put on a kimono, and with her white face and her hair gathered into its towel cone she sat down and read me a few excerpts from the play and then Adele Schwartz arrived.

I asked Adele and her old gentleman friend who was masquerading as a razorblade peddler in the Bowery but was actually a philosopher who'd left the university to discover what he called "life" to be my models for the painting I wanted to do at Sandy's suggestion. In the end I painted them from memory. A tall woman who later would also become Gandy's friend and would be forced to buy a painting from him bought my painting because she thought it was Gandy's and she'd never seen one of his paintings before, or, as Gandy said at the time, of anybody else's for that matter. Adele lived in a huge studio apartment on MacDougal Street. We used to drink there because she had a lover who was a Jack Daniels wholesaler who'd leave her free bottles. I stood at her easel, mounted a canvas, and painted Adele. What came out was something that almost touched on what Sandy had ordered me to paint, but modern painting is not an art through which you can really touch life or touch the hell within us or touch forgiveness or redemption, and painting like Dürer or Rembrandt is no longer possible, and so I began hating paintings. People have written about painting but writers have never fully grasped what Chardin really painted or what Matthias Grünewald painted or created or made out of chaos. Adele talked about her own youth with such enthusiasm. With passion. Oh, Adele, Adele, what a titan you were, Adele. Everything about her was tempestuous. She spoke in a booming voice that scared off at least three out of every four men who tried to seduce her. Adele's eyes carried a perpetual sadness, and behind the exotic curtains of her life she seemed just a frightened woman-child. Adele announced that she'd dumped her Jack Daniels lover, or that he had dumped her, I don't remember. She wasn't affected by that in the least. She said that in any case she didn't trust men. My father, she said, threw me out onto the street when I was only a few months old because his wife died. I finished the painting and Gandy didn't like it. Adele did a series of paintings of birds and announced that she wanted to have a baby. We offered our services but she looked at us with disdain and said she already had brains, she didn't need any more. What she wanted was the body of a real man. For the father of her son she had no need for puny, flaccid Jews who painted and sat around contemplating Spinoza. Adele went to Jones Beach. She wore her tiniest bathing suit. She spread a blanket near a lifeguard station and lay down. Each day she'd set up near a different station. In one hand she had a notebook and in the other a pen. She assessed the lifeguards and made notes: *Object #8. Name: Neil (Irish). Height: 6'1". Looks: Handsome, 6 out of 10. Strength: High, likely an excellent sexual athlete. Total sexual potential: 8. Remarks: Inefficient. Strong. Swimmer. A fine member, as seen through swimming trunks. Blond. Servile. No freckles. Slight stutter.* And that, oh, Adele, Adele, is only one example. After a precise inspection she had nine potential fathers and closed in on one lifeguard whose name, as far as I can remember, was Guy. She wrote about him: *Height: 6'3". Beautiful shoulders. Muscular arms. Not disgusting in the least.* Under "remarks" she wrote: *Good clean bloodline. No hair on his chest. A healthy* goy. *No fool. Though not intelligent either.* This was followed by: *And he can lift a boat. Saved a little girl and an old man from drowning. Keeps his temper. Maintains composure and doesn't drink lotto much. Has stamina and is patient. Skin doesn't get very red in the sun. Eats lettuce, yogurt, and steaks. Sexual potential: two hundred thousand orgasms. Excellent potential longevity.* Next she witnessed him saving an old lady from drowning. He pulled her ashore. Sweet, she said, and he spoke to her gently, though she always felt the strength in him. She let him notice her and chase after her for about two days and then agreed to go to a motel with him. They were there for two nights and she left before he woke up.

It was summer and the story of Adele on the beach, taking down notes, made me miss the sea. I went to Jones Beach as well. There were thousands of people there and I stripped down to my bathing suit and swam while an entire white blazing city was swimming around me; the sky was gray, the heat stood like a giant tree, and there was no air. When I came out of the water the heat dried me up. Everybody around me was in bathing suits and it was so hot that I couldn't help look at the wonderful bodies of the young ladies and then I noticed a man in a business suit sitting on an old deckchair holding a walking stick, wearing a tie, a hat on his head, and he was watching the bathers and smiling a kind of malicious but not evil smile. He looked over at me because I was looking at him and I said it was hot. He said it was hot. I said it was very hot. He said it was very hot. I said the water was cold. He said sure the water's cold and where are you from, my dear sir. I told him. He said, It's probably hot there. I said it was. We exchanged a word here and a word there and I finally couldn't restrain myself and asked him why he was waiting on the beach of all places. He said he wasn't waiting for anybody. I said, Then why the hat and the suit, this isn't the opera. He said, See here young man, don't flaunt your youth. It's a fleeting matter. I'm eighty-six years old. Don't ever get old. Old age is a disease. My wife died six years ago. I met her one Sunday in Central Park as she was taking a walk with her nurse and she was wearing a crinoline. All the young men were trying to catch beautiful young ladies and I caught her. I loved her at first sight. She was beautiful and with the permission of the nurse who encouraged me we talked and afterward we met the same way on numerous occasions and to cut a long story short, we decided to marry, her parents agreed, they lived in Rhode Island and we went there to get married. Anyone who was anybody was there. It was a magnificent wedding. We drank champagne and danced and then they sent us to a lovely building in the park which surrounded the estate and we went inside and what do you know—after we'd been to bed and there was a faint light I discovered she was bowlegged. Do you see? For sixty-three years I lived with a bowlegged woman. I come here every week to envy the young men who can watch their ladies swimming and see who not to marry. But on the other hand, I also come for revenge, because your generation knows nothing about the mystery of a man's courting a woman. The journey of it. Having to imagine. Having to talk nonsense for a year in order to get her into bed. But it was an exciting sort of mystery and your generation has no mysteries. You've lost all your surprises, even the nasty ones, like my wife's bowlegs. He bought me an ice cream and I ate it and he laughed: Oh, bowlegs.

The guy who'd impregnated Adele had apparently been looking for her but didn't find her. Her belly swelled and we sat with her like you sit in a house of mourning. According to Reich's theory the embryo's character is formed in the womb. So she sang it songs from Westerns. She went to see crime and action movies on Forty-second Street so it wouldn't hear only Mozart or jazz. Then she gave birth. She brought the baby boy back to the studio and we had a party in her honor. The Jack Daniels was long gone. She put a tin bath in the middle of the studio and said that the baby could do whatever he wanted, because according to Reich a baby should be free. After about eighteen months he was already peeing standing up in the bath and in the other parts of the studio and also on me. She continued visiting her Reichian therapist who'd hit her so she'd have more orgasms. After her two hundred and third orgasm she took the boy and went to the Rockies so he could experience force and vigor and she taught him the names of wildflowers because she loved flowers and understood them and she began planning gardens.

One day there was a knock at the door. A young woman was standing there with an angry nun's face and a crucifix dangling from her long smooth neck. I saw that her eyes were almost purple and felt her power, endangered but at the same time dangerous. She didn't say but rather fired her name: Mary Frances Hagen. She sat down and stood up intermittently. She said she'd come on behalf of the Union Theological Seminary where she was curating an exhibition of religious paintings. Nobody had ever come to me looking for paintings, certainly not religious ones. I told her that I wasn't exactly a religious painter and she said she'd been told that I was and I asked by whom and she didn't want to say. Maybe it was one of the dancers I'd painted at Anna Sokolow's who danced barefoot and moved like Tarzan. She asked, almost demanded to see some paintings. I gave in to her easily and saw that her body was harsh and that she seemed built more like a model of a woman than a woman. She looked at the paintings I pulled out from behind the closet and asked to see the one of the dancer again and exclaimed, albeit joylessly, Ah, now, if that's not David dancing before the Lord, then David never danced. I asked when David had danced and she said, When he recovered the Holy Ark from the Philistines and Michal, the daughter of Saul, despised him, and then she looked almost happy. I wanted to correct her but thought, she wants David, let her have David. She offered to pay me and I agreed out of the goodness of my heart because if that's what she wanted then that's what it would be. Her angry body was still packed into her clothes as if into a reprimand. The painting, she said in a somewhat complaisant tone, will hang in the exhibition, and you, she said, will be paid two hundred dollars, and she left. I looked at the painting, thought about the two hundred dollars, and already believed that it really was David dancing before the Lord. Two days later she showed up again and this time her clothes were tight on her body but in the wrong places. The priest who was organizing the exhibition had decided, based on what she'd explained to him, and I didn't ask how you explain a painting, that it was indeed David dancing before "a lord," but not before "The Lord." She was angry, because in the days of David there was really only the one, but the priest had made his decision and wrote in the introduction to the catalog that the painting expressed both protest and faith. I knew I'd painted a dancer in the form of a modern Astarte, and whether it was a lord or God Himself he was dancing in front of didn't interest me in the least. I dreamed that Mary Frances Hagen was a nun and I could see her ass. That was the first time one of my paintings was mentioned in the papers. Mary wore purple lipstick and an even bigger crucifix to the opening and emptied a quarter of a bottle of Canadian whiskey without batting an eyelid and I looked at her terrible innocence and like any Jew admired her whorish Puritanism. She came by again at some point, but I don't remember a thing. Just that we parted in anger and I don't know why.

A few years later I went to Ninety-sixth Street to buy the Israeli weekly *Ha-Olam Hazeh* that would always arrive a few days late but only to that newsstand and I read there that Mary Frances Hagen had been arrested in Israel for spying on behalf of the Syrians. The article said that she'd acted so ineptly and amateurishly that her sentence would be lenient. It said that she'd fallen for a Syrian diplomat who recruited her to go to Israel and take pictures and that she was caught on her very first day. Seeing her photograph I had no doubts it was the same person. Mary Frances Hagen returned to America three years later and then came to visit me. The Syrian had dumped her. She was angry with the Israelis but she had to see that painting again and to tell me that I could have prevented the whole affair. I'm a whore with a crucifix and a lot of rage, she said. I looked for the painting. This woman who'd spent time in courtrooms, Security Agency interrogation cells, and then a few years in jail, was weeping now. She asked me why I hadn't loved her. I asked her why it was so important for her to know because after all she hadn't loved me, and she replied, True, but you could at least have loved me!

One fine day—the first day of spring, or at least the first day of spring that actually felt like spring—a few of us artists went to Washington Square to draw on the sidewalk. On the low concrete wall surrounding the fishpond that had no fish sat a young man in shorts, his feet in the water that wasn't there, wearing a Harvard blazer, a tie, the short haircut of someone from a good family. On his lap was a small typewriter, apparently a Hermes, and he was writing a poem. I went up to him. He said he was looking for the fish and spoke exactly like *The Catcher in the Rye* and I told him that they were already dead and that apparently once there were goldfish there. Something lapped by his feet in the water that wasn't there, maybe tiny, prehistoric, stylish, sparkling fish, perhaps just ad for the bigger fish, the giant ones to come, about which he was perhaps writing his poem. It broke your heart to see how serious and lonely he was making himself out to be a poet of waterless water and right there of all places in the strange world of the Village surrounded by people he didn't know, people who seemed to him like enemies.

We drew on the concrete using colored chalks and three girls appeared and sat on the lawn near our drawings and laughed. One was Marilyn Gennaro, the second Mira Pages, and the third was Lee Becker, who was to become my wife. Lee was laughing but her face had a very old seriousness and she acted like a hired clown and amused her friends. I was drawing not far from them and they tried not to look at us and asked the lonely poet to recite a poem and he did and his face flushed and Lee said he sounded like Charles Laughton. Marilyn Gennaro was as beautiful as a movie star. She didn't let even the little sunshine that glimmered through the trees touch her. Lee Becker looked at the drawing and asked if I thought it was good. I said I didn't think, I drew. She said, Its quality can be measured in dance. I said, Go ahead. Mira clapped her hands and Lee danced on my drawing that was quite big, maybe six square feet or so. She didn't describe it but created it in a dance that completely captivated me. She hopped about puckishly. I was a sad man with nightmares and she touched them with her demonic gaiety. She came from sorrow. From a ghetto. After some time it seemed that no misfortune could break her. I joined them. The beauty of Marilyn and Mira was powerful; Mira looked like Hedy Lamar, a Russian with Jewish beauty. Her face was the site of much drama: her eyes were filled with sadness, not sadness, grief, while her mouth smiled secrets when her lips met, and the combination of a malicious smile and a deep sorrow hit you like a punch. Lee's clowning and dancing sparked a tiny flare of happiness in me, from the beginning there was some kind of Russian grace in her and she shifted rapidly between pathos and laughter. She wasn't beautiful in the sense that Marilyn or Mira were, but she had in her the loveliness of beauty, the expression of a woman-girl who already knew the world, and I was swept away. There was something in her that I needed then. A disconcerting desperation that would meet mine and I knew what she was about to say before she said it. I guessed at her life and her endearing sadness. She said, laughing, that she had no further need of men, that she'd had one, a bastard who'd abused her, all men were bastards. I said I wasn't interested in her problems with men because she was telling me about them only to annoy or impress me. Mira told me that Lee had fallen for me. They asked where I was from and I told them and Lee said, A kibbutz? The Haganah? The *Exodus*? Marilyn smiled at me, perhaps scornfully. She was brimming with sex. I realized later that there was a soul of shattered glass inside her. She looked like she didn't belong to this world. And eventually I found myself sitting with Lee in a small restaurant on Waverley Place. She lit the candle on the table and burned my hand by mistake. I quickly applied some ice the waiter brought. Lee laughed because she'd seen who she was dealing with and I realized that nothing would break this girl. She turned serious. She hardly spoke. She said that she and Marilyn were dancing in *The King and I*. I said that was impressive. She said it wasn't. We started whispering. My hand unintentionally touched hers. She looked at me ruefully and across the table I sensed our hearts beating in harmony, a phrase suiting our youth. She wanted a life partner back then. I didn't know what I wanted. She had a somewhat broken but brave strength, a profound and enduring beauty that remained gentle, and she had a wonderful smile too. We ate. We were already holding hands like children. She invited me to the show. I went backstage and Yul Brynner, the star of the show, asked

Lee who I was and she said, The man I love, and he shook my hand and asked me where I was from and I told him, and he asked where my parents were from and I said that my mother was from Odessa and he started speaking to me in Russian and we drank whiskey, and I don't remember how we got to my room. I think it was only there that we started talking again. Her name had been Leah and was changed to Lia and then to Lee. She was a ballet dancer but also danced in musicals and did concerts with jazz musicians. She was one of the funniest people I'd ever met and maybe that was the secret, because I was a snob about beauty and plain women made me angry and I was ashamed of it, but people know something about what they need and want and Lee, who was less beautiful than most of her friends, exuded warmth and I needed her so I could love her and she demanded that I promise not to leave her and in the end we each became the other's retribution. We moved in together to an apartment on Morton Street that cost sixty dollars a month. She was well paid and I painted and thought I made her proud. Our relationship was tense and full of pleasure at the same time. We understood something buried deep inside each other. Each of us wanted to be something we weren't. She was a great dancer but what she danced was before its time. Back then jazz and Nijinsky didn't go together. We both searched for the betrayal that would bring love with it. We both perceived infidelity as a common denominator. She provided for me and although I wanted to work I needed the humiliation of her working while I wasn't, because she was afraid of the freedom I'd have if I made my own living. I'd wait for her at the stage door at eleven-thirty at night, ten minutes after the curtain came down. We'd have a bite at a cafeteria or the Stage Delicatessen. We'd set ambushes for one another, like enemies, and end up in bed. Neither of us believed in love but we wanted to love. But whatever it was between us, it never managed to become love. We were each other's punching bags, but still, we were good friends. We were incapable of really loving, but at the same time we both didn't want it to end. We were scared of remaining alone. She danced in shows and was on the road a lot. I slept with most of her girlfriends. One day I met her brother who was married to a beautiful Jewish princess. I went to visit them in upstate New York and tried to make out with her. She was furious and her husband outraged. I left their house and walked down the street. I met a woman. She took me into her house. I told her how my sister-in-law's husband had gotten angry and how she'd rejected me and how I'd told my sister-in-law that I'd come to their town looking for Dr. Mengele because I worked for the Israeli Mossad, which was like their CIA. The night was sad but satisfying. Cold. And it snowed. I can't remember exactly, but I wanted to go someplace and kill myself. I walked the streets and slipped because the cold was bad for my leg wound. A woman stopped her car and helped me in. She said she lived in the neighborhood and took me home to care for me. I liked her and we spent a nice night together despite the pain in my leg. Next morning she saw I was still in pain and took me to the hospital. They put me into bed and a young intern with fantastic legs and devious-looking eyes came to see me and I fell for her. She said she liked me. She asked who the woman was who'd brought me in. I told her she was my lover. The doctor turned jealous and said she wouldn't come between lovers. I wanted to explain but they brought a phone to my bed and the woman who'd saved me warned me that I shouldn't go back to her because her boyfriend had returned, and she was in love. I tried to find the intern but she'd disappeared. I didn't have any money for the return journey. I called my brother-in-law collect and asked for a loan. He came to the hospital. He was livid and threw fifty one-dollar bills on the floor at my feet. I picked up the bills and took a Greyhound back to New York. Back in New York my wife and her family had already heard everything, and Lee went to bed with Ed Jameson who was gay but who'd always wanted her because gay guys loved her and one had even proposed marriage to her and Ed wanted her to knock him up, what he called a phantom pregnancy. Lee was mad at her brother and gave him back the money he'd given me for bus fare and said, I'm the one who's paying for the ticket. Her aunt Raya gave me a heart-to-heart. A sweet woman who told me about the family's life as communists in America. Lee went to Houston, Texas with a show. Her father came to see me and told me that his wife's cancer had taken a turn for the worse and that Lee didn't know about it and that her mother was dying. That night Lee went to a fortune-teller in Houston who told her that her mother had died. She called and asked about her mother, wept, said that I'd deceived her. I calmed her down and told her that everything was fine because that was what her father had asked me to say. She came back to find her mother dying. She went for me kicking and punching and then her mother announced from her sickbed that if we didn't get married she wouldn't be able to die peacefully. We had blood tests, took Mira, Marilyn, Jerry Tallmer, and Gandy to City Hall and got married. It was no party. No rice. No singing. A pigeon shat on my head as we left City Hall and the justice who married us and was just leaving the building laughed, and I told him, You should be so lucky. We went back to Lee's parents' house on 107th Street. Her father stood there bleak and dismal but at the same time was trying his luck with the chubby nurse. Our friend Al Brown—one of the best viola players in town, who was later the New York Philharmonic's first black musician—came and Lee's father took him aside and asked him what they should play at the funeral and Al said, But she hasn't died and you can't plan it like that, and Lee's father said, But when she goes I want you to play, and Al didn't want to upset him so they agreed on what Al would play at the funeral. Lee's mother died a month later. At the cemetery her father stood despairing at the graveside and when he saw Al and me standing a reasonable distance behind him he jumped in the air, he shouted *Oy, oy,* how can I go on without you! And when he was about to fall into the freshly dug grave, Al and me, who were both ready for it, caught him; he struggled but only weakly and the ones who really wept were Lee, Marilyn, and Mira. Before that, Lee had gone away with a ballet show where she had a painful and tragic affair with a Japanese man and she came back having forgiven me but I didn't forgive her. We went to hear Bird and he asked her to dance to his music and she gave a concert at the Henry Street Playhouse, south of the apartment where I'd lived with Pat, and danced to Gerry Mulligan playing "Makin' Whoopee." At the time he was living with Judy Holliday. She was captive to the persona she'd created: she was the woman who really established the image of the dumb blonde that was later taken up by Marilyn Monroe and many others. But not one of them was an actress like she was. She won an Oscar and acted in the theater and one of her movies was *It Should Happen to You* where she played Gladys Glover. I loved it. Holliday played a naïve secretary who wants to be famous and sees the huge wall facing her in Columbus Square, and for many years there really was a huge wall there like an empty five-story-high billboard. Gladys Glover looks at the wall and dreams that one day her name will be up there. She's saved a little money during her years in New York so she rents the wall and a poster artist puts her name up in giant letters and she sits there loving it. People start asking who Gladys Glover is and of course the world of illusions bubbles over, the gossip columnists, reporters—she's discovered, gives interviews at the drop of a hat, becomes a star and talks nonsense that becomes truth because next to her the wise are fools and she's practically elected President of the United States. 1952 was the first year that the presidential campaign made a lot of use of television. We all gathered at Jerry Tallmer's who together with two friends founded the *Village Voice*. I was sure that the race was between Wallace, the socialist, and Adlai Stevenson.

We read almost exclusively the socialist newspaper *PM* and I was completely shocked as the results began trickling in declaring Eisenhower the winner. In the Village nobody even remembered that he was running for president. Nobody knew what he'd been doing. But there was a whole scorpion's nest of trouble hiding behind that forgettable exterior. Romain Gary said he was the greatest president in the history of golf. Meanwhile, as he beamed his sweet smile, the best of America's minds were dismissed from their posts and either sank into depression or evaporated or committed suicide or were arrested or went into exile. In *The Emperor Jones* Eugene O'Neill writes: "Man is born broken. He lives by mending. The grace of God is the glue." Ike was a meager sort of grace. He couldn't talk and listen at the same time. Lee had voted for Wallace and all of a sudden said, We've lost America! She brought home a day-old chick that Yuri Milstein (who had two wives, one of whom—or so he said—had been killed, and he didn't know which) had given her as a gift. It ran around the apartment and Lee came home tired from a show and asked me to cook because she'd been working and I'd been playing with the chick all day. I took some frozen chicken from the freezer and she shouted, Not in front of the children! She was accepted into the Ballet Russe de Monte Carlo, which had then been reestablished, and she asked me to come with her so we'd have a belated honeymoon. We went by bus to numerous cities in the Midwest. Arrival, check-in, rest, practice, performance, and sleep. On the bus the boys knitted and hugged each other and the girls sat on their own, bored. At night, after the performance, black, curtained Cadillacs would be waiting and the boys were swallowed up in them and driven to hotels or the homes of wealthy ranchers. The girls would come back from the performance and sit alone in the lobby and I was the only man there. And I took advantage of it. There was sadness there. The prima ballerina was Alexandra Danilova who was then in her fifties. Her glory days—when gentlemen had stood in their stirrups in her honor in St. Petersburg, Paris, and New York—were long behind her, though she was still a brilliant professional. She sat stitching and repairing her ballet slippers and told stories about Russia and her lovers and husbands, including Balanchine: she was the first of his six or seven lovers even though she refused to officially marry him. When we'd reach a city everybody would go to the hotel for a rest while she went to the theater and walked the stage, slowly pacing its length and breadth and measuring it with her bare feet to feel its bumps and obstacles. In Red Rocks Park, Colorado they were booked to dance in the outdoor amphitheater, where there were strong winds, and I went along with her on her inspection. She walked across the stage and then collected some pebbles from the river that wound around the amphitheater and sewed them into her tutu. She never stopped practicing and although her body was no longer as supple as it had been her arm movements were the works of a master. She prayed with her hands. Her back was lithe and her gestures dignified and she said that was how you worship the God of the Arts. She thought that sleep was something that great artists cannot allow themselves to enjoy. She said that the Crusaders used to say that a ruin is half a fortress. I am half the fortress I once was and so I have to work all the more. Through the wild monotonous vistas of Utah, Iowa, Nebraska, harsh and frightening landscapes, sometimes cruel and desolate, she'd hold a sewing needle up to their light to stitch her delicate ballet slippers. Somebody joked rather sadly that Danilova surely hadn't danced before the aristocracy of St. Petersburg so that in her old age she could amuse the hick ranchers of Wyoming, but she treated each and every member of her audience as if he were a St. Petersburg nobleman, regardless. She said that ballet was a miracle. Was sculpture in space. Nijinsky was asked how he jumped so high and he replied, I jump, wait a while, then land. Ballet is a form of wisdom descended from royal whimsy—a magnificent rabbit pulled from a nonexistent hat. Danilova liked me, but she turned a cynical eye on my habit, in stolen moments, of consoling the poor dancers who had nobody waiting for them but me, and how Lee would pretend she didn't see.

We reached a small town called Laramie in Wyoming. There was one long street, awkward buildings that looked like the movie set of a town without a town behind them, a church, a huge bar with a dance floor, a few stores, a barbershop, another church, a movie theater, and the silence of an afternoon dying in the heat. We went to the hotel wondering where the audience would come from, although beyond the main street you could see some buildings and a few houses of green wood in the distance. I walked along the street and saw a car speeding by. The street was empty. A cop hiding behind a gate popped out and stopped the driver. The car had Michigan plates. The driver tried to get away but the cop had him dead to rights and took him into the barbershop. I followed them. There was a man in the barber chair having his face lathered. He took out a small card, showing the driver that he was not only the sheriff but also the judge. The driver tried to explain that he'd misread his speedometer but the cop gave him a dig in the ribs and he doubled over, the barber laughed and sprayed him with lather. The judge asked, Guilty or not guilty? The driver saw the cop balling his fists and said, Guilty. The judge said, Ten dollars and costs, right now. The driver asked what costs and the judge said, My shave, a dollar fifty. The guy tried haggling, the cop glared at him and snapped his fingers, the guy paid up and drove off. The judge said, Whiskey on me and he and the cop went to a bar where I saw that they let them drink on the house because no one would take money from a sheriff and a judge and a giant cop, even with two of them being the same man. I moved on. In the shaded, somewhat dark entryway to a hardware store I saw a lantern hanging and a man hidden at the rear of the store. I went inside. There were tractors there. Sprinklers. All sorts of tools. Pruning shears. Shovels. Wire. Electric tools. From a distance the man seemed to be bent over like a monk at prayer. As I drew closer he smiled at me but didn't say anything and I saw he was reading the complete works of H. N. Bialik, in Hebrew, a thick book. I stared and since I was so surprised, all I could think of saying was that Bialik was my godfather. The man recited "The Pool." I asked who he was and he said, Yekutiel Ohev-Zion, a miserable wretch from Rishon LeZion. Then he said he was pleased to meet me and that he hadn't seen another Jew for maybe five years and his wife had died and his son had gone to New York and there was a brother in Tel Aviv who was possibly dead, he doesn't write, he said, because he wouldn't talk to anyone who left Israel for America. I want to go back, but I've been here fifty years already and it's not easy. He told me he'd been looking for someone from the Galilee who'd killed a friend of his by mistake and he'd had enough of searching for him, traveling from city to city, and there was the wife of some rabbi who'd made his way west and died here and he'd married her. She was a good wife, a pure soul, and that's that.

We sat reading Bialik and he said that this was a town of hoodlums. He spoke old Hebrew like my primary school teachers, pompous phraseology mixed with outdated slang, Hebrew intertwined with Arabic and Yiddish and it was getting late, so I said good-bye, went back to the hotel, and fell asleep. Lee hugged me suddenly and said she missed her mother and then she left with the other dancers for the theater and a strong wind was blowing and I walked the streets. Darkness fell and hundreds of people appeared on horseback and driving jeeps. They were wearing cowboy outfits. Most of them were short, no Gary Coopers, mostly Indian, they yelled, drank in the bar, came out and shot their guns into the air, and I followed them. There was a movie theater there. We stood in line and they gave us green eyeglasses for the 3-D screen. The lights went down. A bell rang. Through the green glasses we wore the screen seemed unreal and on it were the same cowboys who were now sitting around me but their faces were slightly different and the town was different and they galloped into town and went into the movie theater and were given green glasses and fired into the ceiling and yelled, and suddenly the Indians around me started shooting at the ceiling. The movie became part of the audience, I didn't know who was who and I became someone sitting watching himself but "himself" wasn't there. The only thing missing from the movie was me.

The barber who was both sheriff and judge arrived and laughed. Reality split open. The contortions of life now became a movie, reality returned as pitiful as always through the glasses now worn by hundreds of people, their lenses cracked, some lights came up, the ceiling was covered with a layer of cork to stop the bullets, the party was over, they returned the glasses and went to the bar. Girls were waiting for them. They drank and at the end of the night they sped off in their jeeps and on their horses back to the ranches in the mountains or beyond them. There was nothing but wilderness there. In the morning the town seemed dead again and a garbage truck cleaning the streets passed by. The graveyard-shift cops split the money they'd collected, beat up a few holdout girls until they handed over their share, and vanished. The giant dayshift cop also appeared and I went back to sleep because there was another show that night.

Yekutiel Ohev-Zion took me to lunch at the drugstore and everyone treated him with due respect and he said they behaved nicely to him because everybody here loved his wife and also because they all owed him money and the sheriff wouldn't let them hurt him because he paid him off. Here's Mr. Kut, they said. He didn't try the bacon and eggs and forgave me for eating it. He asked if I knew Yudelevitz from Gedera and I said I didn't and we talked for hours about Hebrew poetry and he hugged me and wouldn't stop kissing me on the cheeks and said, My son's with a *goya*, the children are *goyim*, I'm a miserable old man, how lucky you are to have a Jewish wife. I said it was pure chance and he said, in matters like that God works for us.

We were on our way the next morning. The ballet went to Los Angeles and I got bored and couldn't resist asking Yekutiel to put in a good word for me with one of the ranchers because I wanted to see where the cowboys came from. Lee was happy about this because she'd had enough of seeing me sidle into our room covered in marks left by her colleagues. Danilova kissed me on the cheeks and said, See what happens when you leave St. Petersburg? A tall ruddy rancher took me to his ranch in his jeep. We drove along dirt roads between cliffs and blue and brown mountains for about five or six hours until we reached an isolated ranch surrounded by hundreds of acres of pasture and cows. I went to the foreman and as he gave me a tour I thought, I could put the entire State of Israel somewhere here in the middle of the ranch. In the evening I sat with the cowpokes in a lean-to. It was cold. They lit a fire and I recalled my days in the Palmach. One of them played a banjo and they sang "Blue Moon" and "Cindy," they told stories, an Indian sang a Sioux tribal song, I asked the rancher if I could bunk with them and he said okay, I'm too tired for a city boy in any case, I don't give a rat's ass about pansy Yankees from the East Coast. I didn't want to correct him. It was late. We drank Kentucky sour mash bourbon and my head was spinning and I sang them songs from Israel and they liked them and said, They sure speak funny in New York, and they fell asleep, some standing up, and I went outside.

I missed Lee and remembered how we hitchhiked from New York to Provincetown in the summer and sat facing the great ocean. The lights of the fishing boats glimmered from far away. There were a lot of artists in Provincetown in the summer and we swam naked on the beach of the Portuguese town that looked like an Italian town and there on the beach I had the longest conversation on painting I'd ever had. I sat with Willem de Kooning who had a summer home there and told him what I thought about abstract art being only decoration and that painters no longer knew how to draw and he got angry, left, and came back about ten minutes later with a black suitcase and he opened it and showed me some beautiful realist drawings he'd done in Holland and New York and I told him, You're wasting your time on splatter painting, give us something about man, about our world, paint from your consciousness and from life, you do fine wallpaper but that's not enough, we argued, and I think that's perhaps why, later, when he did the most beautiful paintings of his life—a series of works on Marilyn Monroe in which he brought the human image back to his turbulent canvases—he invited me personally to come to his new opening and smiled and said, Thank you for Provincetown. I remembered how after de Kooning had left a drunken fisherman came up to me in the bar and talked about painting and about living surrounded by fish and artists. He liked fish better. He talked about the silence at sea at night when the fish glint in the moonlight, about the loneliness of the sea. The yearning, he said. Try to paint that. Melville wrote it, but only one artist, Ryder, really painted the sea. He began to ramble and I was tired and I went to the room where Lee was sleeping and fell asleep.

Outside on the ranch in the mountains it was cold. A bright moon and clear black sky filled with bright stars like you see in the desert. It was a dry cold. The mountain peaks seemed serrated in the light of the full moon. I stepped out and walked and reached a sparkling stream hidden in the sparse undergrowth. I crossed it and stood on the bank and a kind of sorrow about everything filled me. Who, what am I? Where am I going? Why me? Am I just another poor guy who lost his way leaving Rishon LeZion and ended up in a small town like Laramie? How far had I traveled, and what for? I was young and overtaken by a terrible sense of having missed out on something, it seemed that all was lost. The silence was deep, the landscape was infinite, glorious like a cold rocky desert, all chiseled and carved rock. Then in the light of the moon I saw the body of a young girl in the stream. I moved closer in disbelief and from the water, in the freezing cold, she came out. She picked up a towel and dried herself and looked at me and smiled. She put a coat over the towel and sat down and said, "Come here, stranger," and I did. She said she was a mermaid. I said, There's no sea here. She said, I'm Sandra, your host Cooper's daughter. I saw you at supper and you looked like a *kohen* in a cemetery. I asked, How does a pretty girl like you in the midst of all this Christian splendor know that word, and she said, There's a sweet Jew in town, Kut, and he had a wife called Matilda, a wonderful woman, and I'd sit with her and she taught me all kinds of things, a warmhearted woman, their son went away, there was a daughter who died, her husband's brother didn't want anything to do with them and I was like their adopted daughter. They're Jewish. I told her I'd met Yekutiel and that I came from his country and she said, Come closer, I'm cold. I came closer. She was shivering. I asked if it was just from the cold. She said, No, I'm sad. I'm seventeen and there's nothing here for me except a father who hits me and a drunk mother and the cowboys who look at me all the time and undress me with their eyes, so hug me. Don't make love to me, I don't love you and I'm too young to start with that, but you're nice and sad too. I hugged her and she still shivered. She was thin and in that landscape somehow mythical and her skin was wet and firm. Her blonde hair reminded me of Pat. She pressed herself to me, it wasn't easy to keep from doing more than hug her, I stroked her hair and she laughed like a little girl and said she was happy and that she knew a lot of sentences she'd learned from Matilda, like, *Im ein ani li, mi li*? If I am not for myself, who will be for me? She said it in Hebrew. I could have loved her. I walked back alone and lay down to sleep. Next morning I drove around the ranch again, I took a walk. The rancher took me to a small saloon in the middle of the endless fields. We drank beer and ate steaks and came back.

I looked around for her but didn't see her. Then she appeared and asked her father to introduce us, he did, and she said, A nice boy, who was Yoram? He was a king who did evil in the eyes of the Lord, I said, and she replied, That's good, and she left as if the previous evening had never happened. I sat with the cowboys who were hosting some friends from another ranch. There was an Irishman who took out a guitar and sang cowboy songs for hours and concluded with "Danny Boy" and other Irish songs and in the morning the rancher took me to the bus station. It took us four hours. From the jeep I saw her passing like a shadow and blowing me a kiss. I had to ride to some town or other and from there I traveled by train for two days and nights through those vast expanses to Los Angeles. Lee was waiting for me with the company after ten days of performances in Hollywood. She tried teaching me manners and what love is and said I didn't understand anything about it and that she wouldn't let me run away from her and then she continued the tour with the company and we arranged to meet in Dallas in about two weeks' time.

I stayed with Oved and his brother who'd fought in the war with me. Oved, of whom much will be told later, didn't know me then and we got acquainted. He was tall, skinny, pained, quiet, and very introverted. Always seemed to be deep in contemplation. Strong features with no beauty but a kind of unfinished grace, as if his mother had given birth to him an hour too soon. Friends came over in the evening. Fat Paul, the Brothers Karamazov, Handsome David, and in the dovecote in the yard slept Valerie, who was as slim as a feather. Paul was a potential millionaire and although he hadn't yet made his first million he knew he had to work on the second. He lived in an old woman's house and when the first of the month came along and rent was due, she'd doll herself up for him, he'd go to bed with her that night and so buy himself some time to make yet another of his many attempts to get rich quickly, one of which, the most amazing, will be described later. The Brothers Karamazov came from someplace in Israel whose name changed with each story they volunteered, though they'd only say something once every two days. They managed the window cleaning business where everybody worked. I joined them. At the time new neighborhoods were being built in the San Fernando Valley and their job was to clean the windows after the paint job was completed because paint was always left on the glass by the window frame. For this they used a single-edged razor blade and worked by contract, being paid per window. Oved invented an efficient way of working quickly and the gang managed to earn quite a lot of money from this exhausting work in the terrible heat of the valley. The older Karamazov brother had visited Vienna as a Jewish Agency emissary. It seemed he'd fallen in love with a Viennese woman who was perhaps a princess and perhaps not, but whoever she was, she'd left him. In Los Angeles, whenever we saw girls, he'd give them a long look, shake his head and say, She's not Viennese. His brother was convinced that the older Karamazov knew all the Viennese women in the world, because he knew who *wasn't* Viennese.

Handsome David was tall and apparently good-looking and had been in the same class as me for a year when he was a kid but had been held back in the same class for three years. He later worked on an Israeli ship and ran away to Los Angeles. He was scared of cops and guards and even of the poor old guys in livery who stood at the doors of department stores. In New York he used to walk using a system that Oved invented for him according to the theory that the girls on Fifty-seventh Street walked the north sidewalk on even days and the opposite sidewalk on uneven days. The idea was to make a pass at every girl, and according to the Oved's statistics, your chances of spending a night with one of them were about 20:1. David said it worked, he would hit on twenty and always end up with one. In Los Angeles he got a job as a parking valet in front of a hotel that looked like an ancient Egyptian garden called the Garden of Allah, and the younger Karamazov brother gave him a copy of the book named after himself and his brother, or so they liked to think. Handsome David stuck a scrap of paper in the middle of the book and when he'd see a young woman approaching in her car, he would pretend to be engrossed in the page he was reading, and the girl would wait and get curious, because in those days parking valets didn't read heavy books or books in general, and then as if emerging from the fog of the book, he'd discover her, look confused, still immersed in his book, read another line, and she'd ask, What are you reading, and he'd say, *The Brothers Karamazov*, a book most of them had never heard of, and Oved told him he could say Jaguar or Picasso and they wouldn't know the difference. If one of the starlets showed interest he'd explain that he was working on his PhD at UCLA and this brought him quite an impressive crop of pretty faces. In the evenings he'd come over to my place and misspell names of writers, artists, musicians, learn them by heart to then be able to tell a girl, You remind me of Natasha from *War and Peace*. Once he made a mistake and told a beautiful young thing that she reminded him of a Picasso and she slapped him, and that evening we taught him what he shouldn't say, but David, who hadn't completed primary school and moved directly to work on his PhD, got many pretty girls into his bed this way and enjoyed telling us about his performances and we nodded and taught him even more names he should say or not say. His affairs only lasted one or two nights, but he claimed it was worth it.

In the evenings we'd sit and talk about the millions Paul was going to make; I told them about my trip. Valerie came down from her dovecote and put the kettle on for tea and you could see she loved Oved who'd spent his childhood playing and fighting with the Arab children from the neighboring village Qatra. His father's hands were so hard and clumsy that he once killed a donkey with a single blow. His father liked to sleep next to an old fan because he needed the noise to fall asleep. And he liked milking cows. He loved cows more than anything else. Nobody expected much of Oved because he looked distant and drowsy. In 1947, when he was seventeen, he joined the Haganah and from some beach or other swam out to an illegal immigrant ship and was captured by the British and managed to escape. He knew every rock in the desert and had the instincts of a nomad. But he was captured again and sent to an internment camp in Cyprus where the watch he'd been given for his bar mitzvah was stolen and then he was released and came back. Later he served in Moshe Dayan's battalion in Lod and Ramle. He raced ahead in a jeep firing in all directions and the locals fled. When he got back there were bullet holes in his shirt. The Arabs made me some buttons, he said. A Bedouin from Juaresh named Abu Shalouf was married to two wives. He had two camels, two donkeys, and his dog sat on his dead daughter's grave until it died too. Abu Shalouf worked for Oved's father. In the father's opinion Abu Shalouf was a willing slave. Couldn't live unless he worked for him. Oved's father tried to throw him out, he cursed him, he hated seeing his poor callused hands exposed in those terrible dry winds, but Abu Shalouf refused to leave. It went on this way until 1948. But even after he was expelled from the village and the village no longer existed he came back to work. He particularly loved plowing. One day a Bedouin tracker who loved Abu Shalouf's daughter came to ask Oved's father to talk with Abu Shalouf on his behalf. Oved's father spoke to Abu Shalouf and tried to mediate between them, but Abu Shalouf explained that there were two reasons why he wouldn't give his daughter to the tracker: I come from a simple family, I plow and ride camels and this guy who's in love with my daughter rides a horse and is a spy. In their clan, said Abu Shalouf, my daughter will be a slave. The second reason is that I'm giving my daughter to a man from Ramle who wants her for his son because my daughter is the most beautiful and so in return I'll get two of his daughters from him, one for my son and the other, who's fourteen years old, for myself. Since telling that story Oved got the nickname Abu Shalouf, after the Bedouin. Oved had an Uncle Simcha who lived in Tel Aviv and was a prophet. He prophesied that Europe, except for England, would be destroyed. He said that Ben-Gurion would establish a state for the Jews. That one day all the evil goyim would be killed. People would gather round him on Rothschild Boulevard and listen to his prophecies, which even when they made little sense were always interesting. Oved loved him. They met sporadically, and in

1956, when Oved had already been in the States for years, the uncle died, but for Oved he still lived on and soon Oved started prophesying on behalf of his dead uncle.

I worked with them for a week cleaning windows, but a few days later I had to go to Dallas to meet Lee. Oved decided to drive me. For two days we drove through a desert that was darker than the Negev and lacked the unassuming splendor of the Ramon Craters. We stopped at a ramshackle cabin shaded by a Royal Poinciana. An old, disheveled man was sitting on the scorched ground with his back to the wall. Behind a water pump in the nettle-filled yard we saw a huge pile of new Cadillacs shining in many colors. There was no road leading there, only a dirt trail. I don't know how Oved/Abu Shalouf found the place because I was asleep when he made a detour and entered this barren landscape. The old man got up and asked if we'd like a drink. Very much, I said. He went to the well and with a rope and bucket brought us water and glasses and poured from the bucket and we drank. Not far away we saw a field of oil pumps that looked like huge grasshoppers as they rose and fell. The man begged our pardon because he needed a moment of silence. He went into the cabin and came back with an old abacus like the ones we used in primary school. He slid the beads around, scribbled with an indelible pencil on a scrap of paper and said, An hour and ten minutes. Five thousand dollars per pump times twenty. Another five Cadillacs. We looked at him in amazement despite the heat and he explained that he'd lived there all his life as had his father and grandfather before him and they'd go from ranch to ranch, and here the ranches are two days' walk from one another, and pick the left-over cotton. He said his wife had run off. He didn't remember her name or whether they'd had any children. He lived there on his own although up until a few years earlier his brother had lived there too but he'd been shot dead by a crazy sheriff. One day some men came along with instruments and discovered oil on his spread. They came and drilled. He said that each time the grasshopper fell it was fifty cents and the same when it came up, and so a hundred pumps times twenty-five cents a minute was worth something. Every time he needed to he'd call the field foreman who'd call the showroom in Houston. They'd bring him another Cadillac on a truck that always managed to get stuck on the way and he'd put the Cadillac in the yard. He didn't know how to drive. He didn't know why you needed to drive. He didn't want to go anywhere. He didn't want electricity or piped water. There was no real road around there for the Cadillacs to drive on, but this, he said, was how all his ancestors had lived and the colorful Cadillacs were his pride and joy. He didn't know why but it had happened and he didn't want to fight his wealth. He liked us because we came from a distant place that he'd heard of in the prayers recited when his daughter or son had died. He talked right through the night. In the end he told us to dump our old car, the old purple Buick, and told us to get the field foreman who also turned up in a Cadillac and asked him to fix us up with licenses and from there we drove a brand new Cadillac to meet Lee. The foreman had managed to do about a hundred miles in the car before we arrived. We reached a new road that looked good on the map. Abu Shalouf said, Trust me, I've driven along here a lot, and after about half an hour we realized we were alone on the road. No cars. No trees. He'd never been there in his life. Nobody ever drove on this road. No milestones. No road signs. A wide road, four lanes in each direction. Smooth. Burning hot in the desert sun. Not a diner. Not a gas station. No people. Not even half a person. Abu Shalouf was unruffled because he was convinced he'd been on this road before, but I started worrying that it was a new road and I told him that I thought we were in trouble. Oved/Abu Shalouf wasn't a big talker. In a five-hour drive he hadn't said more than twenty words. Fortunately the Cadillac had a big fuel tank and after about eight hours, almost on empty and us hungry and thirsty, we came to a small town with a diner and a gas station and two old black men who stared at us like we'd landed from Mars. There was a small motel ten minutes away and we went to sleep. We tried to find out about that road but nobody would say more than, Yep, it's a road, or Right, not many people use it, or, In the meantime, it's what we've got. The motel was empty. The room looked as if it had never been slept in. There was still a small silk price tag still attached to the sheet. From the window I could see the empty gas station. A lit up Pepsi-Cola advertisement and another one for Pepto-Bismol seemed forsaken in the desert view. A hot dry wind was blowing. There was no air conditioning. In the morning we ate at the diner. We were the only people there. A lively young woman made us breakfast and greeted us warmly and poured coffee and more coffee, and said that my pipe gave me an air of sophistication. I asked who passed through there and she said, Never mind that, the Bible is old but it will always be with us. We left and the landscape began showing signs of life. Huge ranches running for hundreds of miles, here and there a tractor, jeeps, and then a green wasteland and thousands of cows. Oved stopped the car in the shade of a bus stop which said: To the attention of our passengers—Bus No. 76 will arrive on Thursday at 11:00 A.M. It was Tuesday.

Oved got out of the car and through a hole in the fence that he widened with professional ease went over to one of the fat cows and from my place at the wheel I could see he was crying. That was the first time I'd seen him cry. Later, when I told the story, I was told that nobody had ever seen him cry, not when his parents had died, not when his friends had died; he cried and hugged a black cow with white spots. At first she mooed but then warmed to him. Oved whispered in her ear and she laid her huge head gently on his chest. He bent down and she got down on her knees. Oved kneeled at her side and as he stroked her whispered words of love that I could barely hear and later he said that in Gedera they used to speak love to their cows in Arabic so it was a waste of time explaining it to me. In the car Abu Shalouf said, That's how we did things in Gedera.

We reached Dallas and found the theater. Lee wasn't happy to see me but two of her friends were. Afterward, we hugged. That night she was angry at me. I went again to see the show, a ballet version of *A Streetcar Named Desire*, choreographed by Valerie Bettis. It was very successful and the tour even got to Japan. Oved went back to Los Angeles and Lee and I traveled to New York by train and went into the restaurant car to eat. A young man was playing a banjo. Lee began swaying, people moved their plates and glasses, she went into a trance, the passengers didn't complain, their food got cold, the banjo player jumped on the table and danced with her as he played and I don't know or remember how, the others got into it and danced, a small black man wearing a railroad uniform came along and began tap-dancing and Lee accompanied him with movements that grew more and more expansive, the locomotive's horn blew and broken plates lay scattered on the floor. All this apparently came to an end because a day later we reached New York and all that remained was a memory Lee wouldn't share or speak of with me. At night she dreamed that I was strangling her because I was jealous of her success. I told her that the Talmud says that a dream is a sealed letter. She incorporated this into her secret beliefs and with a few of her friends corresponded in dreams and choreographed a new dance to Gerry Mulligan's version of "Makin' Whoopee." It was a hot and humid summer in New York. Lee was working in a show whose name I've forgotten and she and the other dancers used to sunbathe naked on the roof because on Sundays the offices in the Empire State Building opposite us were closed. They'd sunbathe naked so they wouldn't have swimsuit marks in the show.

Bob Fosse called one day and asked Lee to dance in a new show and also to be Carol Haney's understudy. The show, he said, was called *The Pajama Game*. Of course she wanted to. I was angry. She was working on the dance to "Makin' Whoopee" and I thought it was more important for her to dance the things she really loved, as she'd done at rehearsals, rather than get into a musical again and earn good money but what about the soul? Lee, who was the provider for *my* soul, thought a great deal about her own. Already as a girl she'd known that it was important to love your soul, but she had grown up poor and liked her soul to have a body around it. Our argument went on for a few days. I went to watch her rehearsing at the Henry Street Playhouse with Gerry Mulligan and she danced both seriously and with humor and she was wonderful. In the end I persuaded the poor girl not to go. Fosse asked if there was someone else as perky as she was and as good a dancer and Lee recommended Shirley MacLaine who he of course knew and who'd sunbathe with Lee on the roof. Lee did her concert, got a good review in the *Times* and another in *Dance Magazine*. The second performance was empty. Shirley MacLaine danced in the show and Carol Haney got sick, Shirley MacLaine replaced her in the unforgettable "Steam Heat" number. Hal Wallis just happened to be in the audience and five minutes after the show Shirley MacLaine became a star. Lee never forgave me. I told her she was right but it didn't help. Mira, Lee's childhood friend, would visit us every Sunday and we'd argue. Mira's face was a blend of Hedy Lamarr and a Jewish-Slavic princess: the corners of her mouth seemed to hold lots of little secrets. Lee came from a Jewish-Russian-Communist home. Mira and Lee used to shoplift together from record shops and department stores. On one occasion Lee was caught and a complaint was lodged with the producers of *The King and I* and they gave her a talk as she sat embarrassed in the corner, but all in all they thought it was cute. They spoke harshly but smiled at the same time. She recalled the smiles only years later because her childish hunger for love by then had extinguished her embarrassment at being reprimanded. After she begged and pleaded and promised not to steal any more she continued dancing and getting bigger roles but of course couldn't help herself and went back to stealing. She usually stole only what she didn't need. For instance, she took the same record she didn't like five times and each time it was immediately chucked in the garbage.

Mira was only twenty-two, more a woman than a girl. She had a mind like a razor. Got her BA at sixteen. I was scared of her. She was studying at Columbia and working on her doctorate. She had a violinist boyfriend called Yuri. He begged her to love him and she smiled and told him that she'd marry him and then perhaps she'd love him eventually. He asked when and she said in two days. Yuri, who was a talented violinist, everyone said he had a future, loved her even before he was born and out of sheer joy started scratching his hand open so it would be worthy of Mira's ring. They got married and moved into an apartment and Yuri later swore that he'd never had the guts make love to Mira on their wedding night because Boris, her father, had accompanied her to their apartment and joined them and sat playing the piano. After two days she got up while Yuri was sleeping, took her things and left. When he woke up he was already separated. Her father, Boris, was happy. When he saw his daughter coming back home with her suitcases he burst into a hearty Russian song. Her lovely gentle mother sat reserved as always, wearing a hat for all the trips she never took and holding a travel guide with maps and tips she'd never follow. Seeing Mira return, Boris hugged his wife, something he'd long since given up doing, and was thrilled since Mira had left "that idiot," whom he'd actually loved like a son for years. Boris was a chemist who came to the United States in 1942 and was taken immediately to Los Alamos to help build the A-bomb. When I met him we became friends because he was looking for worthy foes and to him I was the Zionist enemy, deforming Jewish history. He quoted Rothschild who'd said that a Jewish state would become a ghetto with the same prejudices as any other; petty, intolerant, narrow-minded, orthodox, expelling the goyim and Christians. He felt he could argue with me and at the time he had a chemical company where he conducted secret experiments. He spoke good English but with a Russian accent and had a small beard like Lenin and he used to sit facing Mira and his wife Zhenya and recite passages from Russian literature. He particularly liked Gogol and Chekhov. Boris had been gifted with a macabre sense of humor, thick wild hair under a beret, a deep bass voice, and he would eagerly deride the absurd idea of a Jewish state, a Chelm, a country of fools, beating the Iraqis. He knew entire books by heart and their English translations too. He also put up with me because unlike the other men around I wasn't chasing Mira and never had sex with her. Mira was looking for love but was incapable of being loved or loving and used her power to hate herself all the better, and more than that, to hate men. Defeated young men with their tongues lolling out like dogs in the heat hung around the building trying to get into their huge apartment on Riverside Drive and West Eighty-eighth Street and Boris would drive them away. Lee had recently choreographed *Once Upon a Mattress*. But Mira was a refugee. Sinister. She was a promise of what would never be. For no one. Everybody wanted to break her. Even being rejected by her was a great honor. All her life she searched for absolute ignorance. Boris had known Stalin. They'd been friends. They'd played chess in the Kremlin and come up with tactics. They would glare at one another and so decide who would lose that day and they would talk about death. They both loved power, the power that was always there in their hands, they'd play with a model railroad that Stalin had gotten from a western communist who'd brought it as a gift for one of the heads of the KGB; later both their heads had rolled. Stalin and Boris would humiliate each other. The Jews of Moscow knew that Stalin had a pet Jew but they didn't know who. When the mood took him Boris would harangue me about my supposedly enlightened ideas, which he detested. The people's love of tyranny, he said, is the great existential secret. The expulsion from the Garden of Eden was the price we paid to know what is permissible and what is forbidden— that is, to be slaves. Human beings prefer to have someone else think for them, and if this someone is a tyrant, they're afraid—but the more they're afraid the more they love him because to live is boring, and it is dangerous and frightening without somebody out there thinking for you. Christianity and the monarchies understood this, they're both based on tyranny and so both have survived and both are eternal. Tyranny is eternal. Both Christianity and all totalitarianism are splendid performances. And in fact even the Christian and the communist rituals are similar. In all of these systems, the Supreme Being resides in a palace. The most wonderful sentence in Russian literature is what Ivan writes in *The Brothers Karamazov*, when Jesus comes to Seville. The Great Inquisitor has him arrested. At night the Inquisitor comes to his cell. He is tall, old, withered, but there is still a light in his eyes. He sits before Jesus and explains that he, Jesus, had founded the Church based on anarchy and justice and compassion while we, knowing the nature of Man, founded the Church on pomp, mystery, authority. In other words, on vanities, on fetters. Ritual is welcome brainwashing. In June 1941 the Germans attacked, but Stalin didn't believe they would because in August 1939 he'd signed a pact with Germany and he admired Hitler. He was convinced that a bastard like Hitler wouldn't violate an agreement with him. Stalin, said Boris, admired the SA commander Ernst Röhm who Hitler had hanged from a hook, because he knew to take care of his enemies. Stalin loved his wife Nadezhda and killed her. Afterward, he said, something was extinguished inside him forever. She was his last connection with the world. Twenty-five million Russians died in the war, half of whom he killed himself. In his view, prisoners of war were traitors, and this included his son Yakov, and so he killed them. Boris drank some tea and wiped his face with a towel and smiled. Eh? Eh? I looked at him. Mira loved telling about how Boris had had lunch with President Truman, and told him that Stalin was a historic hero. Eternal. McCarthy, who devoured communists and anyone who even smelled like a communist, liked hearing Boris out because listening to him he understood what an important role evil must play when it serves a nation that doesn't know what's in its own best interests. Boris despised democracy. Why should fools decide who goes to war and who runs a country? There was something noxious and ugly in millions of ignoramuses electing a fool—anyone who can hypnotize them and convince them that he's just their size—to be their king. A king makes his people, not vice versa. Boris was offended on Stalin's behalf when he learned how eager the dictator's subjects had been not to die for their leader during the invasion.

I remember one of Boris's speeches in particular: The truth is an accepted lie. Somebody once said that the Devil is an optimist if he thinks he can make human beings more evil than they are. Faith has to feed on the blood of innocents because they are the fiction from which a leader is created. I never thought Stalin legitimate. I didn't believe in communism—but neither did Stalin. How can a thinking man believe in such foolishness, that people are born equal and that everyone will get what he deserves? When Mira and Lee were zealous members of the Young Communists in New York, Boris laughed at them—while Mira was admired because she'd once sat on Stalin's knee.

I thought that Boris hoped that Mira and Stalin would both get married. After Stalin died Boris was convinced he was still alive and hiding in South America. A man who'd been at the Kremlin but managed to escape the purges said that Boris and Stalin used to sing sentimental songs together but eyed each other with suspicion. They realized that each of them could happily murder the other. But they loved playing their games and enjoying such sweet anxiety. Boris said, Stalin had a murderous naïveté. But he loved those he was forced to kill.

After the Germans invaded, Stalin put Boris in charge of getting the trains out of the Germans' path as they raced toward Moscow. The very fact of treason, said Boris, is the sign of something deep—just as Mira betrayed me by being her mother's daughter too, because she wanted to and she should have been born from me alone. Boris saw how the Ukrainians were overjoyed when the Germans arrived. At night he saw the German officers embracing and a terrible desire for new betrayal awakened in him. He already considered himself a traitor to the Russian people because of his friendship with the tyrant, but by then he didn't care. Stalin was lost. Trapped by people Boris thought were fools. Stalin was diligently retreating from the Germans he so despised, didn't listen to his officers' advice, killed the generals who wanted to save Russia, and Boris watched them all get shot in the back. When he was in Kiev sometime later he met an American agent sent by Allen Dulles, who was pulling the strings from Switzerland. Boris was a specialist in something or other I know nothing about, and Dulles wanted it. Boris took his wife and Mira, but not before writing a letter to Stalin. The family went by train to Eastern Siberia and from there, via a rather strenuous route—as Greek refugees to Iran and then through Egypt—reached the United States. On his arrival he fell in love with America's shallow happiness. The twenty-eight flavors of Howard Johnson's ice cream. Coca-Cola, the Automat, cafeterias, all that space spread out with no purpose, without culture, beyond the big city, and Allen Dulles came on a private jet and took him to Los Alamos for the Manhattan Project, despite everything they knew about him. For two years the family lived in a small house in Los Alamos. He loved the town in the desert. It reminded him of Stalin's anger and the barrenness he so yearned for. He was angry when the bomb was used against the Japanese and not the Nazis. After Los Alamos he moved to New York and set up a laboratory. He chased around after Mira who'd become increasingly lost.

His overwhelming love for Mira. His rage at his wife who had dared bear her. He was dangerous when it came to Mira. Mira buried herself in study but didn't find what she was looking for in Judaism. She claimed that Judaism was colorless, it lacked ritual and God had no splendid palace—He was wretched, pathetic, He was theology without a hierarchy, without metaphysics. She drifted from theory to theory, from belief to belief, she studied Zen Buddhism which was only starting to be popular in America then, she studied astrology, attended consciousness-raising workshops, went to all kinds of psychiatrists, talked with priests of every stripe, studied Christianity for one semester, worked for a time preparing gravestones in a cemetery, read whatever she found and wasn't excited by Lutheran or Calvinist Christianity but was attracted by Catholicism, was drawn by its absoluteness.

She became even more beautiful. He face grew pale. She studied theology for a year and a half, started going to church, was baptized, delved deeper into religion. She learned about medieval monasteries and cloisters. She read St. Jerome and Aquinas and St. Augustine whom she especially liked and was dismayed by his tortured soul, the fact he wasn't born to religion, and then one evening she came over to see us and as usual we argued. This was an upsetting evening because I tried to convince her of the error of her ways and she only felt sorry for me. She emanated a sort of a Christian concept of sin and compassion, and then, after a stupid and futile argument about faith, which probably can neither be substantiated nor refuted, she left for a convent in Ohio. She wrote every now and then. Boris was happy. He said she wouldn't marry a strict and obstinate Jewish God, but His Son instead, so she'd sin in her mind only with Him. Mira studied for about two years and became a nun.

We didn't attend the ceremony. She came to see us in her nun's habit. She said she'd cried for us, for our errant souls. She went to Spain, to Vejer de la Frontera in the Cádiz province. I still have her address: Frontera Rauch, Queipodel Lahauo #3, Vejer de la Frontera, Cádiz, Spain, and sometimes she'd even reply when we wrote to her. She was in the convent for about two and a half years. It was an ancient and remote place for old nuns. The mother superior was senile. Supplies would arrive from Cádiz every now and again, and the high mountains enclosed the convent and in winter the winds blew with what seemed like hate, Mira told us later. The nuns stayed inside. Mira arrived there in May, when the Holy Cross of Cádiz was carried in the Corpus Christi procession by forty men before a huge statue of the infant Jesus. She walked through the town that seemed to be shrouded in a veil of ancient terror, preserved in the very stones. She traveled a road between magnificent crags that touched the sky and reached the white-painted town of Vejer de la Frontera that looked over the valley from the heights of a rocky cliff. The houses of the town crowded together, she walked along a path between stones and wild vegetation and reached the convent. It was surrounded by thousands of acres of dried vines, neglected groves, a huge rotting winery and abandoned farmland, fruit orchards and withered apples. The nuns were completely apathetic, prayed and giggled and at night she heard them groaning and mumbling. They no longer had any contact with the outside world.

After some time Mira decided to save the convent. She found old accounts ledgers and began taking care of the property. The mother superior fell ill and no one was chosen to replace her. Mira did everything the old woman wanted and the nuns came back to life slowly, and young nuns were sent by the local bishop after Mira went to see him and begged for them. She began tending the vineyards, renovating the winery, she brought in a local winemaker who still remembered how his forefathers used to make the region's famous wine. She brought in workers, paid them well, sold fruit at good prices, cultivated the fields, the orange groves, reached a new productivity record after bringing in a noted expert from France, and the convent began to show a profit. Word spread. Bishops came and were amazed by the newly invigorated convent and said, There's a living, breathing Church here despite it all. Mira painted and renovated the convent, went down into the cellars and found important manuscripts there, some of which were in Hebrew, she found Shabbat candles, an old Chanukah menorah, she discovered that it was customary for the nuns to fast on Yom Kippur and the ninth of the Hebrew month of Av which was adapted to the Gregorian calendar in an old book she found where the Gregorian months were listed in accordance with the Hebrew dates up to the year 2050. She sold part of the non-Hebrew manuscripts in Milan for huge sums. She became famous, wrote us that her life was wonderful and that she felt like she was founding a new nation, and said that she now knew how they used to sing in the Temple because here, she said, they had preserved those ancient psalms. The archbishop came to bless the place. More nuns arrived. Her ex-husband Yuri converted to Christianity. He studied and became a monk. He spent some time at a monastery in California, gave up his music, and two years later settled in Spain at a neighboring monastery. She had no contact with him but he was seen walking around the convent. He wrote to her, but Mira never told us what. She received a singular invitation from the Holy See. She went to Rome. She was granted an audience with the Pope—for a simple nun it was almost unheard of. The Pope knew about her past, her father, Stalin, and wanted to hear more. She told him. He permitted her to kiss his hand. He said she'd brought the roses back to the cheeks of the Church in southern Spain. Mira requested that her marriage be annulled. It's very rare that His Holiness intervenes in the annulment of a marriage because there is no divorce in the Catholic Church and the Pope is God's representative on earth, but he granted the annulment anyway. She went back to the convent and introduced more and more innovations, the region flourished, the villagers became prosperous, she adjudicated local disputes, fasted a great deal, sang Hebrew songs in secret, and one day took the Hebrew books and sold them to a Jewish dealer in Genoa. Mira, who in her youth had studied the piano, composed an oratorio in the Gothic style using the text of her father's letters and after it was sung at the Easter festival she traveled to neighboring Gibraltar and crossed to Algiers. She bought two cans of hashish and boarded a ship. She wrote to us asking that we meet her at the port and marked the number of the pier.

She arrived wearing her nun's habit and looked so beautiful, with her pale face and the habit and coif. She was carrying packages and the cans, which emitted a smell that even the seagulls could probably have identified. But the Irish and Italian New Yorker cops crossed themselves, their sense of smell having abandoned them. She looked completely pure in her habit, likewise crossing herself, and she even held a short prayer for the cops while the hashish sent out its aroma and Lee and I shook with terror. We took a taxi to Eighth Street. Mira hadn't explained a thing but went into a small club and came out half an hour later with thirty thousand dollars and we went to our apartment and she took off her habit. She asked Lee to steal a purple or brown dress and shoes for her from Macy's, which Lee did, and then, after she got dressed, Mira went to see her father and we went with her and she told her story and everybody, except Boris, was overjoyed. He hissed some words in Russian that sounded angry. And from then on she went to bed with anything that moved.

At that time I was in an exhibition. I was showing the paintings I'd done of Sonia and Alex. Somebody said derisively that if only they could, my paintings would sing as well. One critic, who at the time was fighting with somebody, I can't recall whom, wrote something about me, and one day I saw Alex and Sonia in front of my paintings. They had their arms around one another. They looked like a glass sculpture. Transparent. I told them that with them I could fulfill my greatest dream and make sculptures of water. Alex said something about humanity. Sonia spoke about Jewish values. I had a sudden attack of conscience. I called the Union Theological Seminary and introduced myself. At first they refused to give in but eventually I persuaded them to give me Mary Frances Hagen's phone number.

I wrapped *David Dancing Before the Master* in cloth. I took the painting in a taxi to her home. I rang the bell. An old woman opened the door and I found I'd got the wrong address. The woman was slightly drunk so although she wanted to be angry with me she smiled and from there I went to another address I found in the book, also under the name Mary Frances Hagen. I reached a big, fancy house. The doorman, wearing a brown uniform with golden buttons, asked who I was and I said I was a messenger from the

Sidney Janis Gallery. He called her, I heard her say she was in the middle of a call to Chicago and he should send the man up. I gathered that she hadn't really paid attention, which helped me get into the old elevator, and a young man took me up to the seventeenth floor and I rang her bell. I waited a while and she opened the door. She was wearing a kimono and her hair was tousled and she was barefoot and arrogant but she recognized me. She didn't seem surprised. I went inside, she led me into a big room devoid of paintings or furniture except for modern couches, standing lamps, and a single abstract sculpture. She asked, To what do I owe this honor? There was bitter mockery in her voice. I said, I owe you this, and offered her the painting. She peeled off the cloth, looked at it for a long time, I could see tears rising in her eyes but of course she wouldn't allow me to see her crying on my behalf, and she said, How sweet, how much is it? I said, Nothing, it's a gift. I've never put it up for sale because between David dancing before the Lord and a dancer whose name I forgot, I always figured it belongs to you and that you should have it. She asked if I wanted coffee and I said I very much wanted coffee because I'd walked a long way because earlier I'd gone to a different Mary Frances Hagen's. She looked at me with a smile that still carried a certain bitterness, brought in a tray with two cups, poured the coffee and milk, I took a spoonful of sugar and she said, In your prison they count the number of spoons of sugar you take, and I replied that she might have noticed that I'd never taken it upon myself to go out and photograph American military installations in the Arizona desert. She smiled and propped up the painting in front of her and in all the years I've seen people looking at paintings, I've never seen anyone looking at one with such force and for such a long time and without saying a word, stunned by some ancient emotion. I knew it wasn't because of the painting, there were many far more beautiful, it was just a hint of something I'd wanted to reach in those days, I'd wanted to touch a primeval Hebrewness in modern terms, without losing sight of the human aspect and without sidestepping the need to say something personal and without breaking up the canvas with stupid blotches. Then I saw that she was actually crying and she got up, went to the window, looked out, and said, I once asked you why you didn't love me. You had to. You could have saved me. I'm here. Who I belong to now isn't important. You can see I'm not poor. The Israeli policewomen no longer shout "Stop it," or "Spy," or "Slut" at me; the Security Service no longer shines lights in my eyes. I'm my own. I've got nothing in my heart. I exist, not live. You're a Jew and these days I don't like any of you. This is the most beautiful painting I've ever seen and it's not even such a good or important painting. It's me and he's dancing before the Master, and don't call me, I've got a man, he lives with me, he's not like you and he's got a heart. If another war breaks out I'll be on Hitler's side because he knew Jews from the inside. You could have loved me. I would have become a devout Jew for you even if I hadn't loved you, now go. Thanks for the painting. On the way out the doorman looked at me with a smile, I asked him why he was smiling and he said, In ten years only one man has come to see her, and I pressed a dollar bill into his hand like a big shot. He thanked me, poor guy, and I left.

About a year after she got back to New York, Mira met Avi Shoes and nobody really knows what happened between them, except that she cheated on him and as usual was pretty wild, but she was never cruel just for the sake of being cruel. She had an enormous desire to put an end to everything. Religions had destroyed her mind, said

Avi Shoes. Her Catholicism and a convent without God, all from the need to create another Boris out of Jesus. Mira begged me to go with her to Niagara Falls. No way, I told her, take Wally Cox away from Marilyn, or take Gandy, or take Avi Shoes, but she said she only felt free with me because I wouldn't want anything of her and we both knew, she said, how I really felt about love. Lee had gone on tour with a new off-Broadway show and she finally persuaded me to go along with Mira. I had a second exhibition. A museum bought a painting. I invented a method of mixing metallic paints with gouache and oil and then with a concoction made from egg yolks and linseed oil that I found in my school textbook on Caravaggio's color techniques that I then completely revolutionized. I wrote down my dreams and Lee got on my nerves with phone calls that filled me with revulsion at my own ostentatious pangs of guilt and back then I was missing her all the time.

Mira and I went by train. We hardly spoke on the ride up. When we got there we checked into the Falls Inn. It was a clear winter's day, the snow glistened on the roofs and fences, the falls were domesticated in the old windows, hung with red drapes. There was an electric fireplace decorated with golden fringes and cherubs, slightly faded, a small fir tree was lit up with tiny lights, with old paper flowers stuck to it. At the hotel entrance stood a toy general with medals and epaulettes with fringes, and over the threshold was the legend: Be Thou My Spouse. Mira and I took separate rooms and when we went first upstairs and stopped at my door, she announced, Remember, here you don't know me and I don't know you. You just look. After a rest and a shower she began wandering around the streets and stores like a spoiled cat. She wanted me to follow her and she kept turning her head to make sure I was there.

She went into a flower shop. I stayed outside, watching. There were lots of young people there. I saw she'd singled out a young man and gone up to him. He looked like Mr. Clean. Gray-blue eyes, light brown hair. He wanted a bunch of flowers. I couldn't hear the conversation but I saw that he was looking alternately at the flowers and Mira and seemed embarrassed, confused, and angry. He put a flower into a vase and took it out again. Then he went out and stood as if waiting. She played with the bunch of flowers he had touched earlier, and looked at him with innocent curiosity. The man holding the flowers turned around, fixed her with an angry glare; I could see it clearly through the shop window. He looked insecure, and when he turned to go, as if remembering for whom he was buying those flowers, Mira came out of the store alongside him, and he realized he still hadn't shaken her. Now I could hear them. He told her about his wife, he said she was waiting for him, it would be their second night together.

At dinner in the hotel restaurant Mira sat alone sipping a martini. She fished out the olive and chewed it sensually, and there facing me sat the young man with a young woman and his eyes followed Mira's every movement. She ordered something to eat, wine, by this time he wasn't paying the least attention to his wife. Afterward I didn't see anything. Later, in the lobby, I heard her say to the young man, Listen, my husband died, I'm Jewish and I need a man to make up the *minyan*. He didn't understand and said, What? What? And she said, He died. The man was trembling. What do you mean Jewish? She said, He died, dead Jews need a *minyan*, a quorum of ten men. Late that night he came to her. An hour later he crawled back to his own room and a few minutes after that crawled back to Mira wretched and humiliated and miserable, dragging the flowers he had bought for his wife. His wife came out into the hall in her nightgown and couldn't find him. He went back to her and in a loud voice begged her to forgive him. She cried. Mira came out of her room and handed her the flowers. In a tinny voice Mira said, Take them. Later I told Boris what had happened and he said, There's no place like America, she'll be the first Jewish woman president yet. I told him that first off she was a Catholic, second, there'll never be a woman president, and third, she wasn't born in America. He said she was no longer a Catholic and if Ike could be president, so could Mira.

We moved to Gramercy Park, on Sixteenth Street, an old place with mahogany-paneled walls, next door to a locked apartment on whose door I remember a plaque that read: Sherlock Holmes lived here during his visit to America (but that can't be right, can it?). Right next to the building was Union Square and there was a May First demonstration. Lee joined the demonstration and sang the *Internationale* while brawny Irish cops stood around laughing. She went away for a few days. I came home from a night of drinking at the San Remo Bar near the Calypso on MacDougal Street, and found an old man standing naked under the staircase that was now our kitchen, making soaping movements with his hands. I didn't understand. He reeked of cheap whiskey. He suddenly realized what was happening and got dressed awkwardly and explained that he had once lived here and came out of habit to take a shower and hadn't noticed that there was no water because the landlord was always shutting it off anyhow. I fed him.

Sondra Lee was playing in a musical called *Walk Tall*, I think, that Lee had done with Larry Kert. She lived on Fifty-first Street and Eighth Avenue, and told me that she had gone into the kitchen once and turned on the gas oven. It was funny, she said in tears, I put my head in the oven, took my head out for a moment to check that the windows were closed, and I saw light coming through the window and shining on the box of Quaker Oats cookies on the shelf over the oven. It seemed a shame not to eat the cookies, so I missed the chance of dying with dignity. Sondra, who was Brando's lover at the time, wanted to take me to meet a guy who collected folk songs. A studio on Fifty-eighth Street. I went. A man with a beard and a tortured face and thousands of tapes. I could get ten dollars a song. He recorded and I sang songs I'd known from my childhood. I sang Israeli-Russian songs that I translated into back into Russian, which I didn't understand, but knew how to fake. I remembered a Turkish song from my days at sea and I invented a few more. I invented songs in Arabic. In Greek. I went home with two hundred dollars. The poor guy tried to find me again afterward but Brando told him I'd gone to sell peacocks in Alaska.

I met a girl and we went to her apartment and she had a parrot that mimicked me but I just couldn't do it so I told her I was gay because I didn't want to offend the beautiful bird that laughed in my voice as I ran out of the apartment.

Sondra Lee again decided to commit suicide. She told me that this time she got everything ready, didn't look at the shelf so she wouldn't see her cookies, opened the window to jump, put one leg outside, but the air was freezing, a strong wind was blowing down Fifty-first Street from the river, and so she just couldn't jump. I told her that anyone who couldn't commit suicide with a razor blade would never get anywhere. I went back home and Boris called to say that the universe is fluid. That the universe no longer actually exists. It's all in our mind. We are part of a consciousness called the universe. Time is over, we're simply a shadow, a ray wandering between lost galaxies. Mira's no longer a Bride of God, I told him, what do you want from me? And he said, I miss Stalin but the bastard went and died on me.

A Russian woman from a radical right-wing California paper wanted to interview Mira on her experiences in the convent. She researched the story of Mira and the convent and told her that Boris had a brother. You had an uncle. He died in the gulag. Boris knew he'd be taken away. And Mira told her, My father certainly knew why his brother was being sent off to die. Mira remembered how they'd been taught sublimation in the Young Communist League; they were revolutionary cadres who would put an end to the decadent capitalist regime of the United States of America.

I got a call from the *New York Times* radio station after a favorable article appeared about a painting of mine that had been bought by a museum. A man with a German accent asked me to take part in his weekly program called, "How Others See Us." My gallery owner, Mr. Feigel, thought it might help. I went to the station with Gandy and he found some friends there, and he went off to get drunk in the room of a fat woman he'd known since his childhood on the Lower East Side and told her that I was a nephew of the Czar's cousin. The man who interviewed me was serious, pleasant-looking, and ascetic. He asked how an Israeli sees America and I told him that I really only knew the Village and Harlem. We chatted after the interview and he said it had been interesting. He added that he'd like to invite me to dinner. Despite the sale of my painting to the museum I was not in good nutritional condition and couldn't refuse. I went to his apartment on Park Avenue. An upper floor, I don't remember how high. The doorman called up. The elevator had an operator. It was a lovely apartment. A small framed Piero della Francesca fresco that had been brought to the apartment from Italy using a technique I'd learned about when studying art and the transport of frescoes at the Beaux Arts in Paris. There was a Rembrandt hung there too, one of his self-portraits, a few Noldes, a rare Chardin, and more.

He took me into the dining room. A big table, sixteenth century he said. And straight-backed chairs likewise sixteenth century, from a Scottish castle. On the walls were photographs about three feet square of a woman he said was his late wife. He seemed lonely and we ate almost in silence, surrounded by the huge portraits of his dead wife and tended to by an old manservant whose hands trembled from old age. The food was delicious. We drank wine. He said it was wine from Baron de Rothschild's cellar. Suddenly this sad man surrounded by his wife twenty times over began smiling and said that a man once approached a sausage seller standing opposite the Rothschild palace and asked him for a loan, and the sausage seller replied, I have an arrangement with Baron Rothschild, he doesn't sell sausages and I don't lend money. The servant approached almost without touching the ground and served dessert and then coffee. On my way home I recalled the never-ending theological arguments with Mira who claimed that Christianity began where ethics ended and God began. She said that the Church is a way, and a way is greater than the distance between two points— like life and death in Judaism, where we don't even have a heaven! A person searches for a way, wanting to reach hope, because he always needs hope. And then I remembered that for her, all that wonderful Christianity had ended up in two cans of hashish.

It was summer. A friend took me out in his red Porsche and put the top down. We went to see a show that Lee was dancing in. It was so hot that birds dropped out of the trees cooked. Half the cars were smoking. A woman outside a fruit and vegetable store was holding a skillet and frying eggs in the heat. The traffic lights had died. The city's electric grid had shut down. We couldn't move. Evening began to fall apart. We were in the Porsche at night stuck between thousands of cars, smoking buses, trucks, and they were all trying to move and running into one another. A line of people came out of one of the buildings. They walked slowly, measuring each step, and didn't say a word. There were maybe a hundred, two hundred people there; old people, young people, women, men. They walked in perfect order. They were holding candles so we could see them and pocket flashlights and they started directing traffic. My friend shone the lights of his luxurious car at them. They explained that they were blind and wanted the drivers to listen to them, and they seemed to move as if they'd been waiting all their lives for this moment. In the oppressive heat, in almost one hundred percent humidity, they unraveled the traffic jam, sending some of us down side streets and some off to the park, not far from there, so people could find a place to sit and shut down their boiling engines. They went from car to car, from bus to truck. Everybody did what they said, the jam was eased and the traffic started moving: slowly, but it moved. The electricity came back on. Thousands of drivers applauded the blind people who made their way back to their building on Broadway and bowed like they were actors. Then it turned out that the monk who'd been Mira's husband had followed her home and reached a monastery near New York. He had an outdated, naïve, and credulous innocence and though he had only joined the priesthood because of Mira was still completely unable to renounce his abstinence. Completely by chance I bumped into him as he passed me on Fifty-seventh Street by the Russian Tea Room, and he inquired about Mira and whether she ever talked about him and I said yes. He stared at me. With a certain curtness I asked him why he was still a monk. He looked at me for a long time, thought a little, his sandals were dusty, his hair short, his face pale, and he said in a whispery voice, She'll never be mine, I watch out for her and the Good Lord helps me. You'll see the light too one day. God loves you.

Avi Shoes and I had grown up together but we'd never understood one another. The truth is that we liked each other so we didn't even try to understand. Our relationship was fluid. We'd met in kindergarten. We used to swim together at Gordon Beach. Ever since he was a kid all Avi wanted to do was rest. He was born to go through life in a daze. We enlisted together in 1947 and we fought together. We worked together on illegal immigrant ships. We went around Naples and Marseilles together, and in Yugoslavia through abandoned castles where thousands of shattered Jewish refugees had congregated on the grounds and we rounded them up and led them to the ships. I studied in Jerusalem, I was squatting in the top floor of a monastery while he stayed in Tel Aviv and worked collecting luxury taxes. I never stopped being haunted by the horrors of the war but he forgot it the day it ended. In Paris, not far from the Café de Flore, he met a German girl who sounded crazy and whose name was Martina. We were both there they day they met. We flipped a coin to see who'd hit on her. I won but she was looking at him the whole time I tried. Then he tried and she melted. She'd wanted him even before she was born, she said. She made herself into a chameleon for him. She became whatever he needed. He knew all about chameleons; when he was young, he used to pick them off trees and stroke their heads. Martina said she was in love with him and nobody had ever told him anything like that before. She photo-graphed him in the nude and started literally chewing glass because of him. After some time her glass chewing began to worry him, sometimes blood would drip out of her mouth and he began to hate her and used to hide all his glasses, but he also started feeling rather guilty about her. Maybe because she was German and so he thought he *should* hate her. Or maybe because he worried that she thought she only needed to love him because he was a Jew. She sometimes even called him "My Jew." Avi came to America a year later, to get away from Martina, but it was no use, she was determined and followed him. He came to me. Lee couldn't stand him because he never looked at her and wasn't interested in her dancing. Martina's family had a small estate in New Hampshire. Avi Shoes, who didn't want to see her, suggested that she go to up to the family estate to rest. He began working for a moving company and one Sunday, in May 1956, he had an attack of remorse about the way he'd treated Martina—or so he told me—and decided to visit her. He bought a ticket for White River Junction on the 1:04 train from Penn Station. He went there from the studio I had at the time on Charles Street and went into Rikers to order a sandwich and a bottle of Coca-Cola, and he sat down on a high stool facing the street. He was staring into the street and found himself focusing on the figure of an el-derly man walking slowly along. He noticed that the man's shoelaces were undone and trailing behind him. The man, who began to feel that his dragging laces were hampering his progress, stopped by the window. He found a hydrant that looked like a top hat with a little head, glanced embarrassedly from side to side, put one foot on the hydrant, and tied his laces—with no great success. Avi remembered that a few days earlier, in a dusty toy and games store on Delancey

Street, where he'd bought a present for Martina's nephew, he'd seen a flexible but strong leather strap one end of which was smeared with some sort of weak adhesive that would stick but also come apart again and never dry up. As Avi watched the man tying his laces he thought—and this was nothing new for him, because he was perfectly capable of thinking about a single wave at Gordon Beach for an entire hour, staring at it and following it from afar, and when he'd go on to see a ship on its way into port he'd decide the ship must have caused the wave, though they were two or three kilometers apart, and feel as though he'd solved a great riddle—that if the man had laces made out of the straps he'd seen at the toy store, the man could bring one lace to the other and they'd simply stick together on their own. Avi left the diner, forgot about his train ticket, went to Delancey Street, found the straps he was looking for, bought a whole bunch of them, and then—unable to do otherwise, given his stubbornness—went back to Penn Station anyway, even though he knew he'd missed his train. He called Martina's brother from the station and said that due to his feelings of moral obligation toward her he would be unable to come. She then began coming to New York, sitting on his doorstep shouting, and in the end he'd take her inside and she'd make noises like greaseproof paper and draw butterflies on his chest and finally something strange and completely inexplicable to Avi burst out from within her and she asked him to give her a child. Avi was vehemently opposed to this.

At this time Yochai who had served with us in the war came to America too. Avi told him about his shoelace idea, which was giving him no peace. He cut the strap into thin strips like laces and played with them, stuck them together, tore them open, experimented, and really, I had my doubts as to whether this was worth all the trouble. Yochai was excited. With the little money they took from their savings they rented a room on Broome Street and immersed themselves in their work for weeks. They started producing strips as thin as laces, which if they came undone and then came into contact with each other would stick themselves together again. Avi Shoes said, It's a small thing, not like a new jet plane, but something. They went to a shoe store owned by a Jew in Brooklyn who Yochai knew through a cousin he'd met when he first arrived. The shoe-store owner took a shine to them: Israeli soldiers manufacturing shoelaces! It made him laugh, but still, Israeli soldiers, what wouldn't we do for them! He told the story at his temple and invested five thousand dollars in development. Avi said that one day they'd find a way of sticking the straps to the shoes themselves so that laces wouldn't be necessary at all. They threaded their way through town, selling their laces from store to store in Brooklyn, then in Manhattan, the Bronx, Coney Island, and as far as New Jersey. To their great surprise, demand increased. Within a few months they were producing thousands of pairs of laces, black and brown and white and red. They employed Israeli students who were saving money to buy electrical appliances before returning home, paying them to go from store to store and sell the laces for a commission.

One day at my apartment Avi Shoes met Mira who'd come to argue with me. He fell for her. What amazed me was the way Boris received him. He didn't throw him out and didn't insult him. They spoke the same language: Avi Shoes understood Boris and Boris understood him. He is a shoelace genius, he said, not radio, not television, laces, and that's what's wonderful about inventions, it's more important and more difficult to invent scissors, the wheel, a fork, than another sophisticated bomb! Boris went one better and made Avi some stuff to add to the original adhesive that made it last even longer. Their innovation, the simplicity of the process, did their job for them. Avi registered a patent, not because he really thought that potential big-time competitors would be deterred by it, but he still hoped his business was too small for them to notice. Mira warmed to Avi and began to hate Martina, though hating had never been difficult for her. She didn't love Avi Shoes, or maybe she did later, but I have no proof, and anyway I don't understand how Avi Shoes, usually so sharp, could have fallen in love with her. He rented a big loft on Avenue A. The Jewish storeowner who'd invested the first five thousand dollars wasn't really interested in whether the shoelaces worked or not, but he was happy for his pro-tégés. People always buy shoes, he said, and in shoe stores you don't make money from laces. But within two months Avi Shoes and Yo-chai sold thousands of laces and later tens of thousands of pairs all over the United States, and with the help of a friend of Mira's they embarked on a successful advertising campaign and began export-ing. Yochai returned to Israel to marry Aliza, the love of his youth. They've got four children and three grandchildren now and live in a *moshav* near Tel Mond. Yochai invested the money he made in his children and for pleasure he raises parrots and teaches them to talk. Avi forgave Mira for her quiet contempt and admired her malevolent intelligence, and what softened her heart toward him was the fact that he wasn't scared of her and he said that she was a one-woman theater. Before he sent Martina away again Mira came and slept in the next room and Martina said something nasty and they had a fight. Left with no choice, he hit her, or she hit him. Avi Shoes gave Martina some shares in his company and a considerable sum of money and sent her on a long world cruise from which, he told me years later, she never returned. Lee's cousin who worked in a shoe factory in Jersey taught Avi to chew leather, smell leather, she taught him about sewing leather, about glue, nails, cutting. He began learning what made Italian shoes so special and what was worthwhile about American production methods. He learned the structure of the reliable American shoe compared with the elegant Italian one. Despite the piles of money he'd made from his adhesive straps he began working at a low salary as a salesman for the big shoe company, First & Co. He worked hard. Mira, who'd left him dangling, didn't drop him completely. She needed his love as much as he needed her. Avi didn't care. He loved her simply and with the same honesty that had always set him apart from other guys. He slowly acquired the majority of Furst & Co.'s shares and when he was ready, took over the whole company. Three years after he'd become a shoe salesman, Avi became a shoe giant. He began manufacturing shoes that didn't need laces that were tied with adhesive straps that were now built into the shoe. Being an Israeli he came up with an idea for buckle-less sandals too, but didn't neglect the lace business. Whatever happens in the cutthroat shoe-sales business, he said, laces won't attract too much competition. And indeed, his personal business continued to thrive, and soon he acquired a company that produced elastic stockings and doubled its output. He took over and expanded a boot manufacturing company too, setting up a subsidiary specializing in cowboy boots that he began marketing in ever-increasing quantities in Japan, Korea, and Taiwan. In 1958 he headed a concern incorporating some twenty different companies. He lived in the Hotel des Artistes, an old listed building on Central Park.

One day Avi decided he had to find the old man who was tying his laces while Avi watched from Rikers. We sat down in his apartment and he said, Get a piece of paper and write down exactly what I say, it'll come to me as if in a dream. I concentrated. He closed his eyes and I sat writing down what he said, an imprecise description of a man: white-haired, nice eyes, apparently quite timid, feels a shy sort of discomfort. The Avi he noted the day, the time, the place. The man, Avi recalled, had been wearing somewhat bohemian clothes, out of place in the summer, maybe even corduroy pants? A threadbare coat? And he was wearing a strange watch, something you don't see too often, it wasn't even round! An artist? An art lover? A professor? We went to Sotheby's. I had contacts there and we were given catalogs of rare watches. After a while we became experts in watch collecting. We went through dozens of catalogs until we came across the 1929 Rolex Prince, valued at between seven and nine thousand dollars, which reminded Avi of the watch he thought he'd seen on the old man's wrist, since when he was working to tie his shoelaces, his sleeve had ridden up. We headed to several antique stores, hidden collectors' nooks that specialized in old fountain pens, medals, stamps, watches. Stores without signs. After cross-referencing what we'd been told by a number of store owners—who were, of course, not unsuspicious, and each of whom we had to work on for quite a while to gain their trust—we got what we were after. We now had a list of ten people in the city who were known to have bought the 1929 Rolex Prince. True, we thought, the lace-tying man could have inherited the watch, bought it years ago in Berlin, London, or Paris, it might even have been another watch, but Avi said, We've got nothing to lose! Something about that man reminded me of a beggar I saw photographed in the *New York Post*—they found a million dollars hidden under his mattress after he died.

To gain the man's trust, Avi asked Boris to recommend a rare watch to us. Boris went to the city library, sat there a whole day, and brought back a list of suggestions in which the most significant was an IWC Schaffhausen watch, which he said was the most expensive of all. Our search took a long time and we went through a lot of ups and downs and disappointments—a crazy woman even latched onto Avi at once point, claiming he was her husband—but in the end we heard from one of the salesmen, who decided to try out the old Hebrew he'd learned back in Krakow on us, that there was a gallery owner at the end of Greenwich Avenue whose name was Hauser and who was well known for his abiding love of old fountain pens and watches, and who had a large collection, though he himself wasn't at all wealthy. From a watch collectors' store on Eighty-ninth Street Avi bought a Schaffhausen for $90,000 and a Patek Philippe made in a limited edition of three hundred for $49,000 dollars. His Schaffhausen, so we were told, measured seconds, minutes, leap years, non-leap years. It was completely error-free and beautifully designed; built to work without breaking down, gaining or losing time, until 2499! And the expert explained to Avi that inside the watch was a tiny glass tube that should be replaced in 2100—at any IWC Schaffhausen workshop in the world—to ensure the watch's precise timekeeping for another 399 years and probably more, though obviously there was no scientific proof of the latter, he said. Similar watches, said Boris, had been worn by King Ferdinand of Bulgaria, Winston Churchill, Pope Pius IX, Brezhnev, King Ibn Saud, the Sultan of Borneo, and six Japanese tycoons. The best watch in the series cost four hundred thousand dollars.

We arrived at the gallery. Hauser was wearing worn corduroy pants and a corduroy jacket with threadbare elbows. Before seeing our faces he lit up at the sight of the watch and started breathing heavily. Excitedly he mumbled, Amazing! Amazing! A Schaffhauen! A good watch, said Avi. Hauser was wearing a watch but not the one Avi remembered. It later turned out that he had actually been wearing a Cartier Cougar that day—the Cougar was a women's watch and the company had made only one men's edition in 1938, which indeed resembled the 1929 Rolex Prince, and was a beautiful old watch in itself. Hauser spoke excitedly about the Schaffhausen as though he were praying. Avi, who didn't know what to say, asked how much it would cost him to buy all the pictures on the gallery walls. Hauser laughed. But when Avi told him how amazed he was by his 1938 Cougar and that he viewed his Schaffhausen as his greatest treasure—and how if he only had the money he'd buy a 1929 Rolex Prince—the guy suddenly started looking suspicious. But I felt that Hauser was more inclined toward belief than suspicion. You know watches, he said, collectors are a dying breed, today everything is plastic, batteries, no design, Mickey Mouse, and I can guess that you're no big art maven, so what's with you and these pictures? I'm a compulsive collector. The pictures are my children. They don't have much value. Collecting is a disease. In any case, when any of these kids makes it, he leaves me for a bigger gallery.

Avi asked Hauser whether by any chance he remembered walking down Fifty-fifth Street and his shoelaces coming undone so that he had to put his foot up on a hydrant to tie them. The man said it happened frequently. No, he didn't recall that particular occasion, but it was certainly probable that he'd passed by there. Despite his protestations Avi bought the contents of the gallery. He also put two hundred and fifty thousand dollars into Hauser's bank account, a sum identical to the one he'd made from the laces during the initial period of production. Hauser pleaded and grumbled that it wasn't right, that he hadn't worked for the money, but Avi explained that he had more millions than he could count, and that Hauser deserved it. Avi said it was humility and humility is a kind of conceit. Hauser yielded. He got confused. He invested in new paintings. Avi continued to buy paintings from the gallery through acquaintances and people who worked in his companies. Hauser began to look haggard. He begged Avi to stop. He bought watch after watch and pen after pen with the money, even when his purchases drove the market up, but he still couldn't spend all that Avi gave him. And then, one day, in his Packard with Gandy and me, as his chauffeur was taking us to his office in Manhattan, Avi read a small item in the *Post*. It said that an antique collector and art gallery owner had been found dead in his apartment on West Ninety-second Street. It said that he was found holding a pistol in his mouth. It went on to say that the police had found a sheet of paper with no addressee, on which was written, "Much is little. Victory is catastrophe." Avi Shoes sat and wept. I'd never seen him cry before.

We went to Hauser's home. Relatives told us that Hauser had died a wealthy man. Avi Shoes told me that now he realized that Hauser had died because he could no longer look forward to his new acquisitions with the same desperate desire he'd had when he was poor. Because of him, because of Avi, Avi said, there was no more tension, no mystery, no triumph in his victories, in his perseverance. I killed him. Once he had all that money he could go right to Christie's or Sotheby's and buy every fountain pen or watch he wanted, never getting excited, never having to beat out the cunning stratagems of his competitors, and so, said Avi Shoes, he had to get out of the game. Avi never got over it. He tried to atone for Hauser's death. He found Hauser's daughter Rita and tried to help her as much as he could. She hated him. But that story doesn't belong here.

Since Mira's return from the convent her mother had become a wispy shadow of herself and looked like a moth stuck to a lamp. Or, Avi Shoes said she was a fly who'd managed to escape the flypaper. Boris looked old now. He said that the difference between Russia and America was that in Russia life is a drama. Tears. The more horrible the ending, the better. America on the other hand is a fairy tale, a musical, a Western with a happy ending and good guys and bad guys and bad guys who turn out to be good guys and good guys who turn out to be bad. Life here is a musical. I had a show, Lee danced the part of one of the three girls in the *Nutcracker* and her friend Marilyn started visiting us again, bringing along her domesticated gypsy beauty and a childhood friend of Brando's, Wally Cox. Bird played at Minton's for a few enchanted nights and one night he took Gandy and me to a Chinese restaurant around West Fiftieth Street to hear Lennie Tristano. The second floor was almost empty. I drew this handsome blind man. A beautiful young woman was sitting there who didn't take her eyes off Tristano's hands. Tristano caressed the keys with a kind of tenderness but from a secret place hidden inside this tenderness he would sometimes strike the keys with a sudden smack though his fingers were the most delicate things in the world, said Gandy. Once I even kissed his fingers after I'd finished drawing some of them and the woman looked at me enviously. Bird liked him and said he was an Italian bastard and a wonderful musician. That he was white but of Benny Goodman's magnitude and he had black rhythm in his hands. Somebody once called blood "dried-up water," maybe it was Borges who I'd then begun reading, and here the blood in the music was like that. Sometimes Bird would pull out his alto sax and join Tristano, but only as an accompanist, because he didn't want to steal a single note, a single second, from that man. They threaded a crumbled tune stuck with thumbtacks of brilliant lightning and at the same time going crazy with notes sneaking one into the other. The woman cried. Lenny asked that Gandy and me bring some paintings. He fingered them and described what was in them. I asked him to describe my face. He moved his hand over my face gently, his fingers touching it like a pianist playing Chopin, turning it into the mirror of a blind man, and it was nice. The young woman's name was Jane. Maybe it wasn't Jane, maybe I don't really remember, but when Tristano stroked Bird's huge head his description was perfect and beautiful: the high forehead, the sensual lips, the sad mischievous eyes, the rounded cheeks, who can remember words so mysterious and so extraordinary, something about a fluttering of forms that cannot see but can feel, something that moves, waves, a sense of something that touches it with wings, a song that remains a song but returns by a roundabout route to be the words that that the song really wanted to sing and the caress calling forth delicate, quivering, invisible forms . . . Go figure today what it all meant and how that brotherhood between Lennie and Bird and Gandy and Jane was formed. At the end of his time there, after the restaurant had lost a ton of money, we took Lennie to Minton's. Jane came too. Lester Young, who knew about love, brought them together officially. They were married in the Chinese restaurant by a justice of the peace we brought and afterward they went to a Catholic church and a black priest conducted the ceremony even though Jane was a Methodist but the priest was kind enough not to mention this. When Lennie played after the ceremony you felt he was taking pity on the music, perhaps he wanted it to burn up with his own happiness. He enthused and played and said, I'm playing windmills, playing the leaves of trees in the park. His pale pink fingers whispered the music. Bird wailed. Mingus wept. Bird said, Lenny's taking pity on his music. Billie Holiday, who called Bird the Black Angel, said later that Tristano was out of the ordinary, abnormal even, and that's why he would eventually just fade away. Like when I heard Bird I thought it was the voice of God, like the Brahms sextet or the coda of Beethoven's Ninth. As always Lenny was wearing a fashionable black suit and a wide kitschy purple tie, and he asked what was the difference between pink and red and what are eyes when you don't have eyes to see them. Bird, who was trying to quit heroin and had the shakes and drank a whole bottle of sweet Manischewitz wine and chewed through the contents of an entire big bottle of aspirin, just sat staring. Next day, Jane told us later, Lenny had said to her, Let's travel the two hundred and fifty miles to Virginia by taxi. It cost him hundreds of dollars. There he met Jane's father, who was terrified by this apparition, got blessed by an old drunk, and when he got back, he played the same melodies but something was lost. He knew, he said, that such happiness tends to make bad music and Bird said, Tell that to all the other fools in this fucked-up town. Let them be happy that they're stupid and that life's good to them and they've got all the money in the world. Twenty people attended Rockefeller's funeral, the man was a giant, he had more money than God, but everybody hated him, couldn't he have bought two hundred people?

We went to a gig with Bird. They didn't want to let him play, because of the drugs, but somehow he managed it. On the way we stopped at some hole-in-the-wall town in Pennsylvania near New Hope where he and his wife Chan lived in a little house surrounded by green lawns. New Hope was one of the few places where a mixed-race couple could live undisturbed. But nobody loved America like Charlie Parker. Europe admired him and America beat him to the ground, but he went hurtling on anyway, he was in love. He collected guns and loved Westerns. He made a religion of fried chicken. A fat black man asked Bird for his autograph. He told him he was the greatest. He said that Dizzy Gillespie had said that Bird plays the way the music should sound. He said that his music came out of God's ass. Bird laughed and the guy sang, "Hey Bop a Rebop, Mama's in the kitchen, Daddy's in the jail, Sister's on the corner singing 'pussy for sale,' Hey Bop a Rebop." More kids came along and sang too. I forget who turned that great work into a beautiful piece of jazz. A few weeks later I went to Minton's Playhouse with Gandy. A black kid was tap-dancing by the subway. A limousine drew up and Fred Astaire got out. He danced a few steps with the kid and gave him some money and yelled, You're great, kid! We clapped. And Slavenska from Lee's ballet company said that when a great Russian dancer had come to America and was asked how it felt to be the greatest dancer in world, he replied, The second greatest! The first is Fred Astaire.

Wally Cox stopped making the beautiful jewelry he put together so skillfully and began appearing at the Village Vanguard, this time without the help of applause from Gandy and me. He was ugly but funny. An evil little man with a talent for hurting people. We'd laugh till we cried at the parties he came to and it was suggested that with his cynical, sharp, witty, and rather British sense of humor—and maybe because of his screechy voice and ludicrous appearance—he'd do well on the club circuit. In the end he had his own television show. He claimed he'd fallen in love with Marilyn Gennaro even though he'd been dating five strippers and had beaten them all up. I tried to avert a disaster but was told not to interfere.

Ilka and Aviva came back from a tour of American cities and started working for Leo Fuld who'd opened an Israeli nightclub called Sabrah. I was asked to paint camels and Bedouins on the walls. Leo Fuld would sing, "To see the *Yam, Lir'ot Ha'am, Ha'shemesh* all day long." He'd trill the words with his hair dyed orange, wearing plastic teeth, make-up, singing in Yiddish-English-Hebrew. The murals I did were usually left in darkness and nobody saw them and Avi Shoes brought Mira who said that the paintings looked good in the dark. Lee came with me once or twice and that was more than enough of the world she thought I came from. Two Israelis from Haifa danced the Israeli "national" dances: the Zionist Fisherman and the Arab Hunter.

Steve Allen, who was dragged to Sabrah and laughed, decided to do a show for Israel's Independence Day. I was asked to bring a big painting to the studio that I'd done of Shabtai Zvi riding a horse. I was to show the picture to the camera and say a few words about Israeli art. The big day arrived. I found a huge disorderly stage. Dozens of people were running back and forth and back and not-forth and writing things on little blackboards and shouting and there were masses of cameras and microphones and huge piles of cables. Allen was sitting wearing a djellaba and a kaffiyeh with a red akal on his head, which is, of course, Israel's national costume. An old man wearing a yarmulke set up a falafel stand and next to him men and women in various costumes wandered about, some in djellabas and others in regular clothes. It was hot. Allen drank whiskey and played the piano. Off to the side I saw a strange camel that had been brought from the Bronx Zoo, and at its side a short Pakistani; the camel spat and looked angry, Allen was already drunk, and five young men were running around him holding big boards and chalk and writing gags that might suit the moment. It was a kind of electrical musical hell, an orchestra playing tunes like "Hava Nagila" and "Mein Yiddishe Mama." The hunter and fisherman from Sabrah hunted and fished. Israel Fuchs, wearing a tarbush but without a djellaba, was sitting by a bonfire protected by terracotta-colored stones and making coffee in a jug and pouring it into little *finjans* and then he spoke about the fighting spirit when we fought all the Arab nations. I wandered around, getting under everybody's feet. Steve got drunker and drunker and told jokes he read off the boards and also made up a few of his own and played something that wasn't Israeli but dragged in some Yemenite singer called Zemira I'd never heard of and who was introduced as Israel's national singer and she just sang away. The camel didn't like the sound. It groaned and Steve told a joke about a Jew, an American, and a Frenchman, and then they signaled that it was my turn. I was positioned in front of a camera, and back then the cameras were huge, the one in front of me started rolling, they shouted at me to talk, I showed Shabtai Zvi on his horse and began talking about the first Israeli exhibition at the Tower of David in Jerusalem, when the camel suddenly jumped forward, detaching himself from the Pakistani who was holding on to it for dear life and it galloped toward me hawking horribly, the Pakistani hanging on behind, and it tore cables as it ran, hating my painting and hating me, the painting had been sold and I was scared it would be damaged and I didn't have the money to give back to the buyer, and so instead of talking about the historic exhibition at the Tower of David I started running holding the big painting, Steve Allen loved it and told the cameramen to follow me, the camel attacked, the Pakistani smacked his head on some cables, I retreated, trying to think up escape strategies, somebody ran after me with a microphone and another said, Go on about the exhibition at Solomon's Tower, I said David's, but the camel abhorred the Tower of David and the Pakistani was wheezing like his camel, words, words, Steve Allen was laughing and his writers who were already as drunk as lords were laughing too and running after me and the camel with the Pakistani who hit a wall and the camel was trying to attack again and again and the Pakistani was trying to it and more electric cables were torn, Steve was lying on the floor half dead from laughing and was scalded by some Arab coffee, the camel trampled on all the falafel and the guy cooking it ran, the camel licking him all over, the writers wrote a gag about a licking camel and I panicked, the camel was strong and butting the painting and belching, we were all running, somebody threw water on the bonfire, and the fisherman and hunter lost their costumes because the camel didn't want them to feel ignored and they were running naked looking for their clothes, Zemira seized the moment to sing another song, her Hebrew sounded like Arabic, and Steve, who'd lost his kaffiyeh, went over to the piano and took out a clarinet and played a little more and the writers were writing words for the song he was improvising, and then he sang a song they'd written on the board for him about a camel and an artist and I don't remember what else. I ran for it. Happy Independence Day Eve. I ran down Seventh Avenue, people saw me and yelled, it was one in the morning. They shouted, A madman with a fucking horse, because the camel had managed to break free and run after me. The passersby fled. I was trying to get to the subway entrance and the camel knocked down two people who he thought looked like me, and I with the horse and Shabtai Zvi shouted, Watch out! The Pakistani ran after the camel and I managed to get into the subway. I waited for a train. I got in and almost passed out. Next day I got a call from Steve Allen's office and they begged my pardon, but they couldn't stop laughing. How the camel fought the horse. What did it have against you, maybe the camel was the brother of the horse's real father who wasn't a real camel, and then a guy named Bill Dana came on the line and said he was one of the writers I'd seen on the stage and he invited me for a drink the following evening.

We met. A sad Jew. He could easily have played an Italian gangster. Or maybe it was the other way round. He spoke ten dialects. Hated himself with gusto. A strange guy. I liked him. Later he did a funny bit about a character named José Jiménez and it made him a star. A year or maybe more after the Independence Day with the horse and camel, he suddenly called and asked how I was. I told him. He invited me to his office to see how they got the *Tonight with Steve Allen* show ready. It was broadcast nightly from eleven-thirty to one and was the mother of all the late shows. I went to the office. A cold winter's day. The coldest day of the year. The room was overheated. In the middle of the room stood a table holding a bottle of Four Roses bourbon and around it sat the five saddest people I'd ever met, their faces long and longer, looking as though they'd just come out of a pogrom, and one of them was Bill. They whispered among themselves. They drank. And one said sad-faced, What about Jew 4 with Scotsman 7 and a Puerto Rican on a plane? The second said, That's fine, we just have to add German 6, and a young woman was sitting writing down everything they said, and Bill said, Indian 4 with Jew 25, a Pole not a Russian, plus Scotsman 8, plus a wheeze, and then maybe Brooklyn 6. During a break, during which they finished off the bottle, Bill explained that he'd been writing gags for five years, first for Jack Benny and now with his friends for Steve Allen. Good money. There were thirty or forty basic gags. Or maybe it was a different number. They were so clever that all they needed was the tiniest hint and they could tell you the rest of the joke. I didn't believe them, I tried them, I told them about how Ben-Gurion asked his old Minister of Religious Affairs, Rabbi Toledano, who had recently gotten married to a young girl, to get to the cabinet meeting early in the morning. Rabbi Toledano said to Ben-Gurion, If I can't come, I'll be there—if I can, I won't. They finished the joke when I was still in the middle. Then they gave me four other possible endings. They didn't laugh once during the four hours I spent with them, then Bill opened the door to the hall to let in some oxygen, or so he said.

On the other side of the hall, through an open door, a beautiful girl sat typing. Bill, who saw me looking at her, introduced us. We talked. She finished work and I went out with her. I couldn't think. Sex oozed from her. I could feel my body tensing. We went to Macy's because she had to buy something, and no more than a few minutes passed before we were making out. She went into the store and I suggested that afterward we would go to my place—Lee was away on some tour or other—but she said not now, and asked me to come by her place at nine that evening. I wrote down the address. I went home and waited. On the radio they said that the temperature was dropping and that this was without doubt the coldest day in fifty years. I left the house at eight forty-five and, completely frozen, managed to hail a taxi. The driver was wearing gloves, the heater was on, the windows were covered in condensation, he managed to mumble that I was his last fare that night and then he was going home, he said, it was worse out than when he was in the army and was stuck in Alaska one shitty January.

On the radio we heard the announcer saying belligerently, A cold night. Cold. Cold. You could hear his teeth almost chattering in his heated booth. There was excitement on the radio. America loves it when it's the coldest or hottest or longest or shortest day. A woman phoned in and said she'd been outside and found a bird that had frozen in flight. A man phoned from a call box on Ninety-second Street and he couldn't move because his feet were stuck to the ice on the sidewalk. The driver said he hoped for my sake that I wouldn't need a taxi later because they were all about to freeze up. I got out and looked around. It was on the corner of York and maybe Sixty-eighth Street. A big building, it looked like a warehouse. The walk from the taxi to the door was short. Excitement enabled me to reach—albeit frozen—the doorbell with her name underneath. She called me from inside to come in. I went inside. I went upstairs. A huge room, like a studio. Through the cloud of my breath I saw that the big hall was devoid of furniture. From a distance I saw a big bed lit by a ceiling light that came down to the bed and facing it a sealed window and door and she said from the bed, I'm sorry, there's no heating, it's a coldwater flat, and I remembered Pat's apartment on Division Street. She told me to get into bed right away. I was confused and it was hard to think in that cold. I realized I had to use some kind of abstruse strategy to get even partially undressed and get into the bed that looked like an island in the middle of an ocean. I was shivering, she laughed and said, Get in, get in. Everything misted over, I managed to take off my coat and sweater and shoes and jumped in. I was shuddering. And how I was shuddering! My teeth chattered so much so that my mouth ached and she giggled and shoved a bottle of Cutty Sark into my mouth. I managed to ask her how she knew I was a Cutty Sark man, and she told me, but my ears were so frozen that they were about to snap off and fall down and I didn't hear what she said.

I drank, I gargled, and after a while managed to stop shivering and my teeth stopped chattering. There was a radio next to her, a woman was saying that things were getting worse by the minute, New York was freezing to death, and I thought longingly about the drive in the Porsche in the heat when the blind people came to rescue us. And suddenly it hit me, maybe because most of my brain wasn't functioning and some of the dormant cells had come to life in a brief flash of memory, that when we saw the blind people, a nun was marching ahead of them, and I realized, in that freezing hell, that Mira must have found her nun's habit and gone to the shelter for the blind and had been there when we passed by. I thought, How come I didn't realize this before? and I tried to think about the heat and gradually calmed down. I slipped one arm out from under the covers to tidy up my clothes that were scattered on the floor, but suddenly I had no arm with which to continue undressing, nor the strength to continue. My teeth were chattering again and with a cry of despair I got out of bed for a moment, undressed completely and hopped back in. I couldn't see a thing on account of my breath clouding in front of me in the cold and my frozen arm hurting and I had to thump it to get rid of the tingling in my fingertips. My heart was pounding fast.

I looked at her. Her face was incredibly beautiful in the glow of the small bulb that shone above us. She had the face of a little girl; there was sorrow in it. She had brown eyes, lips that looked as though they'd been taken from a Holbein print, and a high forehead. Her cheeks were pinched—and then I embraced her. She pulled a cord and the light rose up, only a thin faint light remained, she wept in my ear, our bodies drew close, and then, beyond the intoxication of the moment, beyond the cold outside the blanket, I sensed that something was wrong. My brain hadn't yet reactivated the synapses required to for me to draw conclusions from stimuli. Through the cold vapor hanging above, battling the warmth of the bed—from which I didn't dare out stick my head—I slowly realized that the woman I was embracing had hair on her shoulders, back, breasts, legs . . . not like a hairy man but more like some sort of animal. I was lost and the tears that started trickling from my eyes froze and remained as icicles on my face. I could see the trees near York Avenue through the window. A cold moon hung in the sky. She smiled and said, Sorry, but I thought they liked it in Egypt. I whispered that I wasn't from Egypt. She said she'd been told that I was. I asked who'd told her and she said, I don't remember. But what *is* this? Hair, she said. I lay there and thought. Tried to think. It's difficult in that kind of situation to know how to be polite. I was a prisoner in her bed because what had gotten me into it would hardly get me out of it again, and I asked, But why? Why don't you shave? She said, I don't want to because some people like it. She closed her eyes sadly and I was holding a woman covered in a thick, black down. She laughed nervously, but there was no sign of empathy with my predicament in her voice; there was a concrete and unyielding innocence in her, a demand perhaps, something exotic, some kind of obdurate feminine cunning; there was a harsh critique of the world in that voice, as if her fur was something she'd deliberately covered herself with for the sake of some secret portion of humanity. Perhaps she thought she it was her hair versus the world. I suddenly wished I were Egyptian. Never in my entire life had I wanted something as badly as I wanted to be Egyptian at that moment. I would have given years of my life to be Egyptian. She smiled shyly, her face mournfully yearning, despairing. I made no effort at pretense, although I muttered a few polite words, and tried to flee, Egyptian or not, it was impossible. The cold enclosed the bed like a glacial wall. Then, left with no alternative, with the knowledge that there was nothing to be done, I took the bottle, gulped down its contents, and sank into a stupor.

In the morning, when I awoke through the mist of a terrible hangover, I looked at her and seeing the laughter in her face, realized that I had done my duty after all. I was filled with revulsion but also compassion for her and myself. The cold had lessened slightly and with enormous effort I managed to drag my clothes over to me and get dressed under the covers. She got up with a sorrowful smile, put on a pink robe as if it wasn't at all cold, and brought coffee to the bed. The coffee was delicious and aromatic. She didn't want me to leave yet, said that I'd sung her songs in Egyptian during the night. She started begging me to stay, brought delicious cookies, it was difficult for me, embarrassing, and I said, Look, I have to go, and she said, I understand, her sadness now subsumed in a voice filled with a wistful sort of challenge, Go, go on, people are waiting for you, you didn't complain last night! I don't remember how I managed to get away. I hailed a taxi and made it home. I took a long shower in almost-boiling water, sat in my heated apartment, and waited. I didn't know what I was waiting for and in my mind the beauty of her face blended with revulsion and loathing and anger at myself for being so cruel. I tried to separate the vast black fur from my body, and when the phone rang and it was Bill Dana, I realized what I had actually been waiting for. They knew, those sad comedian bastards. And how they knew. Each and every one of them had apparently been had once, but not on the coldest night in the past millennium. They at least had the option of running away, or perhaps they were Egyptians in disguise, they wanted to teach me to laugh with my mouth closed too. I yelled at Bill, but he just laughed, and that was the first time I'd heard Bill laugh, Bill the great comedian who wrote thousands of gags in his lifetime, Bill Dana who was immersed in eternal sorrow, laughed at me. His lips smacked the receiver and I told him I hoped they'd break and that he would choke on the laughter that he didn't even know he had in him, maybe he thought he was sick, and then I hung up on him. Ten minutes later, she called.

She sounded cheerful and asked if that sonofabitch Dana had already called. I told her he had. Those bastards, she said, but you're sweet, at least you stayed till morning! You were decent to me. I told her that maybe I had no choice, the others hadn't visited her on the coldest night in the last ten thousand years, but she said, You did have a choice, you're decent, don't be ashamed of being decent, it's all right, bye. Then I painted Icarus with golden wings over and over using a paint mixture I'd invented. As I worked on the painting, which took quite a while, I couldn't find an appropriate face for my poor angel, I wanted the face to be beautiful but a kind of Renaissance beauty that could be either a young woman or a young man. I went down to a nearby cafeteria and sketched faces of young women, but none of them was who I wanted, none of them had the profound feminine spirit I was after, reminiscent of those ancient

Madonnas who seem promiscuous at the same time as holy and give you the agreeable impression of mocking everyone who dares look at them. I sat gloomily in my small studio and drank Cutty Sark when suddenly the image of the girl from Naples sprang to mind. A hundred years had passed since then. I painted the memory of her on Icarus but it was difficult to capture the basic structure of her face, the foundations on which expressions are built. I put the Icarus aside and started painting Israeli flags. They were laughed at. Years later, Jasper Johns made a career out of American flags. I painted a picture covered with paint-tube caps that I stuck to the canvas and then Lee came, we became a couple again for a time, moved to Fifty-second Street over a strip club and the building shook from the echoes of the drums below and people yelling: Take it off! Krissoula, our Greek friend, purchased my Icarus.

Forty years later I came back to New York and Krissoula was there, Krissoula who had managed to be the lover of four Greek tycoons one after the other, and who was always wise and practical, and who said that all she had left was nostalgia and Valium. In the old days, she would come back to New York just to spend time with us. We were close but didn't know much about her. Krissoula said that one day the painting had disappeared, and she looked everywhere for it. She didn't find it. Eventually it returned. But then the face disappeared. A big lump, a dark stain, had replaced the beautiful face. And then, quite recently now, the face had returned, but it was different from the original face, it looked like a whore's face now, but an angel's too. Sadness and a hint of disgrace. And forty years later, I was in New York looking for friends, and most of them had either died or disappeared. But I found Krissoula. A great lady.

But no one had seen Adele Schwartz for ages, Adele Schwartz who, with an unknown father, had had a baby boy with a body like Superman's and the brain of some Jewish Amazon from an orphanage in Brooklyn—Adele Schwartz, who ran workshops for non-orgasmic women and once asked Gandy and me to take care of two workshop attendees who had never experienced an orgasm until then. And Gandy and I did our thing in two different apartments, and Gandy's one looked happy afterward, and mine told Adele that I'd given her what she wanted but that she'd run off home straight after, and she said, I can't be his mother for one fuck, and so Adele decided to explain to all her women about the custom practiced by certain men of taking off right after doing their thing, and asked me to introduce her to Marlon Brando. A picture I had painted from an old photo of my mother in high school hung on the wall above his bed. I went to his apartment on Fifty-seventh Street. He was playing with Russell, his raccoon. A journalist was sitting there and Brando had had enough of lying and set Russell onto her. I told him about Adele and we called her. She came over and I went back home. The journalist was still standing downstairs crying. Afterward, Adele said that he'd been great, but then wanted her to leave right away, and she did, and she said, Now I have something else to teach the women in my course tomorrow about men who don't like to hang around afterward.

Forty years have passed. I want to find Adele. Someone said they thought that she worked in gardening. My friend Jerry Tallmer had seen her and heard that she'd changed her name, and not to Barak Ben-Avinoam. I investigated for several days and discovered that she'd once danced, possibly belly-danced, at a Turkish restaurant on Christie Street to the accompaniment of a bouzouki player who looked German. I found out that she'd changed her name to the name of an American flower she liked and did indeed work in gardening, and then someone said that the flower she'd named herself after was a rare mountain flower. I went to a botanist acquaintance who found the name of the rare mountain flower for me. After some more sleuthing, I arrived at the name Kalmia Deveraux. Kalmia is indeed a rare flower that grows in the mountains and Deveraux—she later explained—was a French film actor who absolutely no one remembers anymore: she was his last living fan but couldn't remember what he looked like and had lost the only photo she'd had of him.

I went to see her in a rather shabby apartment somewhere around Seventieth Street and Amsterdam. Living alone. No sign of a child. She still had the tin bath. Adele was painting pictures of huge flies and living off a pension she had from her gardening work but with no money for medicine or food. I went downstairs and brought a big bag of food and we drank coffee. She was already over sixty-five and all wrinkled with sorrow. She pretended to be happy but it was obvious that she was going through hell and the rooms were crammed with memories of her son. She told me how he got sick and she called for her Reichian doctor who misdiagnosed him and the child died. She asked me if I'd seen Pat and I told her I hadn't, and she said she'd heard that Pat was still looking for her daughter. The doctor killed my son. And what now? I see a different Reichian since I put the first one in Mount Sinai Hospital with broken bones and did two weeks in a women's prison for it, but it wasn't the same prison you remember from next door to Alex's Borscht Bowl, the one on Sixth Avenue and Eighth Street was demolished. I asked and she told she didn't have a living soul in the world. Just like when her father ran off and left her with her mother and her mother died and they found Adele almost dead and put her into the orphanage. I'm an old orphan. The kid's gone. But she keeps the tin bath for him. She sat facing me and I could see that the ancient, gypsy, frightening, brazen light that had kept her alive had disappeared from her eyes and how all the safety pins she used to fasten herself together had loosened. I asked if there was anyone she could telephone if God forbid something happened to her, and she said she sometimes talked to the storekeeper downstairs. He's Mexican and gives me food on credit and sometimes I even pay him, he's got a good heart. And no, she said, the truth is I don't have anyone. Then she suddenly said, D'you know who I saw on television at George Bush's inauguration? Mira. Standing there in a fur coat, her eyes closed, looking like she'd fallen asleep on her feet. I was surprised because I'd been looking for Mira for years. Adele said, I tried to get hold of her but it wasn't possible.

I said good-bye and left her all the money I had and went back to Tel Aviv. Two months later, I felt kind of guilty and called Adele, or Kalmia to be precise, and the metallic voice of the impersonal world of telecommunication announced that the line had been disconnected. I went to the library at the American embassy and a pleasant and polite young lady gave me a videocassette of President Bush's inauguration ceremony, and suddenly it wasn't Mira I was seeing, but Adele standing close to the President. She was wearing a fur coat, locked into herself, as if she didn't belong there. I flew to New York two months later for one reason or another, a stifling, unpleasant flight, and I looked for Adele. Someone said she knew the President and had found an old friend of yours called Mira or something, and then this someone's brother said she'd painted pictures of fifteen-foot-tall flies and Clement Greenberg had written wonderful things about her. I found her new number through a friend of Jerry Tallmer—who, as you'll recall, was one of the founders of the *Village Voice*—so I called. She said she didn't know who I was or who Mira was but didn't manage not to cry. I asked, Why are you crying, and she said I'm rich and there's no one for me to be rich for. I said, Barak Ben-Avinoam, and she shouted, Yoram Yoram, and hung up. When I tried again, her number had been changed to an unlisted one.

But back then, when I was still living in New York, after the business with Bill Dana and the monkey-woman, Lee, Gandy, and I went to drink wine with Bird. He was trying to kick again, but he just couldn't help himself, he went crazy, he came over and took the ring off his wife's finger, she cried, her finger reddened with blood, and he slipped away like a thief and then came crawling back on all fours like a dog because he'd bought some stuff, he looked relaxed now and sad and she forgave him and we all went to drink some wine and he played. He already looked half dead. I translated the lyrics to "Lullaby of Birdland" into Hebrew for him and he memorized them and repeated them all sorts of places he wandered into during those bitter nights. Sometimes it seemed as though all that was left to him was devastation and a childish arrogance. He played compassion and indignity, Sarah Vaughan once said, or something like that. He's wise, Gandy said, Wise and as old as Methuselah, he plays tough, and I once told him that he and I are the day and night of the same twenty-four hours, not because of our colors but because I'm born out of his devastation . . .

Gandy said there was a surprise party for Tennessee Williams at the Hawaiian Room and we were invited. Bird didn't want to go. I asked Gandy who invited us and he said, You remember the woman Adele fixed me up with for an orgasm? She's a friend of Tennessee's. She looked angry when we arrived because apparently she hadn't exactly invited Gandy, but she soon vanished into the beautiful and respectable crowd and Gandy managed not to notice. Young Jewish ladies in Hawaiian costumes and garlands of exotic flowers on their heads and chests stood at the entrance to the hall and they looked exotic when they swayed in their Hawaiian grass skirts to what they call the hula-hula, and whispered to one another in Yiddish so that no one would understand what they were saying, and they sang Hawaiian songs between jokes at the expense of the arriving guests, mumbling something in an ancient Hawaiian melody that I remember my grandfather Mordechai the baker singing in his bakery on a crowded street in Tel Aviv. The girls served us drinks: Cointreau in avocado goblets and pineapple juice laced with Drambuie. The lights were dim. People were dancing and laughing, eating and drinking. We were given leis to hang around our necks and were decked out in all kinds of exotic flowers. There was a big pool in the middle of the hall and some boisterous friends threw Williams into it and laughed and he laughed too, but when I stood near him I saw no sign of happiness on his face. Some guests were less polite than others and wondered where they knew Gandy and me from, but we managed to mutter something that sounded satisfyingly mysterious and so no one wondered any more. We ate and drank as much as we possibly could and Gandy shoved fruit and delicacies that looked Chinese but had Hawaiian names into the pockets of a big coat he'd brought specifically for this purpose. I saw Ginger Rogers from a distance. She was radiant. She was wearing a white dress, smiling a white smile. Rogers and Fred Astaire were always what the world was supposed to be. Magnificent. Beautiful. Eternal. America. Shirley Temple had conquered India for us and the children of a Tel Aviv full of sand and sycamores, and Rin Tin Tin was the voice of yearning, and the most sensational thing we saw at the movies in the community center was when Flash Gordon or some other hero rescued an Indian boy who was hiding in a barrel of apples and the bad guy stuck a knife into it but couldn't reach him. Ginger was a Yankee Doodle of a woman. The world in divine Technicolor. It was said of her that she really did have a heart of gold. In a wonderful film I saw numerous times, a rich suitor buys her everything and drives her around in a Rolls-Royce, as I recall—but she is undecided. She wants to hate this man, but she's poor and the jerk buys her expensive jewelry and she almost succumbs to him, so finally the idiot takes her to his psychiatrist friend, who is Fred Astaire, of course, to persuade her to marry him. He waits downstairs drinking in his Cadillac. Fred, like any typical psychiatrist, sits in an office the size of a football field with mirrored walls. A fairy-tale New York can be seen through the window. A large desk in front of him and a couch to the side of it. They look at one another, Fred and Ginger, music playing in the background, then he gets up and dances a little Freudian dance for her. She smiles sadly and dances a Jungian dance for him. He sings to her. She sings to him. I said to Gandy, Look how probability theory is nonsense. We just saw Fred Astaire in Harlem, and now her. I would have given five years of my life to dance with her. Gandy was just happy because he wanted the chance to sell her some of the sketches he'd brought with him, of course. As he showed her the sketches, he whispered something into her ear and I could see her rummaging in her purse and taking out bills and at the same time staring at me in amusement. Her jaw dropped and Gandy, with the money stuffed into his pocket, walked past me quickly and whispered, There's no time, she's coming, you're a Russian refugee, you jumped over the Iron Curtain and you were wounded, you limp, you adore her. She came toward me. I limped toward her. We met halfway. She said, A pleasure, and I said, I no speak English, I Russian, Stalin, admire for you, see cinema with you and husband underground, KGB. She was excited. She said, Sweetie, Fred isn't really my husband, but I didn't understand of course, she said to several people who were standing nearby, Look at this brute, jumped over the Iron Curtain and got wounded, poor thing. Naïve, doesn't understand anything, it was all on account of me, he saw my movies underground. I put my arm around her waist and she drew me close, it was intoxicating. She guided me with all the affection of a nurse tending to a wounded child, we started dancing, me hopping like someone who had been wounded jumping over Iron Curtains and she explaining to all the people drawing near—wondering at the sight of this beautiful woman in white dancing with a brute skipping ungraciously—how nice I was and that I had jumped over the Iron Curtain just so I could dance with her. All the who's who were becoming jealous. Gandy was standing next to the buffet table picking it clean, and only Tennessee Williams was still standing over there and Gandy whispered something in his ear, Williams looked from me to Ginger and back again and laughed uproariously and almost fell back into the pool. I whispered to her, Me cellar, film with you and Fred, friend go Siberia because you, I pulled my arm from her back for a moment and made as if I was slitting my throat with a knife, people sighed, one woman blew me a kiss. I said, This do people who love Ginger Rogers, and I saw the tears well up in her eyes, and at that moment someone turned up the lights so that they could photograph the occasion.

Only we remained on the dance floor. The stars and starlets stood around us in a circle. Their diamonds sparkled in the light and looked like the Milky Way. She asked, What did you dream about most in Russia? I said, You, only you. She was delighted and said to the people surrounding us as we danced, Cute, he sat in the camps and thought of me. I was surprised that no one asked how a curtain could be made of iron and how you jumped over it anyway. Those were the McCarthy days, everyone hated the Reds. People on the street rehearsed rapid evacuation into atomic bomb shelters. They purchased gas masks. Some of the guests at the party were out of work thanks to McCarthy. I was a young Russian who had dared and was now a source of hope. Ginger put on her best PR face. She was no longer a young girl. She was Fredless. She fluttered like a charming butterfly and the crowd applauded and I said some words in Russian Hebrew that I remembered from the Habima Theater, and she called to her friends, What grace this poor guy has, and pressed me close to her. I put on an expression like a wounded dog, the lights got brighter. Startled women fled the light lest their ages be revealed. Being so close to her, I could see Ginger's radiant face, her sparkling white teeth, but I saw too, all at once, that her neck was furrowed, wrinkled. Her face had been lifted and was still boyish but you can't fool the neck. I stared as if hypnotized, embarrassed and sad for her, and she saw me staring, she put a hand on her neck, startled, shouting, Turn the lights down! Everyone moved aside, apart from the younger partygoers, Ginger looked at me with a mixture of entreaty and anger, perhaps hate, drew away from me, the Iron Curtain had been forgotten. She hurried away with her hand still stuck like a knife into her neck. Gandy grabbed a bottle of brandy and Williams smiled and pushed a bottle of Four Roses into my hand, and we left.

Grasshoppers hear through their knees, I told Gandy, and he asked, So what, and I said that if I could paint what had just happened through my knees I'd be Rembrandt. Lee left again and came back. Wally Cox became more and more attached to Marilyn Gennaro who'd come to visit with her beautiful eyes painted with blue kohl as though she were an ancient Egyptian, but there were other blue marks on her face as well, and Lee explained that Wally beats all his women so he beats Marilyn too, he can't help it, he has to beat them, and Marilyn didn't want to hear a single word said against the man she loved. Ugly, and he could barely see through his thick glasses, and he tyrannized women, but they still wanted him. Marilyn, the Madonna who attracted men like moths to a flame and never gave in to any of them was now completely overwhelmed with her total devotion for Wally, who hadn't even courted her; she would lay in bed and he would just smack her over and over. He starred in a summer replacement series called *Mr. Peepers*, about a bumbling teacher, and he was a huge success; I went to his house with Lee. He made a face and said I was jealous of him. I didn't say anything because I preferred for him to get all his anger out on me. And Lee, who had remained a communist at heart, decided to assist with a revue of former stars who were unable to work because of McCarthy. The stars were Zero Mostel—who had been famous and now went hungry with a flower in his lapel and an artist's hat from Montparnasse from the last century and who was spending his time painting—and Jack Gilford and Sono Osato, who was a half-Japanese, half-Irish dancer whose husband was a Moroccan

Jew who imported Volkswagens to America. The revue was funny, but people were afraid to come, people dressed like FBI agents who really were FBI agents and wore Humphrey Bogart-style fedoras sat in the empty hall and scribbled in notebooks. Even the press were afraid to write about such an excellent show filled with such stars. It didn't last long.

Then I became friendly with Professor Irwin Corey who was known as the World's Foremost Authority and wasn't a professor at all, but had what he called a PhD in the science of laughter, and who was in many ways the inventor of modern stand-up comedy. But when he started appearing at the Copacabana with a hat to collect money for the children of the recently-executed Rosenbergs, he was gently dismissed. He continued appearing at the Blue Angel because Max Gordon wasn't scared of anyone and said that if Hitler hadn't managed to kill him then McCarthy and Ronald Reagan wouldn't either. Irwin would take me to his home on Long Island and used to buy paintings from me. Irwin liked to try and avoid paying toll on the highway and so would stop at the booth and mumble, looking for the right words, coughing, fumbling, his face red, the drivers behind him all honking their horns, until finally a cop would wave us through, yelling, Corey, you're not funny!

He would come onstage wearing shabby clothes and a long tie that trailed onto the floor and with his hair all disheveled, holding a sheet of paper. He'd mutter something to himself, read what was written on either side of the paper, then think for a few minutes, grimacing. No one said a word. After thinking for a long time, he'd start with, However . . .

One day he called and said he'd heard that my friend Chan Canasta, a Jewish magician from British television, was in New York and he wanted to throw him a party. Chan arrived in New York and called, as if he knew. He said he wanted to see my new paintings and we met at my home and he looked at the paintings and then we went out and sat at Nedick's on Second Avenue. Canasta was a tall man, pale eyes, an officer who'd deserted from the Polish army and joined the British. He fought in Greece. He was wounded and came back, but he had no name because he didn't register when he first arrived as a deserter from the Polish army.

He went to England and became a success. He always said he wasn't a magician. Claimed that something in his brain was just fucked up, that's all. He explained that he knew things but didn't know where from. He had this crazy thing in his head, he'd say, that's all, same as Mozart had but in reverse. Mozart composed music at the age of five. You, too, have the same ability as me in your brain but you don't know how to activate it. No one knows how to activate this ability. It's self-activating. In my case, due to a defect in my head that might be called "positive," if that doesn't sound conceited, whatever happens happens, and then everyone accuses me of pulling some sort of trick on them. But I don't deceive people. I don't know how to saw a woman in half or escape from a barrel wrapped in chains. But I can read the whole of today's *New York Times* in one hour or even less and you can ask me whatever question you like about what's written on any page and I'll know what it says on each and every page and even on which line it says it, and I'll be able to recite what it says back to you, so is that a trick? Surely there's no sleight of hand there! So they say I'm a cheater, because if I'm not then how do I know? True, the next day I won't remember, but look, I don't even read the paper. Who has time to read? All I do is glance at each page and you've seen how I can photograph what I look at and retain it in my head. I'm the negative, and part of my brain transforms it into a positive again. So what? Is it my fault? What else can I do if people like to be tricked and like to disbelieve that the tricks aren't real? I've got a camera in my eyes and a darkroom in my brain and I'm the only one. I make money from something I don't even like doing because I always have to convince people that I can really do it and I don't like having to convince people. Do you know many people who can absorb a hundred newspaper pages in a single day? Chan Canasta's Hebrew name was Chananel, and sometimes he failed but that didn't deter him because he claimed that it only served to prove that he was a freak and not a magician, because if he was a magician he wouldn't make mistakes. His dream was to be an artist. He wanted me to help him. He was always asking. He said, I want you to help me like you promised me in Paris. I told him I'd help him.

I asked him to come to Bill Dana's and he agreed. There were about twelve of us there, including two of Steve Allen's writers. Wally came with Marilyn who Bill asked to pour drinks and she already looked like a shadow of her former self. There was Lee and I and Irwin Corey and Al Brown, who must be the only man in New York to live in the same apartment from 1947 to the day I'm writing these words, with the same telephone number, the same cheerful smile, the same talent for playing his viola the whole while. There was somebody else too and we drank. The air was filled with tension, tension of the "Let's see how this schmuck gives us the business" variety. Everyone looked at Chan Canasta like doctors examining a wound. He started with card tricks, moved on to a *New York Times* that he knew backward and forward, and then, as expected, they started mumbling that he'd just managed to memorize the paper. Bill said, Page six, in the sports section, line five, from the words "There is," and Chan Canasta recited it. It made me laugh how they believed that an ordinary man could learn a newspaper like the *New York Times* by heart in a day. Canasta, who didn't rise to their bait, asked Bill Dana if he had ever visited Bill's home before. Cynical Bill was forced—and I could see how hard it was for him—to answer in the negative. Canasta smiled and told me to take a look in Bill's bookcase and think of a book. Don't move your head toward the book, he said, move your eyes over the books and decide on one. I did. He told Bill to think of a page number from one to fifty. Bill thought. Chan told Wally Cox to think of a line number from two to twenty and then without even thinking or pretending it was difficult, he rattled off something about Dryden. Now there was a heavy silence. I pulled out the book I'd looked at and read, *History of English Literature*, by H. A. Taine D.C.L., Chatto & Windus, London, 1906. Bill opened the book with a look of absolute hostility and said, I chose page twenty-three, and he looked. Wally, withdrawn into himself, said, Line fifteen, and Bill read the line that Canasta had declaimed. Wally shook and screeched, It's a fake, it can't be! Chan smiled and asked him to look in the bookcase and think of a book and again he gave them the rules and knew the correct line. Chan spoke quietly like someone who knows all about people and said, Let's say I snuck in here last night and read all the books and learned them by heart and learned every paragraph, each line and its number on the page, yes, since I've only been in New York for three days, it's stamped in my passport, and I spent two of the three days with my cousin in Long Island, which can be proven, so let's assume that I came here last night and read the entire library, about a hundred books. No, let's even say that I'm lying to you, that

I came here who knows when, came some time ago and broke in here and read a hundred books, which is millions of words, and still remember them today. Do you have any rational way of refuting what you've just seen?

We relaxed afterward and they asked questions, but there was still a deep suspicion in the air.

In the end Chan stopped making a living from his strange mind and successfully devoted himself to painting in London and Tel Aviv. He hated himself so he came to love gimmicks. Once, during his show on British television, he said that in another second all the TV sets showing him would be turned off. And then the TV sets all over England turned off. Twenty seconds later they all came back on and Chan said he was only joking and the BBC apologized—but he never explained. Chan wasn't a big one for explanations. He was contemptuous of his powers and said that they were nothing to be amazed at because they were just nonsense and what was so miraculous about a miracle anyway? In his youth he had been a talented mathematician and still said that one simple equation was more interesting than all his tricks. He actually said, I'm a genius who doesn't fall into any real category, so I became a circus clown. I joined him for a two-week tour once. He also appeared on various television shows, including Steve Allen's. On every show they asked him the same stupid questions. In his screechy voice, Wally accused me of aiding and abetting a charlatan. Marilyn, who was upset, saw that Wally was angry, and behaved abominably by agreeing with her husband.

A week later Canasta was supposed to go to Hollywood and Lee always liked saying that Hollywood was a nice place if you were an orange and she told him and he replied, I'm going as a Polish orange. She was fascinated by him and went along. She loved magic. She loved mystery. Maybe that's what connected us, that's what she told her Aunt Raya once. She loved watching burlesque shows. She asked Canasta and me to go with her to one. There were still a few clubs of that kind left in New Jersey. We went into a huge hall shrouded in antiquity. It was a faded place, where American comedy had been born, but the comedy had gone on its way, leaving only a memory behind, an ember of the laughing man. Now there were hundreds of men leering, not laughing, as an ugly female dwarf danced. She was followed by a fat triple-chinned stripper. And then the ancient vaudeville artistes performing sketches from the twenties—still alive and kicking. The audience reveled in it, ate popcorn, smoked cigars, belched, shouted encouragement and jeered and played with themselves and then more strippers came on and they all shouted, Take it off! Lee loved the place. It's where she learned how to comport herself on stage, she told me. And then, Wait, she said, watch this. The star of the show came on. Silence. A beautiful stately woman wearing a high-necked blue gown. She stood quietly and looked disdainfully at the audience, like a queen. The audience was quiet. She took a book from the purse she was holding and began reading a Yeats poem. She read it slowly, stressing each word, with perfect precision, and the audience waited patiently. A few new visitors who were apparently there for the first time shouted, Take it off already! But the others, most of them old timers, shut them up. Chan mumbled something and sounded like he was choking.

After she'd finished reading the woman put the book down in a corner of the stage and music came on and she began stripping and the audience roared, and she smiled a sweet smile and she had a terrific body and Lee said, Look at her movements, she's a black-magic ballerina, look at that showmanship. She's in control of her body, the audience, she's precise down to the last detail, she does nothing that's not planned but still leaves room for improvisation, half the dancers in the world would love to know how to work with their bodies the way she does. She knows exactly when ninety percent of the men are going to start with the heavy breathing and she doesn't rush things, she wants to draw it all out and for it to be an experience, not just voyeurism, she's really great. Watching her is how America's greatest comedians learned how to make people laugh, and Lee clapped and I almost loved her. And then the woman stopped for a moment and called out, Chan? God! Where did you spring from? Come here, give me a kiss. Amazed, they all looked at Canasta who sat there pale and still. And the woman went on stripping and staring right at him all the time. When she'd finished and was standing there almost nude except for a small triangle between her legs, she stopped all her stage business and said, Sitting here is one of the greatest artists in the world. He can tell the future. A man from another planet. Come up here, Chan, for me, I'm begging you. The audience sat in quiet shock. Lee was excited. Chan came to his senses and went up onstage. The woman kissed him and he kissed her and she asked him to do something with the whole audience. He looked embarrassed, I'd never seen him embarrassed, he asked everybody to think of a word and jot it down on a cigarette pack or a bit of paper, and when they'd done it he said to them, You over there, you wrote "Bastard," and you wrote "Dream," and you in the gray hat, you wrote, "Fraud," and that's very nice of you, you in the brown derby, you wrote "Looker." There was commotion in the audience and the woman hugged Chan and he got down off the stage and we left and he said, You see? If I was a mathematician and knew complex equations by heart and invented a new way of solving a three-hundred-year-old problem I'd be lauded and be made a professor at Columbia, but who am I? A freak who excites fools, like someone with six fingers, or a midget or a fat gaudy stripper. Lee was more excited than I'd seen her for years and that night she danced in our apartment. Chan stayed a while, applauded her, said, When you dance nobody thinks it's a miracle and your dancing is much more of a miracle than what I do. He went on a tour of nine cities and came back and claimed there was still no explanation for the positive defect in his brain. His paintings weren't any good yet, but he persevered for years, always alone and always feeling rejected, contemptuous of his own great talents, making money and hating himself. He had a boyhood friend, an Israeli writer who came to New York and lived for a while with a bellicose woman photographer he had a thing for. He was a good-looking man and he moved in with the woman before they'd even managed to talk to each other. She didn't know Hebrew and he only spoke beginner's English. They'd have fights in languages they didn't know. One day Chan told me I should help them because people said I'd saved Frank Sinatra from hitting rock bottom with my applause and so maybe I could help this nice couple. I knew the guy. He had a good imagination and was boundlessly optimistic. Before he even wrote one page of a new book he'd already sold it like it was a bestseller and had won the Nobel Prize and been translated into twenty-eight languages.

I went to the photographer's apartment on Fifty-sixth Street a few times, not far from the Plaza. She worked for *Look* and was nice to look at and pretty wild. And so it happened that, on a few occasions, when they got mad at each other, they'd call me, and I'd go, they'd hold back until I sat down and once I was down they'd start. They were livid. Clenched fists. She was on one side of the room and he on the other. And she said, Tell him he's a bastard and a motherfucker and a fatherfucker too and he doesn't know how to write. So I translated. He said, Tell her she's a cow and ugly when she's naked and that she sucks cucumbers. I translated. Now and again I got stuck, motherfucker and fatherfucker sound natural in English, but not in Hebrew. And *kus emek* doesn't sound right in English. They waited patiently while I translated and when he said "daughter of a whore" in Hebrew it was hard for me to find a good substitute so I said "sonofabitch" but they were patient and always waited for me to come with a solution and then they continued. When I was a kid the subtitles always used to run at the side of the screen on a separate strip. The projectionist would get tired and fall asleep every so often, so the translation was never in the right place. Then projectionist would wake up and roll the translation fast. During particularly sad scenes the parts of the audience that didn't know English or French or Russian would burst out laughing because a joke had arrived late. After about an hour of sweating like a horse with the writer and photographer they'd make up and slip into an animal-like trance and growl at each other and wait for me to leave and I'd run for it. I told Lee about it and she said, That's how it is with us too, only we both understand English.

Back then, and even beforehand, and actually years later too, there was a woman who had grown old and lost everything and was always smiling, a wonderful woman and not beautiful at all, yet despite that she was lovely and somehow got power from her ugliness. When she told me that ugliness is a disease, I told her that she was creating a new beauty with what she called ugliness, feeding on itself. Power is weakness you know how to use. The intelligence of this woman, Sherry Abel, oozed from every hair of her head. Her husband Lionel was a professor at Columbia who wrote metaphysical plays that nobody would stage and he even wrote books on what he called "metatheater," as in "metaphysical," and his friend e. e. cummings liked to go to Sherry's place on Saturday evenings and read his poetry and they let me come along. Sherry introduced me to her daughter Mary who was fourteen. Black eyes, slim figure, she seemed frightened of life, there was an innocence in her, but she was cynical beyond her years when it came to marriage. Her father and mother were among the Village's first bohemians and separated when Mary was a little girl. Lionel had a "life partner" and Sherry had a boyfriend. She lived with the boyfriend who was always lying in bed in the next room and thinking secret thoughts, while Lionel lived with a woman nobody had ever seen. But Lionel and Sherry were still very close. He would come to her apartment every day and they'd argue for hours, and Mary was spellbound taking in all the witticisms and verbal projectiles and she knew what coitus interruptus was when she was six. She also knew that Spinoza had been ostracized out of vindictiveness but she didn't understand her parents' love because they didn't know how to put it into simple language and used metaphors and Virgilian and Dantean aphorisms and they absolutely forbade her to have any ideas about love in language they called billingsgate. Mary was their guinea pig, and out of their metaphysical hostility and love for one other, they'd managed to turn her into a terribly frightened little girl. Each of them wanted her to be his or her special something in the world. Sherry was a warm woman, though sharp-tongued, quick to laugh, she'd worked as a deputy editor on *Commentary* from the day it was founded; but Mary wanted her father, who was busy solving metaphysical problems and writing literary reviews for the *New York Times*.

Sherry told me that she wanted Mary to study painting with me because she'd liked a painting I'd given to her. Later, years later, whenever I visited Sherry and we talked about Mary, she'd bring a sealed green bottle out in which she kept Mary's ashes. She'd put it down between us and we'd talk about Mary. But when we met, Mary was alive. I was twenty-four and she was fourteen. She would come into the apartment as though hovering; she had no scent. How profound and serene was her sadness.

One day Freddie came to our ground-floor apartment and asked me to lock him in the bedroom for a few days so he could kick his habit and demanded that no matter how he might yell I shouldn't answer and he even told me to throw away the key. The room had a small window that overlooked a neglected garden. He really did yell; for three days and nights he screamed and banged his head against the door. I didn't want to throw away the key but then his hooker girlfriend came along, weeping, and took the key from me by force and threw it down the drain. Freddie beat his head against the wall and begged and yelled and his woman said, Don't pay any attention, he's got to get clean, otherwise he'll die, I got clean too, I don't have the strength to go on turning tricks for him. Mary came on Tuesday as usual for her lesson and heard the yelling. She went into the garden, stood like a scarecrow, and recited a poem. Birds perched on her. Freddie went silent. Mary came back and sat down and painted while I supervised and made comments, and then she flew away. A day went by with no shouts. I started worrying and called a locksmith who smashed open the lock. Freddy wasn't there. In the yard

I found the jacket Mary had been wearing when she stood outside. Freddie had gone back home. I don't know how she made an opening for him to crawl out. He said he didn't know who Mary was. But when we painted in the small cemetery in the neighborhood and Mary saw the stone angels on the headstones she said she wanted to fly like them or anyway be a stone angel with wings who can't take off. She painted angels. She loved me and used to hug me and cry.

I got Chan Canasta to entertain her. She sat unmoving and used to repeat every word he said. Chan told me later that he was concerned about her. He said she was alive but didn't understand where or why she was living and that scared him. I talked to Mary and she tried to explain to me how she saw life through what she called cobwebs. She said, I understand characters in books, I understand characters in plays, I understand them because they're not real, but people, who are even less substantial than fictional characters, I can't manage to understand them or touch them. I only know how to touch you. Two days later Sherry called to tell me that I had to sleep with Mary because she needed to know real physical love before some bastard took advantage of her. I refused. Her father came over and brought me several learned treatises on adults who had made love to young girls and how it had helped both the girls and the adults. I told him that he could go to bed with her himself because maybe that's what she really wanted. I went on teaching her. She was a rara avis in my life and she knew it. Once I had a dream. There was an angel in it. It was nice. Lee wasn't home. I woke up and saw Mary standing over me, watching. I asked her, How long have you been there, and she said, An hour. You were sleeping and you looked so tranquil and sweet. Freddie came over to drum for Mary and she danced with me, trembling and frightened. Some time passed and she went to Smith College in Northampton, Massachusetts. I visited her because she wrote me that she was sad and that Lionel was writing to her about Proust and her mother was busy with a book on Franz Rosenzweig. It was a small sweet town with sweet scenery with sweet houses and lots of sweet young girls. In the evening they rang sweet bells, lots of little bells, and the melody sounded like the voices of angels. Mary said I was her older brother and that I'd come from Paris. There was something nice and sterile about the town. All the girls there looked alike. It was depressing there but revelatory. Thirty young girls would come down to breakfast in identical pink or blue bathrobes and Mary said she was only here so as not to be there and all her life she was where she was not.

Then I didn't see her for a few years. Sherry used to report back to me, and Mary wrote me lovely letters. Lee was jealous of her but there was really nothing to be jealous about. Later Lionel would come over and say awful things about Mary's lovers, whose numbers were growing, and then Sherry told me that Mary had met a young doctor, married him, and moved to Chicago. One day Sherry and Lionel were called to Chicago urgently. According to the report they'd been given, Mary had fallen from the roof of her building and been killed. The police and Sherry and Lionel suspected that her husband had killed her, but despite numerous inquiries there was insufficient evidence. The husband denied it. He hinted that she had been suicidal. There was no great love between them, said Sherry; he had killed her because she wanted to fly and he wanted her in a cage; Mary's monument was a graveyard angel. In the bottle that stood between Sherry and me were her ashes. A Jewish princess in a bottle. I said to Sherry, Mary could only have cheated on her husband with God, that's what that bastard was afraid of.

I'd look at Mary's paintings and try to understand who she really was, and then, I remember it was a rainy day and the room was hot and I was doing a drawing based on an Etruscan burial site I was interested in at the time, thinking that the Etruscans must have been even greater than the Greeks or Romans. Mary looked at the painting and did something in watercolors that looked like a huge wadi and she wrote next to the wadi: Betrayal! I tried to understand. I thought and thought. I suddenly missed home. I recalled a line from the Book of Job: My brethren have dealt deceitfully as a brook.

Then I got a call telling me that I had been invited to come and exhibit my works at the Bezalel Museum in Jerusalem and the Tel Aviv Museum too. I collected paintings from various people who'd bought them from me and added in a few new ones. My parents were excited about my coming home. I was surprised when Lee asked to join me. She was acting and dancing in some show and could only take three weeks off though I had to travel by sea along with the paintings. We arranged to meet in Rome and she said she'd fly there. The paintings were loaded together with me aboard the SS *Saturnia*, an aging luxury liner. My cabin was comfortable. As happens on sea voyages, I got pretty friendly with some of the passengers, as friendly as you can imagine, friends for life with people who swear that they'll see each other again and of course never do. Lots of affairs started up. We'd all dress up in each other's honor. There was an Israeli woman on her way home from New York where she'd been looking for her son who'd disappeared after her husband had died. On board she discovered a man who'd courted her late mother when the Israeli woman was young. In her youth she'd liked him, unlike her mother who'd gotten rid of him quick, and she'd been jealous then of her mother because this man had been in love with her, but now, after so many years, on deck, in the torrential rain, she met him again, and a new love story was born, and they were even talking about marriage. And during a storm a woman whose name I've forgotten was standing on the bow, standing and shouting that the captain didn't know the way. She'd already sailed this route a few times. She was the one who said, with the utmost seriousness, that there is no nothing, because there is something.

A week later we reached Barcelona. It was 1955. Spain was all policemen and fear. The passengers disembarked to see Columbus's ship, the *Santa Maria*, here where he was called Colón. It was a Sunday and quiet, the church bells were ringing and the entire city went to the corrida. We sat in the huge arena, there were matadors or toreadors, the shouts of the spectators and the handkerchiefs thrown by women. After the first matador had slaughtered his bull, and after all the other noble participants, in contrast with the corrida in Mexico, had stuck the poor bull with their lances and tormented it to the roar of the spectators, I fled and walked down the broad La Rambla. The street was almost empty except for the policemen in their peacock-like hats. I was walking in the direction of the ship, looked down a side street, saw a fountain, walked toward it, saw that it was beautiful. Then, from an upstairs floor I heard the strains of Dizzy Gillespie's "A Night in Tunisia," and I stopped to listen. It was nice and it was strange in the middle of a city of toreadors, Franco, dueling, swords in the cellars, castanets, so many citizens screaming to see bulls slaughtered, to suddenly hear the rhythm of jazz. To hear the right intervals. The right rhythm. Professional. A young man peered down from a balcony and was joined by another, and they stared at me. One of them called out in Spanish and

I gestured that I didn't speak Spanish. He called to me in English and asked if I understood English and jazz and I shouted yes and yes and they came down, dressed in black, and took me upstairs. A big apartment. Photographs of New York on every possible surface, and photographs of Sarah Vaughan, Billie Holiday, Bird, Louis Armstrong, Hawkins, and musical instruments everywhere, then they gave me coffee and beer and went on playing and I listened. I don't know if it was jazz, because there was something missing, something you only get in America, the echo of whips lashing slaves, of joyous southern funerals, of brothels, which were the only places where blacks and whites came together—but the desire and the passion and the etiquette were there. They spoke New York-accented English between themselves and used jazz lingo: Groove. Pad. Hey man. They called Lester Young "Prez." They asked who I was and I told them. They asked what I knew about jazz and I told them. They began touching me. They wanted to know which hand had shaken Bird's hand and they kissed it. They danced around me. They knew the names of New York streets. They knew what the entrance to the Lincoln Tunnel looked like and where to get a shoeshine on Lennox Avenue and Eighth Street outside the second building from the corner by the empty church, in Harlem, and the tobacco store on Madison between Fifty-fifth and Fifty-sixth Streets, and they knew what the buildings looked like, where and what Saks Fifth Avenue was, what the Apollo Theater looked like, what was happening at the Fremont, what Katherine Dunham and her parties were like and her dance company on the roof by Shubert Alley. They knew how long it takes to walk from Charles Street to the Cedar Bar. Where Circle in the Square was. But they were naïve. They had all submitted visa applications for the United States. They had to wait. How long?

One would wait fourteen years. The other only ten. There were some who would have to wait twenty years. No problem. The main thing was to get there. We've got patience, they said. They'd wait. Maybe something would happen to Franco. There's a future. Then they got a little timid because they weren't sure if I would inform on them. They said, frightened, There's nobody like Franco, and I said, It's okay, guys, and left for the ship. I met my friends from the ship still all excited by the slaughter of the bulls and the ship got underway for Naples; a sea of silk; from Naples I was supposed to board the *Negba* for Haifa, after a quick side-trip to Rome.

Lee and I met in Rome. The ship was due to sail in three days' time. We walked the streets. Rome is the city of the world. We couldn't stand one another all that much, but not being able to stand one another only helped our marriage because we expected nothing from each other and dependency seemed better than freedom and love anyway, and so we got closer again in Rome. There was magic in our time there, maybe because we were on foreign soil. The people were poor but friendly, they wanted to steal and screw, but were pretty agreeable about it. Lee and I laughed, even though we hadn't laughed together for a long time. There was pleasure in our relationship again and so she demanded that she travel with me by train to Naples, accompany me to the ship, and from there go back to Rome and fly to Israel. We made love on the train. Me and my wife—love on a train. We watched the passing scenery through the window. The Italians couldn't have cared less and they drank wine and laughed. We reached Naples.

I looked for Angelina, the hooker I'd fed at Santa Lucia. There was the same Vesuvius. We ran into the happy couple who'd met onboard ship. They wanted to get married right away and were looking for a rabbi. I introduced them to Lee and we looked for the hooker and a rabbi. I found the hooker. She'd aged, she saw me, recognized me, got scared, started to run. From a faded hotel nearby came some rabbi who was shocked at hearing Hebrew. Angelina didn't want me to see her in the doorway of some cheap hotel. I yelled to her to come back but the crowd swallowed her up and we went back to the port. The rabbi ran after us asking if we understood him. I said sure and he asked if I wanted to put on phylacteries. I saw he was terribly excited so I told my wife to kick him where his pants were bulging. For some reason she started thinking about the story about me and her lovely sister-in-law and so she kicked me instead. I was writhing with pain and she told the rabbi, That's because he messed around with my sister-in-law. He put phylacteries on his head and arm and at the sight of the box on his forehead Lee asked him if he could get the BBC as well. The woman asked the rabbi to marry them. He took us to a small synagogue and didn't ask about papers. Lee and I were the witnesses and they were married in accordance with the Law of Moses and Israel and went back to America on the first ship. My paintings were already aboard the *Negba*. Lee stood on the gangway to say good-bye and suddenly fell in love with me after three years of living together. I'm going with you, she said. We arranged it with the company; the Shoham shipping company was associated with El Al and they changed her ticket. She sailed with me.

On the deck like a shadow walked an elderly and slightly hunch-backed man who nodded his head and seemed to be talking to him-self. Lee followed him and studied his steps, as she always measured people's steps, and said she thought he wanted to die. I didn't argue with her but the man saw us, came over, and we started talking;

he took a shine to us, and he knew about my exhibition, and we went to lunch together and one might say we became friends. His name was Chaim Karniel, big wide light-brown eyes, thick brows above them, two half crowns, and this whole bent man seemed to sit inside those soft, well-proportioned eyes, his whole tiny body seemed a timid extrusion from the concavities of his eye sockets, which were, apparently, or so Lee said, the breadth of his heart. His English was excellent and in the evening we sat on deck, in deck-chairs. It was hot and he said he'd come from France in 1934 and joined Kibbutz Avivim. He was educated and so they made him into a high-school teacher. At night he cleaned the dining room, on Saturdays he worked in the fields. I said to Lee, when he got up for a moment to look at the water, If it wasn't for his huge clear eyes, you could easily say he was ugly.

He had married an unhappy woman and had had a son. In 1945 a young Austrian girl who'd been brought to Israel by the Youth Aliya rescue organization met a group of kids from the kibbutz and came with them. She fell, so he said, into my lovable eyes and didn't see my ugliness. I left my wife and son for her, she told me that she knew I understood her sorrow and we got married. When he wanted to touch her he used to knock on the glass of her body to get in, he said. And then some party leader came to lecture, talked a lot of nonsense, seemed authoritative and impressive and saw the girl, whose name was Lili, and became obsessed with her, begged her to spend a week with him, begged in front of everyone, including her husband, and she went to Beersheba with him and he became less and less interested in politics and they settled there and he opened a big store and prospered. Years later Chaim's son from his first mar-riage had fallen in love with and wanted to marry the daughter of

Lili and the man from Beersheba. After the wedding, where Chaim had needed to support his son and smile at his ex-wives, he shut himself up in his house. Lili got sick then and her second husband threw her out and she came to Chaim's home to die. At that time in the kibbutz he began writing poetry and went into the Jerusalem hills to look for a cave to sit in. On the way he stopped at phone booth, he called his son, told him he'd had it with everything, that he was going to go hide in a cave and that no one should come looking for him. The police traced the call. They searched and searched and didn't find him. In her will Lili had asked to be buried next to Chaim and he told us that night on deck that Lili was waiting for him in the ground and he didn't even know if he still loved her. Lee sat with him on the last night onboard ship and, after we'd passed Cyprus, she said, his head dropped. His eyes remained filled with wonder, as though the death that had settled on him there was simply a curiosity, and he smiled at it. Lee shouted to one of the sailors to call a doctor, the doctor came, Chaim looked at the doctor and said, Next to Lili, what a beautiful death this is, and Lee saw how he closed his eyes, opened them again, and then his head dropped again and what remained of him, she said, were the eyes.

When Lee saw Mount Carmel she asked what it was and I said it's Mount Carmel and she didn't believe it was a mountain. Then we went to my parents' home, lots of people came to welcome us. Ze'ev Shiffman took me out to the balcony. We sat down. He wanted to tell me a secret. He said he'd heard himself on a tape recorder his daughter had brought from America and didn't recognize his own voice. When I realized that this was the secret I consoled him, and afterward there were the exhibitions in Jerusalem and Tel Aviv and the guys from the Havurat Ha'esh palmach unit came and invited

Lee and I along on their annual trip to Masada. It was July and hot. We went in jeeps. There were a lot of us who gathered at the foot of the mountain and Gandhi, the army officer who organized the whole thing, sat his son on his shoulders and made sure that the kid had a nail in his shoe because it was important for a Jewish soldier to suffer. We went up the Snake Trail to Masada. The view even impressed Lee. I took her to the cliff edge and we looked out; Hebron's lights were glimmering, the moon was full. Magic, said Lee.

When you see Paradise, I told her, like this one, with shimmering lights, always make sure that you're not standing on the edge of an abyss.

Afterward we went down. It was nighttime. They lit a bonfire and five hundred people sang around it. They fired guns into the air. They yelled. Because that's the price Jews pay for a state. Being right means shouting with all your might. Back then the Israeli style was ho-ho-ho and ya-ha-ha, and Avshalom the Yemenite dancer came, they said he was the greatest, and he asked Lee to dance and for years people talked about that dance, which was accompanied by nothing more than shouted singing and drumming and which went on for hours, until they both dropped.

Then we toured around Israel, Lee didn't believe that the narrow stream flowing through the scorched land, between the granite hills and the heat, was the same Jordan River that the black singers sang about in Harlem's churches as if it was the Mississippi. We sat in Café Kassit. Everybody looked busy, hunched over their glasses, they were experimenting with Nescafé, which had only reached Israel a few months earlier and was known as *Nes*, the Hebrew word for "miracle," because it was a miracle to put a spoonful into a cup and pour hot water onto it and get a cup of coffee. The more meticulous among us conducted a variety of experiments, putting a spoonful of sugar into the cup, for instance, pouring a little milk onto it, stirring it for a while and then, when they at last poured in the water, they got coffee with foam. You could go into Kassit and see an entire nation sitting with strained faces, focusing with maximal concentration upon their cups, earnestly mixing sugar, coffee, and milk. I met up with childhood friends, comrades in arms, my parents were happy, Lee played the loving wife who would soon provide them with grandchildren, and we flew off on an El Al DC-6. The plane bounced, there were what they called air pockets that made it feel like you were about to drop down onto the mountains below, but no, we ate sausages, reached Rome many hours later where the plane landed and refueled and from there we flew to London. We stopped over there for two days.

I had a friend in London I hadn't seen for five years and whose name I've forgotten and who was engaged in planning the global Trotskyite revolution. We walked in the city and met an angry and horribly rude policeman. The sun was shining and we went into a restaurant and the food was excellent. Lee said that in twenty minutes flat all the English stereotypes had been refuted: a rude British policeman, a lovely and sunny summer's day, and good food. We flew back to New York via Scotland, Iceland, Greenland, and northern Canada. Together for about thirty-five hours. When we arrived Marilyn Gennaro came over and asked us to hide her from Wally. He came looking for her right away, he didn't like people running away from him, even people whose faces were already all black and blue. They'd had a daughter by then. We tried to persuade Marilyn to stay, but she claimed that she couldn't leave him, she loved him and had to go back to him. Mira appeared from somewhere or other. She didn't say from where and didn't talk much. She wanted to go to sleep and so slept for twenty hours and then said that Boris was sick.

A few days later I went to Boris's house and Mira said that last night she'd been asleep and when she woke up she'd seen her mother standing over Boris's bed, watching him dying, weeping her heart out. She wept until she died. We found her mother's will. She'd written it in Russian. Zhenya asked us to remember that she and Boris had also lived another life, when there were no people around, that they had been in love like the children they once were in Odessa, and she left money so that her body could be kept in cold storage until Boris died and then, only then, she requested, should their funerals be held—together. Mira decided to adhere to the terms of her will and Zhenya was put into the refrigerator of the Chabad burial society, who for a great deal of money had agreed to turn a blind eye to this unusual practice, but two days later, Boris couldn't wait and died too. Mira got into her dead father's bed, hugged him and slept with him all night long until they came to take him away. Avi Shoes, who we hadn't seen for a long time, came with Rita Hauser, the daughter of the man he claimed he'd killed. She looked confused, clung to Avi Shoes, and Mira fixed him with a look that, despite the pain, was basically a look of amusement. He came over to her with Rita on his arm and said, Mira, I'm sorry about Mother and Father. She replied, They're not your mother and father. He shook her hand and Mira looked at me and tried to laugh, but it seemed that for the first time in her life she was truly sad. She stood there powerless, weak, and didn't manage to act unruffled and sarcastic, and then she suddenly fell onto Avi Shoes's neck, hugging Rita as well, and burst into tears, and that was the first time we'd seen her crying. She said that to everybody's surprise Boris had asked for a proper Jewish funeral in his will, not the modern nonsense. Even so, she said he'd look up from his grave and criticize how they were carrying it all out, and he'd correct the cantor's singing. I found the old Hebrew bookseller who looked yellow now from some sort of illness, and he gathered a few Orthodox Jews together and we brought a rabbi from the Chabad Hasidim who had kept vigil over Zhenya's body and we stood by the two graves. Mira was silent. I said Kaddish for Boris, because there was nobody else. After I'd blessed the Almighty for being so good as to take Boris and Zhenya from us, the rabbi prayed some more and then they began filling in the graves. It was hot. New York knows how to be hot. The sky seemed like it had sunk into a viscous grief. The air was still and in it we could see flecks of dampness; like passive-aggressive rain, Gandy said. And then a black automobile drew up and out of it got Professor Oppenheimer from the Manhattan Project accompanied by some people who looked like scientists, one of whom said his name was Teller and he was an admirer of Boris's, and they asked to stand by his grave. Oppenheimer asked to say a few words. Mira thanked him. He smiled at her with a good and heartwarming smile and said, You've grown up since we last met, and Mira said, Yes, but I'm no wiser. He spoke of Boris's work and of what a great contribution he had made, but didn't go into detail. To Boris he said, About that matter, you know which one, you were right, but we can't go public about it yet.

Boris and Sonia were put into their graves, in their coffins, she first and he after. Mira said that they were lying side by side for the first time in years, and when we got back from the funeral we found his laboratory burned down. Somebody had torched the laboratory and his files, all the protocols and the scientific notes. At the funeral I'd recognized Yuri, Mira's ex-husband. He was still wearing the garb of celibacy and was staring at Mira. She looked at him but didn't see him. He prayed. I went over to him to offer a word of consolation. He sounded confused and contradicted himself and said that one day he'd remarry Mira, even in heaven, when his holy vows and hers were no longer binding. I told him that she'd left holy orders a long time ago and he said that you can't leave holy orders.

Afterward Lee began rehearsing in the studio we had on Fifty-second Street and I painted in the next room and in the evenings I walked around with Gandy. I was still trying every possible way of finding Pat; there were rumors, but they all proved unfounded. Adele Schwartz disappeared and Mira left her parents' home a few days later and did not return.

I went out with Tony Scott the clarinetist and at night we met Bird on Delancey Street. It was the last year of Bird's life. He would die at thirty-four; like Jesus, Gandy would say. Something inside Bird had broken. He had stopped using heroin because he could no longer afford the expense, his daughter, Pree, had died, and Bird knew he was going to die because of his kicking the habit so late, because his body could no longer function without heroin. The man had invented a musical language. He never used curse words; you'd never hear a "fuck" from Bird, and he had an old-fashioned gentlemanly respect for women. He chewed aspirin and drank sweet and disgusting Manischewitz wine, which calmed him. Chan, his wife, was the daughter of a Runyonesque character in the sense that Damon Runyon had actually written about him in his stories. Her mother had been a Ziegfeld girl. Chan had a lovely smile that seemed to challenge the world.

I was in the lives of all these people by mistake. A time of anarchy in America. I was passing through, younger than all of them. Once I was walking down Bleecker Street and saw Bird. He was stamping his feet hard on the sidewalk. I went over. He said I shouldn't be his shadow and I should get going. I said that I wasn't a shadow but if he wanted me to go, I'd go. Don't be stupid, he said, and we walked together. He spoke about Chan, Pree's funeral, how they'd played jazz, and he talked about his music, about the young Chet Baker. That wild young guy's got the music, he said. We passed Louis' Bar, the San Remo, the Calypso, we walked farther, far into America, and stopped. He said he wanted a cup of coffee and I saw we were outside a Chock Full o'Nuts. When we went in he said that the place with the small shining white squares probably looked like the men's room in a millionaires' railroad station that you'd go into and because it's so squeaky clean you never want to leave. That happened to me once in Paris. What really made him mad was the sign at the entrance—same it was in each of the chain's hundreds of stores— "No Tipping." He said it was crime not to leave a tip. He was dumb-struck. You could tell Bird was angry by his clenched fists and his head tipped to the right, like Gary Cooper when he had no place to run in *High Noon*, which Bird said was the best Western ever made. And he knew all about Westerns. Bird looked around and said, Man, this is the whitest institution in town. The waitresses were all free when we got there. There were sitting in a row on a long bench and smiling into the restaurant. They were hired because of the whiteness of their teeth and lovely legs and were ordered to smile even if there were no customers. They were sitting cross-legged with the gleaming whiteness of their teeth shown in smiles of polite malice that Bird envied; they were like porcelain statues, their hair identical, dirty blonde, with gray or blue eyes and that simultaneous smile plastered over their faces. The fact that the place looked like a synthetic temple also captivated Bird, who'd found himself raised to this moment from one of his lowest—when his body was crying out for what he couldn't give it.

A waitress got up smiling and asked Bird how he was today. Good, he replied. She asked me and I said a little less good today than yesterday. She seemed taken aback and stopped, she wanted to say something but whatever it was didn't reach her lips, and Bird asked for a cup of coffee and the waitress, still baffled by my reply, served Bird his coffee with chilly ceremony and I ordered pea soup and a roll. She said, The roll comes with a hot dog, soup comes with a cracker. I asked, Can I have the soup with the roll from a hot dog? She looked confused, her jaw dropped, the smile vanished for a moment and she said she was sorry but she'd already told me, the roll comes with the hot dog. Bird looked like a pensive old man and he smiled at me as if to say, They're your people, not mine, and I said, So what about soup and crackers and a hot dog without a hot dog, I'll pay for the hot dog I don't eat? Now there was murmuring all around. The waitresses' smiles turned mean. She brought me what I'd asked for and looked frightened. I put the hot dog to one side and ate my soup with a roll. I asked for coffee and she asked, With cream? No, I said, with milk, and a glass of milk! What milk? she said. Coffee with milk and a glass of milk, I said. She served me contemptuously and Bird told her that he thought not leaving a tip sounded anti-American. She smiled and said, Thank you, but we're not allowed to give an opinion.

Bird looked like he was enjoying the place, he said, I'd live life all over again if it could be Chock Full o'Nuts with music, like that pretty boy Liberace. He talked with unexpected excitement about Liberace and his pink clothes and the smile stuck to his face and that pink voice. And pink piano. And pink hair. And pink teeth. It's a shame I'm not him. Money drips off him and thousands applaud. Go be a jazz musician in America—you play the nigger of music. It's not Hopalong Cassidy, because he was a man, he had a long-barreled Colt 45; and Bird talked excitedly about some Hindemith he'd heard recently. As we left I said something pompous about his music being the link between the sewer and God or maybe something about its being terror shrouded in cotton and he yelled at me, Yo, jazz is jazz. It's rhythm. Rhythm. Rhythm. Syncopation, something banal, some preplanned improvisation and phrasing, and most important, timing and timing and timing; I asked him why he was called Bird and he said it came from yardbird, I asked what a yardbird was and he said, The chicken I loved eating when I was a kid, and I said I'd already asked around and hadn't ever come across such a bird, and he said that a yardbird wasn't only a chicken but also a guy who cleans shithouses in the army, or a deserter, or a rookie, but I ate the bird, he said, and maybe there aren't birds like that in New York or Jerusalem, but there are in Kansas City. He suddenly said, Let's go to your studio. I took him to Broome Street where I'd rented a new studio that was slightly larger than the previous one. He said, Now, you sweet white boy you, open the door nicely for the nigger. He wasn't making fun and I understood what he meant and said, It would be an honor. He said, Don't be a creep, it's not such a great honor. He came in and had some of the sweet wine he'd brought with him and looked at the paintings. He saw a new painting of Shabtai Zvi, also on horseback but different from the one I'd shown on Steve Allen's show. I explained that I had a soft spot for kings, angels, and messiahs. I said there'd been hundreds of messiahs in Judaism and he asked who's the guy that isn't Jesus, and I told there'd been a guy, Abulafia, who'd gone to the Pope to warn him that if he didn't convert to Judaism right away his end would come, and he hadn't been heard from since. Bird liked the painting and said, Nobody's ever painted me from life, I don't have too much time. Don't talk that way, I said, there's time, and he almost yelled at me, Don't tell me what there is and what there isn't and don't be my grandma and don't say what you think should be said, and listen, do you want to paint me or not? I said I very much wanted to and he asked if I'd paint him with a revolver in his hand and I said I'd paint him playing the saxophone and I didn't have one here so I'd give him a stick and I'd put the saxophone in afterwards. He said, I want royalty in the painting. Negro splendor. You like kings, so let there be a king in this Negro that's me. I gave him a stick I had and he held it as if he was really playing and I began painting. I painted for an hour and a half at a speed I'd never known.

I thought of Giotto who was the first modern artist to come to the Pope, though not Abulafia's, and he painted an absolutely perfect circle that resulted in his being given the wall of the church at Assisi that the older artists had fought over. He talked and I talked, but I was on a trip now and he evidently understood and was happy to see somebody on a trip and apparently also went into a trip because he was humming and singing bebop without the instrument in his hands and without words, scatting like Ella Fitzgerald or Sarah Vaughan. After knowing him for a few years I was now seeing him for the first time. The high forehead was now a single canvas crammed with expression—the smiling cheeks and the terrible sadness covered with thick oily skin and the eyes wide with childish wonder and a kind of troubling and heavy old age in them. I reached his sweet, dreamy, and submissive expression that was sometimes strong, his gentleness that appeared frozen in the jaws of defeat. In his eyes was an adult understanding, but at the same time the child seeing rain for the first time remained in them. I saw all this, but I also painted the royalty, Ellington the Duke, Lester the Prez, Lady Day, and although the painting wasn't realist but was a new interpretation of the man, a new expression, there was also royalty in it. He got up and looked at the painting, didn't say a word, and left. I found a photograph of him with his saxophone on the sleeve of a record he'd made under the name of Charlie Chan, because for a time the Mafia controlled the record market and he had to appear under another name. I painted the saxophone into his hands and put it in his mouth, it wasn't easy because in the mouth's meet-up with the instrument there is a certain trembling, the cheeks blow up and then sink back, the mouth is clamped onto the mouthpiece and small wrinkles appear in the lower part of the face and the chin juts outward. I painted through the night and all through the next day. I didn't eat, then ate a little, until Lee came looking for me. She looked and said, You've painted a dead man.

Ruth Sobotka was waiting for me outside. We went to her nearby home so she could feed me. Her husband, Stanley Kubrick, was hunched over his old manual editing machine in the other room where he was editing his first feature film, *Killer's Kiss*, in which Ruth played Iris the ballerina and Kubrick stopped on a freeze of Frank Silvera and enlarged it and there was something in Frank's expression I recognized from drinking together in the Village and that I'd already seen when he played with Brando in *Viva Zapata!* I rushed to the studio and brought the painting back. Kubrick looked at it for a long time and said, Bird's a genius. Ruth and Lee were doing ballet exercises in the studio. I looked at Kubrick's stubborn and tormented work and told him that in Hebrew we had an expression about "a man wise in his work." The scene in the huge warehouse with the naked mannequins, the thousands of plastic women, the ax fight, all contributed to New York's narrowing the gap on Hollywood as far as full-length feature films were concerned. By the time the film hit the screens I was no longer seeing Kubrick, because Lee and Ruth, those two Jewish-Russian girls, had apparently drifted away from one another.

I went to see the movie with Bird. Next day, at the Five Spot Café, he did a variation on the movie's theme music and said, That bastard's made a great movie. In that last year of his life Bird went through a lot of mood swings. There were days when he sounded like the black power revolution that would erupt years later, but what he was really proud of was the recording he made with a bunch of white violinists in tuxes who played with Parker at Carnegie Hall. The violins and the white musicians. It was a triumph for him, but I still felt the sword of black anger that America had left in him, in his blood, the slavery and the heroin and the disgrace and the Pullman porters. Lee had said, Bird is about life, and then he started talking about Thelonious Monk who wasn't popular yet but Bird took me to hear him and said, This cat is great.

On March 12, 1955, Tony Scott called to tell me that Bird had died at the home of a friend from the Rothschild family who had been looking after him. We went over and I sat with his wife, Chan. At the funeral I stood holding her trembling hand. Bird's black friends brought a previous wife who he'd left when he was young and who'd refused to divorce him. His only real wife was Chan, he'd said, who he couldn't marry because he couldn't get a divorce. He left everything for Chan and she bore his two children. But his family and friends got back at her. Solidarity with the black woman he'd left overcame emotion. Even his best friend, Gillespie. It was as if they had been given permission after his death to walk all over Chan, and so they paid their respects to Doris; and I'm talking about Bird's very best friends, though not Gerry Mulligan. Not Art Blakey. Not Ben Webster. They paid their respects to the white Chan. And Doris didn't want them to play jazz at the funeral, so they didn't play jazz at the funeral. Chan felt angry and betrayed. Bird's mother too was on Doris's side. Somebody said, The Negroes won't forgive Bird for his wife, and Chan was quivering like fine down in my hand. They brought a priest who prayed. They held a service in a church where they sang gospel songs and swayed, and although the ceremony was beautiful, Chan was all alone and felt unacknowledged, and then they took Bird away for burial in Kansas City, the place he'd said so many times that he wouldn't want to go back to even if he was dead.

A few months later Chan and a few friends held a memorial at Carnegie Hall, the place he'd been so proud of playing at. Chan stood next to me. Gerry Mulligan and Art planned everything. When they played "Now is the Hour," Chan wept. They say there's no second act in American lives. Just a memorial. Before the event, Chan asked me and Lee to look after little Baird. She had lots of things to arrange. Too many women claimed that Bird was the king. Chan took care of her son and the recordings. She sent the Mickey Mouse wagon on little rails that Bird loved so much and his big old model railroad from the thirties, an original Lionel, a Model M, one of the 10,000 originals. Each car was huge. The terrifying locomotive sent out sparks, and when it passed through a station the lights would flash and bridges would open and close and there were grade crossings and points that switched and a station from which porters appeared when the train arrived and the locomotive whistled. The train that Bird loved to play with and when he did he wore an engineer's cap, took up almost an entire room. Now it was sent along to little Baird in our apartment on Fifty-second Street.

Little Baird wore his father's cap and played. Charlie Mingus came by to play with him and asked forgiveness for the funeral. Chan didn't answer, but she didn't not answer either. I was afraid that Miles would come along and ask for the painting of Bird because he was the only one who knew I'd done it. But it wasn't appropriate and later he forgot. It was nighttime. Little Baird fell asleep in Lee's studio and we in the small bedroom and we woke up in panic in the middle of the night to the sound of screaming. The train was going around, roaring, the engine was shooting out sparks, the lights were flashing and the bridges opening and closing, and someone was shouting, running like a maniac around the dark room, banging into walls, the door, the closet, fleeing the train, Lee and I could see him running around in fright, shouting, What is it? What is it? And Lee, who at first had been frightened by the noise and the lights and the clattering of the train, started laughing, Poor guy, she said, he came up the fire escape to burgle the place and ran into the train, and the scared burglar shouted, What is it? What is it? And Lee, who knew the seamy side of life better than me said, And what did you come up here to knock off, anyway? What did you think you'd find here? The frightened burglar tried to find a way out. The door was hidden behind the angle of a small wall. The train went round and round and went on making noises and shooting out sparks and the guy was hysterical. Little Baird clapped his hands and laughed. Like an idiot I ran after the burglar with a skillet I'd picked up in the kitchen, I threw a shoe at him, I threw a little stool, the guy turned and tried to get back to the fire escape, but the widow had closed behind him and there was the train flying around, sparking, and the guy was begging, Look, let me out, I'm sorry, let me out, I'll never steal again, and I almost punched him, wanting to impress Lee who I'd always told that I had been a brave soldier; the guy found the door finally and ran down the stairs, I ran after him but he was too quick and I came back. Lee stopped the train and switched on the lights. Little Baird said, Poor man, he wanted something and we interrupted him. I told him I'd go downstairs and give the guy something because he was probably waiting. I took a wedge of cheese from the fridge and an old pan and I went downstairs and threw them into the garbage. Little Baird asked if I'd given them to the burglar and I didn't want to lie to the kid so I said I'd left them downstairs because he wasn't there, but he'd be back. And then Lee and little Baird sat on the floor and laughed their heads off.

At the time Lee had made friends with a Yugoslavian dancer who said she was in love with a doctor called Arthur Brandt. One day she brought him over. He looked at us and smiled and the first thing he asked was whether we'd ever had an Indian meal. We said we'd never had an Indian meal. He came back next day, this time alone, carrying a huge sack filled with ingredients. He begged our pardon and told us not to disturb him in the kitchen. He started preparing an Indian meal. The house was filled with exotic aromas. Little Baird went into the kitchen. Arthur was tall and pleasant and we watched him go in and out of the kitchen wearing an apron he'd brought with him. About two hours later we began to smell smoke. We went in and saw Arthur fighting flames. The meal was burned. Bottles were standing on the table, the draining board was full of empty bags, strong aromas vied with the smell of burning and Lee saw how apologetic he was and said we'd eat the food even though it was burned. She said afterward that she'd never eat Indian food again. Arthur looked at the paintings and asked if he could buy one and pointed to a painting of a woman. I said yes. He explained that he was interning at a psychiatric hospital in Brooklyn and would be able to pay me ten dollars a month because his salary was forty a month. I didn't really want to take money from him but my pathetic pride got a kick out of the idea and so he began visiting us frequently. He married his Yugoslavian dancer and after completing his internship he opened his own clinic. He had a good name because right from the start he had a bunch of clients; it began with the dancer, who went through life going from shrink to shrink, and moved on from there. I wondered who'd want to tell their problems to a kook like Arthur, because in the meantime we'd realized that he was as nutty as they came, and I told him so and he said that only a nut was capable of understanding another nut and his clinic thrived.

He met Mira and wanted to treat her, but she said she was past it. His Yugoslavian wife started pacing their eighth-floor roof balustrade like a cat in heat, stretching, and he ran after her begging her to get down and she'd dance a bit, like a high-wire artiste, and Arthur lost his patience, he'd had enough of her, and some time later she started sneaking down from the roof to his office window and spying on the women who came to see him. She was unpredictable and irresponsible and threw things at him whenever he came out of a session with a woman. There was a certain malice in her, and it was a pity because to all appearances she was a gentle woman. They separated, shouting, at our apartment, and then Chan came and took little Baird and the model railroad away, and Adele turned up to say that Wally was in a bad way and was taking drugs and Marilyn wouldn't last much longer; Wally was bringing women home, hookers, strippers, and they were leaving their smells in her bed, and Marilyn just brought them coffee and begged Wally to love her and forgive her for her jealousy.

Krissoula came back from the Greek shipping tycoon who'd died on her and threw a party and she invited Avi Shoes, but Stephanie, Krissoula's sister, had a boyfriend, Baron Hans von Noy, who lived downstairs and got angry about the party and called the police. All the stories that were around at the time—that he'd been attacked by his comrades in an Allied POW camp because he sided with the United States—were of no help to him then. A young man came out from the party and yelled to a cop that he was a Nazi. The cop left and the young man who'd yelled was James Dean. He started talking to me in all the racket of the dancing and Avi Shoes's shouting and Dean said he had a friend, or maybe he said a teacher, a Jewish musician, and for some reason I reminded him of that guy and the man had influenced him a great deal. He said his role model was Brando. He spoke in a whisper with a shy, sweet smile on his lips. He asked if I was really Krissoula's artist friend and I said yes. He said he'd heard some good and not-so-good things about me from Brando and I said that for me the subject was *verboten* and then he asked if he could come and watch me paint. I said that would be fine.

Next morning I was in a deep sleep after all the whiskey and at nine o'clock Dean showed up. Lee, who was only half awake, opened the door and said, Jimmy Dean's here. I made an effort to wake up.

He'd brought a brown bag with hot coffee and rolls with butter and jam and Lee looked around with her despairing morning expression and sipped the coffee and closed her eyes and started to say something and fell asleep in the middle of her sentence. I carried her back to bed and locked the door. Over two weeks, day after day at nine in the morning, Dean would show up with coffee and rolls with butter and jam. He sat behind me but a bit to one side so he could see the painting too, he sat on a not particularly comfortable barstool I used for resting my palette on, he sat and watched as I worked. I bought a small round mirror at a five-and-ten that I hooked up so I could see him looking intently at every movement I made with the brushes and what happened with them on the canvas. When he thought I'd succeeded he'd smile his captivating smile. I don't know why he kept coming. I asked him if he was doing research for a movie and he said no. In Lee's studio meanwhile with its huge mirrors they were rehearsing a number choreographed by Lee. The music enveloped the painting. Dean sat watching and appeared not to be hearing the music at all. He spoke very little. I don't know how a guy can sit on a barstool hour after hour just watching, but that's what he did. When he did speak, he was entirely self-effacing.

He sometimes thought for a long time and then it seemed that the words came from his mouth unintentionally and not the way he'd planned to say them. He talked about his love for girls and for Sal Mineo and Billy Gunn. I said I thought he was stubbing out cigarettes on his soul. He said I was only throwing fancy words around and making a celebration out of bullshit. I said that in the mirror he looked like a whimsical prince, childish but sweet. His expression was sometimes malicious, because in the mirror I could see everything that passed over his face, but the malice was hidden behind a mischievous sense of shame. He fidgeted slightly as he sat, as if trying to catch the rhythm of the painting in his body. He'd wait until I dipped the brush and mixed the paints and then, as I painted, he'd follow the tip of the brush, swaying gently to its rhythm and a smile of joy would appear on his face if the brush managed to capture something that seemed right to him. He looked like someone waiting for something dangerous to happen, as though the brush might set off a fight. He looked like he was preparing to launch into some elegant ceremony in honor of something or other and I honestly didn't know what he was thinking or thought he was doing, it was a strange feeling to paint with this man behind my back and I tried to talk to him but by and large was unsuccessful. He'd growl some indistinct reply. Every now and then Lee would peek in from her studio and he'd tell me it was hard for him to talk, not because of you, the artist, but that because of the painting—I'm trying to understand you. At times he sounded as though he was listening to himself more than saying anything for my benefit and I realized that he was connecting to the painting, the work, the doing, not to the doer. He said, The doer is a shoemaker, in the end you've got shoes or a painting, what interests me is the shoemaking not the shoemaker and not why he's a shoemaker or whether or not he was beaten as a child.

One day he asked me to go with him to the swanky 21 Club that was only a few buildings away from where we lived. Outside there were statues of jockeys and when we went in people nodded to him and greeted him and he underwent a transformation. He became a different Dean. Like a chameleon. Uninhibited but meticulous in his movements, as if he was absolutely refined but nonetheless parodying himself. He looked at the people waving to him and feigned revulsion. He spoke sentences that were disjointed and absurd. We sat down and a waiter brought a telephone to the table and Dean said, Take it away, and right now! And the man bowed and took the telephone away. A quiet young woman came over and sat down next to us. He didn't introduce us. She tried talking to him about some movie she wanted him to play in and he stuck a fork into the steak that had been served in the meantime without him ordering it and stuck a piece of it right into her open mouth. And he laughed. He had an impenetrable, sad laugh. She tried to laugh too but choked. Tears flowed from her eyes and then suddenly stopped as if she'd cut them off with a knife. She chewed the piece of steak until she managed to swallow it. He took no pity on her. She tried to understand exactly who I was but he gave her no help, and I looked around at the wealth and the stars and that beautiful old place steeped in nostalgia, and then she gave him a submissive look and said, I deserve it, James, I deserve it. Yes, he replied, but on the other hand I won't do it again. She said, Remember not to do it again. I'll remember, he answered. Jimmy, Jimmy, she said, sounding as though she was pleading, but at the same time there was a kind of threat behind the words and her expression turned less submissive and more hostile. She went on sitting there and he pretended he'd forgotten who she was. He looked at her and asked, You? Yes, me, she replied. She suddenly turned to me like a wildcat and snarled, So you're the Israeli artist? I nodded. She said to Dean, If you want to be spiteful be spiteful to the artist from Palestine, and I knew immediately that she was Jewish. She smiled and said, I've got uncles and aunts there. In Ramla. Pioneers. She used the Hebrew word, *chalutzim*, and there was derision in her voice. Don't teach me.

You're all teaching us. We're the *galut*, the Diaspora. I said I hadn't said a word and hadn't tried teaching her anything and she said, I saw your frowning forehead, and I said I'd had a frowning forehead from childhood and it frowned even more during the Arab-Israeli War and she asked, What do you think, that I'm putting on a performance for you? I told her it had nothing to do with her and don't involve me in your problems with Jimmy Dean. She got up to leave and said, Don't tell me I've got problems, he's got problems. I said fine and Jimmy said, She's a semi-agent of mine, now smile and say good-bye nicely and pick up your feet and get lost. She stood there like a frozen lioness and mumbled good-bye and slowly walked away. We went outside and stood in the street. It was raining and all the neon signs over the clubs on the street were shining and flickering and Dean said, She's actually a nice girl, let's go. He dragged me back inside. She was standing with her back to us talking on the phone. He went over to her, got down on all fours and started yowling like a cat. She was holding the phone and turned to him. She wanted to appear surprised but there was something desperate and tough in her. She waited until he finished mewing and he kissed her shoes and she pulled his hair. When he got up he said, You're not worth it but you and me will get married someday and she told me, Get him out of here, there's no love here, and Jimmy told her, You're weak in your strength, you haven't learned the rules of acting yet, we're all whores and sell ourselves on the meatmarket and this guy here, my friend, he sells magic in painting and he paints like he's a dancer. And we left. He said, What a sweet whore!

I met his girlfriend who I think was called April, she worked as a waitress on Fifty-sixth Street. Nobody ever mentioned her. She was a lovely person and we talked a lot when I visited her where she worked at the first café in town, except for the Village, but Jimmy lived with Billy Gunn, a black actor who would later become a director, and we'd go to the movies, Krissoula, Lee, Jimmy, and April. Sal Mineo, who was murdered years later in Los Angeles for drug-related or "homosexual motive[s]," would sometimes go with us, and he liked Jimmy and whenever someone recognized Jimmy in the street Jimmy would pretend he was blind, which wasn't difficult because he was myopic and knew how to squint pretty convincingly. In the end, April said, Jimmy leaves his heart with me but always goes home to sleep with Billy who knows his prey can't help but come back to him. April knew how to steer clear of the spotlight and she gave Dean warmth, but his dark side came out both with Gunn and any woman who the studio wanted people to think he was having an affair with. One day, maybe the last day he sat behind me while I painted, he said, I've always had a basic feeling of unease, maybe that's what I've found in your paintings. Not in you. You and me are a bit alike. You've been, he said, the painter of the paintings that are me. A few weeks later he went to Hollywood for the last time to work on the picture he never completed. It seems today that perhaps death was already in him and was eager to get going. The way he looked at life was basically playful. He said he loved gambling and experimenting, testing the limits he could reach in car races.

When he talked about cars you could hear the longing in his voice. He said he loved them more than he was capable of loving people, that he trusted them more than he trusted people. The night after that last day, after he'd sat behind me for five hours rocking and mumbling and talking to imaginary cars, we went to the Blue Angel to hear Anita Ellis. Dean listened and flapped his hands like a suffocating fish. Gunn came along and tried to calm him down. When Anita sang Brecht and Weill's *Mahagonny* songs he cried. For me she sang "Put the Blame on Mame," the song she dubbed for Rita Hayworth in *Gilda*, and I was over the moon. I remembered the sublime Rita's gloves, the smoldering sex of her, the archness of her false naïveté. Dean said he'd wanted to meet me since he saw my *Icarus* at Krissoula's and her sister's place, the sister who had the Nazi boyfriend. He said he loved the angel and the angel burning and that's why he'd struck up a conversation with me. I told him I'd noticed that he had no barriers between himself and the world. He said good-bye to me and told me he'd learned a lot, and flew off to California. He called from Los Angeles to say he was starting work on a picture and that he missed my back in his eyes and he missed the paintings and asked whether I'd finished the big painting of Isaac's sacrifice, and I said yes. He asked what I was working on and I said I wanted to do something with the verse "And the wolf shall dwell with the lamb." He said that in any event he'd prefer to be on the wolf's side. Then he thought a bit and said he stood no chance of getting in with the wolves. He something that's stayed stuck in my memory like a dart: I'm looking for the razor's edge, how far I can go, there's nothing sexier. I've got a new Porsche. I want to reach the speed of thought in it. A few weeks later, at night, Lee was asleep, April called and Krissoula called to tell me that Dean had been killed and they asked me to come to his apartment and that Gunn was waiting there.

We cleaned up the apartment, got rid of all the filth that Dean had collected and kept. We wanted Dean to be seen as clean and nice and a good American when the police and press got there. We left before dawn, tired and sad, and went to a coffee shop on the corner. We were drinking coffee when we suddenly heard a siren and saw a speeding car. Four in the morning and a patrol car was chasing someone. Back then the cars had running boards and two cops were hanging onto both sides of the car, holding onto the doorframe with one hand and firing at the car outpacing them. Krissoula said, That's a fitting epitaph for Jimmy Dean.

That was a month or two after Lee and I got back from Israel.

Bird died in March and then Avi Shoes made an unsuccessful attempt at suicide. He came over and sat in silence all night. Avi Shoes, I told him, with all your millions you can buy anything, even death, and he replied, But not Mira. He said he'd been with her, that he'd sworn not to tell anyone where she was. That she was searching for something, that she was raising cats and loved him, he said, but she felt it was forbidden, and I've had it, he said.

Then Lee was invited to dance in a show called *John Murray Anderson's Almanac*, an attempt to recreate the Ziegfeld Follies. She didn't explain why she wanted to dance in it. I asked her if it was the need to stand onstage with all those amazing women, all of whom were six foot two and sculpted like goddesses, and show them who was really important, but she didn't answer. Belafonte sang. There were a few comics. There was an old woman who played the cello and looked like Yom Kippur and told dirty jokes with the cello between her legs, and there were a few funny pieces and some less funny and the usual filth and of course there were girls. They came down a staircase. They wore beautiful costumes. They took off the beautiful costumes. They really did look like the sirens. They walked around and all looked like they'd been made in a factory. Lee competed with them. It was brave of her said Belafonte when we went to the Waldorf-Astoria after the show.

Among the sirens there was one woman who was especially stunning, Monique van Vooren. She had a body that only comes along once in a very long time, but inside the body was a woman that no man really needed. She had a distinct and calculated corruption about her but she had self-respect because she sold only what she actually had, not what she didn't. She had a head on her shoulders. We talked one day. I was embarrassed at looking at her half naked and she pointed at her breasts and said, They're just tools, like your brushes. She said she knew exactly what she had and what she didn't have. She looked in the mirror and studied her face and said, This will all pass one day and I've got an idea exactly when, and then what will I do? I didn't go to Harvard. I've gotten used to the good life. There's no good life in old age. And then what? Stand in line for a pension? I've got to think about that day because I won't do any modeling if I'm not just as beautiful as I am now. I was standing at her side at the fiftieth performance party for the show and she was watching Lee dancing. Monique admired dance and said she envied Lee and me. Nobody cheats, she said. There were two performances on Wednesdays, a matinee and an evening show. Every Wednesday Monique would put on her fur coat—which, once, she took the trouble, grinning, to open up and show me she wasn't wearing anything underneath—and go to the stage door where a limo awaited her, and drive off. Sitting in the limo was the man who was to become President Kennedy. Once a week, she told me, I get to sit in a senator's lap, and that's something to think about when I get old.

Lee and I went back to the Village, to a lovely apartment on Sullivan Street, and she went to her shows and one day a friend of hers came to pick up something Lee had promised her and of course, before I'd even taken in her features, I looked into her eyes—I was shy as usual but desire always wins out—and she agreed with her eyes that I was almost too shy to look into, and it was business as usual, and I touched her by mistake and she didn't bat an eyelid and then another brief episode began on Lee's and my bed, but when I got to opening the zipper on her jeans I saw the word "Lee" shining on a metal button and I just couldn't. After all your cheating, said Lee later, poor boy, your conscience got in the way, and on her sweet clown-like face there was an expression I suppose of schadenfreude. Sandy Sachs heard about the Lee jeans story and wrote a radio sketch that was adapted into a short play for the Philco Television Playhouse, because she occasionally wrote scripts for them and made a melodrama out of the Lee story; not funny, not sad, quite dirty. It was broadcast, and let me tell you, it didn't do me much good. Sandy took me aside for a talk in which she made herself sound like pretty hot stuff and announced that masturbation was an excellent way to kill time if you were too lazy to go out and work for a living so maybe I should stay at home more often and not open the door to every woman who might or might not have a button on her jeans. Afterward Sandy swallowed a pill and started going wild and climbing the walls and cut herself and fainted and some friends came and we took her to the mental hospital she'd already been in a few times before.

I went to the small café on MacDougal Street and had an espresso and Robert De Niro Sr. came in with his young son, and he asked how I was and I asked how he was. I liked the softness of his speech, the modest melodiousness, he was looking for the good in things. I paid and we walked slowly and talked and wandered over to Little Italy. He suggested we go into a restaurant and invited me for a meal. We went inside. It was quite dark. The tables were mostly empty at that hour, and at the far end was a table that stood apart from the others, and there was a man seated at it dressed like a banker with a wide face and a heavy jaw, and next to him were a few energetic young men and two older men who seemed scared. In the corner sat a police officer who had removed his cap and was drinking coffee and the banker tossed him a few twenty dollar bills. De Niro went over and the man got up and hugged him and kissed the boy and asked who I was and De Niro answered in Italian and the man said, Israel poof-poof and fired into the air with an imaginary pistol and shook hands and invited us to eat with him.

The table piled with salads, small fish dishes, and then beans and cannelloni and what I called noodles and they laughed and said, Pasta, pasta, and the man sat down with us and for a few minutes stopped throwing twenties to the cop who sat there hunched over and I couldn't see any sort of happiness on his face, he just grabbed the money, didn't look at it, and stuffed the bills into his pocket. The man said he was a friend of De Niro's. We were suddenly surrounded by young men whose guns could be seen a week's drive away, and the Don sent them away and asked me about Israel. I told him that a few years ago I'd been a deckhand on a boat and I'd visited Naples, Rome, and Sicily. This pleased him, he ordered glasses of a fine liqueur and we drank to the health of the survivors we'd brought on the boat that he said had come from the greatest calamity known to mankind since God created the universe in seven days. Six, I said. On the seventh even God had to rest. Two young guys went for me, I'd insulted the Don, but he smiled and sent them away. Afterward De Niro and I talked about art, about white on white, black on black, Mondrian's *Broadway Boogie-Woogie*, which had always bothered me and that De Niro praised, and I mentioned the names of artists I liked and said that Hopper was the greatest. And Wyeth. Who looks at Hopper today? I do. Painters and critics don't. He's passé. He's the greatest American artist today, I said. And he said maybe and that I could buy a Hopper for only a few hundred dollars and I said I didn't have the money and then he said, Maybe they'll go back to him one day, and I said I hoped that would come to pass. Hopper's city. The lonely houses. The play of light. The distance. The subdued scene of the man at the bar or the reclining woman, the sad, empty, dejected city, like Vermeer, in a light that came, with both artists, from some unknown, unexpected source. We left and it started raining. He put up his umbrella over me and we returned to America.

Adele Schwartz called and said that somebody called Gilbert had said he'd seen Pat in Yonkers. She'd buried what she called her daughter in Yonkers. I went there. In the cemetery, on her stone, was a wreath, but she'd left no other trace. At the time I met by chance a Jewish detective whose surname was the same as my mother's maiden name. He was a sergeant in the NYPD and was following someone when I met him at Washington Square and West Broadway. Suddenly there was a commotion not far away on MacDougal Street. I went over to see what was happening, bumped into the sergeant who was running and we saw a guy dressed like an English lord with two good looking girls being driven in an open Chrysler by a Chinese chauffeur wearing a tux, and he was shouting: Anyone who can sing a Hebrew or Jewish song wins a TV set and electrical appliances. The open car was filled with TV sets, radios, toasters, and people began clustering around it: young blacks, artists, and all kinds of bums, and they all tried to sing. Some sang "Hava Nagila" and "Shalom Chaverim" and they got a TV set or a toaster or a phonograph, one guy seemed to be avidly slicing the air with his hands and then suddenly burst out with, "Tse-na, tse-na ha-banot ure'ena . . ." and another ran up and yelled, "Hevenu shoilem oleichem," and another, red-faced with effort, sang "Bei Mir Bistu Shein," and others tried other songs, not strictly accurate, but close. The guy looked pleased and handed out expensive gifts to whoever sang first, and the girls giggled. Somebody sang the Israeli national anthem and "Mein Yiddishe Mama," one guy who'd heard Ilka on the radio sang "Eretz zafa halaf udegash" in broken Hebrew and the man yelled, Wonderful, and gave him a TV set. He threw the gifts at them, they had to hold out their hands to catch them, and the guy said, Remember that the Jews have got a state with pioneers and soldiers—despite the fact that most New Yorkers had never heard of it back then. Now they very much wanted to hear about it. Two young Jews knew a couple of prayers from the Yom Kippur service and the guy was happy, the people blew him kisses and I looked at him in wonder and asked who he was but nobody knew. And there, on that spot, the sergeant and I met. We were both moved by the same thing: fear of a pogrom.

After he introduced himself and I told him that his surname was the same as my mother's maiden name, we were both excited by the suspect closeness that was apparently the product of some obscure longing for the past, which he'd always said was a dead country. We had a drink at the San Remo. The Italian bartender wanted to entertain us and told us not to worry so much because the Pope had recently pacified the Christian world by saying that in the next world there would be no need for sex. I told the detective about Pat. He told me I'd met exactly the right man and that he was part of a national police operation to smash a network of gangsters selling babies and so Pat's story meant something to him. We went back to my apartment.

Lee was rehearsing a dance and from the phonograph came the sounds of Bird with his violins and I found the piece of paper I had with all the details I'd once written down about Pat, like the date when it had happened in the hospital, what the lawyer looked like, and which Broadway hotel Pat had stayed at. The sergeant promised to help. I told Avi Shoes who came and went and whose secretaries never knew where he was and where he wasn't, and he said he'd help too. Mira came and she and Avi Shoes looked up material on Boris because his laboratory had been burned down. At the Atomic Energy Commission they said they'd never heard of Oppenheimer or Teller or Boris. Mira didn't look her best, she looked like a shadow of the woman she didn't want to be. She'd completed another master's degree at Columbia, started teaching medieval philosophy and Renaissance art, and made Avi Shoes's life a misery; he was possibly the only man—with the exception of Boris—she'd ever loved, or so at least Lee said, and in my wife's voice there was a touch of longing. The sergeant, my pretend cousin, fell in love with Sandy Sachs who we went along with to meet a medium who claimed he could see thousands of abandoned children all over. Sandy believed in him and we said, What have we got to lose? The sergeant stayed with her and she devoured him like she'd consumed eighty-one other men before him, notwithstanding the two slip-ups that had left her with two sons. The sergeant told Lee about the so-called family connection between him and me and he really did make inquiries and came up with the name of the family that had adopted Pat's baby. With Avi Shoes's help I put ads in ten newspapers in New York, Chicago, Philadelphia, and a few more cities in the South. I wrote: Pat from Division Street. I have news. Call Yoiram (and I added the telephone number). I waited. All kinds of cranks of both sexes called at all hours of the day and night firing poisoned darts of evil and filth and terror at me, and in the meantime I went to the adoptive family's home with Gandy.

They were a family from South Carolina who'd come to New York two years earlier because the husband had got a job at the Chase Manhattan Bank. Gandy dressed me up like a clerk and forbade me to utter a sound while he pretended to be a department head in Chase Manhattan's internal investigations department. It was, of course, on a Sunday when the banks were closed. We were shown into a fine apartment on Lexington and Fifty-something and on the way we saw the El at Third Avenue that was almost dismantled and there were huge heaps of iron piled all around. The dead buildings that had been hidden were still desolate and bent but the sun was now hitting them for the first time in a hundred years and you could see in your mind's eye their forgotten youth beneath the patina of ugliness caused by the El as the trains passed by their windows for decades. There were all kinds of *machers* sniffing around, they all knew that property values would soar. The adoptive father spoke in a Southern drawl and sounded surprised, but as someone who'd come from the South and wasn't familiar with the rules of the game here in New York, he didn't raise a fuss. To complete the charade, my "cousin" appeared wearing the uniform of an NYPD sergeant. It should be noted, to his credit, that he never deceived anybody because it was all sort of part of his own investigation into the baby trade and it was he who had found the family for us. He reassured the man and his wife, a nice woman who served us drinks and whom I was immediately attracted to, but Gandy saw it and whispered to me to restrain myself, maybe because it was unthinkable for me to end up as Pat's daughter's stepfather, and as they all talked the conversation slowly shifted to family and the South and from one of the rooms a beautiful little girl of about five came out and kissed her mother. She and Pat were like two peas in a pod. My heart lurched when I saw her. In the end there was no choice and we told them who we were. The woman looked at us in astonishment and I could see tears coming to her eyes. She said she'd been crying for a long time. She said she hadn't slept for the past two years. Poor thing, said her husband in a soft, loving voice. One day, she said, I looked at our daughter and saw how little she resembled me and him, and I dreamed about a poor mother somewhere out there who had been forced to get rid of this blonde angel, and all the time I was thinking about the mother's eyes and what she wears and the color of her eyes and I want to know who she is. The woman said she was a devout Christian although she hadn't been before, but she'd undergone a spiritual rebirth and now belonged to the Methodist church. Sometimes, at night, she said, I look at the child while she's asleep and I love her so much and I know that maybe someone is weeping over her right now. She told us that five years ago they'd been looking for a child and somebody had told them he'd heard from an agency that later proved to be nonexistent that they'd found a little girl and then there was a doctor who'd shown them his license and a city official came and they'd legally approved the adoption. I told her about Pat. I didn't disclose any details, neither her surname nor her place of birth. Just that she was from the South and how she'd wanted the baby after she'd nursed her and how the baby had been snatched. I didn't say that Pat had searched for her. I didn't tell them about the cemetery. I said that Pat would surely be happy to know that the girl was living with such a lovely and loving family, and the woman kissed me, and Gandy too, who tried to sell her a drawing, but she said that she didn't understand modern art, and she even seemed filled with innocent surprise at my long appraising looks, but likewise restrained herself. My sham cousin Braverman—who maybe wasn't sham and was indeed a third cousin or something, although my mother's family had only changed its name eighty years ago because my great-grandfather hadn't wanted to join the Czar's army—questioned the parents a little further because the parts of the puzzle he was interested in were linked to a big organization that had been trafficking in babies for years.

Oved, my friend from Los Angeles, arrived from Guatemala and said he'd come through Europe. How, I asked, do you get to New York from Guatemala via Europe? But Oved, like Billie's flower and fire and love, wasn't in the habit of explaining himself and didn't say much. He said he'd gone to Guatemala, seen Mayan statues, a Dutch hotel owner he'd met in Guatemala wanted whores, had given him money to buy Mayan artifacts in exchange for importing whores from Italy. An Italian had provided visas. So Oved or Abu Shalouf bought a dozen whores in Genoa and sent them straight to the airport in Guatemala. He stayed with us and didn't stop talking about a system for beating the craps tables in Las Vegas. Lee and I were already at the end of our road together and perhaps that's why we'd only fallen in love with one another then because when you're *falling* in love you don't actually have to love, but in any case we couldn't live together any longer. My cheating hurt her more now than before, because before there'd been a chance and no love, now there was love and no chance, so it hurt.

I went down to the Lower East Side because I'd heard that Pat had visited the woman in black at the entrance to the *Forward*. The paper had already become a weekly, but the woman still sat there erasing the Jews who were left. She admitted that Pat had dropped by and told me, If you're looking for her keep it to yourself because she doesn't want to see you, and don't put stupid ads in American papers unless you really can't help yourself, and then only in the *Forward* and in Yiddish. I bought an ad, it only cost a few pennies, and sent a message to Pat. I went to the house at Canal and Division. Most of the Jews had gone, including the great Morom, and now Chinese people lived there.

The bookseller looked like an ancient butterfly. He was still alive because he was just a bunch of burned paper. He was glad to see me despite his hostility and the woman in black told me it was because not a single other potential customer remained.

He started talking about his girlfriend from Odessa who'd gone to Eretz Yisroel on the *Russland* and caught malaria and died, and he'd been told that if she hadn't gone she could have been a queen of the Jews in America, because they hadn't had a queen since Pat disappeared.

I went back home. Lee was doing a scary dance with two tall black dancers who said it was a Watusi tribal dance. That night there was a party at Ruth Sobotka's, who had already split up with Stanley Kubrick.

On one side of the huge room stood the male dancers dressed in garish colors, made up and reeking of eau de cologne, hugging and kissing, and on the other side were the women dancers, you could tell they were women by their legs because women dancers—Chinese, African, American, or Russian—all have the same legs, and they looked at each other in despair and there was me in the middle, someone who was neither here nor there. And there was Jerome Robbins, who loved Lee and liked me and who'd made a fortune with *The King and I* and *On the Town* and who'd taught me how to save a dime crossing Times Square on the BMT Broadway line and he invited me to paint at rehearsals. For two weeks I sat in City Center and painted for hours every day. What interested me was painting movement and capturing it in the serene frame of a body melting into motion. I painted a world of images, certainly not great art, maybe superficial photographs of the moving human being, and I think I managed to touch or cage the movement itself, and the dancer remained enveloped in the movement, expressing it, part of it. Robbins bought ten drawings from me and so I had a little money in my pocket.

Oved asked me to accompany him to Los Angeles. A trip of four days and nights was short for him. He'd already been from Los Angeles to Guatemala six times and we didn't know why somebody would drive for seventeen days along mountain roads just to sell the car in Guatemala and make enough to buy an air ticket back to Los Angeles. He said that this time it would be worth my while because he'd worked out a system and we could get rich. Since I didn't have anything urgent to do—Lee had had turned into a miniature lioness, wonderfully cute, dancing not only in the studio but also on me and she'd started inventing nonexistent lovers to make me jealous and it worked—I told her I was going with Oved and would come back rich and she said she was starting work with Robbins on a show called *West Side Story* so in any case she'd be too busy for lovers and especially for a cheating husband. I joined Oved and we went to Detroit by train. He took me to the Lincoln car company.

We were given a brand-new Lincoln that we had to drive to Los Angeles. Transporting a car by rail cost the automobile manufacturer four hundred dollars while having the car ferried from Detroit by people like us saved them two hundred, and if you multiply that by a few tens of thousands of cars, said Oved, you can understand that they're making more on us than we're making from them. They told us not to hurry. If it rained hard or there was a hailstorm or sandstorm, we should stop right away and let them know. When the car reached Los Angeles the company people would zero the odometer and sell the car as new. They gave us enough money for gas, oil, and routine servicing along the way. All the rest was up to us. We drove slowly. We didn't hurry. Oved looked for cows. He kissed a brown one. All during that day's drive he talked about that brown cow, the likes of which they didn't even have in Gedera. Wait a while, he said, and you'll see a *Casuarina*, and in the middle of America there was the tree just where Oved said it would be. Sometimes it rained. We'd stop and watch. He said there was no sight as wonderful and sad and touching—or he didn't actually say this but mumbled it, and I made gestures in reply to his mumblings to the effect that there was indeed no sight to cause such supreme and moving sadness as torrential rain. At first the wind came from one end of the horizon to the other, fields, trees here and there, and a smokestack or barn or big silo that looked like a fort and a lonely house and car on a long journey, and then the clouds sailed slowly by and fine windblown rain fell and a flock of birds swirled brilliantly in the fire of the sun that flickered briefly between the clouds, and then the hard rain came, buffeted by the wind.

We drove through breathtaking storms, the sky glowered, and Oved was happy, we saw how a storm built up in the distance and came closer and then the torrent, the wipers were useless, we stopped in small towns whose names the inhabitants didn't even know. At gas stations we got fed up explaining our accents and where we came from and where that country was and so we said Paris and they said, Paris, Texas? And we said, No, Paris, France, and then they'd remember that they'd read about the Eiffel Tower and the naked girls and we drove on. We called to tell Lincoln it was raining and that there was a sandstorm in Michigan and hail in Iowa and a flood in Colorado. We drove into the mountains, we looked down at huge valleys, and one evening we saw a thunderstorm not far away. Lighting began splitting the heavens in zigzags, thousands of bolts of lighting that together looked like a ballet in half light shooting across the sky and hitting the ground and leaving the night far behind. And after an hour's driving the sky cleared, there was just the darkness of the desert, and next day we saw a meteorite shower. And I looked and saw the sky slashed. Blackness filled with sparks. We stayed at godforsaken motels. From afar we saw a man plowing in the infinite space. Herds. Horses galloping or nibbling grass. Dusty pickups, and for half an hour it hailed with each hailstone about two inches around. We stopped. The hailstones fell on our heads and fortunately not too far away there was a farm and we got the car under cover and the people were friendly and we drank whiskey and ate stew from which came the smell of winter by a fireplace.

We reached Utah. A Technicolor movie. We didn't linger in Salt Lake City but Oved wanted me to see the Church of Jesus Christ of Latter-day Saints so we stopped. From outside it looked like a temple of kitsch, but we went inside because it was hot and it was supposed to be cool inside. The first Mormon we saw was Shimon from the Florentin Quarter in Tel Aviv who'd worked with Avi Shoes in the luxury tax department in 1949. He was standing with his back to us and talking to a few girls in colored skirts and socks pulled right up. He hadn't seen us yet and I said, Abu Shalouf, let's get out of here, all I need is Shimon the Mormon, because Shimon used to be Shimshon and then Simone and he was told that Simone was too Jewish and he decided on Simon but at different times he'd also been Gad and Nimrod and Haimkeh, and when he'd lived on the Lower East Side he sometimes said he was born in New York, sometimes he said Jerusalem, but in fact he had been born in Tel Aviv, in the Shapira neighborhood, though he even claimed to be Swedish once or twice. He had witnessed his father's murder. His father, Menahem Pritzker, had imported five thousand pairs of shoes from Italy. Back then you were allowed to buy one pair a year with ration points. And crude shoes at that. But here came Pritzker with beautiful shoes. Shiny. The latest styles. In two days he sold five thousand pairs. Then the rains that were supposed to come on Tuesday fell on Thursday and everyone who'd bought the shoes realized they were made of cardboard. A journalist investigated and discovered that Menahem Pritzker had purchased the same shoes from Italy that were put onto corpses about to be buried. So, made of cardboard. So, five thousand angry people, including poor women who had bought the shoes for their lovers, sons, and husbands. Five thousand people looking for Pritzker. On Friday everything was closed and Pritzker was unable to get out of the country in time. Five thousand people were looking for him. Tel Aviv was small. They found him in about two hours. An hour and a half before the Sabbath. And one of them murdered him. And five thousand people minus one knew who the murderer was and they all kept quiet. They were ashamed at being conned. The state was new. It was a Jewish state. History couldn't know they were fools. They kept quiet. Shimon saw it happen, but couldn't identify the killer, and in the end he didn't really care. When he grew up he worked on a ship and tried a similar scam in Italy. He took tap water and said it was from the Jordan. Thanks to memories of his father, he got away in time. In America he joined the Episcopalian church, but then said he'd gotten disillusioned, he didn't say with what, only that he didn't find the true Jesus there, as if Jesus actually interested him. I'm searching for myself, he said, and then joined another church. Avi Shoes had told me Shimon went to Utah and became a Mormon because they were allowed to have more than one wife, although even one was probably too many for him.

But by the time Oved came up with a response Shimon had noticed us and smiled as if it had only been a couple of hours since he'd last seen us. He motioned for us to wait and we heard him explaining to the girls how he'd gone to Bethlehem and heard a voice and followed it to the Church of the Nativity and he'd seen Mary and she told him, Shimon, the Mormons see the truth, she said, their Law of Abraham is the true law, and back then I'd never heard of the Mormons, I was just searching, there was a holy man in Jerusalem who was a Mormon and we went to Tabgha and saw Jesus delivering the Sermon on the Mount right in front of us.

Those nice innocent girls were listening to him and eventually we interrupted and called him over. He came over and whispered, What are you doing here? What, the woman from New York told you to look for me? I don't owe her a cent. And I'm fixing up a wedding for myself and then I'll have a Green Card and that'll be the last you hear of me. We told him that we just happened to be passing through, and he said, Since when does anybody just pass through a thousand miles from any real city, and we said that we wanted to convert and marry those pretty girls and he said they were very devout, like the *goyishe* version of the people in the Mea Shearim quarter in Jerusalem. *Yalla*, do me a favor, I've got it good here and if I'm seen with you too much I'm finished. I'll have three wives and Jesus too. With God's help, I said, and he said, Yes, with God's help, and added, *The choine on my boike is bwowken,* just like he used to say when he was still Shimon and thought it was funny and so we left.

After hours of monotonous driving along deserted roads we reached a small town called Provo and were surprised to discover that we'd run out of money. We found a public phone booth and made some calls, me to Avi Shoes—collect, of course—but he wasn't there, and Oved called his brother Hanoch in Los Angeles and he wasn't there either. The hours passed. When we picked up the receiver the operator would ask, Is this Oved or Yoram? Our voices were similar and sometimes when I hear myself I think it's him and she knew by then who to connect us with and we were getting hungry. A flotilla of young girls from the local college passed by. We looked at them. It was sad. They were there. We were here. The wonderful telephone operator who wouldn't give her name sent us coffee and sandwiches via a nice little boy and Avi Shoes finally arrived at one of his offices and wired us a money order and we drove on.

We came to an empty gold-mining town. All made of wood. Not a soul. No name. Collapsed buildings. Neglected empty streets. Dogs roaming around. We found one old man living there, so he said, because all the people who'd left were fools and soon they'll be starting to look for uranium and after all there was gold here once but to-day's gold is uranium and I've got a Geiger counter. He was waiting. And no, he wasn't bored, he went hunting sometimes, he said, he talked and dreamed a lot about uranium with passing travelers like us, and he'd never been all that fond of people to begin with and all his wives had been cruel and he hoped they were all dead and now he had ten dogs and he trusted them, he called them and they came and he told them to behave themselves and they obeyed and he said, Don't trust people, they're all cheats.

After an hour in the desert by canyons gashed with sunlight it was decided that Oved, Hanoch, and I would go to Las Vegas and try out Oved's system for beating the casinos. He'd learned the system from his late grandmother of blessed memory who had prayed for him and saved him in the war and now he'd had a dream about her and she'd told him what to do. For a guy who came up with the idea of hiding the fact that his Israeli passport had expired by covering it with Jewish National Fund stamps, this all came pretty easily. We had a little money left over for this trip and Oved found an old Dodge and we drove for seven hours across the Mojave Desert and Death Valley and reached Las Vegas—wide streets and one-armed bandits in every gas station. We found a small motel, had something to eat and drove to the Sands, which was considered the best. We checked out the territory. We were interested in the craps tables, because the roulette wheels had two greens and the house took you for all you had on both.

We saw that free drinks were being served all the time and there was a bar where people were eating and drinking without paying, but we discovered too that the minimum at every casino on the Strip was a dollar. We didn't have enough money to gamble whole dollars so we went downtown. Going there was like going back in time, before we'd even been born. Poor, withered, sad-looking people were shouting, Seven! Seven or eleven! and shooting craps or playing blackjack. The pit boss sat on a high chair looking like a brawny lifeguard at the beach. Down below a few guys we wouldn't have liked to meet in a dark alley were moving through the crowd. The minimum there was a quarter. We got some chips and Hanoch went to sleep at the motel and Oved and I played. He stood behind me saying, Put it on the red or Put it on black. Or, he'd do a quick calculation and say, Six, and I'd put it on—No, no! Eight! And I'd move it. After a day of playing we saw we were winning about the same sum over any given two hours. After deducting expenses and losses we had won twenty-five dollars.

After the second day a short, heavy-jawed man came over and asked who we were. We told him. He was overjoyed, Ah, boychiks from Yizrael! Then all kinds of bosses and semi-bosses came over looking like the gangsters from *Guys and Dolls*, and they gave us drinks and awarded us the house medal and a Las Vegas medal and invited us to the wedding of one of the owners. We went. We danced. They'd brought a rabbi from Reno. They said that the sheriff was a Jew as well and that he'd spent five years in jail. Most of the security people and the bosses had been small-time gangsters and now they were running the most crime-free city the world had ever known. People would forget huge sums of money on a table, come back and find it was all still there. But everything in the club was shoddy and cheerless. People lay drunk and half dead on the floor, a passing winner would toss them a coin and suddenly roused from sleep or a drunken stupor they'd manage to catch it, get up, stretch and become men, go to the cashier, buy some chips, put them on a number, and then if they lost they'd yell something to some god or other and lay right back down. Every few minutes the bouncers would frog-march somebody to the door and throw him into the street. Not far away, in the desert, you could see the green of an enormous golf course, and a police station with the waving hands of prisoners sticking out through the bars, all the guys shouting, Let us play! Let us gamble! Whiskey bottles were passed from hand to hand and in the halls, in the jail, in the parking lots you could hear pleas, like a melody. The Jews asked me and my friend to sing for them, I think that Hanoch who had woken by then was the one who agreed, and they sang something like, How pleasing it is the Sabbath of Israel together, because their Hebrew education had apparently only been so-so. Each morning we went back to the motel room with twenty-five dollars. Oved said, The system works but we don't have a safety net, we're not showing a profit, we're breaking even; if we had two hundred dollars in our pocket we could go to the Strip and play for whole dollars and make some real money.

After four days during which we were hailed national heroes, the nice Vegas Jews told us, stone-faced, that they were going to give us a few more medals, a bottle of whiskey, some candy and chocolate, but although it pained them to say so it would be better if we didn't show our faces in their clubs any more. Why, we asked. They didn't answer. Do yourselves a favor, they said, we're all brothers, the People of Israel, but get lost. Oved smiled because he understood that the system was working, but when I asked our friends what would happen if we went back, after all these were casinos in an American city and there was law and order here, they told us, Look boys, we're the law here, nobody's ever been robbed or murdered in Las Vegas, there's no death or theft here, but on the other hand there's a big hot desert and all sorts of people who asked too many questions are out there in the ground. And I, poor little me, said, But what will happen if we complain, because it's not fair to throw people out just because they've been winning twenty-five dollars a night, and then one of them kissed me on the cheek, hugged me tightly, his hands were like steel bratwursts, and said, Who would you complain to? We're the staff, the bosses, the cops, city hall, the courts, the bailiffs, and we're all graduates of Sing Sing and Attica and a few more universities that aren't exactly Yale, so don't play tough guy with us, okay? We won't snitch on you because you're flesh of our flesh and we're all our mother's boys. Go up to the Strip, maybe they won't catch on at first, go break the bank and don't forget that you're the most honored guests we've ever had and *shalom*.

We consulted.

Hanoch had to get back to Los Angeles. Oved and I cased the biggest joints and again decided on the Sands because everybody said it was the best. For the food too. Part of it, so they said, belonged to Frank Sinatra, whose career, after all, I had restarted, and to good— not bad!—gangsters. We learned the lingo from the hookers, who were not called hookers, and what they didn't know you could write on the head of a pin. They lived at the same motel we were staying at and liked us; Oved was tall, he had the face of a despondent Swede, and we'd meet in the mornings, have breakfast together after they'd been working all night, and they told us all the secrets. We started playing. It was a classy joint. More than four-star. Seven-star at least. We were there for two weeks. We swam in the pool, ate in the restaurants for free, heard the greatest performers without paying, just as though we were high rollers. The hall was vast. Every hour along came a half-naked girl with a tray and served drinks to the gamblers. Unlike downtown, here we saw the who's who arriving in their private planes and winning a million and losing a million and it had no effect on anybody. The house won on the 12 that was like the green in roulette but in craps it was called 12, and there was only one, because one was enough for them.

One day, or one night, a huge Indian came in dressed like a chief and surrounded by ten young fierce ladies. He came, played, we stood near him, we stopped gambling, he won two million dollars and lost three and went on winning and losing, laughing all the time and hugging the duty girl and after two hours he went to eat with his troop of virgins, that's what he called them, and we followed him. He was happy to talk. The virgins moved around and made eyes at all the gamblers who were ogling them and we asked why he was willing to lose so much money. He asked where we were from. We told him. He said he'd heard there was such a place, and explained: As you can see, I'm a goddamned Indian. My father lived on a reservation. My grandfather too, who had a great name, died there. And his father too. The tourists would come to see real Indians and I had to go Woo-woo-woo and my wife had to embroider, and the children—I had children then—had to dance with feathers stuck in their hair, and the FBI came and got everybody drunk because the war against us was still going on, it never stopped, it would never stop until not a single Indian remained alive. I was supposed to be given some land outside the reservation, some hole in the desert, to build a hut for selling Indian clothes to the tourists. But I was given a big plot of land by mistake so I was forbidden to sow or plant and only cacti grew there. And one day a young man came along and put his finger in the soil and smelled it and said, There's oil here! And he took pity on me. He knew something about Indians, and not only from the movies, and ran me to Oklahoma City where you can see those big metal grasshoppers pumping oil at the entrance to the Oklahoma State House of Representatives, and I got official confirmation that the land belonged to me because they'd thought it was just a little old useless piece of desert for giving to Indians who don't know how to think clearly without whiskey and are only good for John Wayne to kill. They took me back to my land and the young man came along and drilled. They put in a drilling derrick. That was in 1946. There was a gusher and in one day I was rich. Then they tried to get rid of me. It reached the Oklahoma Supreme Court, but with all their power the law was still on my side, because that nice young man brought in reporters from all over America, and then the government fumed and sent in some thugs but I rounded up a few tough Indians and we beat up the thugs and they left me alone. They said, Okay, so there'll be one Indian with oil, that'll be good PR for America. People wrote about me in all the world's papers. They wrote what the press attachés at the embassies told them to write. They did a TV report and said, One Indian with oil, but there won't be any more. And then I started buying things: I bought a ranch. A yacht. Why a yacht in the desert? For kicks! I bought a plane. I hired pilots. I bought a restaurant just for me. I bought twenty young girls for a hundred dollars a day and they get a tip after a good night. I'm seventy years old. I can't even count my millions. I can buy anything. All of a sudden I wanted to buy a big company in Texas. I bought it. They tried to stop me, but money is the real law in America. And then one day I realized I could buy anything I wanted. I thought, there's got to be something I can't buy. I searched. Classy women? I bought them. A church? I bought one. Until I passed through here by chance. The city was tiny. I gambled.

I suddenly realized that there was one thing I couldn't buy—luck. Here they say luck is a lady and when I come here I get excited not because I win or lose but because I don't know if I'll lose or win when I roll the dice or wait for the croupier to shout, Seven! Seven! Or eleven. Or three. Or twelve. See? It's wonderful to feel yourself hanging in the air and not knowing, because money can't buy that throw of the dice—because even if I buy five croupiers I can't buy luck. He looked happy. He tossed two hundred dollars' worth of chips to us, which helped us to play for real money and win a hundred a day. But we still didn't have the big, big money.

I called Avi Shoes but Miss Hauser answered and said dryly that Avi Shoes had sold most of his shares, bought a ranch in North Dakota, and taken Mira with him. She told me he'd said he wanted to learn to fish and he didn't have a phone and didn't want to hear from anybody and he'd call if necessary and that bastard, my father's murderer, told me he loved me. And he said he loved you too. But he doesn't want to talk with you now because you're a loser who's trying to gamble instead of painting.

The wives of the gamblers who frequented the casino and didn't play roulette or craps would crowd around the one-armed bandits and play on them. The casino, which knew its clientele, built niches in the walls around some of the bandits and the wives would hide there, and if word got around that someone had been playing a long time without winning they'd run like crazy to grab the machine as soon as it was abandoned, out of an erroneous belief, hard to up-root, even if they'd studied statistics at Harvard, that if the machine had been working for a certain time without yielding results, then the next player would surely be a winner. The guys from the casinos knew better than all universities in the world how to con people, the bandits only paid out at random and the hiding women had nothing going for them.

We continued playing and it wasn't easy. I'd stand close to the table, one hand stretched out with a chip, I'd wait, and Oved stood behind me making calculations in a tattered notebook and saying, Red! No, black! Or, Eight, no, no, no, six! And I was forced to concentrate and know exactly where my hand was in the face of the croupier's calls and Oved's shouts, and sometimes I thought that his voice was mine thinking aloud, and sometimes he lost his voice and I didn't hear what he said, or there was some commotion, a gambler who didn't know how to lose, and some of the nice guys quickly dragged him outside, and we continued, with the best will in the world, to play for single dollar, we couldn't raise it to five because if the losses and gains stayed at the same level we would still only win a certain percentage, just like downtown, but we'd also be losing more, and we just hadn't reached the point where it was worth our while. To get to a five-dollar bet we'd have to play for another four and a half weeks. The girls at the motel kept us entertained and told us what had happened to them and who they'd worked on the night before, and we drank together, and one day a one-eyed man came along and told us we were wanted upstairs by the management. We followed him because from the way he looked we could tell that running was out of the question. We were taken into a spacious room. At the far end sat a friendly looking man who got up, came toward us, it took him a few minutes to impress us and he said his name was Jack Entratter and he wanted to show us something. He led us into the next room where there were TV screens showing every blackjack or poker table and everything else in the house, including the one-armed bandits. We looked and saw how we'd been watched for the past two weeks. Everyone was being watched. Even the Indian chief. And then we were taken back into the big room.

The man asked us to sit down facing him. He ordered coffee for us. He asked some innocent questions like whether there was a casino in Israel and had we fought in the war and whether we knew where we were. We answered as best we could. He said, Look, my friends, I'm here to make money, not to be nice. When I was nice they stuck me in jail for it. So this is how it is, two of your good friends from downtown were discovered found dying of thirst in the desert, maybe because one of them, or both of them, hinted that you should come gamble at the Sands. This is the Sands. The Sands is me. They really were nice guys, but they talked too much. Sure, they've come back now, they weren't buried out there, but they've got histories in town and they know what a mistake they've made. I mean, they were helped to understand what a mistake they made with the aid of a certain party who can smash through a concrete wall with one fist. Here on the Strip, systems vary. As you must have noticed, we don't care how much you win here, even if it's ten million in an hour. But—we do care that you're winning the same amount every night and that one of you takes notes while the other plays. We've had hundreds of miracle system players here and they all learned soon enough that we don't scare easy. Because, you know, here in Vegas there's only one fear: like at Sodom and Gomorrah, which went up in flames because of a vengeful God, the fear here, which keeps us up nights, is that somebody will come along with a real system, and that system will finish the whole city off. So we don't know if your system is really that system, or if you've just been lucky, but we don't like worrying or taking risks. So it's like this: You're going downstairs right now, I mean right now, in a minute, and you'll cash in your chips, take your money, go to your motel, pack your things, pay your bill, go to the parking lot, get into your shitty Dodge, drive to the first Gulf service station on the right as you leave town, fill up, and then head out in the direction of Los Angeles. Just remember that, until you pass a certain point—and this is wholly out of concern that nothing unpleasant should happen to you on your drive—you'll be tailed by a black Packard with Nevada plates that'll keep an eye on you until you cross into California, we don't cross the Nevada state line, and then once the Packard disappears from your rearview mirror just remember to continue driving in the direction of Los Angeles, and I'd like to say this in the nicest and fairest way possible, because I like you and I'd even adopt you both if I could spare the time but there's no free time in my life and I work hard since my bosses—who are both partners and friends—aren't around to keep an eye on things themselves, but you've got to go, you're hitting the road today, and I'm going to ask that we don't see you here for a very long time, not because you're not nice, on the contrary, you're very sweet, but we've got a situation here where our love for you blinded us for a while and we don't like being blind. So come here a second and take a look. Look—he took us to one of the TV screens—look, see over there? Groucho Marx. See? He's just won half a million. Water off a duck's back. Tomorrow he'll lose. Or somebody else will. But winning that much every night, or even a small sum, consistently, that's dangerous. Look, a gambler comes along. He knows that if he loses he'll double his bets and if he wins he cuts his losses by half. That's the sort of system we allow, the pros use it, and it doesn't scare us because whatever a pro wins he'll lose, or somebody else will lose it for him. The guy's come to gamble, but how long can he gamble? How many hours? Five? Six? A day?

Two days? You've got to sleep, eat, drink eventually. And we're here with a hundred craps tables and twenty roulette wheels and they all work twenty-four hours a day because in the normal course of events a man can beat the machine, but you can never beat the system. So here's a little something for you, for the road, a few cigars, club lighters for the both of you, despite that one there not being a smoker, and we'll even give you back the cost of the call you made to Avi somebody in New York, but now, regretfully, I want to see you going through that door, and out of our deep respect for you both you'll be shadowed by some nice guys who want only the best for you until you are in your car and driving.

He got up, embraced me and embraced Oved and I felt a tear falling onto my lapel, then he turned his back on us and said, It's been a long time since we had such honored guests, it has nothing to do with money, I mean what you've brought from your country, but I've got no choice. Business is business in America. It's not about doing or accepting favors. And that's how it really was. I was disappointed, but not Oved. He said this was proof the system worked, we'd made it onto their list, which meant that we'd get rich yet, we just had to bide our time because with us it was the other way round, we'd beaten the house but lost the table. Next time we'd come with more money and instead of here we'd go to Reno or Europe and play for a short time for big money and get out before anyone invited us to take a nap in some hole in some desert even there are no deserts in the south of France but look there are plenty of lonely mountaintops nearby and those Nazis, added Oved, who was already thinking about the Mayans and Mexico and Guatemala where he would spend most of his life, those Nazis will shoot us one way or the other.

After about two hours the Packard following us disappeared from the rearview mirror and in the middle of nowhere we saw a small town: a gas station and a diner, a few houses, a small street with stores, a police station and a bus station; we saw that the town was called Mojave. We bought a cold drink. It was very hot. From behind the station appeared a cop wearing a huge wide-brimmed Stetson and who looked like Gary Cooper . He went over to Oved who was at the wheel and said he wanted us to get out of the car because he wanted to ask us a few questions. There was no point in arguing. He pulled out a notebook and wrote down Oved's name and asked where he was from and Oved said he was from Gedera, California. Then the cop said that the car had Kansas plates. Oved said, Right, that's where the plates must be from, and that he'd been in Kansas too, once. But they're 1949 plates, the cop said, and it's not enough to be somewhere to get plates from there, I've been to Arizona but I've got Nevada plates, and Oved said he'd been to Arizona too, and the cop gave him a long look and Oved added, It's good you noticed, but 1949 was just a good year, you know? Especially in Gedera, California. We still feel that way today. And the cop was taking a liking to Oved, you could see it, and he smiled and said, Okay, so where's your license? Oved looked and said that for some reason he couldn't find it. The cop looked sympathetic and asked about the insurance. Oved said he'd left it in Las Vegas. Tell me, asked the cop, have you got any papers at all? Just one piece of ID? Oved showed him his tattered passport with the Jewish National Fund stamps and the United Jewish Appeal stamps and stamps from the honorary consuls in Italy, Mexico, Guatemala, but the cop said it was written in a language he couldn't read and asked, Have you got a single document proving that this is your car and that you are you and that you live where the license says, wherever it is, because if you do, I'll help you out. Oved said he did have those documents, but that the cop would have to let us drive on to Los Angeles in order for Oved to find them, and that he didn't understand at all who'd taken off the California plates and replaced them with plates from Kansas through which he'd passed only once and he'd seen wheat and corn fields and the moment he got to Los Angeles he promised he'd bring the papers to the nearest police station. The cop spoke from such a height that I had to stand on tiptoe to hear him. He was the most decent man I've ever met in any desert. He really tried to help, and asked questions like, Have you got enough money to get a license right now so you can keep driving? And, Have you got insurance, which Oved had already told him he hadn't. In the end the cop told us sadly that even with the best will in the world he had to impound the car at the police station and if Oved brought him proof of ownership and a driver's license at the very least, even without the right plates, the car would be returned to him. Meanwhile you should wait because there's a bus in two hours' time. Oved asked him, Who takes the bus home from Vegas? And the cop said, You. And he laughed.

The car was put into the yard behind the diner and the cop had to take off on his motorcycle after receiving a message on his radio that a Ford driven by a drunk had been spotted doing a hundred and fifty, and he left, but not before he apologized. We only had enough money for a few sandwiches because buying gas had swallowed up most of our winnings. Eventually a bus arrived packed with people who it turned out had all gambled and lost their cars and their money and their watches and rings and fancy suits and their savings and their daughters and wives and children and jobs, and they sat defeated, downcast, bent over, smoking and mumbling. Some tried to snap out of it and shouted, What am I going to tell my wife? She'll kill me, and she's right to, because I also mortgaged her brother's house! We arrived in Los Angeles a few hours later and Handsome David came to pick us up after Oved called him. Hanoch had apparently wanted to come over too, but a search of his wife's purse—she already knew where not to keep her money— yielded nothing. Paul came to ask what about Guatemala and when would we make some money and I managed to get a small loan from Nick Conte, an amiable actor I had befriended, and I bought some paints, brushes, and canvases and did a few paintings and to these Hanoch added two of my paintings he already had and we put up an exhibition in Billy Wilder's apartment, who said his name was Shmuel and was a warm and funny man and I told him that my father had only seen one movie in his entire life, Wilder's *Ninotchka*, after which whenever anyone asked him if he wanted to go to the movies he would say, but I've already seen *Ninotchka*, and then repeat the joke about I want coffee without cream and the waiter who comes back and says, I'm sorry sir but we have no cream, would you like it without milk. And Wilder asked about some of his friends from Vienna who had come to Israel; I knew one of them, he had a clothing store in Tel Aviv and they gone to high school together and Wilder bought a painting from me and said Israel was a good thing because he had been pretty lucky to make it to Hollywood and survive after he first fled to Paris, but others couldn't come and he lost his family over there. He had a friend, a Jewish doctor who lived in the hills above Hollywood in a neighborhood where Brecht and Thomas Mann used to live and where Stravinsky still did. Wilder took me to this Doctor Morrison; he was an austere man with a silent rage in him and a bitter smile and he owned four private hospitals in Los Angeles, and he was nice to me and bought two paintings and we talked about the war. He said Brecht was egotistical and devious but he liked Thomas Mann. I envied that he'd known Thomas Mann and he invited me to a garden party. It was pleasant. Japanese paper lanterns suspended from ropes. Several guests arrived in Swabian peasant dress, and an orchestra played on the never-ending lawn. I finished selling my paintings and Oved vanished to Mexico but not before I gave him money for traveling expenses to get the car back from Mojave, and I flew to New York.

In New York, everyone had disappeared. Gandy had gone to Florence and found an artist there, a woman called Jocelyn, and he loved her, and they got married and went to live in Vermont, where he found peace and painted and taught to the end of his short life. We saw each other infrequently after that but we corresponded and I always remembered how he painted like Bud Powell played. He'd start in a whisper, searching for the right note, then make the most of it, crushing it, letting the eighty-eight keys of the piano bring back his faith and his hands would caress the keys like velvet, repeating a musical phrase, the way Bird sometimes ran through variation after variation and only then played the theme. His face would be stuck to the keys, then he'd smile because he'd found something good and he'd rise with the note, put rhythm into it and change both the melody and the beat, bring in the theme and wring it dry and emerge from the depths of something deep like a barrel of manure and suddenly shout, I'm playing clouds, because Bird once said that the clouds are the only artists who make art out of their own forms, they change constantly, they're the only artists in entire world whose shape is their art, is all their art, and that's how

Bud Powell played, he'd extract from within himself and transform himself with his playing and beat the keys or stroke them like a butterfly and ravish the music and love it and beat the living daylights out of himself to reach for and realize the tenderness he held in his eyelids though he didn't know it because he was crazy. That's how Gandy Brodie painted; he'd go into a painting and conquer it and let the painting kiss him and he'd celebrate, skip, let the painting come into being. It's a shame that he didn't get an exhibition at the Sidney Janis Gallery until after he was dead. Gandy had wanted to be exhibited at Sidney Janis's his entire life.

I hadn't found Pat. Sandy was hospitalized near Boston. Adele had disappeared. I had another exhibition but suddenly my heart was in writing, what did I have to do with contemporary painting, I couldn't see myself in contemporary painting, I didn't like my paintings, Lee was in a run of *West Side Story* in Philadelphia. I called and she wasn't nice to me at all.

I went to see a movie at the Museum of Modern Art. The who's who were there in force but only a few real cinema lovers. They were there so that everyone would know they how interested they were in High Art—they and a few intellectuals and wiseasses, there was giggling and laughter and a kind of chuckling or affected throat-clearing at the emotional and touching scenes, what they probably called kitsch, and kitsch of course makes cultured people laugh. They were showing Lewis Milestone's 1930 *All Quiet on the Western Front*, adapted from Erich Maria Remarque's novel. I had once been a soldier. I had been wounded. I knew what despair was. And the people around me were clearing their throats to seem "in." Suddenly, without thinking, as if in an epileptic fit, I got up, grabbed one of the throat-clearers, with all his choked laughter still in his throat, I wasn't thinking, it just happened, I didn't know I had this violence in me, the stunned man flapped his legs, he was twice as big as me, and I dragged him outside, threw him onto the sidewalk, went back inside, people murmuring angrily. Somebody went out and came back in; two policemen came and asked me to accompany them. They took me to the police station and asked for an explanation. I said I had been a soldier and I'd gone to see a war movie that had touched me because I knew what it was all about, and sitting next to me were these intellectuals who were laughing because otherwise nobody would know that they were such big mavens. The Irish officer couldn't resist asking me if I'd used force on the man in question and I told him that I'd barely touched him and he'd fallen right into my arms and I thought that maybe he was overheating so I dragged him outside because there was air there and a sidewalk that maybe he would enjoy resting on. The cops looked like they weren't the biggest fans of the MoMA crowd and couldn't really care less what happened to what they called those snooty faggots, and the officer told me that if I ever threw anyone like that out of a movie again on Thursday at four-thirty in the afternoon, if I ever threw anyone like that out of a movie called, what was it called? *All Quiet on the Western Front*, I replied, if I ever threw anyone like that out on Thursday at four-thirty in the afternoon when they were showing, if they ever showed *All Quiet on the Western Front* again, they'd be forced to haul me in front of a judge. I asked what about Wednesday and the officer said, We're busy on Wednesday. And Tuesday too.

I went to see Lee in Philadelphia. She wasn't happy to see me. She said she was busy with the show and if I wanted to see it I could stay but she'd only talk to me in New York and only after the premiere. I could see there was no point in arguing with her. I felt she was planning on leaving me and I didn't like being left. I saw the show that night and afterward Leonard Bernstein took me and the actor playing Tony, Larry Kert—the brother of Anita Ellis, she who sang *Gilda*'s song—to a restaurant. In the restaurant Leonard and Larry hugged and looked at me as though I was someone lost who didn't know what love was and I said how moving the show was and how lovely the music was and how wonderful the choreography was and Larry said that Jerry Robbins, who'd never been with a woman in his life, had proposed marriage to Lee. I said that he'd once proposed to Nora Kaye too but Larry said that this time it was serious and that his love for Lee was touching. I felt betrayed and tried talking about it to Lee, but she refused to talk and said we'd speak only after the premiere and when we got back to New York, and then only at our apartment.

In the meantime Sandy Sachs wrote me asking me to visit her in the psychiatric hospital near Boston. I went, thinking about Lee cheating on me with Jerry Robbins. In the hospital there were catatonics limping along and Sandy said I was a lowlife because I'd never loved Lee but I told Sandy that now I was sure I did. Sandy said I was a typical macho man with abandonment issues and that she was being treated by a young doctor who played a twelve-string guitar and was apparently even crazier than she was. They'd had a brief affair and she suggested I meet Hughie, who people said had discovered oil in Alaska by using telepathy. I went with her and her doctor to another wing of the huge building. I met an elderly man, Irish, who was being treated with LSD by Sandy's doctor, because this doctor was one of the first to use hallucinogens in therapy. In the hospital's opinion, Hughie was the sickest patient they'd ever had, and now he was recovering, not because they had cured him, but—said the doctor with a certain sadness—because there'd been a miracle. Hughie was what Americans call a con man, a guy who could sell refrigerators to Eskimos. He was uneducated, clever, charismatic, imaginative, and an unstoppable rhetorician. A kind of Chan Canasta whose freakishness and greatness had found their outlet in illness—he was a genius at being sick. When he got sick, he got sick because he had decided to get sick, announcing his intentions in advance. He decided that on a certain day he would have diabetes, and so he got diabetes. He thought about heart disease and then he got it. He elevated his blood pressure and had been in the hospital for ages now, empowered by his madness, enraged at the world. He was funny and pitiful, cursing everyone around him and at the same time always getting everyone on his side—his day was night. But what had happened was that quite by chance he met the second-worst case in the hospital, a boy-dog. The boy was tied up with a rope in a room that had become a kennel. He was covered with a sheet. He barked instead of talking. He hadn't straightened up since he was four and ate on all fours. He was incapable of standing on two feet. The only treatment the hospital had come up with for him was to let him make up his own mind whether or not he should remain a dog—and so a dog he remained. But then Hughie ran into this dog. He started taking an interest in him. I said that maybe he was jealous because he thought that the boy was sicker than him. Hughie showed me his diaries, which were almost entirely incomprehensible, but they had a few lucid sentences relating to how Hughie had sneaked into the dog's room with an electric shaver and then with a battery-operated radio and later with a typewriter and how he'd taught the dog to type and how the dog made contact with the world through the machine and how Hughie and the dog had corresponded and how, a year later, Hughie had taught the dog to talk—but also how every time Hughie made progress with the boy-dog he'd make himself sick again and insult the boy and both of them would withdraw but then Hughie would go back and get interested in the dog again almost in spite of himself, and I learned how, with his power, he finally made the boy stand up and afterward recover completely and at the same time Hughie recovered as well. This story about how two lonely dogs cured themselves captivated me. I sat in the hospital mesmerized. The boy, who had recovered after a four-year confinement in the stench of his own isolation, tied up and speechless, left the hospital healthy, with his parents waiting for him. Hughie was happy and went to the cafeteria with me, took a glass, asked how much it cost, and the guy behind the counter said thirty cents, so Hughie paid and threw it against the wall and said, That sonofabitch will be healthy!

A week later Sandy was discharged, and I said that the story would make a great movie and she agreed and we decided to write a television play based on it. She said that since she'd just gotten out of the hospital she didn't feel up to writing just yet, but she'd put her name on whatever I came up with. So I wrote the synopsis and she sent it to *Playhouse 90* and one day she came to my apartment naked, a bottle of whiskey in her hand, shouting, Do you remember Hughie and the boy? Yes, I replied. Joyously she announced, I've sold the adaptation I did of your adaptation to *Playhouse 90*! I was in shock. After about a month however they rejected what she'd written because it was too realistic, too depressing. I guessed she'd taken out Hughie's black humor and they said she'd basically done *The Snake Pit II* without the love, the jealousy, the humor, and I decided I'd had enough of her, but I felt bad for her, and even though she'd hurt me I thought I had to save her and get her married off so she'd have a chance at staying alive. She had suffered so much and I thought she deserved something good in her life.

I had a friend, Steve Scheuer. He was the founder and owner of the *TV Key* column that gave the week's television program times as well as cast and crew, recommendations, a bit of gossip, and so forth. The column was a real success story. Steve's father, a Jewish emigrant, had dreamed of the country whose streets were paved with gold. Well, the gold wasn't on the streets, but at times he earned well and at others not so well. One day he was walking down what's now Park Avenue. The trains would rumble out of Grand Central Station, escaping New York. The buildings on both sides of the enormous, black, soot-covered area were in awful shape. And the noise from the trains was very loud. He stood there and asked himself, America? Is this what happens in America? And he decided that it was indeed America and that the trains would eventually be put into tunnels, a subway, and he borrowed money, some from his relatives, he mortgaged his home, bought a few pieces of land for what now seems like peanuts. A few years later the trains were indeed put into tunnels, Park Avenue became Park Avenue, and now on his land you've got the Waldorf-Astoria and so forth and so on; this guy, I thought, beat the house, not just the table. And it was his son Steve, who was shy and polite and goodhearted and a good friend, that I decided to marry Sandy off to. She was crazy enough for an introverted, charming, unsuspecting guy like Steve. I introduced them. They hit it off. They had a son. They lived on Eighty-seventh Street and fought sometimes, she naked with a knife and he with a breadboard and lots of shouting and her older kids and their son would hide and somebody once called me to intervene. Sandy was covered in blood, I poured a bottle of whiskey over her, and so on and so forth. Gandy wrote me that I shouldn't do favors like that to any of his enemies. Sandy said she was writing a proposal to city hall on how to teach eighth graders in elementary school how to take off bras. Speaking from her own experience, she said, if you could cut down on the time it takes for an excited boy to open a bra, which are all made differently, and the girl is sitting there trembling, it would save them trouble for the rest of their lives, just think of all the problems they'll never have. She was writing, she said, such a proposal, and was looking for people with contacts in the education system. I told her I didn't have any. She said, But you need the course more than anyone!

Lee was still with the out-of-town production, now in Boston. Oved called one night and his voice was screechy, pitiful, remote, he said, I can make only one call. Listen. Hanoch isn't home, I'm stuck on some island, there's no way out, it's like Ellis Island but for Mexicans, there's one guy who's been here since the Indian Wars, it's terrible here, call Hanoch, he's sure to be home soon, get hold of Brando to put up five hundred bucks' bail so I can get out of here, and he hung up. I called Hanoch. I told him. He knew about the island. Next day Oved called again, but this time he used our system, a person-to-person call for Mr. *Hakol Beseder*. ("Everything's OK.") The operator asked him to spell it, he spelled it, and then he said, if Mr. Hakol Beseder isn't available he'd speak to Mr. *Echtov Machar* ("I'll write tomorrow"). She asked him to spell it, and he said, No, no, actually, I have to speak with Mr. *Oved Yatzah*. ("Oved's on his way.") It took half an hour but I got the message.

Two weeks later Oved reached New York. Lee was on her way home from Boston. Oved told me that Shpilke, who had been in

Mexico, had found Laundromat tokens there you could buy in packs of a thousand for a dollar and they were just the same size and weight as quarters. He'd brought some along to New York. Hordes of Israelis were suddenly standing at public phones and calling home, their friends, Café Kassit, Paris, all over the world, until the phones filled up with the tokens and got jammed. The Americans checked, realized what was going on, and brought in a few Hebrew-speaking girls to the Bell Telephone Company. Two weeks later, our Israeli system was a thing of the past. I asked Oved about the island and why he'd been there, that island you called from. He asked, Remember the car in the desert? With that cop? So I went back to get the car. At the bus station there wasn't a bus going to Mojave, but there was one going to Mexico City. In Mexico City I ran into Harry Gemora and we went back to Los Angeles. I asked, What about the island? Oved said, All my stamps didn't work at the border this time and I was caught like a Mexican and taken to the island. There are people there who've been locked up for years. Scary. I said I understood now. That it was entirely logical.

I told him that Lee wanted to leave me and he said it was a shame, come to LA with me for two weeks, get over your broken heart and we'll find something to do. I've got an idea, that's why I came here, I want to take you back to LA. That's nice, I said, but why didn't you call, I would have come and saved you the trip, and Oved said, My Uncle Simcha said that the closer you get the farther you go. I said I didn't understand. Oved said that neither did he but remember his Uncle Simcha was a prophet. Oved bought an old Oldsmobile from a repossessed car lot. The price of each car there was just the remaining outstanding payments plus something to cover overhead. We drove to Los Angeles. Corn, cows, horses, alfalfa, and wheat.

Just one kiss for a cow. A farmer who told us the story of his murdered wife. The same old motels with their lifeless rooms. We went down to Utah and instead of driving directly to Nevada or Idaho or California, Oved wanted to go to Arizona, and not to cross it from east to west, but from north to south. We began driving through Arizona from north to south because, Oved said, of two reasons: First, he had a friend he wanted to talk to who lived in Phoenix, and second, he knew a shortcut to Nevada and that when we got to Nevada we'd find the car we'd left at Mojave and come up with or just invent some kind of paper or document that would convince the police to let us take it back and I'd drive the Buick and he'd drive the Dodge. The color of the land changed. Hours to Phoenix. Not far from the Grand Canyon we saw flocks of birds and the guy in Phoenix didn't really know who Oved actually was and what he wanted. The guy thought that someone would be coming to deliver him the Mayan urns he'd asked for, while Oved thought the guy would be able to tell him where to find some Mayan urns next time he went down to Guatemala. The whole thing could have been sorted out by two phone calls, but Oved loved sneaking up on an idea and pouncing without warning on whatever it was he thought he might be planning, or wanted to think he might be planning. We left town for the desert. After a day's driving we sat down for a few minutes in a small diner and had something to eat. The sky was clear and the sun was shining and from a distance we could see the huge yuccas and the adobe houses the people here had learned to build from the Indians, and I looked at the map and reminded Oved that Nevada was north and we were going in the opposite direction, but he said that the scenery was interesting and that there was a place nearby whose name he couldn't recall where there was a house he just had to see. I didn't argue. A day more, a day less. The talk with Lee could wait. I saw a small cloud sailing overhead. It looked beautiful, like a bunch of feathers rubbing up against the sky. A few moments later Oved said we should speed up. We were soon doing about a hundred and twenty miles an hour. The sky gradually darkened. Gray clouds came and black clouds came and there was noise in the sky and eagles could be seen winging away from the rock fissures looking like small fighter planes, a strong wind came up, there was a loud honk, like from within a huge bassoon, and we stopped the car. We saw the storm heading for us. Lightning cleft the sky and hit the ground with a bang. The earth trembled. Snakes could be seen squirming out of their burrows and from afar we saw the funnel of a cyclone emerge from the towering clouds, crushing everything in its way, magnificent. The funnel whirled out of the sky, very wide at its top as its narrow end reached for the earth and hit it and everything went mad, the car began sailing backward. Oved jumped out and stopped it rolling down who knows where. It was a sky-quake at the same time as an earthquake. Then the clouds began dispersing. Torrential rain fell for a few minutes, the sun even came out for a moment, then the sky darkened again and we heard thunder and it began to hail. A vast rainbow sliced open the sky and the sun reemerged from the clouds. We drove quickly to the spot where the cyclone had hit and reached a small town. Destroyed houses. Overturned cars, one hanging from a tree bent over beneath its weight. A gas station at the entrance of the ruined town. The roof had blown off and we saw it stuck in the ground not far away. On the main street people were lying crushed under a roof that had landed on them. Not far away a young woman was trying to free one arm from where it was pinned by a beam from what had evidently been her house, while in her other arm was a baby sucking at her nipple. At that moment another wall collapsed and Oved pulled her and the baby out and she was saved from being crushed beneath a wall that was just a bunch of shattered adobe now and the earth was sending out a hot vapor, it was burning inside, fires could be seen starting and going out again all around town, people were running in a panic, the sheriff came by and saw us saving the woman and shouted, Come with me. We helped him get a few more people out from under the rubble, they crawled out from what remained of their homes, terrified, and only one building remained intact: the town hall. The mayor came running and stopped by the sheriff who was trying to restore order in the general panic. The mayor thanked us and brought a bottle of Kentucky bourbon and we said something about sorrow and he said, You build rockets and go into space and fly airplanes at supersonic speeds and crack the brain's secrets and with a giant telescope you see the point where the universe begins and where time ends and then along comes the Good Lord and shows us who's really in charge—nothing made by man could ever destroy a place like this, even a little town that's barely on the map, in so little time . . .

We drove on and stopped the car at the Nevada state line. It was unbearably hot. Oved said that if he were a chicken he'd eat himself roasted. We drove on through scenery that soon became monotonous and Oved's silences didn't much help pass the time. Oved had three expressions he liked to use, the rest of the time he kept quiet. When he got into a traffic jam he'd say, What's this, a funeral? When he couldn't find a house he was looking for he'd say, They've moved the house, because when he first came to California from Gedera he'd seen a house on the back of a truck, and then for no reason at all he liked to talk about "The List" in Vegas and how he'd gotten onto it. Now he said, They've moved the first desert to the second. I laughed because I knew that if I didn't I was a goner. There was music in the car. We finally reached the Mojave Desert that we could have reached two days earlier and saved a lot of gas if we'd only come direct and we went right to the police station. It was noon and everything was quiet. Everyone was hiding in their air-conditioned lairs. Our cop came along. He laughed and patted us on our backs and said, I'd started to think you wouldn't make it. We had a hamburger with him in the small diner that was empty at the time and we had a drink and gave him the bottle of bourbon we'd been given by the mayor, as if it was a gift we'd bought specially for him as a token of our esteem, and he said that only a few people he'd arrested had ever given him a present, actually none at all, and he thanked us. He brought the Dodge around and said, You've proba-bly got all the paperwork now, and Oved said in his sleepy voice, Of course we do, just give me a second to find it, but the cop apparently took pity on us and didn't ask us to show him and so we carried on, me driving the Buick with Oved stuttering along behind me in the Dodge that didn't know it was on its last journey because on the outskirts of LA it started to limp. I saw it in the rearview mirror and pulled over. Oved got out drenched with sweat and said, Blessed Be the True Judge, and abandoned the car. In any case nobody knows who it really belongs to, he said, and it's died its final death. We got to Oved and Hanoch's house and all the guys came over right away. In the meantime Handsome David had found an American woman who thought his English was broken and who didn't know that ev-ery language he spoke was broken. She married him and was in the movie business. He said he gotten a green card and now he was a film producer and according to what was written on his business card he was really slumming by hanging out with us: Handsome David Productions. And Valerie came down from the dovecote and told Oved she'd missed him and he replied, Hmmm, who, me? You missed me? And she cried. She was paper-thin. When she stood in profile all you could see was hair and a head and feet, all the rest became part of the scenery. Oved gave a brief report on our trip and the moment the Brothers Karamazov heard that we hadn't met a single Viennese woman they fell asleep, bored, because any sentence of more than six words without Viennese women in it was too long for them. Hanoch told a story about the war. About a certain event that had happened to him when I was with him in the same platoon and I'd made a laughingstock of myself because I wanted justice, and then Oved smiled and Valerie tried to hug him and he went outside with her, went up into the dovecote with her and slept there. In the morning Oved declared that my driving the Buick without a license had been a success and he took me for a driving test. I went in and they gave me a paper filled with yes or no questions. I guessed right and a tired man took me out for a drive. It was the first time I'd driven in a big city and he asked me to park. I had nothing to lose so I parked. And then he said, Make a right. I made a right. Make a left. I made a left. Stop. Go. Have a nice day, you've passed. I had a mug shot taken right there and I paid and was given a license. Oved was pleased, because his license had been revoked so many times that it would be better, considering what had happened in Mojave, that he drive around with someone who had a license. Fat Paul came with Harry Gemora who brought a girl who wanted to be a star and meet Handsome David the producer. Paul asked if we'd found our police station in the Mojave Desert and

Oved said, No, they moved it. Everybody laughed, including the actress who had a pretty good figure and nice-sized breasts, but Paul, for the first time after all those years, didn't laugh. Oved tried him again and again he didn't laugh. Oved turned white for a moment, looking at Paul. Waiting. Oved had a drink then and told us almost casually that on his last trip to Guatemala City he'd gone with the Dutchman, and along the way they'd seen a flower market. The Dutchman, who loved cows and flowers, said that they had the latest thing there, flowers made of plastic that looked real and cost ten cents a dozen. We didn't really understand why Oved was talking about flowers, but Paul went pale and asked for a drink and he downed it and then his voice became weak and he whispered, They were beautiful? Like real ones? And Oved replied, Paul, absolutely like the real thing. The Guatemalans are renowned flower lovers and they buy those fake things like crazy. The younger Karamazov brother said, What? Like in Austria? And Oved said, Even more so. And they're like real ones, I'd bet anyone a hundred dollars that they can't tell the difference. He knew that nobody there had a hundred dollars so he was on safe ground, and besides, his system worked and was just waiting to cash in once he had a little money to get to Reno, this time with a bigger safety net, so what did it matter what he said. Fat Paul's face was the most interesting thing about Oved's story. First his features seemed to sink inward as though trying to reach the bottom of his soul, then he began quivering more and more, his huge ears flapping hither and yon. I kept watching him, there was nothing else too exciting to look at in there, notwithstanding the big-shot producer whose nose had started running because the effort of following the conversation had gotten him all worked up. Then Paul really collapsed in on himself, his face seemed about to be torn apart by muscles pulling every which way, desperate and uncontrollable like the cyclone that had been sent down by the Hand of God, his eyebrows were seeking a foothold in his eyelashes and his big belly seemed to expand and his feet tapped the floor and he managed, after much effort, to get some sounds out, and now he was clearing his throat so that some actual words might follow. Almost whispering, with his body trembling, he asked, How much? How much? And Oved said, Ten cents a dozen. And what color? All colors. Lilies? Sure. What else? Roses. Narcissi, and more. Where? In the market. And is there a factory there? There is, plastic flowers don't grow by themselves. Paul began straightening up in his seat. His eyes opened wide as if he'd just witnessed a miracle and Oved said that his Uncle Simcha had said, That's just what Moses looked like when he saw God on Mount Sinai. I looked at Paul and saw the lust in him. Paul grabbed the notebook that Oved had taken notes in with all his odd and even numbers for the system in Las Vegas and began scribbling. Everybody was staring at him. He was apotheosized. His belly was flat. A light sparkled in his eyes. We all agreed, later, that we had never seen anything like light in his eyes before. Yes, his eyes and even his hair all radiated great excitement and he started talking slowly, but gradually his pace increased and in the end he was actually chasing the words because they were faster than him now: Ten cents times a hundred thousand times two million times three, times four less expenses, ships, planes, trains, New York, Brussels, Paris, London, Tokyo. A global empire. After a few minutes Paul had already dispatched a fleet of ships and trains and planes and trucks to the four corners of the earth, selected possible ports, calculated how many people would be working in his company, how much each of them would earn, he said there'll be no employee discounts, salaries are best so the staff doesn't steal, It's a matter of principle for me, he said, and we'll have representatives in Guatemala City for security, each of them will be given shares in the company—Paul was talking as though in shock. He excused himself and ran outside and said, Wait for me, wait. And we waited. All of us, that is, except for the Brothers Karamazov. One of the reasons they're so wealthy today and have built thousands of homes in Los Angeles without ever really saying a word is that they never stopped to think about anything, which just makes everyone else think they're brilliant. We thought that Paul might have suffered a psychotic attack and Hanoch said we should call Susie, whose father was the brother of a psychiatrist, and I thought about calling Dr. Morrison in the Hollywood Hills with his four hospitals to ask for help.

We were hungry. Hanoch went out and brought back hot dogs, French fries, and brown beans, and he made an omelet. The elder Karamazov said, Why didn't he mention Vienna? Vienna crossed his mind, replied Oved, but he didn't want to take it away from you. *You* will be the representatives in Vienna. We ate. We listened to music on the radio. Valerie danced a little and came on to Oved. She wasn't pretty but she oozed sensuality and eroticism, if not actually sex. She looked like a handsome young boy while still maintaining a careful femininity. Two hours later Paul came back. He spread out business cards on the table that he'd just had printed at a press in Hollywood he'd worked with for years: "Paul, Oved, and Yoram Inc"; "Flowers and POY Inc"; "All Kinds of Flowers, Ltd—POY"; and a few more besides. The only one to get excited by the cards was Oved. He said, Why not Abu Shalouf, Paul, and Yoram Inc? Paul wrote it down. We've got to think, he said. Meanwhile it had gotten late and everybody was leaving. Two days later Oved came and said he was going to Guatemala City in a few days time to see the flowers. Paul got excited and said he was going too. Oved said, You don't know what a hard journey it is. You're soft, Paul, and you'll break down on me on the trip. Paul said that he'd been in the Haganah too, maybe he hadn't fought in the war but he'd heard bullets whistling by his head and had been a sergeant, and an Italian bomb had fallen next to the shoe store that belonged to his family on Allenby Street during World War Two, and he was going and that was that. In the end Oved got a big brown Mercury and Paul, Valerie, and me all decided to go together. The day Oved announced that everything was set but complained how low we were on cash, I met up with Nick Conte and told him about the trip and he said it would be hard but that he had a friend at MGM who had lots of diamonds and was married to the same woman for the third time now and who wanted to buy him and her a suitable burial plot with candelabras and music and sculptures of all the dogs they'd ever owned but that he was out of work at the moment and so had asked Nick if he knew of anyone going to Central America because the currency there was weak and there was three-figure inflation and lots of middle-class people were looking for diamonds to invest in because the banks weren't safe and the price of diamonds was soaring.

I told Oved. We drove to the valley where Mr. Smith lived, whose real name was Cohen but who had settled on an American name of equal rarity and we sat down with him; a big house, two pools, one for him and the other for his wife, and she said that the most wonderful thing was to get married every few years, the same woman to the same man. He trusted us and we drove to Paul's friend who had been a diamond merchant in Tel Aviv and before that in Warsaw and then not so much of a diamond merchant in Treblinka, but the kids who used to find diamonds in rectums and sell them to the SS used him as an expert appraiser and so both he and they had survived. The small, tubby man wearing a thirties pinstriped suit, a wide, side-buttoned collar, and what they called high-buttoned shoes—Jimmy Cagney wore ones like them and the guy loved Cagney—scrutinized the diamonds for a long time through a magnifying glass and with his pinky nail and pronounced them good, nothing special, but worth thirty thousand dollars, But you should know, he said, that you can't insure them because they're unreported, and we said, It'll be fine, and one morning we set out to make Paul rich. Oved told Paul that at the Mexican border they were checking all non-Americans—Me and Yoram, he said, have got green cards, and Valerie is a citizen, but Paul wasn't yet, and so at the border crossing he had to hide in the trunk.

It was a bit difficult for Paul to scrunch up into the trunk but greed won out and he probably lay there all squished calculating the riches awaiting him and about half an hour past Tijuana Oved let him out. He was dazzled by the light and smells and sat next to Oved with me and Valerie in the backseat. It was a long trip but the scenery was rich in contrasts. The north had stone houses in the Spanish Colonial style. A gigantic waterfall. Canyons. Bays. Boats. Noise and poverty vying with great wealth. We stopped in villages that looked like Europe. We stopped in Indian villages that looked like they were from the first century. Mayan villages. See: any book about the history of Mexico and its antiquities and the richness of its scenery. See: Acapulco, with its beach leading to its mountains that vanish into the sky. Deserts, wildernesses hidden in thick vegetation or sometimes dying from drought. Magnificent haciendas facing tumbledown villages and haciendas in ruins, souvenirs of the Pancho Villa revolution. Whorehouses and cantinas. Restaurants in the cities and food lines in the villages. See: the boulevards. See: the stones of every color. See: the beauty of Mexico in any book about the beauty of Mexico. We're not tourists, said Oved when I asked him to stop by a waterfall or a house built and decorated in an ancient style, and I kept quiet. Every now and then we stopped, we slept and ate in little inns. By this time Paul was sick. The food was killing him. The flies. The mosquitoes. Fear of the Indians. The Mexicans in their sombreros. The mariachis were killing him. He said it sounded like the same song all the time. The dirt roads caused him no end of suffering and he lost weight, about half a pound a day, but he had plenty to lose, and after a few days—I didn't count—we reached Mexico City. We passed through delightful neighborhoods where the rich drove Cadillacs and there were beautiful girls with bandannas on their heads and lots of churches and monasteries, and when we reached the city center Oved warned us that it would be difficult and told us to hold on tight.

Cars flew by through the city, which was crisscrossed by narrow streets, one on top of the other, and since the streets were only wide enough for one vehicle at a time, whenever two cars tried to pass each other, they would both end up climbing the walls of any adjacent houses—just seconds before a head-on collision. There were a few traffic lights, but nobody took any notice of them. People wanting to cross the road looked lost and exhausted; There are people, said Oved, speaking from his own experience, who grow old at those intersections, and only when they die do the cars stop, so their relatives can collect them for burial. I went to see the Diego Rivera and Siqueiros frescoes and was less impressed by Rivera than in the days when Mexican communist painting had captivated us in the Israeli youth movement. I wanted to stay looking at the Siqueiros frescoes but Paul pleaded that we go on. Many eyes gazed from cars that didn't move but simply idled, and trains passed by above. It was hard to get out of the city—all the exits were confusing. Abu Shalouf managed it, however, and we drove from village to village, stopping in towns here and there, here and there saluted by policemen to whom Oved tossed coins. More and more Indians. Less and less beauty and splendor. More wildness. White treeless cities at the feet of mountains. After four days of driving we were almost in the mountains ourselves. The scenery changed. The peaks arched above us and Paul asked, What's that over there, and Oved replied, More mountains, and Paul said, How do we get around them? And Oved said, We don't get around them, we drive up them. Paul asked if you could breathe at such an altitude and Oved said that most travelers said it was fine but then again it wasn't too easy for the ones who couldn't breathe up there to come down again and tell us about it. Paul was destroyed. We were tired and Oved said that before we started the climb we'd better have a day's rest.

We reached a white, picturesque Indian town and found something resembling a boarding house. Oved explained to the owner what we wanted and the owner was happy and said that very few strangers had passed through in recent years and he rented us an apartment with a huge adjacent porch and there were two fans there possibly dating back to the last century and it was hot. Very hot. Very, very hot. Paul sat sweating in an armchair that collapsed under his still excessive weight. Valerie took a shower and when she was done she came out naked to the porch to wrap herself in the pleasant wind that had started blowing. I fell asleep and woke up to a loud commotion. I looked out at the naked Valerie and in front of the boarding house I could see a swarm of people: men and women, priests and children, and they were all staring at Valerie, who just looked back at them serenely. They seemed less incredulous than openly aroused. They whispered. Sang with emotion. The priest brought a flute and his flock sang hymns. A boy lay on his back and screamed: *Diablo! Diablo!* Paul got out of his armchair— this was before it collapsed—and went out and yelled at Valerie. She told him it was none of his business if she liked to stand naked in the heat with the wind caressing her all over her body. Soon most of the people outside had taken off, just leaving behind a few old-timers, smiling, many of them toothless, the women buzzing and giggling, and a couple of hours later the men returned. They were carrying a large salver with a pig's head decorated with flowers and its genitals sitting next to its eyes and one of the men, finely dressed, and who didn't wear bones in his hair like some of the others, and who spoke Spanish and not Mayan or another Indian dialect, delivered a speech, and Oved translated for us. The man said that this was a big day for the village. Once, he said, a movie had come here. That was ten years ago. Horses galloped across the screen and there was a white woman who fled from the horses. For years they wondered what had become of her, and now they could see that she had returned. He said that everyone had missed her, and those who hadn't yet been born had heard the legends, and everyone in the village adored her. He said they wanted to buy her. We've brought a pig's head. A wonderful delicacy. And we've brought its genitals too, which are particularly delicious. If we gave them the white she-devil, we were told, we'd get the salver and beads as well as the head, and if necessary they would even throw in one of their women, who could cook anything we might desire. Oved explained that Valerie wasn't for sale. The man pleaded. Some of the men fell to their knees and prayed to Valerie with outstretched arms. Some wept. The women giggled. The children fondled their genitals. A wailing lamentation rose and increased until it became a ferocious roar. One man tried to lift the pig's head onto our porch but was gently pushed back by Oved. The lamentation continued. They wouldn't leave us alone. Valerie went inside then and fell onto Oved and kissed him passionately and he, embarrassed, went into a room with her. I stood bewildered on the porch, looking at all the people. They didn't leave until morning.

In the morning we got dressed, most of the crowd had dispersed. The distinguished man, his clothes crumpled now, asked if two pig heads would help, and Oved said we wouldn't sell even for ten, and the man said, We don't have ten heads anyway. Then the man bowed and said—and Oved translated—We're not animals, we are ancient Americans and people of honor, and if you come again the priests will sing for you at our church.

We started driving up the mountains and the air became thinner, rarified, and it was indeed difficult to breathe. Paul, who'd managed until now to concentrate on his future millions, became scared. He started coughing, looked ill, looked like a broken man, and I was afraid he was going to die on us. He gradually shriveled and all that seemed to remain of him was his outline, his dry screeching voice, whereas Valerie slept like a baby. The road was narrow and winding, over a void. The clouds would sometimes gather in the chasm below and sometimes rise toward us. On the brink of real despair Paul asked Abu Shalouf, When will we get there, and Oved, uncertain of the answer, said, Soon. And then Paul asked the question that led to his utter defeat, he asked if the route we'd take home would be easier. Oved delayed his response as long as he possibly could, and then, almost whispering, said to Paul, We're coming back the same way. Paul asked: Why? And Oved answered: Because there's no other way. Above us we saw people crouched wrapped in serapes working in the tobacco fields, the height was dizzying and Paul thought for a while, Oved's words sounded so dramatic to him that they took him some time to digest, and then he asked, Do you mean to tell me that there's only one way there and back, and Oved answered, Yes. And then Paul dared to look down. We were so high up that it was difficult to discern what was going on down in the depths. And Paul, close to fainting, asked, And what happens if there's a car coming up from the other direction? Oved said, It's difficult to explain, but you'll find out soon. And sure enough, after a while, during which Paul lay passed out on the floor of the car whimpering, a truck, not a car, loomed up in front of us. Oved stopped and the truck also stopped. Oved and the driver acted as if they'd spent their entire lives getting two vehicles across a road that only accommodated one. Oved looked back the way we came and spotted one of the turnouts hidden along the way. He reversed and began guiding our car into the little side path. And then Oved and the other driver commenced evasive action. The truck turned a little and Oved turned a little. Paul got out of the car and stood there shaking all over, half our car was hanging over the chasm and then the truck pulled up closer. For twenty minutes the two drivers played this game of mountain roulette and again and again we hung over the chasm, alternately trying to get more of our car our more of the truck into the turnout. Paul shouted, shaking all over, poor thing, What would happen to me if you guys fell in while I was standing over here? I told him that there was nothing to be done and if he was left on his own he'd have to go on on foot and then all the millions would be his. He asked Oved what would happen if his maneuvers with the truck didn't work and Oved, as he drove, explained: Look down into the valley, do you know what it's called? And Paul said he didn't and Oved said, It's called the Valley of the Crosses, because if you look carefully you'll see the crosses marking the graves of the ones who didn't make it. Paul didn't look but Valerie and I looked down, way down, and sure enough we could see crosses scattered among the boulders. Finally the truck went on its way, but not before Oved and the driver exchanged a few joyful words in Spanish, and we forced Paul back into the car. He wailed that he wanted to go home. Or he said, Drop me off and I'll fly the rest of the way. Oved said that it was all mountains around there and the nearest city wasn't near at all and there's nowhere to fly from until we reach Guatemala City. Paul yelled: Why didn't you tell me, Oved? And Oved said he'd warned him that it wasn't going to be easy. We continued on our way, holding Paul tightly so that he wouldn't jump out of the car. Here and there the track widened into the quarried mountain, now and then we encountered a car and another truck and Paul almost faded away entirely, that fat man disappeared into himself and could no longer be seen at all, all that was left of him was a shell, burning with fever, thin, sobbing, and then occasionally reviving as though in some delirium and shouting at Oved through the clouds in his brain: Oved, how many wreaths can you fit onto a truck? And onto a ship? And Oved would hurl numbers at him and go on driving.

I don't recall now how long the trip lasted. I remember we slept at a small inn on the mountain where the air barely reached and

Paul lay there half-dead and muttering astronomical numbers, and eventually we came to a valley, still at an enormous altitude but not quite as high as where we'd just been, and we checked into a small hotel and ate and bathed and Valerie was happy and we stayed the night and a day later we were close to Guatemala City. Paul started feeling better. He combed his hair and seemed in good health. What was left of him anyway. His initial enthusiasm was restored—Paul's ships, and Yoram's and Oved's, crossed the ocean again, planes flew wreaths from here to there, enormous cash registers registered, but what about income tax? Where will we pay? In the States or Guatemala? What's going to be left after we pay our agents? Perhaps we should concentrate on funeral displays, what did we think? And we drove into town and Paul looked around amazed at the beautiful houses, the Spanish-style palaces, the weird churches. I looked at the beautiful city. Mighty in its beauty. Solitary in its sublimity. We drove. About an hour later Paul said, Tell me, Oved, that church with the big cross, didn't we see it earlier? And Oved said, Maybe, but most of them look the same around here. And we continued driving around in the city for about two hours until Paul yelled: We've driven past this house five times, five times! I've been counting since the third time and I remembered that it was the third time, Abu Shalouf—where's the flower market? And Oved looked around, distantly, as though none of this was really happening, and checked the landscape quite thoroughly, and said sadly: The market's been moved.

I was sitting next to Paul, Valerie was sitting next to Oved, and Paul fell forward, writhing, trying to speak but choking and starting to move like a Chasid in prayer, mumbling something and finally screaming, You son of a bitch, to get me to laugh at your lousy jokes you haul me through the mountains for seven days in search of a made-up market? Tell me, was there ever a market? Oved said, There was, but apparently it's been moved. Poor, lost, thin, sick, dreaming, depressed Paul, who'd yet again seen one of his schemes collapse, broke into sudden, wild laughter, and Oved put the car into gear and sped toward a hotel that wasn't particularly large but nevertheless very impressive, painted pale green, and shouted something, and a light-haired man came out. Oved said, Hi, what's new, we'll talk later, take care of him, will you? He's losing his mind. Oved said to me, Say hello to the Dutchman, and feeling sorry for Paul who was convulsing in the massive arms of that bulldog-faced man, who was about six foot four, I asked Oved what the man's real name was, and Oved said, We're friends, I have a room here. He's always waiting for me, but no one knows his name. He can read upside down, and can read a letter that someone sitting in front of him is writing. He calls himself the Dutchman, but he might be Belgian. I met him at Seymour's. Seymour's job was to clear derailed trains off the tracks. In return he got anything that fell out of the trains, and he kept it all in his warehouses and then sold the stuff wholesale: Sardines. Guns. Tanks. Small aircraft. Chairs. Kitchen utensils. Refrigerators. Air-conditioners. Parrot cages. Once there was a train carrying wine and he made off with tens of thousands of bottles. And once a shipment of the pinkest pants in the West. The Dutchman used to visit Seymour to buy animal cages from him and we met there. The Dutchman has a separate balcony for the girls I imported for him from Italy. Valerie disappeared into her room and I into mine and the Dutchman took care of Paul who mumbled and spat and laughed and cried; the Dutchman brought a Jewish doctor who happened to be nearby, since he'd just dropped his eldest son off at a neighboring whorehouse. He was a pleasant man and spoke a little Hebrew and treated Paul for quite a while and told us in the hotel's kitchen that Paul had suffered a psychotic attack and wrote a prescription for some pills. It'll pass, it's not severe, he just needs to rest for a few days, eat well, and not see anyone by the name of Abu Shalouk, I said Abu Shalouf, and he said, Yes, is he an Arab? I said he wasn't, his name is Oved. Ah, Oved, *ovedet, ovdim, ovdot*, he said, reciting the Hebrew declension, and left after having a cup of coffee and said that he'd go for a walk and come back soon to take his son home because his wife had prepared an eighteenth birthday feast for him. The whore he'd left his son with, who wasn't up to the standard of the Dutchman's Italian women but the doctor didn't want to ask a favor of the Dutchman because to ask for a whore for the boy was all right but the Dutchman was liable to ask for a bottle of wine afterward, the whore, he said, who isn't even Jewish, was a present from him and the boy's mother. Paul locked himself up in his room and got treatment from the Dutchman and Oved suggested I not ask what kind of treatment. A beautiful Italian woman is potent medicine. Valerie hung out with some young people who were staying at the hotel and found out from the Dutchman that they were fugitives from the States because the States and Guatemala didn't have an extradition treaty.

Oved and I went for a walk, I bought a hat like a Texan's but with a narrow brim and Oved found a group of Mayans and greeted them and they greeted us. The Dutchman entertained us with stories. Oved sold the car because there'd be enough profit to fly back to California. He talked to the Dutchman about the diamonds we brought. The Dutchman got an appraiser to come around and he said that it was forty thousand dollars, and that someone would come the day after tomorrow and bring the money. On the third morning we heard Paul grunting and he came down to eat with us. He looked terrible. He swore that from now on he'd laugh until Oved cried at every joke he heard. We saw Valerie hanging out in the yard with one of the criminals and a day later we saw them together again. A messenger came with the appraiser. They examined the stones at great length and said they'd come with the money tomorrow and take the diamonds. Then Valerie came in, pale. She stuck to Oved. She said, Will you marry me today? And Oved answered categorically that he wasn't getting married.

She wasn't around in the evening and we went to a musical performance in the city square and came back late. Valerie was nowhere to be seen. I went to my room and tried to figure out what I was worrying about and couldn't come up with an answer. Then Oved came in, trembling all over, saying, Valerie's gone, the diamonds are gone. The Dutchman was summoned. He found out that Valerie had befriended a lady-killer by the name of Bobby Tennet. From Minnesota. He'd done five years for armed robbery. Escaped. Got caught. Did another year on a prison farm in South Carolina. Escaped and sold drugs to tourists. He knew how to charm women. He had brains and knew a lot of fancy words and was good looking too. Oved didn't feel betrayed, he was just angry. He'd looked after Valerie for four years. Supported her. Perhaps, in his own way, even loved her. He sat around silently for a whole day and then Paul, who had already started to recover, saw how upset Oved was, and the Dutchman sent some of his people out to investigate and soon he said he knew where Valerie was hiding and if Oved wanted, for a hundred bucks—which the Dutchman would lend him—he could see to it that certain people would finish the thief off and for another fifty they'd finish Valerie off too and bring back the diamonds. The Dutchman had asked around and found out that the stones hadn't been put up for sale yet so no one would know the difference. Oved thought it over. He told me he'd rather kill them with his own hands, but then again maybe he wouldn't be able to. The Dutchman brought us a pretty Italian woman we didn't sleep with. She'd known Oved back in Italy and gave us drinks. We chewed some peyote, and Oved told the Dutchman not to kill them just like that. Then he left for four days during which cartoons ran through my head nonstop and between times I ate and looked after Paul. Paul liked Oved and still hoped that maybe some of the Mayan marvels that Oved was always looking for and occasionally found would wind up rubbing off on him too. Four days later Oved returned. He said nothing. He didn't have the diamonds. The Dutchman said he thought Oved had found them but hadn't killed them. He said that Oved was embarrassed for Valerie. He didn't get the diamonds because maybe he'd decided that if they wanted them so badly perhaps they deserved them.

Eventually we flew back to Los Angeles and held a consultation that Hanoch also took part in. The owner of the diamonds wept bitter tears. His three-time wife yelled. He understood that he couldn't sue us because the deal had been illegal to begin with, but he'd counted on us and he really cried and Oved promised him Mayan urns and Aztec paintings and all kinds of things, but he wouldn't calm down. I asked him finally if I could use the telephone in another room. I called Avi Shoes. Rita Hauser picked up. Now she was all sweetness. She said she'd just married a Spanish prince and was happy. She was happy to give me the number to Avi Shoes's hideout—to disturb the bastard, she said. Mira picked up. She was happy to hear my voice and said she'd heard that something had happened between Lee and me. She always understood what other people were going through. I asked for Avi. He picked up and said, Avi Shoes at your service. We had always liked one another but had gone our separate ways because we no longer had anything in common apart from the terrible sore called Mira. I said, Avi, all these years I've never asked you for anything serious. This time I need your help, and I told him what had happened and Avi Shoes listened and asked, Exactly how much do you need, and I said, Forty grand. He said, No problem, let me speak to the man. I called the guy to the phone. They talked for a few minutes and he gave Avi his address and came back to us and said, He's amazing, this guy I've just spoken to. We went back to the house. Oved slept for a week. Hanoch split up with his wife and Paul slept with his old landlady one more time and it was the last because two hours later she died of a heart attack.

I thought of going back to New York, Lee sounded angry that I wasn't crawling back so that she could score a final victory because she knew that I hate being left even when it's inevitable. Nick Conte told me that he was going over to a friend of his to swim in his pool and invited me to come along. We drove to a house that looked a bit like a fortress and went inside. German paintings by Nolde and Kirchner hung on the walls. We undressed and changed into bathing suits. We went out to the pool, which was in a yard facing the valley below. Lewis Milestone, whose house it was, sat in a bathing suit and was wrapped in a large towel. He was big and fat and looked like a Roman senator. On the other side of the pool sat Akim Tamiroff in a bathing suit and a white toga, and Peter Ustinov was there too. Sitting together they looked like a meeting of the Roman

Senate. Milestone introduced us to one another, and of course I had pleasant memories of *All Quiet on the Western Front*, which he'd directed. They spoke Russian and drank vodka and talked about who I was and what I was doing and after swimming for a few minutes we sat down in Milestone's study, and somehow I got to telling the story of Hughie and the dog and how it had occurred to me to write a script about them and make Hughie into a kind of Chan Canasta working as a Jewish clown in a Nazi concentration camp. Milestone had directed *The Front Page*; *Hallelujah, I'm a Bum*; *A Walk in the Sun*; *Edge of Darkness*; *Of Mice and Men*, and other movies, but then, from 1953, after several Oscars and great success, he'd been blacklisted and couldn't work. He was the cousin of the violinist Milstein and told me he was born in Russia. Nick Conte took me back to Hanoch and Oved's house.

The next day, Milestone called and asked me to come over for lunch. We didn't sit in the dining room but at the pool and Milestone, who was a pleasant man—apart from the occasional Russian-style outburst: very familiar to anyone who'd grown up in Israel—asked me to tell him again about the man and the dog because he hadn't slept all night and he asked me to tell the story in as much detail as possible and not leave anything out, even if it seemed unimportant to me, and to take as much time as I needed. We ate and drank chilled wine and I told him about Sandy Sachs and Steve and the hospital near Boston and about Hughie and the boy-dog and about a woman I once met on a street in New York at night who told me about the Auschwitz Orchestra, not much was known about it at the time, and who told me that in another camp there had been a Jewish clown who entertained the commandant, and then she talked more about the pitiful Jewish orchestra that played German marches at the entrance to the camp and about how the SS soldiers would beat and abuse them, and I said that I thought that if Hughie was the crazy clown then the encounter with the boy-dog would be even more interesting, because then it works out that dog heals dog but is still *envious* of dogs, and perhaps I even said that you can see how they would be living in a sort of kennel, and that would make the story very touching. I said that when I wrote the treatment I had ordered the sequence of events precisely as they'd occurred in real life and tried to be as realistic and accurate as possible within the bounds of this crazy story. Hughie meets the boy-dog. The dog barks at him. Hughie brings a battery-operated radio, and later an electric shaver, and then a typewriter, which they use to communicate, and in the end he puts him back on his feet. Milestone listened attentively. His face was taut. He said, This is a good story for a movie. He said he hadn't made a movie for a long time because he'd been blacklisted, but he could now and he'd like to make a comeback with a good movie after a long absence, and asked me to go see his agent Paul Kohner the next day and discuss details. After that, he didn't let me talk. He was thinking aloud and started skipping from one topic to another. There was something nice about him and he looked like a wise old bear. His eyes talked. He asked, What time is it now? I told him. He said, I'm calling Chaplin. I asked if Chaplin was in town for a visit. He said, No, he's in Switzerland. I had never dared to dream that I'd see a man calling Charlie Chaplin. I would be there to see a man hearing Chaplin answer the phone. After a few polite words, What's new and how's Oona, Milestone started telling him the story and I heard barks coming from the phone, I asked quietly: Is that Chaplin barking? He said, Yes, he understands dogs, and then went back to their conversation. They spoke at great length. This could be an excellent project, Milestone said to some man who appeared suddenly and then Milestone laughed and told the story and embellished it and the next day I went to meet Paul Kohner on Sunset Strip. He was one of two Viennese brothers who were agents and we talked and he seemed happy that Milestone was going to be directing again and asked me to rewrite my synopsis and gave me some money so that I could work for a few days. I was sent to the luxurious Beverly Hills Hotel where a room was waiting, and I wrote on a typewriter that had been brought in especially for me. The hotel was nice and I saw more stars in the gutter than in the sky and I wrote, and four days later I brought the synopsis and Kohner read it and Milestone read it and then we sat in Kohner's office and they wanted to sign a contract with me and I said I couldn't because half the synopsis belonged to Sandy and I had to get her permission. They looked at me in astonishment. I told them how I'd gone to visit her in the hospital. How we'd thought of writing the story. How she'd been too weak and I had written the whole thing. How she had tried to improve and revise what I had written and sold it to *Playhouse 90* for fifteen thousand dollars but how they rejected her version in the end and said that it was too depressing. How she had taken out the humor and the love and made our story into something like the movie *The Snake Pit* and we had parted ways but she had dreamed it, lived it, Hughie was her friend, not mine, and Kohner asked a hundred questions about the sequence of events, asked about contracts, there weren't any, said that Sandy had no rights unless I wanted to grant them to her because she sold a synopsis that you wrote following a structure you invented and based on diaries that Hughie gave you to read and didn't give her, hence the rights are yours. He called his attorney who listened and said a few minutes later that Kohner was right. I said, Maybe so, but I have to act according to my conscience and I'm confident that if I call her she'll be happy to grant me her permission and then I'll add her name to mine and it'll be at my expense. The looked at me like I was out of my mind but agreed to let me call her from the other room. There was no answer at her home. Steve didn't answer in his office. Two friends I called next hadn't heard from her. Finally, I asked Avi Shoes to find her for me. Avi Shoes would have found my grandmother and grandfather for me if I'd asked. A day later he called and gave me a number in Canada. I called and Sandy answered. She sounded happy and said that she and Steve had gone on a second honeymoon, or perhaps a third, and they were happy, happier than she'd been on any of her previous honeymoons throughout her four marriages, including her current marriage to Steve, and she couldn't think about dogs and messiahs right now, because she told me I'd made Hughie into a kind of messiah, and she had no interest in Hughie right now because she was in Steve's arms and he was giving her foot massages and feeding her fruit mouth-to-mouth and she was sorry, she'd be back in New York in a few weeks and then she could think. I appealed to her. For the first and last time, this poor woman, who had been mercilessly battered by life, sounded happy and said she was in love and didn't want me to talk to Steve even though I'd introduced them, and hung up. Kohner and Milestone tried to persuade me but I said that I'd be in New York soon and sort it all out and they looked at me with pity and Milestone felt it was all for nothing and Kohner said that he was going back to his earlier plan to make a movie about the Korean War, *Pork Chop Hill*, which he did, and he made another couple of pictures and then the last one he directed was *Mutiny on the Bounty*.

In my final conversation with Milestone we talked about authors. He told me about working with Erich Maria Remarque and with Steinbeck and I asked why he'd never made a movie based on Saroyan who I liked so much and Milestone, who had started talking for a moment about his family and his cousin Milstein, said, With that bastard I won't work. His career is finished. There's a reason why no one reads him anymore. He said that Saroyan was an insufferable man. But if I wanted to, I should meet him. I said I'd tried. That through Brando I'd met Saroyan's wife, Carol, who had once been Brando's lover and was now married to Walter Matthau who'd made me laugh so much one day at the Stage Delicatessen, and I called her and a child's voice answered and said, Aram speaking, who's this? and I said, Yoram, and we both laughed and hung up. I said the first book I'd read in English was *My Name is Aram*. For me Saroyan was a heroic author. *The Time of Your Life* and *My Heart's in the Highlands* were two of the most important plays written in America. Milestone reacted strangely. His got flushed and he said, You have no idea what kind of man he is. I was surprised, because Milestone, who seemed gentle and soft, was really upset. He said Saroyan had killed himself. Killed his career. Killed his wife Carol. He said that Saroyan had killed his children. I said that perhaps great writers have to kill their children and Milestone got hysterical. You'll meet him, he said. And how. And he called him. I heard shouting. Someone cursed a lousy Israeli artist—that was me. And Milestone said something bad about me and then Saroyan swore, I heard his curses through the earpiece and they exchanged insults and in the end Milestone laughed and said, Tomorrow at the Chateau Marmont. He'll meet you at seven. Perhaps he was touched that I liked *My Name is Aram* and that it was the first book I'd read in

English and Milestone said that Saroyan only hears what he wants to hear you've read.

From the outside, the Chateau Marmont—that old hotel over-looking Hollywood which had hosted the top writers and screen-writers for fifty years—seemed enormous and even resembled an ancient citadel, but inside it was a splendid ruin. The wallpaper was dried up and torn and the upholstery threadbare. The staff was so old that it seemed their teeth were about to fall out of their mouths at any moment. Everything was covered in cobwebs and I knew that Saroyan, who had once been much admired, needed the hotel's de-cline so as to hold up a mirror to his own. He came in and looked at me like a king scrutinizing one of the spiders who had helped cover the lobby in webs. He was majestic and frightening.

A big, broad-shouldered man. He sat down and invited me to sit in a waiting room closed in with old, dusty drapes and he ordered himself coffee from an old, quavering waiter. He inspected me for a long time from the loftiness of his sad significance and sipped his coffee. I looked at his coffee. He noted my look. The king addressed his subject: Does the young gentleman need some coffee? I said I didn't need it, but I certainly wanted some. He evidently liked my reply and called the waiter over who read Saroyan's lips because he was hard of hearing, and said, Bring him some coffee, in a clean cup, and you know which kind. He told me, Since they only have one kind of coffee here! The waiter walked away, he hadn't lip-read Saroyan's last few words, and the king asked me: So you're the Jew-ish Aram? Yoram, I replied. He made an effort not to hear me and repeated, Aram. Aram with a Y. It seemed he felt obliged to put me through some sort of humiliating ritual. That he was lowering himself to sit down with somebody like me, so I had to be put in my place. For me it was quite moving. In his books I had found the sad, dark glory of the human condition—something Saroyan's work had in common with Edgar Allan Poe's and James Thurber's. He said some nasty things about his ex-wife, that she had ruined him and robbed him of his good name. He talked a lot about women. About publishers who'd rob their own mothers and make children into orphans. About agents who in any civilized country would be lined up and shot. He said they were all sons of bitches. That they all, without exception, were bloodsuckers. He said his own children were waiting for him to die so they could inherit. That all that interested them about Saroyan was his death. He said he was an orphan and knew all about being an orphan. He said he was alone because of the bastards all around him who just wanted to suck his blood. He said that he hated his children. I made so bold as to say that I didn't believe what he'd said about his children. He said, Who are you to believe me or not? What, do you know them? Are you somebody whose opinion I should consider? Do you think you're smart because you're Jewish? Hollywood is the garbage can of the arts, and who controls it? Jews, just like that bastard Milestone. Elia Kazan and I are the only Americans in Hollywood, because anybody who fought the Turks and was beaten by those bloodthirsty despots knows a thing or two. I said that was probably true. He raised his voice and said, Don't agree with me and don't parrot what I say, Kazan and I are the only two Jews in Hollywood—if a Jew is Einstein and not that schmuck Mayer. And not that bastard Milestone and not his fucking friends either. They're running my life. But the Jews and the Armenians are half brothers. Always against everybody and everybody against them. But you didn't understand God's gift when of all the nations he chose to give you His Son. You didn't even understand enough to kill Him when you had the chance. No, you let Pontius Pilate kill Him so that He would die and you'd be able to keep your hands clean and exonerate yourselves. Saroyan ordered some sandwiches then and asked me to eat because I still had room to grow. There was background music, something classical, and as I ate he said, Tell Milestone he's a sonofabitch. Tell Akim Tamiroff he's a sonofabitch. Tell everyone you meet that Saroyan says they're sons of bitches, and I don't mean the same bitch. Humanity has no future. Once upon a time, people got married landing order to unite their territories, they got married for land. It was business. Today they want love. They spoil and blackmail their kids so in the end they just want your blood. Just want to kill their parents.

I listened to him. His bitterness was mingled with a kind of desperation, a "cry for help." This wasn't the man who'd written *The Human Comedy*—and yet it was. He was angry. He was really angry. He wasn't even angry, he was enraged. Not interested in me at all. He didn't ask questions. He didn't know why the hell I was sitting with him, and moreover, why he was sitting with me and wasting his time with me, and I could see he didn't understand. Maybe it was just because I was there and wanted to meet him. Maybe he wanted to amuse himself. Maybe the boy in him that had written those magical stories was still hidden inside somewhere. He said, Just don't try and be a successful young writer in America. America hugs them all to death. Then there was silence. He didn't look at me again.

I could see a sliver of sky through the torn drapes and a faint light came in. I wanted to get up and go. He said, You're staying until I tell you to leave. And then he sank deep into his threadbare armchair, pulled out an old dog-eared book without a cover from his jacket pocket, opened it, and looked at me and in his eyes I could see that I no longer existed. He began reading aloud. In his eyes I could see that he wasn't reading but looking and wasn't seeing well but simply reciting. His voice became soft and pleasant. Filled with love for the words. He read from memory what he probably hadn't read in years. He read from *My Name is Aram*. He probably hadn't read the book for ages, but must have been in the habit of reciting and possibly rewriting the book aloud. Every now and then I saw a tear glistening in his eye, or actually rolling down his cheek, but he didn't notice. I didn't budge from my seat so as not to sully the moment, his voice was clear and every now and again he remembered where he was, he'd looked up in surprise but then carry on as though possessed, looking at me angrily for a moment before going back to the loveliness of his reading. I could hear his own amazement at the words he was speaking. The words he was recreating. Acuity, precision. An elderly man sitting and reciting—or guessing at—the fruits of his youth. He wanted me to understand something, apparently, something that I would perhaps repeat to Milestone, along the lines of: apart from Saroyan's words, we were all merely sons of bitches. The words were inside him. Still with their old sound. He occasionally gave me a playful glance, because something that had astonished me had amused him. He had brought the book with him. He certainly didn't walk around with it in his pocket every day. Perhaps he wanted the book to tell me about the man who had written it. When he finished and I saw the tears flowing down his face, I applauded. He turned gray and pale. He shot me an penetrating yet good-humored look. Then he turned serious and said, Everybody hates me, there's not a single person who doesn't hate me, and I hate everybody back, without exception. Only Aram doesn't hate me.

And nobody hates him either. I mean the real Aram, not my shitty son. You're acting like an idiot when you flatter a pig like me. And Jews don't applaud pigs, they only eat them in secret. You're a bastard and you're trying to buy me off, trying to get by me, trying to be sneaky with me, just like everybody else. Tell Milestone, no, tell *Milstein* who wanted to be as American as baseball and changed his name to Milestone, tell him to make a film about an aging man who turns love into hate. I'm a guy who knows what life is really made of, the way women know, especially witches—and what woman isn't a witch? None of them are ever good, none of them are ever nice. There aren't any nice witches. He suddenly got up and started to walk out. I said good-bye. He didn't answer. He just looked at me. What a waste, he said, and left.

Afterward I called Lee who sounded distant and scary with a kind of forced cheerfulness and I said I'd decided not to come back. Mexico had been good for me. Viva Zapata. I remembered the movie. Lee was like a gift from a different universe. I felt sad and lonely and didn't want to hear Lee telling me we were through. Oved went away again. I drove with him for two days and then he continued on his voyage in the footsteps of the Mayans and their treasures, which were to become the center of his life for the next forty years and that story will be told in the annals of Oved. He went his way and I went mine, without a map, just like that, I went where my feet took me; the way, not the destination, interested me, as they say, and today I don't remember where I got to, apparently Yucatán. It was desolate. I met Mexicans in remote bars and little villages and who gave me mushrooms and peyote and I had Technicolor movies in my head like Walt Disney's. Lee was leaving me. The conceit was sweet because it hurt. Mexico was filled with forgetting, with mystery. In a small town I saw a matador in his glittering costume, but he wasn't the real thing, and his outfit was a cheap sort of Halloween costume. He was a small, jumpy man. When he stood facing the bull he didn't know exactly what he was doing. When I got into town I went into one of the town's two bars and drank tequila and licked table salt. An immense woman, who as far as I remember found me drunk in a bar near the town's only gas station, and whose name was Maria, took me to her hacienda. She was saucer-eyed and despite her outrageous height, the legs that supported her huge body were slim. She didn't know any English and we conversed in the little Spanish I'd picked up on the trip to Guatemala. Her priest, whose aunt was the stepdaughter of an English trader in Honduras and so knew English, told me that Maria killed her husbands. It sounded romantic and she told the priest to tell me that she was a lioness and I was a poet. What with the hallucinogenic mushrooms, the tequila, the Old Crow bourbon, and some other unnamed liquor straight from Kentucky, I became everything Maria wanted me to be, and our time together was deep, faraway, detached. The soil was sad, arid, and treacherous. All that grew there were churches on which God had turned his back and no longer frequented. He had been replaced by ancient gods with the names of Christian saints. When I asked Maria her name she didn't want to tell me.

The bartender spoke a bit of English to so I told him that Moshe Dayan used to tell a story about a guy who went into a bar in Mexico and there was a man sitting next to him and he ordered a tequila, drank it, and asked, What's your name, and the guy didn't answer and he asked again, What's your name, and the guy still didn't answer, so the first guy pulled a gun and shot the guy and said, I'll get a paper in the morning and find out. The bartender, who managed a laugh, told me, There's no paper here, but Maria, for whom the story was translated, thought it was cute. She was proud that the Mexican corridas were different from the Spanish ones: Here we don't torment the bull. No lances stuck in the bull's neck. The fight is fair: The matador against the bull. Nothing more.

The corrida took place in an almost natural amphitheater in the center of town, and the church bells were ringing. Most of the matadors were local boys. The bulls weren't all that big. The women swooped down on the murdered bull to cut off its testicles and crush them into a powder that would help them bring more children into the world and so that the ones born would not die in their cribs. They were all terrified of Maria who because of her height also served as the local weather forecaster because radio hadn't yet reached them. On numerous occasions she was assaulted by the priests who tried to feel her up but she'd hit them with the black cane she always carried, pinch their balls, and they'd beat a hasty retreat, and as they ran you could see they were barefoot. A matador who several years earlier had moved to a bigger town—which wasn't saying much, because a bigger town in that region meant a few more houses, another bar, another whore, Maria told me— had recently come back home to be a local hero. There were also visiting matadors sometimes who had gotten famous in the larger towns. Whenever they'd come, they were presented with suckling pigs stuffed with vegetables and mushrooms and rice—and, of course, some superior marijuana—as gestures of goodwill. The matadors were short, slim, dressed in their pretend outfits, nobody had the money to buy a real matador's costume, but since the village women knew, from ancient times, and with no small help from their dreams, what a real matador looked like, they put together the matadors' toy costumes themselves, leaving the men looking like chintzy scarecrows, all taking part in a corrida at once a religion, a ritual, and the national lottery.

Maria never missed the corrida. The cheap glitzy materials, the mariachi music, the old phonographs playing New Orleans jazz, the barefoot priests standing around the arena and popping blown-up condoms they'd bought from traveling salesmen who had come in their dusty Fords to buy marijuana. Since blowing up the condoms was so amusing, nobody bothered to inform the priests that what they were popping weren't exactly balloons. So the audience went wild, the matador tried to kill the bull, but sometimes the bull made mincemeat of him. In most cases, because of the bulls being so old, the toy matador would win. There were no perfume-drenched handkerchiefs. No lace scarves. No operatic cries. It was just a simple game played by matadors with sequins on their clothes that fell off the moment the corrida was over.

I was at Maria's hacienda for about a month. We growled at one another. There were servants who took care of me. They'd put me into a bath with dried flowers and massage me and dry and shave me and Maria would hit them. She was nice to look at and she had a body like Monique van Vooren's but bigger. We liked charging at each other, playing corrida in a vast bed that looked like a football field, and once, when I fell out, I was bruised for two days. I no longer remember what exactly went on, because most of the time I was chewing mushrooms and walking through a colored paradise or else going right down to hell. I think she liked me, but I don't know why. The whole village was crowded with suitors she'd rejected. She was the only wealthy woman in the region. The men were strong and handsome. One evening she and I were sitting drinking, earlier we'd watched the sun go down and now it was dark. She cried, but covered my eyes with her hand so I wouldn't see. She gave a speech, or a groan, or recited poetry, or some sort of gospel, from herself to herself, she spoke nonstop for an hour and more, I sat there captivated, I understood very little but in her voice I heard a plea to God because she said, *Dios, Dios*, said it a lot; she asked him for a son so that there would be somebody to remember her after her death. I tried to understand the words I didn't know from her intonation. I thought about Bird, how he would have understood her just from the music of her speech and I tried and tried, but I just wasn't Bird who had such a way of understanding the worst, it was because of his great gentleness, Bird who knew how to read me even when I was walking down the street and he was too hopped up to listen to the words I was saying, but he felt the music in a person's walk. I realized Maria might have been declaiming something like her last will and testament. She was nobody's fool. She knew I didn't understand. She wasn't on drugs, wasn't drunk. That day we hadn't smoked anything and she hadn't chewed any buttons.

Ours was the longest affair I'd had since Lee and would be the longest I'd have before the final one, which was to be very long indeed. In the absence of language, what did we see in each other? I thought about the first woman I'd been with. In that small hotel in Tel Aviv. A new immigrant who hardly spoke Hebrew and with whom I'd had a long conversation almost without words. What did we give one another? For years thereafter, perhaps even now, I was positive that our strange coupling had produced a son or daughter. This was 1956. I sometimes wait for someone to knock at my door and for an adult man or woman to stand there and say, Hello Papa. Maria rode splendidly upright on her horse, which she called

Yum-Yum, though I don't know why. She loved sunsets and turned strong and predatory only when she had to deal with another villager. Everybody in the town and the district admired her and courted her and feared her. One day she asked me to talk to her in the language of *La Biblia*. So I talked. I told her what I thought of her. She listened attentively and brought flowers she picked in the yard and made me a garland and said *Dios, Dios* and I said—God, and she said *amor*, I said—love. There was no telephone and the world outside the town and the neighboring villages and the mountains and the desert and the cacti and the poverty and the Indians and a few Spaniards who remained from the sixteenth century and the churches celebrating ancient gods with Christian names—all remained mysterious and distant.

A short time before I left, a tired elderly man arrived in town and in one of the two bars announced that he could fly. Everybody got excited and paid him something to see. Even Maria, who was rich, paid. We went out into the square, which wasn't a square at all but was called the square because every town needs a square, and which was actually an open field bordered by the two bars and the five churches, which were all mainly empty. Everybody stood waiting. The man concentrated. He prayed. Everybody knelt and held hands and prayed for him. Maria pushed me down into a kneeling position and prayed on my behalf as well. Then everybody got up and the old man looked at the waiting crowd. Maybe they didn't really believe him but they couldn't completely disbelieve either. There wasn't much to do in those towns except dream. And sometimes because there was so little to do they wouldn't even be able to dream for themselves, so they'd dream the dreams of their mothers and fathers who at least had seen the great revolutions. The old man pulled a package from his coat pocket, undid it, and took out what looked like a kind of folded kite. He spread it out, adjusted it here and there, and suddenly he had wings. He strapped the wings to his shoulders, raised his arms, and started flying. True, there was a strong wind. That can't have hurt. But the fact is, he flew. No wind alone could have carried him up to the top of the steeple of one of the churches to scare off a flock of ancient pigeons that I would have thought an atom bomb would leave nonplussed. The man flew. Even Maria wept. The peyote in me was so strong that even I believed that he was flying. His demeanor afterward, the way he drank, his ludicrous desire to be a bullfighter, the way he touched the sequined costume of the bleeding matador at the very next corrida—that wretched costume made of cheap, thin material that some traveling salesmen had traded for marijuana—all that hardly gave me the impression that he was really capable of performing miracles. And yet, he'd set himself a challenge and made sure he was believed. And when the next matador came to town, his sequined costume like play clothes, and everybody turned out for the bullfight, and the bull did a turn that aroused great admiration, and the crowd applauded, but then it butted the poor matador and his outfit immediately fell to pieces, he was standing there in shorts and undershirt and the crowd held its breath, the bull gored the poor guy until he was almost done for, but then the flying man went up to the bull who was now already a little winded and tired of hurting people, and it waited for him quietly, like a trained dog. The old flying man picked up the matador's torn clothes, his sword, took out his wings, jumped onto the bull's back, the bull bellowed, and then he flew, he flew over the bull, the bull just stood there quietly, and people clapped because the flying man had won, but then he disappeared to another town. Maria wasn't happy when I decided to leave. She'd learned a few words of English, had shown me gray fields that one day she would till, but I was already feeling suffocated and the monthly bus came by and I went to Mexico City and then flew to Los Angeles and then to New York to meet Lee and hear her verdict and be sentenced. Oved said later that in this case the man on trial maybe wanted to be punished more than the judge wanted to punish him.

Our new apartment on Cornelia Street near Sheridan Square, where I'd stored my paintings, our furniture, our books and our records, next door to which Lee had a studio—that's where I went from LaGuardia after a long flight in what was then the latest airplane, the DC-7, though because jetliners were coming in, it had a short life. Lee was just standing there when I went in. We mumbled hello to one another. Lee was standing sipping from a bottle of Cutty Sark and she asked, What are we doing here? I said that we had to be in the same place on the same day sooner or later. She asked, Why? She wanted to be angry but she hadn't yet mustered sufficient strength. I tried being clever and said that it was randomness being justified after the fact as having been necessary, like Brother Juniper tries to do in Thornton Wilder's *The Bridge of San Luis Rey*, which is about an attempt to comprehend, theologically speaking, why five people die when "the finest bridge in all Peru" collapses—why they were there in Peru in July of 1714 in the first place, and why them in particular, at that precise moment, why he of all people, Brother Juniper, happened to be standing there to witness the disaster, which it made no sense for God to allow. Lee thought for a moment and said, We had some great years, and we had some interesting years. I made you laugh. With you everything is always a drama, that's why you're sad even though inside the sadness you're funny too, but you really hurt me when you went off to have an affair with my sister-in-law, I hated you but I also admired the depravity you're capable of, which you try to hide by overcompensating with your guilty conscience but your conscience isn't always on the right side. How sad your face looks and how convenient your so-called shyness is, every woman you meet wants to breastfeed you, the sweet baby from Tel Aviv, and you really are sweet, sure, a real sweetheart with a tragic and beautiful face. But all your insecurity always leads to suffering because you don't know how to love, because you don't believe that someone is capable of really loving you. I know that people can love me. That's not why I've got problems. All your life you've been apologizing. You love wallowing in your own self-righteousness. Each one of your paintings is always the last one. Each day is the last. Tomorrow you're always going to die. The day after tomorrow there'll be a funeral and I'll be sorry I didn't come to see you sooner. You go to a funeral and think, Ah, I might as well stay put, it's coming in any case—and how old are you? Twenty-seven?

You ruined my career, said Lee in a empty voice. I could have been a star but you worked on the Jewish Russian in me who had to be a penniless artist and because of you I let Shirley MacLaine become a star and I appeared at the Henry Street Playhouse. But I loved that about you too, if "love" is the right word, I wanted you to be my enemy because you wanted the most important things for me, you wanted to purge my soul of impurities, you wanted me to stand on the razor's edge and touch eternity, but it wasn't me you saw in your glass-bottomed boat in the sewers, but yourself. You realized that unlike art, literature, poetry, or music, which can all have a forever, dance and theater have only a present and you robbed me of it so that I'd be, as your precious Dostoevsky puts it, worthy of my suffering. You, you're both strong and weak. On the one hand you've got the strength to do what you want and believe, while on the other you want to succeed not like yourself but like the people you despise for not doing it the same way as you. You want to be my performance at the Henry Street Playhouse but still to succeed like Shirley MacLaine. You're frightened of everything. Arthur used to bring you pills and say that you suffered from every phobia under the sun. And now I see it, I see how scared you are, I see how after you left me for years and weren't with me when I needed you, when I was deep in the shit, when I've finally had enough, when I want to leave, to live, to breathe, instead of thanking me for releasing you, for sending you off to the life you want and are worthy of, you beg me to stay, beg without shame, because you've got what Arthur called autophobia which is, as far as I remember, the morbid fear of being alone. Marlon Brando saw something noble and strong in you but he despised you too though he was as curious as ever about you and you used him and he hated seeing you envy his money and success but he admired you for understanding that what he wanted most in the world was to be a botanist because he loved flowers, but you betrayed him anyhow, and you know what I'm talking about. You cheated him. He said that not only are you the only person in New York who actually replies when asked how you are, but also that you're a talented man—but not a decent one. That the greatness in you, if it's there, will be in the art you hate and will surely run away from because it it'll never lead to thousands of people applauding you, will never give you the success you both desire and mock. The stupid story about your night with Barbara, the one whose jeans had that button with "Lee" stamped on it, that story did the rounds all over town and everybody laughed, and Sandy wrote that idiotic TV play, and I thought, Why does it have to be that way, who's that fat cow anyway? I'm a thousand times smarter and sexier and just better than Barbara, and when you got Billie Holiday up onstage with Percy Heath while she was high, and everybody cried, what interested you was that you were part of a historic moment that wasn't yours; being Charlie Parker's friend was more important for you than Charlie Parker himself, who you didn't understand because you didn't believe that somebody could like you for who you are, for better or worse, you didn't believe that he needed you and loved you and let you, only you in all the world, paint him how he was.

Lee stood there, pale. She was proud of all she'd said, but it hurt her to say it. I tried to say something. Don't talk, she whispered, and sat down in our old armchair and buried her face in her hands and spoke as though from inside a vacuum-sealed room and it sounded like a controlled explosion and she said, I'm happy in *West Side Story*, you want to be like everybody else but you're different, it's not your fault, why do you try to be like everyone else when you can't? It's infuriating. It's just self-flagellation. You even enjoy being wrong. You've never liked or hated what others saw and liked or didn't like in you. Marlon said that you went to a movie house on Broadway and stood in the balcony to see *Viva Zapata!* but he saw how you were turning your nose up at the movie and he thought, This schmuck is here with me and still he's acting like a snob, I'm not sure about him, he doesn't look all that good, why isn't he home with Lee, but you never were. At least you saved me from dependence on you. Marlon showed *me* respect, not you. When you asked him that infuriating question, why he was so attracted to Movita, and he told you that she screws like a motorcycle, you spread it all over town. He broke off all contact with you, but to this day you still think you're friends because he hung that picture of your mother over his bed. I loved and still love your mother too. I write to her. You can't hold a candle to her because you're not warm and unassuming like her. You like to humiliate yourself and you like to believe that you're worthless and you actually enjoy wallowing in it all. I'm happy with Jerry Robbins. He loves me more than you're capable of. He's only loved two women in his lifetime: Nora Kaye and me. Both of us aren't beautiful. He doesn't need us as decoration, he isn't just some faggot who wants to look good in company, he loves us. He's considerate, he listens to me, he doesn't judge me, he doesn't think I'm too fat. You've got a nice side too, sure, you know how to love, but only for a moment, only when you conquer someone new. Yeah, you're sensitive, you're very sympathetic about other people's sorrows so long as it doesn't get in your way. If there's a funeral and you liked the person but you want to finish a painting, you'll always find a way of lying and not going because, even though you liked him, that one painting is more important. No, you don't know how to really love a woman. To love her pettiness. You want someone angelic and queenly. That's why you like elbowing your way to the stars. What have you got to do with Eva Gabor, who you tried to cozy up to like an idiot? Or Monique van Vooren for that matter? They're larger than life, larger than *your* life, and so you kiss their asses and do them favors and throw your brain out the window and act so proud of the fact that you can walk down the street with a floozy from TV. Have you ever noticed that you brag about having been a soldier, but never about your paintings? Hanoch and Oved are always saying, So what if you fought in a war? There are millions who fought and were wounded in wars, but how did you learn how to paint? Have you ever told anyone what really happened to you along the way? You really are a genuine bohemian because unlike the rest of us here you didn't rebel against your parents, against the bourgeoisie, because you didn't have to, you came from a rebellious country. But look, I no longer want any part of it, I don't want to be your excuse for legitimizing your sadness anymore, for those demons that live in your paintings and tell you their stories. I hate you and hating is a wonderful emotion, because I also have the love of a genius like Robbins.

I sat in silence for a long time and then I told Lee a few things about us and her and me. Not a lot. A few. She listened and burst out laughing and then into tears. I went to the Cedar Bar, drank, and told everybody there that I loved Lee Becker and she'd left me.

Years later, when I went to New York to look for the footprints I'd left in the city, I went to visit Larry Kert with my friend Jerry Tallmer. Most of the people I'd known were dead. Or had disappeared. He was the only one of all the people I'd known who hadn't died and still lived in the Village. Wally Cox was dead. Marilyn Gennaro, Wally's wife, had committed suicide. Their daughter the belly dancer had committed suicide too. Gandy was dead. Bob was dead. Lee was dead. Larry said that Leonard Bernstein would be dead in six months, and he was. Jerome Robbins would die within a year. Mina Metzger was dead. Dolores, who'd changed her name, was dead. Ethel was dead. Beulah Weil was dead. Marshall was dead. Frank Silvera was dead. Julie Gibson was dead. Eva Gabor was dead. Cyril Johnson was dead. Mara Lebo was dead. Melita was dead. Al Elliot was dead. Fanny was dead. Kubrick was dead. Sherry was dead. Mary was dead. Hiram Hayden was dead. Louise was dead. Arthur Cohen was dead. Lewis Milestone was dead. Ruth Sobotka was dead. Mira had disappeared. Beautiful Marie Barr was hiding in Idaho. Miles, who towards the end looked like a Cro-Magnon with thinning hair, was dead. Libby and her Indian Ambassador had vanished in England. Freddie's wife was dead. James Jones was dead. Jerry Robbins was dead. Bird was still dead. And years after he'd died, when they made the movie, *Bird*, I was asked to go and interview Chan Parker. I said I wasn't sure she'd remember me. I had been a passing shadow in her life. Two days later they told me to go anyway. On a rainy day at Orly a Renault 25 limousine was waiting, whose driver was a Frenchman who looked like an FBI agent from an American movie. Traffic was heavy. The driver put a blue light on the roof of the car and used a siren and the other cars moved aside and we passed through like the Children of Israel in the wilderness. It was an appropriate way of arriving at Champmotteux, a small village whose houses were two hundred years old, with a church in the square and lots of empty fields, and I told the driver he'd worked wonders and he looked at me as though I'd just complimented the chef at La Tour d'Argent for managing to make boiled eggs.

Chan was standing at the door of an old house. On the refrigerator behind her was a poster: Bird Lives! There were paintings and drawings hanging in her house that looked familiar and it took me a few minutes to realize that they were mine. No, she hadn't forgotten. The ice was broken. Chet Baker was dead. Prez was dead. Louis Armstrong was dead. Little Baird was a chef in Kentucky. But I went to Christopher Street with Larry Kert. In the area around Bank, West Eleventh, and Fourth, people shuffled along slowly, looking like shadows. They walked holding hands. Pale, dying old people leaning on consumptive young people. Bodies like shadows of bodies. Hundreds of frightened people. Eyes gaping from fallen faces.

Like the Vale of Tears, for those who've seen it. Hundreds of lonely, shivering people. Larry Kert looked bad. His face was sunken. His cheeks smooth. His hair shorn. Almost nothing remained of the beauty he once had. He hugged me and we sat down. Two silent men were in the room, gazing into space. And he said, All the people you see here will be dead in one to three years. Me and all the rest. We tried talking about Lee. Larry said he hadn't seen her before she died, just like nobody else had seen her, he would ask her to help a sick dancer friend and she wouldn't come and then he would spot her in a wheelchair because she had cancer and she would turn her face away so as not to see him. It's sad here, he said. If they don't find a drug in the next three years none of the people you see here will be alive. My sister Anita was here and she fainted when she saw me. Her husband's a doctor who hunts wild animals in Africa and hangs their heads on the walls, and there's an empty space on the wall and she said it's waiting for her head between the heads of the bears, wolves, and deer. Maybe I'll be hung there, but who'd want to put up a head like this? I sat there stunned. Hundreds of gray people. Without hope.

But at our sad parting ceremony, I'd tried to persuade Lee to give it another try, I was scared to death of living alone and without her, and she said, Look, let's put things in order. You're staying here. I'll take care of the divorce. It's easy to do in your Mexico. I'm not going to wait around for you to lie to me again. Now we have to decide what each of us is taking. She asked, What are you taking, the books or the records? And what furniture? She waited for an answer. There was no mercy in her voice. I tried to say something, but without success. In the end I said, The books because you don't read, and she got insulted and really finished me off by taking all the records, some of which were valuable, some were presents from Lady Day and Prez and Bird and Ben Webster. The radio was playing plaintive, winter afternoon music. It was a tough room. I tried telling her stories. To amuse her. To bring her back. She was cold. She took a few pieces of furniture and the records. I got the divorce papers by mail from Mexico two years later. The last twenty years of her life were shrouded in mystery. Even her best friends didn't know exactly what happened to her. She died of cancer after founding the American Dance Machine. Even her brother couldn't explain what had happened to her exactly. Nobody believed she'd died of the disease. It was thought that her husband had killed her. She'd had a nose job. She didn't want to see any of her old friends. Her father died. Her brother visited Israel and forgave me. She even refused to say good-bye to him. Her husband's name was Paris Theodore, the son of Nenette Charisse, sister-in-law of Cyd Charisse, who was of Egyptian-Coptic extraction. And she called herself Mrs. Theodore, not Lee Becker. At the end of her life she drew a curtain and demanded that it remain closed over her past and the world. She erased Lee Becker and created a new character who died of cancer. She was no longer liked. Dancers spoke ill of her. She gave her children Arab names. She became an anti-Semite. Paris made weapons. He designed and sold guns. He claimed he was a descendant of King Farouk. Al Brown says he was maybe the grandchild of an Egyptian Jew, but others claim that Lee had converted to Christianity, and if she did, why did she give her two children Arab names? Paris treated her as if he was an effendi and maybe she tried to kill him and ended up sticking to him out of hatred. He had made a bundle, but didn't agree to pay for her burial. I don't know who did. Not her brother and not her sister. They only read about her death in the *Times*. It was said that she never mentioned her earlier life. She never admitted that she'd been married to me. Jerry Tallmer, one of the founders of the *Village Voice*, one of my friends who survived the old days, didn't even know where she was living. He sent me Lee's obituary from the *Times*. It didn't say a thing I already knew. Nothing about her family. Nothing about me. Nothing about her friends. Nothing about the shows she'd done. Or maybe just a bit about that.

A few years before she died I met her after not having seen her for almost thirty years. We sat looking at one another. She said, Can you tell me what there was between us? I said no. Do you remember being close? I said no. She told me about her children. She looked good, she was pleasant to me, and I told her about my daughters and she asked about my mother, I told her she had died, and we parted. Then she was dead.

But after we separated, after her speech, I was broke again. My few paintings and drawings had almost all been sold. A hot summer's day. You could have swum in the humid air. I bumped into Lovejoy. I hadn't seen him since he used to shout to his hookers on Sixth Avenue near Alex's Borscht Bowl. He said he was very happy to see me. I said, We haven't seen one another for years, how come you're happy to see me? He explained that he'd just been thinking about me because a good friend of his was urgently looking for a painter and asked if I wanted to make a little money, and this was my chance. I thought, Why not? Lee had left. There was nobody around. Gandy was in Vermont.

Being alone with some paint, the quiet, some brushes was good for me. Painting apartments is nice. It's serene, and I know paint and think about it and nobody expects you to be an artist. So I went to a building on Central Park West in the afternoon, because Lovejoy had told me that the friend slept late. It was a splendid building, big and old with two art nouveau turrets and windows of different shapes, lots of decorations and sloping roofs. I got into a well-tended elevator of the old type, completely covered in a brown weave, and the elevator boy, who in fact was so old that he quaked on his feet, took me up to the top floor. I rang the bell and a woman was waiting because she'd already been informed by the lobby that I was on my way up. I told her who I was. She opened her mouth in a yawn you could drown in and asked, Who? I explained and said, Lovejoy sent me. She was wearing a faded robe and her breasts were visible through her nightgown and her face was pale as if she'd removed her makeup with sandpaper though there were still traces of it by her ears. Her lips were white. She said it wasn't such a great pleasure to meet me and they'd told her from downstairs why I was coming but she didn't remember exactly and so I told her I was the painter and she said, Ah, yes! Come on in. The great artist has arrived. The living room was shrouded in darkness. The door to the next room was open and on the big round bed lay sleeping a young woman who didn't for a moment stop writhing and grinding her teeth like a rabbit. The woman who'd opened the door said her name was Mary Lou and she took me into the kitchen and put on some water. She yawned again and said, What? Isn't it early in the morning? You've got an early-morning look about you and anyway you woke me up so I'll make you some Colombian coffee that you won't forget in a hurry. We had a conversation that didn't begin anywhere in particular and led nowhere. We sniffed each other like dogs. She talked about goldfish, about Texas, how somebody could die of a heart attack without feeling it happen, about sleeping pills, sex improvement pills, pills for apathy. I drank my coffee, which was tasty, and told her I'd once been down on the Panhandle and met an old guy who bought Cadillacs, and she said it was a cute story. It came out, it just came out, because I didn't know what to say and I didn't understand where I was and how it could actually be early morning despite being afternoon. She didn't really hold up her end of the conversation and in any case whenever there's a silence I get scared and start talking even more and that's just the way I'd already missed out on a few of my life's more beautiful moments, and Lee had once said that I could have got twice as many girls into bed if I'd talked less about Tolstoy and death and the divine depths of sorrow, and I told Mary Lou because it just came out that I'd had a grandpa just like the old man in Texas and I saw flashes of anger cross her face and she told me, Get it into your head right now that there'll be no intimate or personal relations between us. And then, after her anger abated, she added that the story about my grandpa was a trick, but let's move on. Her hair was unkempt and she looked as though she'd replaced her skin with something else beneath her faded robe. She said that she and Tina, the beautiful girl asleep in the next room, worked on what was called the telephone. I smiled. She asked why I was smiling, and I said that telephone operators didn't live in fine apartments like this and she said it wasn't actually that kind of telephone. If you're a friend of Lovejoy's then you'll know. I said I wasn't his friend and didn't know. She said he'd said that we were like brothers. I said I had a sister and almost no brothers, sort of like this girl I knew who was almost pregnant. Mary Lou said that was cute but I'd been asked to paint and not to tell her the story of my life. In this apartment the stories end as soon as you walk through the door. A guy comes, goes, and comes. There's no connection between the beginning and the end. And my name isn't exactly Mary Lou. And the room where Tina's sleeping is the one I want you to paint. You look good and that'll make it difficult for me, but I'm not interested in good-looking young men. Are you married? Not anymore, I replied. She asked, What does your wife do? I said that she was acting and dancing in *West Side Story* and she said she'd seen it and it was nice and who was she in the show, and I explained and she asked, How did you get along? And I said that we'd made each other's life a misery and she said, But she's a good dancer, I saw her with the Ballet Russe too in *A Streetcar Named Desire*. Marriage gets in the way of a love life. I said I hoped her clients wouldn't smell the fresh paint at night and she got angry. A real rage. She almost shouted, Who do you think you are? Do you think I'd take a client into my own bed? Into my own apartment? Are you crazy? This is the temple of my life. Here we play jazz. We have a ball here. This apartment is for me and my friends. There are enough hotels in town. She took care to keep my coffee cup filled, but I wanted to go see the room I was supposed to paint so I'd know what I was in for. She paced up and down looking as though she wanted me to feel that she was a lifeline, that she provided a real service to the upper echelons of humanity, and she said she loved art but she knew humanity mainly from the ass down. Lovejoy told me that you killed Arabs in the desert and that you beat out seven nations.

I tried to move into the other room but she didn't want me in there yet. There was something pathetic in her attempt to make herself seem like a big deal in the eyes of someone who was an artist and poor, and I remembered that the whores I'd known in Paris were neither dramatic nor tragic. They hadn't come from homes where their fathers raped them, they simply sold their bodies because they needed money and didn't make a big deal of it. Mary Lou seemed like an affable but dangerous woman, because she'd conditioned herself far too well. I thought that maybe her way was actually easier, given her profession, since she could despise a client and still relate to him, because he hadn't chosen some street whore but had come to a penthouse on the Park. She showed me a case of Dewar's she'd been given that week by a wealthy client who liked bringing gifts. Tina van Haas who was asleep in the round bed woke up and was nice to me right off and didn't put on a show. She came out of the room, came over to us, and smiled. She had to touch to know and so she touched me as if feeling her way and only then took in my name. She wrapped herself in Mary Lou's arms and said that her real name was different but she'd been married to a guy who said he was a Dutch aristocrat and who spoke in a cute accent like mine and he loved to suck her nipples and talk like a baby and she'd diaper him until he'd come into her hand and on her belly and then she left, he called her Layla Day. I told her that in Hebrew the name meant night that is day or the other way round and that made her happy. We talked about payment, how much my materials would cost, I said I didn't have the wherewithal to buy them myself so Mary Lou gave me an advance she called small to buy paint and maybe she meant me to paint Rockefeller Center. We talked about the colors they wanted. Tina wanted pink with gold stripes and said that Lovejoy had said I was an expert on angels and knew most of them by name and had painted angels for churches in Chicago. I want gold in a room filled with angels because it'll look cute. Mary Lou said she wanted something more conventional and beautiful but she trusted Tina who knew about colors and angels. I had some more coffee from the pot and they gave me breakfast—in the world

I'd come from an hour earlier it had been after lunchtime—and we chatted and they said I seemed nice and next day I brought paints and brushes and knives and a ladder and a variety of other tools and began stripping the paint from their walls.

There was a kind of hunger for beauty in those two. They talked about colors the way children do. Tina showed me a box of Crayolas and said it contained sixty-four crayons, and I said they were an ingenious invention. A combination of paraffin wax and industrial paint, an oil-based crayon, an invention that changed the world; and she said that she too liked to learn little facts about things and that it was a good thing she was still such a little girl really, because that way she didn't have to think about the things she does at night. I just close my eyes and see angels when disgusting people are playing with my body. But no matter how disgusting they are, they can't penetrate the soul of a little girl. It touched me and she drew an angel in Crayolas and said, See? I can draw an angel too. Mary Lou said, What I like to do most is to put makeup on and hang a pearl or diamond necklace around my neck, smear bright lipstick on my lips and go to a movie on my own in the middle of the day—which isn't your middle of the day!—and buy popcorn. And when she talked about it, her voice took on a velvety quality. She was happy at the sight of the gold paint I had prepared, everything was ready, buckets of paint, spray paint, palette knives, and I wanted to get down to work. I worked for about an hour before Mary Lou came in, stood behind me, and said that I looked tired and should rest. I said I wasn't tired but she said, Believe me, if there's anyone who knows about tiredness it's me. She led me to the balcony overlooking the Park. There was a big swimming pool there, a barbeque grill, chairs, loungers, rocking chairs, a garden with flowers and vines climbing up the wall. Someone was playing a gleaming grand piano. A tall black man wearing an apron was grilling hamburgers and hot dogs. Small tables were laden with bottles of whiskey, gin, and fruit juice and pickled herring. Miles Davis, whom I hadn't seen since Bird's funeral, sat drinking, looking somber, deep in thought.

I said hello and he didn't respond. He sat there like a bored prince and when he raised his eyes looked lackadaisically at Tina and three other naked women who were swimming in the pool. Tina came out of the water and stood there naked and dripping. Her dripping pudendum was a precise triangle. She saw I was impressed and said proudly: Nice, eh? I have a French hairdresser who fixes everything. Even the insides of my ears. Miles mumbled something in his deep, husky voice and no one understood what he'd said, and as he stared jadedly into the pool he fell asleep sitting up. I was invited to come in for a swim but said that I had a hard time with naked women and Mary Lou said, We're not women, we're telephone operators. I said I wanted to get back to work but Tina wanted me to give her a massage because Lovejoy had said that apart from the war and the angels and art, I was also a renowned masseur, famous throughout the Middle East, and that I painted peacocks the way they should be painted. I gave her a massage the way I'd seen it done in the movies and she said that there was divinity in my hands. After that, I'd come every day at about the same time, work for less than an hour, and Tina or Mary Lou would come and have a look and make admiring noises and then announce that I was tired and hungry and call me out to the balcony. I'd eat and listen to jazz played by musicians, some of whom I knew. They started calling me "electric fingers" because of my massages. What they apparently needed was some-one who just wasn't half asleep and full of heroin. From the room where I was working I overheard them saying that you could talk nonsense to me and that I'd answer seriously. They wanted someone who would tell them about Leonardo da Vinci or Shakespeare. This suited me. They knew, as did the rest of their friends, how to lock their shame and sadness away, and I apparently woke some sort of regret in them—not for what they had or hadn't done but about life in general, Mary Lou said in a moment of melancholy, a trickle escaping from her well-sealed eye. The musicians showed up exhausted from nights of playing and most of them were saturated with drugs. Hairdressers came and fixed the girls up on every part of their bodies. They had delicate skin and they took great care of it. There was a body-wisdom about them that sometimes led to Miles mumbling something about the fucking skin of angels.

One day, after I had painted a gilded angel on a pink background and was playing around with the paint, giving the angel different hues and a kind of shadow with wings beneath it that were more implicit than visible, they came in and applauded, and they were pleased and we drank Cutty Sark because they'd figured out what I liked to drink most, and the black man who tended the barbeque said, Ah, now I remember this guy, I remember him, he used to work at Minton's Playhouse. He washed dishes. Wore black. Miles woke up and stared at me witheringly and said, Him? He never worked at Minton's, he doesn't know what Minton's is. I said I remembered him from Bird's funeral though he hadn't necessarily been standing on the right side. He shot me an evil glare and said, Go to hell. He was working at the Hickory House and I went to listen to him the next day. He saw me, gestured for me to leave but I insisted on staying and he was flattered. He was working on a wild refinement—if you could call it that—of jazz that he'd inherited and he played jazz without a piano. I went with Gandy, whom I hadn't seen for a long time, and he said to Miles, You come from a good family, not from the ghetto like Bird, you're a lousy bourgeois but a great one and a sonofabitch, and suddenly Miles, who was always stony-faced, smiled. I realized then that he went to Mary Lou's to unwind, and there I was, showing up all of a sudden, a white guy with connections to Minton's Playhouse, Bird, Lady Day, and it annoyed him. It shouldn't have been me he saw at the funeral, it shouldn't have been me who'd seen him play with Bird and Ben Webster so long ago, and I was also the only one who'd ever painted Bird and now he was being reminded of it. He didn't want to talk to me, it was more convenient for him to say that I didn't know Bird because I'd had no right to know him. Who are you compared to him? he asked angrily. Mary Lou went quiet for a moment, gulped air, Miles muttered, she dove into the water and waved her arms and Tina showed her the angel she'd drawn and Mary Lou waved her arms like Tina's angel and sang a song from Texas. I told Miles that when I'd seen him at the Five Spot I'd realized that he wasn't a decent man but was a greater musician than Ben Webster. But Ben Webster was a better instrumentalist and a decent man into the bargain, and Miles gurgled and whispered in his characteristic rasp that if he was more of a decent man he couldn't be such a sonofabitch. I said that Bird was a decent man and he said that Bird was a genius and thought for a moment and added, You're right about one thing, I'm a great artist, and then he fell asleep. I continued painting. Mary Lou drove me crazy with all the enforced breaks. It took a month to paint half the room. I had no life apart from that. I came. I painted. I drank. I ate. I talked to the whores and then went back to the room I rented and I don't even remember where it was. Mary Lou could see that I was preoccupied about something and she said, It's written all over your face, she wanted to know what it was. If I said that I'd been thinking about De Kooning or about Dr. Stern, with whom I was having empty conversations about my condition because he bought paintings from me and wanted to delve into and investigate all the emptiness in my life, Mary Lou immediately wanted to know how he, whomever it was, lived too. And I'd tell her that the doctor ate boiled chicken and sat around in dark rooms and she'd want to know why and what the rooms looked like and what he said to me and what I said to him. Once she pressured me for an hour to talk about Spinoza because I'd said something to Miles, who didn't listen to me, about the line that Boris was always quoting about how will cannot be termed free but necessary and how only God acts from laws stemming from His own nature and is not controlled by external forces. I begged her to let me finish my work because although I was happy there I was thinking about my own work and how I was going to stop painting, something that had been on my mind for a long time, and she said, What's wrong? The money? Isn't it enough? I said, More than enough, and she got angry, she said, There's no such thing as more than enough. Your salary is doubled retroactively as of two weeks ago. And once she told me that she was the greatest moaner in the business, and added, I'm a thousand times more honest than you. You don't mind making money from a whore. My clients pay me just so I can pay you, so who's the prostitute here? I said that I hadn't expressed an opinion one way or the other and that it made no difference to me whether she was a whore or not or whether she fucked over the phone or in a bottle of gin, and she started sobbing bitterly and a few seconds later stopped as quickly as she'd begun. And she saw how the room had progressed and didn't want me to stop, and to punish me for what she said I was doing to her she brought over an Arab she said she was in love with. And he went into the room at the end of the hall, slept all day, and took money from her to gamble with and he'd chuckle in front of me and say, There's a Jew for you. It made her happy. She didn't say anything about what happened at night and I'd sometimes stay over and in the morning, in the late morning, she'd come back tired, her makeup streaked on her cheeks, and we'd drink Columbian coffee together. Tina said that Mary Lou despised the Arab but swore that she was in love, which was why she didn't sleep with him but only kissed and then he'd go to a plain, fat whore with the money she gave him. He wore an earring. He asked for more money. He went out and they discovered there was some jewelry missing and Mary Lou called someone and said, Finish that Arab off because he stole jewelry and money, and by the time I left the apartment for good, a tragic episode I haven't mentioned yet, he had been missing for ages. I worked hard. I fought Mary Lou when she wanted me to come out and relax, and Tina became a bit hostile and claimed that I was offending Mary Lou but I decided I just had to get out of their reality. Finally, the room was finished. A lot of young women came over. Stony-faced people came, musicians came. Miles came. Apart from him, everyone praised the beauty of the room. The huge round bed was put back in the center of the room and Tina and Mary Lou got into bed and embraced and looked at the walls and were also pleased with the white ceiling instead of the purple one they had requested and I said, That's it. I'm done.

They didn't go to work that night. Friends came over. We sat in the room rather than on the balcony and drank. The black pianist brought his piano inside and played. He sounded a bit like George

Shearing. Miles sat staring at me, an evil look in his eyes. Suddenly he said, That's the illustrious painter who knows how to milk innocent women like Mary Lou and Tina and who caught Bird stoned one day and painted him and Bird didn't even remember. His words hit Mary Lou, she collapsed beneath them. She bent over and her hands touched her feet, she stretched up and her expression was both exultant and frightening. Everyone stared. I hated the horrible silence and said, Miles, you're a liar! And Miles said, I'm not. You've got the painting, or you've sold it. I said, Yes, I painted him, but you know very well that Bird was clean then, that he couldn't take any more, that that's what killed him, and you know that he chewed whole bottles of aspirin to kill the craving, the shakes, the pain, and drank whole bottles of revolting Manischewitz wine, and he liked my paintings and was happy to come and sit and I painted him and he liked the painting and I have it. Mary Lou went pale and glared at me, like a fox looking at me, like a wolf, and she asked, Where's the painting? Her voice sounded different, perhaps it was her professional side. She got up and stood over me and Miles laughed and fell asleep and woke up and she said in a steely, merciless voice, First he comes to paint my bedroom, takes my money like a pimp, and then it turns out that he has a painting that belongs to me and doesn't say a word about it. She slapped me and I slapped her back. She said, A painter with the hands of a faggot and the fingernails of a dyke. There was violence in the room now. All the angels in her eyes died when this anger, this malice began to ooze out of them. Why didn't you tell me you had a painting of Bird? she shouted. I said that no one had asked me and anyway, how come it belongs to you? Miles said, Why did I forget you? Because you're easy to forget. You came here because that pimp Lovejoy wanted to fix you up with work.

Mary Lou was furious. Her face looked like a clam shut tight. Her lips shrank until the gap between them became a thin line. Bring it here, she said quietly. Bring it now. Miles looked at me and grinned. Everyone in the room was against me. She wants it and she'll get it, Tina whispered. Miles said, Bird wouldn't have allowed this nobody to paint him. You probably painted from a photograph, Mary Lou said venomously, and lit a cigarette, but the smoke choked her and she coughed and shouted, No Bird by you won't be mine. You faggot. Mary Lou stubbed out her cigarette, went into the other room, and our silence waited for her to return, and she came back with her purse and said, How much? I said it had no price. She named prices that I didn't even know existed outside of the movies. Her voice died down to a whisper and the numbers just kept coming out of her. She was determined to have the painting at any price and was oozing hate. Tina tried to calm her down, mama's little darling, but Mary Lou wouldn't give in. Her lips remained clenched. Miles was sorry to have to miss the show but he had a gig at Birdland and said, Bird, your nigger, your boy, made music and Benny Goodman leeched money and fame off him. I said that that was nonsense, Bird came after Goodman and he admired Benny Goodman and that now Miles was being anti-Semitic, and as he was leaving he said, You people! You're always right!

In the end the pianist from the barbeque and two friends I didn't know—and when I took a closer look at them, I didn't want to know them either—drove to the Village with me to fetch the painting. We brought it for everyone to see, but I knew I was going to lose. After Mary Lou looked at the painting she said in a harsh voice, Name your price, whatever you want. I said I wasn't selling. But I wavered and left the room because the prices were making me dizzy. She wanted the painting more than I'd ever wanted anything in my entire life. I hadn't seen such passion in years. I told her angrily that even the thousand men who had fucked her had never sounded so ruthless, so full of lust, and she said, You don't know anything about it, you stole a painting, the men who fuck me pay and leave, you didn't get inside me and you're still not gone. You're going to give me the painting. Silence again and everyone looked from me to the painting and back. Tina started whimpering like a kitten. I looked at the painting and this was the crucial moment, it was the best of my paintings but I also realized that it wasn't good enough, that I would never be the painter I wanted to be, would never be more than just another painter. Like a high-speed movie, I saw in my mind all the paintings I liked and knew that I was finished, that like the piano player in the Wild West who hangs a sign that says: "Don't shoot the pianist, he's doing his best," that my talent was meager, I was only doing my best, but my best was shallow and conceited. Each and every one of my paintings could have been different, and a work of art is measured as it is: it's a work of art *because* it can't be other than it is. They all drank and someone brought out a joint that was passed from mouth to mouth and after a while they seemed to be enveloped in fog. The painting became more and more foreign to me. I could already see it through Mary Lou's eyes. She pulled out a stack of hundred-dollar bills and started throwing them at me one at a time, laughing sardonically. Dozens of bills fluttered toward me and I gathered them from the table or from the gleaming red wooden floor and I looked at them but didn't drop them or put them into my pockets. I tried to fight but weakened with every hundred-dollar bill she hurled at me. In the end I said, You win. Beggars can't be choosers. She said, It's not your money, this money is a payoff. She touched the painting as if it were a Christian icon and then said that she loved me and that my hands had created a miracle and I looked at her. I stood up and kissed her and she pressed her lips onto mine and kissed me hard until my lip started bleeding and she grabbed the painting, threw a few more bills at me, I'd stopped counting by then, my eyes filled with tears of shame, the telephone rang, it started raining buckets outside. I looked at her, went into the bedroom, and looked at the room I had painted. Tina came in and touched me and I went back and said to Mary Lou, It's just a painting, Mary Lou, it's not an icon, it's just a painting I happened to paint, and it doesn't really belong to me, it belongs to Bird, but Bird's dead, so take it, and I left.

It was raining hard and I got soaked to the skin, but I couldn't stop walking. I was overwhelmed by the thought that what I was most worried about was keeping the money in my pocket dry. I got home and hardly ever painted again. (Years later I tried to find out where the painting was. I enquired about Mary Lou. About Tina. Tried to find out where Lovejoy was. But time and America know how to make people vanish.) I called Avi Shoes and we went to the 21 Club. We had something to eat and I told him what had happened and he said that now he wouldn't ever leave me. We went for a walk and I told him that I was giving up painting to write, that I couldn't make painting into just a mistress on the side and didn't know how to be married to two women at once, and that my gallery owners were furious and collectors were cursing me and that I had begun writing a play about Mira. Avi Shoes took me to a party at Krissoula's who had returned from Greece from one of her shipping magnates, and I looked at my *Icarus* hanging on the wall, and

Avi Shoes talked about what I'd done in the war and someone sat next to me and said his name was James Jones and that he'd been a soldier too. Not in the navy, in the infantry, though he'd been at Pearl Harbor. He said he'd seen the attack up close and tried to write a book but had given up and had written about his own experiences in Hawaii, *From Here to Eternity*, and he asked me if I wrote. I told him I'd read his book already, that the book was powerful and moving, and that I used to write but stopped so I could paint but that the painting had died in me and that I felt that I had no choice but to write.

We spoke a long time that evening. Krissoula danced a Greek dance. Avi Shoes called a catering service and ordered steaks for everyone, and the next day Jones came to visit me in the squalid room I lived in and I told him about Mary Lou, and Avi Shoes came to take us for a drive in the park in a convertible and then Jones said that what I had to say should be written and that he would take me to his publishers and get them to give me an advance. I was too weak to refuse and we went to the office of the editor-in-chief at the legendary Charles Scribner's Sons publishing house and we sat there and the guy stared at me in bewilderment and Jones finished singing my praises and the man asked what I was actually writing and I said I was writing a play or a story about a woman called Mira, and I told him a bit about her and about her becoming a nun and about Boris and about my war wound and about Pat. He said it sounded interesting but that he had to see something in writing. He must have pressed a concealed button because I could tell by the look he directed at the door that he was waiting for something, and indeed a secretary rushed in and asked Jones to step out with her for a moment because he'd forgotten to initial one of the pages of his new contract. He left and the editor told me quickly, Listen, Jones is naïve. This isn't the way to sell a book. Jones doesn't understand business, he's achieved a huge success and thinks that anyone can do the same, the editor's voice was arrogant and disdainful, but he said that when I had a book written in good English I could come to him even without going through an agent. We left. Jones was confident that within a week I'd have a contract in my hand. I didn't argue. He lived comfortably from his book and from the movie that had been made out of it and a little from the other books he'd written that were less successful. There was a beauty in him, he was naïve and wise and pitiful with a million dollars in his pocket and him feeling that he wasn't worth it. He liked me and I liked him, although we didn't have very much in common. Jones made me into a character in a book he was writing in his mind, I interested him as a model, not as a person, and neither of us understood the other. In 1976, I would meet him entirely by chance at the Île Saint-Louis in Paris. He looked terrible. He said he was living on this prestigious island. He said that he was just another American in Paris and that everything had fallen apart for him. That women had disappointed him. That he'd forgotten how to laugh, and that he felt like a terrible failure. He'd say that he'd been happy when he read the reviews of my new book and had remembered our meeting at Scribner's, and I tried to tell him how important he was to me, that there was something childish and beautiful about him, that I loved his naïveté, he was unsure whether he even knew how to write and said that he was fortunate that the Japanese had attacked Pearl Harbor while he was there. He told me he didn't have anything much worth living for, and two years later I heard he had died and I was sure that he didn't die of an illness.

Avi Shoes and I saw a partially demolished building across the street. It was a nine-story building. Avi Shoes said, It looks like a Buchenwald of toilet seats and bathtubs and washbasins. The building was split as if a huge sword had cleaved it in half; the street-side façade had been demolished and only the interior of the building was visible. The toilets and basins and baths from all the apartments were hanging out, decades of toilets and baths. I quoted a line from Natan Alterman for Avi Shoes, It is the fate of buildings to fall, it is not the fate of buildings to stand.

People were starting to leave the Village. Fancy cafés opened up on MacDougal Street. The rich began moving in to live near the artists. The apartment in Morton Street now cost a thousand dollars a month. Artists who started getting rich left the city, the poor were shunted aside and started drifting east, to SoHo, to the Lower East Side, and art became commercialized. Larry Rivers who'd combined abstract expressionism with realism had reached maturity, and abstract art began losing its fashionable appeal. People tried to wrap the world in pink paraffin paper to disguise the shame of their disillusionment, and the rich went after all the artists who had left town one after the other and Senator McCarthy was finally defeated after a long struggle. People could go back to work and those who had been arrested came out of the prisons. Artists returned from Europe where they'd lived as refugees, and a new era seemed to be beginning. I moved from the Village to Eighty-seventh Street between West End Avenue and Riverside Drive. The building belonged to Carl Marzani, a communist with a kind face who in his youth had been one of what were then called "Roosevelt's Whiz Kids." His secretary had been Ethel Rosenberg. He worked in the Office of Strategic Services' economic division. During the war against the Reds he was thrown into jail. Following his imprisonment, his wife fell or was beaten up and ended up in wheelchair for the rest of her life. Marzani believed in Ethel Rosenberg's innocence and when he spoke about it I remembered how Boris claimed that he'd known she was a spy. When Marzani got out of jail he bought a building to support himself but only wanted poor tenants. I still had the money from Mary Lou. I ran into Millard Thomas on the street. He'd been one of Belafonte's accompanists and lived in Marzani's building because he was a broken man and poor and couldn't get over what he called Belafonte's betrayal and he suggested I come along, and I did, and Marzani was courteous and the rent was low. He was still editor of the *Daily Worker*, which was the paper of a party that barely existed anymore, and wrote revolutionary articles. He ran the party's small publishing house too, which had few customers but he was loyal to them and quietly fanatic. He didn't try to force his opinions on anyone. His wife, a beautiful and sad woman, would smile from her wheelchair and they'd hand-bind the press's books and prepare invitations to assemblies and demonstrations that usually ended with police beatings because they outnumbered the demonstrators and were not overly inclined to be sympathetic toward Marzani. I got a basement apartment that had a bedroom and another larger room that included a kitchen and even a small refrigerator, and a window that looked out onto a garden was set above my bed. There was another small rectangular window above the kitchen sink through which I could see the legs of passersby on the street, and I used to try to guess things about them from what little I could see. I wrote a lot, erased and discarded and then wrote more. Sandy and Steve Scheuer lived in an adjacent building and I would go up to see them and Steve would be standing, resolute, holding an ironing board as a shield, and I'd rinse bleeding Sandy off with whiskey, just like I used to, and I'd go back down to my apartment so that they could patch things up for another week. The landlord made a habit of pasting notices in the stairwell: "Comrades! Help needed! If you possibly can, please pay your rent." Millard played a guitar most of the time and two young women lived above him, one of whom wasn't very pretty and the other had huge breasts and was learning how to tap dance, which had long since gone out of fashion. Once in a while I sold a painting or a drawing, but sales gradually declined. There was a pleasant and pretty woman without breasts; and there was the brilliant daughter of a vice-admiral who came over with a broom and a toothbrush and was sweet and wanted to be my mother; then there was a painter who restored antique furniture in Hartford, Connecticut; and a tall girl I found in the subway; and there was Sally too; and I went to suicidal Sondra Lee's and lived at her place for a couple of days and came back, and then Oved called from Mexico City using the "Israeli system" said that there was a woman coming to town he wanted me to meet.

The woman called two days later. She said she was visiting relatives in Brooklyn and would be coming to New York on Sunday morning and would I meet her. I said I would. She said, I'll be arriving at the station on Lexington and Fourteenth Street, or perhaps she said Twenty-third, and if you really can, wait for me on the platform because I don't know the city. I asked how I would recognize her and she said, Don't worry, I'll recognize you. I went to the deserted station on Sunday morning. A train pulled in. A lone woman alighted. Six foot two in her stocking feet, but she was in heels. She was wearing a red dress, and walked toward me. I came up to her chest and she said how pleased she was to meet me and that we should go for a walk, and after a while she bent down to tell me that she was wild about short intellectual Jewish types like Frank Sinatra, Marlon Brando, John Garfield, Chaplin, Einstein, all short men. She wanted to walk along Fifth Avenue and feast her eyes on the store windows. We walked. Children laughed at us. I kept trying to shove her onto buses and get her to sit down so that we'd be the same height, but she wanted to see things up close, and people stared and we talked almost as though we were on the phone, first floor calling third floor and vice versa. It was difficult to communicate with her, and then the nightmare ended. We agreed that she'd call and she did and said that she'd found a big bed that would suit her dimensions with a mattress to match and had rented an apartment, and I asked whether the ceiling was sufficiently high, and she said that it was an old building with a high ceiling. I invented excuses but so as not to offend her I said that most of my women had been taller than me but at least we'd been able to meet midway for talking and listening. And I went over to visit her and her robed body seemed endless, she sat with a dramatic air, a glass of wine in her hand, and said, Wouldn't it be nice to jump into bed. I did my best. Lying down, her head was so far away that I had to take it on faith that it was there in the first place and that it was a proper head, but it wasn't easy. I felt like a Lilliputian walking along Gulliver's nose. I got off her, said I'd remembered that I was sick and fled. And there was a whole string of girls to come; there was the sweet black girl who danced at Katherine Dunham's and who I swore I was in love with, and I was, but then I cheated on her and she ran out on me, hating me; and there was the Israeli girl who had come to New York to lose her virginity. I was shy and the women could all see that I fell in love easily, but my love affairs lasted two or three days at most before the remorse and the guilt came that both distressed and delighted me; and then there were the women who rejected me and laughed, Why should I be interested in your youth in some youth movement and that you were a soldier and that your father is the director of some museum and how much you like Faulkner?

A guy we knew in the war came to see Avi Shoes and me. He'd lost his entire family in Germany, and after the war went back to Germany and dismantled every church and every grand building he could find and used his Jewishness as a weapon and spoke Yiddish and acquired palaces from frightened Germans and brought them to America piece by piece, and renovated and sold the old furniture and the tapestries and the crystal chandeliers and the ovens and brought them in ships and there was terrible hunger in Germany in those days, while he bought and sold in America and made a fortune. He came to see me with a blonde girl, and we were talking when he suddenly stopped in mid-sentence and froze. I'd never seen anything like it. He froze in mid-laugh, his mouth remained open, and after a few minutes of frozen alarm he snapped out of it and said to me, You're a dreamer and you'll never amount to anything. Painting and writing, you haven't got what it takes, but if you come to work with me in my store on Third Avenue you'll make money. I asked him why he'd frozen like that and he asked, Who froze, we were talking, weren't we? I tried working with him for two days and sold a magnificent crystal chandelier and the customer haggled with me and I sold it cheap and the boss, Nachman was his name, said, My friend, if you want to save the world, don't do it with my *rebbe gelt*, because he was angry with me for not sufficiently believing in the World of Tomorrow and the peace movement but he also liked me despite the fact that I told him that someone had said that over-simplicity is a sign of tyranny. And maybe he was right to think I was criticizing him. I bought a small television. Those were the days of *Amos 'n' Andy*, Jackie Gleeson, *I Love Lucy*, Ernie Kovacs, Jack Benny on the violin, John Garfield and Lana Turner in *The Postman Always Rings Twice* on the late movie, and they started broadcasting *You'll Never Get Rich* with Phil Silvers, my favorite show.

One day I saw a young woman who looked like Ava Gardner and I followed her. She tried to give me the slip and I caught up with her at Nedick's. She was drinking coffee and I told her whom I thought she resembled and that was enough for her to spend a few days with me. She was an assistant to a photographer who photographed film beauties who were blessed with that elusive sort of allure that reads as innocent cruelty, a closed door, unattainable depths. One day Avi Shoes came to me and said he was fed up with life. No challenge, like what had happened to poor Mr. Hauser whom he'd killed. He said he got up in the morning, had a cup of coffee, got into his Packard, drove to the office he'd only rented because he wanted to prove to the Hauser daughter that he was a real businessman, or so he said, and then he smoked a cigarette, drank more coffee, and ruminated on the fact that, between the time he'd woken up and this very moment—nine o'clock in the morning!—he'd earned more money than most people make in a whole year of hard work.

While we were sitting there a guy we didn't know came in and said he was from the NYPD and wanted to know which of us was Mr. Kaniuk. I said it was me. Avi Shoes, who went to a lot of movies, and since the guy wasn't in uniform, asked him, Can you show us some ID? Detective Keenan knew all about people who see a lot of movies and showed us his ID. He said he'd found a woman in a really bad state. There was a chain around her neck with a medallion on it and on the medallion was engraved "Sarah Kaniuk." He said he'd only found one Kaniuk in the telephone directory and had come to me to find out who Sarah Kaniuk was. I was pretty scared. I said my mother's name was Sarah Kaniuk and asked him for more details. He sat down, had some coffee, and told me that a woman had been found wandering by the river not far from the East End and had collapsed. An ambulance had been called. They took her to the Beth Israel Hospital and they'd found the medallion and hadn't found a Sarah Kaniuk in the phone book but since there was only one other Kaniuk they'd called the police and asked for me to come. He drove me to the hospital. We went up in the elevator and into the emergency room and at the far end there was Pat. She didn't recognize me. Her face was more serene than ever. It wore a small smile; there was a sense of peace about her. I told the policeman and the doctor who came to see us who I was and I told them a condensed version of Pat's story, with some deliberate erasures. I explained that I wasn't the father and didn't have a daughter called Sarah but a mother called Sarah, and that Pat, who was not Jewish, had perhaps wanted her daughter to be Jewish, and that there was a Chinese guy called Chao Li who maybe knew the rest of the story. We drove to see him. He recognized me right away and smiled. I told him what had happened and he didn't move a muscle. Not even the tiniest twitch marred his features. He spoke laconically and said that she was his sex slave. He added that he was busy and wanted to conclude this unpleasant conversation. We went back to the hospital. I tried to talk to her. She was in another world and was elated, perhaps even happy for the first time in her life.

Avi Shoes arranged her transfer to a psychiatric hospital not far away and paid a huge sum so that she would have a good room and would be treated well the whole time she was there, however long it might be, with additional payments to be made regularly. We signed an affidavit supported by the Hebrew bookseller from Division Street who was hardly breathing at this point and seemed likely to drop dead at any minute but he was more than happy to talk to me now because almost all the Hebrew writers in New York had died, all the ones who had waged the long war between Sephardic and Ashkenazi Hebrew, including the editor of the Hebrew-language paper he called "the big-shot"; the prestigious journal *Hadoar*, whose importance, I explained to the detective, lay in that it was read by even fewer people than wrote for it. I went to see Pat a few times afterward. She never came back to us. The bookseller died. I was invited to his funeral by the woman in black from the *Forward*—which, as mentioned earlier, had become a weekly and whose pages were now somewhat smaller—and his son, perhaps, said Kaddish. I knew everybody. They seemed frightened and lonely. They held onto one another. I saw too who hadn't come, I thought of my aunt, who at her husband's funeral had counted not only those who attended but mainly those who hadn't, even if they'd already died. Avi Shoes said that Pat had found herself a better world. She looked a bit older than her true age but beautiful and enveloped in a serene happiness and I visited her again and again until I stopped.

Today I have no idea how I met Mina Metzger. She was fragile and beautiful and was eighty-five without a single wrinkle on her face. She did tiny paintings that looked liked bright lights winking out of a dimness painted by Chardin, as if he had joined Mina at the window from which she looked out over the world. She lived on Madison Avenue in the old building where she was born. Her father and mother lived in the building as well, but only her father was born there. And she lived alone and had no children. She walked like cotton wool, she'd been married for forty years and her husband died of a heart attack. When she was a child they still bought their produce and milk from farms on Madison Avenue and the apartment was splendid but frugal and classic in form and always pleasant to visit. She would talk about New York at the turn of the century, not the artists, not the stars, but the honest bourgeoisie, though deep inside her nested the demon of painting and it frightened her and she eventually submitted to it and did such tiny paintings so as not to compete with anyone, hiding her light under a bushel as they say, and years before we met she had been a close friend of the artist Arshile Gorky who committed suicide. She had discovered him and supported him and his family and bought a few of his paintings and taken care of him even when he was sick, even when things were at their worst, and then cared for his family after he took his own life. She said that Gorky had brought Miró and Kandinsky with him from Europe and had managed to insert their ways of seeing into the tissue of American painting. Gorky had also been a friend and teacher of De Kooning, with whom he had shared an apartment in their youth, and there were family resemblances to Frank Stella and Rothko in his work as well. I loved her human gentleness and I loved her paintings, and although De Kooning was a star, I called him up and I asked him to help me organize a show for her. There had already been some tentative steps out of abstractionism and the price of a Hopper had doubled, but Rothko and Pollock and Motherwell and De Kooning and Newman were still *the* art.

One evening Mina had Gorky's family over, as well as Lee Krasner, Pollock's wife, who herself was a fine artist in her own right.

We ate together and drank wine. After the Gorky family left, Mina, Lee Krasner, and I stayed on to sit in the big room and Lee Krasner was looking for somebody not involved in her life and who she didn't know and who didn't know her, and since I was handy she told me something about her relationship with her husband, who in her eyes was the great genius of American painting, and how they had fought, and how they drank, she told the story in a kind of restrained and quiet continuous weeping that was strong even in its restraint and Mina urged her to go on painting because she recognized her talent, she said it was great and I kept quiet. I hadn't liked Pollock's paintings from the first moment to the last, though I had gotten a kick I suppose out of Picasso's statement that Pollock was the Franco of contemporary art, but Gandy always cut me off before I really laid into Pollock's work and one night in a bar with Gandy and De Kooning there was a real argument, I spoke disrespectfully and enviously about Rothko's work. The figures on the subway. The daring play of colors but within a human framework, though that of course was before he took all the beauty out of his work and did his renowned wallpaper, and he said, Jews, always arguing, and I said he should give some thought as to how an artist like him had become a decorator of tapestries.

I wasn't painting but painting was still my home. Like Lee's dancing. Back then everything was unfocused and people came and went and there was no money because I sold my last drawings but their value on what was called "the market" had plummeted as a result of my decision not to paint. Museums and galleries took down my paintings. I wasn't worth anything. I painted an apartment for girl who invited me into her bath and said she admired Schopenhauer and wanted loud garish color and I didn't know which and at last

I found a combination and she waited for me in the bath and suddenly I was invited, me of all people, to a party at the apartment of Clem Greenberg's latest protégé, Helen Frankenthaler—tall, a little De Kooning, a little Hans Hoffman, a little Pollock, a little Gorky, a little Newman, a little Rothko, a little Motherwell. Greenberg, the father of contemporary painting, had discovered all those artists and had Alfred Barr of the Museum of Modern Art in his pocket, and Barr held the purse strings of the whole world of modern art, because Penny Guggenheim and Betty Parsons and Sidney Janis and Kootz were all connected. Greenberg found a woman. He wanted her. He wrote about her. He got her. Prices soared. Barr bought for the museum. Parsons hiked up the prices. Janis paid attention to who Greenberg liked on a given day. People got rich and people were broken and artists became like sheep and out of nowhere the man I'd insulted in the Cedar Bar and who hated me and hated what I painted and hated what I presented in my paintings and with whom I quarreled at every opening I ever bothered to attend, he of all people invited me to a party at the home of his new love and I wasn't about to miss out on this opportunity.

I called Avi Shoes—who only that day had bought an Italian hat company and had started producing gold-colored laces because laces had remained the love of his life—and persuaded him to join me. He insisted on buying me some nice clothes so I'd look important. It was cold. It had begun snowing heavily. We went up in the elevator. A top floor, I don't remember which one. A big apartment, hordes of people talking in loud voices, kissing, drinking, eating. Burning hot. New York was snow-covered through the windows and from above the whipping snow looked like a vast down quilt that had ripped apart. Greenberg, hand in hand or hand in pocket with Barr from MoMA and somebody from the Carnegie whom I'd met when he showed one of my paintings at the Biennial that looked so prominent in its nothingness because it had come from life and myth and when he saw me he told me I was right, that painting had no future. He was drunk as a lord and Greenberg welcomed me winningly, hugging me like we were brothers, it was important for him that everybody liked him, he hated the abhorrence I held for him because it's a well-known fact that kings don't like children who yell the king is naked. He asked me and Avi into the big room. I passed through an empty hall. From a distance we could hear the tumult of the people milling about the infinite apartment as they drank. There were four Ming vases standing in the hall; the emptiness was frightening. I tapped one of them gently and a loud tone that rose and fell reverberated around the room. A waiter wearing a swimsuit ran toward me in panic. A mistake, I said, but the echo continued to reverberate and he said, Be careful, sir, and I told him I was Helen's cousin, and he said, You don't look like her cousin, but somebody rescued me, and my friend Avi Shoes who looked happy in the arms of some woman artist was circulating through the room and laughing. People were walking around like shadows in the heat haze. Artists could be seen squirming like worms in the maze of the mass of people all looking for something they weren't sure about. In the next room somebody I didn't know was standing dressed in a diaper and pontificating about his sex life, and artists and critics were standing around laughing. Fastidious museum directors were trying to mingle and use vulgar expressions they'd picked up from somewhere and didn't know how to say properly and coming from them it all sounded ludicrous. I saw Mr. Kootz from the gallery walking around bent over from the heat, trying to hear what Greenberg and Betty Parsons were saying. And then we reached the designated room. Maybe forty people. We took off our shoes and socks as Helen requested, via megaphone. We rolled up our pants, those of us who were wearing pants, because there were also girls in skirts and men in diapers. A huge sheet was spread out on the floor, fifteen by twenty yards. First Helen daubed a few layers of paint over it and then sprayed another layer of metallic paint and gave everybody crayons and we were all asked to get onto the huge sheet and walk around. Dip our feet and hands into the paint. Color with the crayons. If possible, we were supposed to dance as well. A TV cameraman shot the event. Helen stood on a high dais and with the megaphone clamped to her mouth issued further instructions; You there, Eric, draw in the corner, Yoram, sit and push yourself inward, Dorothy, write out some names; and some people sat on the sheet—I refused—and daubed their bodies on it. One guy put his face into it and then his face looked etched in paint. Helen invited some guy who liked to copy entire Shakespeare plays onto eggshells to take small squares in the corner of the painting and write on them in his delicate hand—poems and curses, whatever he wanted. After half an hour of walking on the sheet and drawing with crayons and fingers and hands and feet, with everybody listening attentively to Helen's monotonous voice as she stood shouting and correcting, changing, warning, directing, we all walked off. Avi Shoes hadn't lowered himself and remained in the embrace of some woman far away in another room. Waiters in swimsuits came in and washed our feet in turpentine and warm water and soap and cleaned our hands and also the face of the man who had stuck it into the painting, and they even cleaned between our toes and managed to remove the paint from the women's fingernails and helped us back into our shoes, and I heard somebody in front of me say, Michelangelo was a mediocre sculptor. Leonardo was an illustrator at best. Dürer was a street artist.

I looked at Helen. She knew that Greenberg wanted her. Her eyes looked like fish eyes but she wasn't drinking. She was the sanest person in the place. The coldest. She didn't touch the champagne. Greenberg came up behind me and said, You don't understand that she's the Goya of our time, it's war, generation against generation, it's conciliation and antagonism and love and a struggle for the future and there's nothing sexier than war. I told him he hadn't the faintest idea about painting or war either, but he was too drunk to reply. About six months later she hung "our" painting in a show. It was bought for a huge sum by Barr from MoMA. Helen was ecstatic. Greenberg wrote about this great breakthrough in the history of art. The last and ultimate word: Stain Painting. Two days later in the Cedar Bar, as I was having a drink with Gandy, and William Steig was there too, he lived near the Cedar Bar and did trenchant and hilarious cartoons for the *New Yorker*, and Gandy was fresh in from Vermont and hated that he'd missed Helen's party, and I got up, little old me, and I began to orate and everybody listened because they were all drunker than hell, and Gandy, who had a sketch pad and a pencil, jotted down some of what I said and gave it to me and years later I lost it though I still repeat my speech in my dreams:

Painting is the most ancient art. People painted in caves to drive out demons. To understand where they were going. Death. There weren't any words yet. The elder of the tribe painted the animals lurking in wait for him and the members of his tribe. The Etruscans begat the Renaissance that begat Giotto who begat Paolo Uccello who painted *The Battle of San Romano*: the horses, the spears, the banners, the colors, the hats, the movement, the composition, the prince, the officers, the knights; and he begat Hieronymus Bosch or was born of him in turn, who begat Dürer and Van Eyck who begat Holbein who was surely divinely inspired and Matthias Grünewald who brought down from the stars the miracle of the Isenheim Altarpiece and he begat Rembrandt who begat Goya and Velásquez and, from Greece, defeated by Titian in Italy, El Greco went to Spain and was reborn there. And Cranach, Vermeer, and Van Dyck and Monet and Van Gogh and Homer and Munch who begat Nolde and Soutine who brought trees from the forest of Poland and planted them upside-down in the landscapes of the south of France and begat Ryder and Bonnard and they begat Hopper and Wyeth and were murdered in turn by Picasso who was art's greatest tactician and technician, likewise Matisse and Cézanne and Renoir whose paintings are not as good as they seem, and he begat Pollock and Hans Hoffman and De Kooning whose work degenerated to the level of tapestry decoration with the exception of his Marilyn Monroe paintings which were the greatest of our time and he begat Rothko who after his beautiful New York works prostituted himself. Art left the churches because God didn't pay. Barons competed to purchase important paintings because they wanted to make themselves look beautiful. There was a longing for beauty in them. At their side sprang up a wealthy middle class that was sufficiently rich to show that it was as rich as the barons even if it wasn't. And they had estates. Yachts. Summer homes. Palaces. Then art began to be what it has become. A man who owns a De Kooning is the only one who's got it. And that's why it's worth a lot of money. Because art has become a marketplace. Owning original work shows that you've got money; money creates a painting anew. Instead of hanging ten thousand one thousand dollar bills, it's cheaper to hang a Motherwell. A Pollock is worth more than the all the Renaissance artists put together earned in their lifetimes. During his life, Van Gogh sold in total what Rothko sells in a thousandth of every second. Art that aspires to comprehend and reveal Man, art that brings him pleasure, touches him, art that investigates the human condition and connects Man with God, is finished. Over. And then I collapsed. I was drunk out of my head.

Gandy was angry but said he forgave me. He was angrier with Mr. Barr of MoMA and the directors and curators of the other museums and the colossal conspiracy with gallery owners like Kootz or Betty Parsons or Sidney Janis. I said they hadn't found a way of putting humanity back into painting and humanity was the mother of the arts: All was Man. There was no fear in the new art, no love or envy or hate, there was just decoration, wall illustrations. The next day Gandy and I went to Birdland; Count Basie and his band were playing there. The place was packed. There was a vocalist I'd never heard of, Joe Williams. He had a voice that could shatter glass. We sat there all night listening to him. We regretted that we were no longer twenty-two. Jazz had started to become minimalist, sophisticated, trying to compete with the classics. The members of the Modern Jazz Quartet were all excellent musicians. Bird had said that the greatest pianist alive couldn't do what Percy Heath did with the bass. They could write a symphony out of improvisations. Tie pieces together with a string that would come out with perfect phrasing and beat. Organized spontaneity. Ordered anarchy. But the new jazz didn't touch me. It left me cold. I'd lost a good friend. Even the best were only making "some ice queen out of jazz" like Brubeck did, he was the prophet of that sound.

Meanwhile I was on the outside. No painting. No Lee. No jazz. And then Arthur Brandt, my sweet psychiatrist, called, Arthur who'd bought one of my paintings for ten dollars a month and said he was bringing me the tranquilizers I'd asked for, and he arrived in his station wagon and honked. I went outside. From the car he brought out the pills and a young, dark-skinned girl, with sparse hair, wearing dirty threadbare clothes, and he shouted, I've brought you a present, I found her wandering drunk around the railroad station, she'd gotten married by mistake and I helped her get a divorce. My girlfriend at home is jealous, so I had to get rid of Carole, she's desolate, take her, she wants someone who'll be nice to her, and Arthur drove off. I was standing outside by the steps down to my basement apartment. Carole looked at me without moving. Standing still as furniture. She looked tired. I told her to come in and she obeyed like an automaton. She looked around, still not saying a word, and then suddenly asked, Where? In bed? What bed? I asked. And she said, Where do you want to do it and come on let's get it over with, I'm tired. I said that wasn't what I wanted, we just needed to find her somewhere to stay, and first of all tell me what you feel more: hungry or tired? She looked at me with the first emotion I'd seen in her face and it took her time to take this in and she said, Do whatever you want, my hands are frozen. She stood without moving. I took off her clothes and she stood there naked next to a pile of clothes and filthy underwear. I picked her up, she hardly moved, and put her in the shower. I washed her and soaped her and washed her thin hair with shampoo that the rear admiral's daughter had left by mistake and I dressed her in an old pair of pants and a pair of panties that the antique furniture restorer from Hartford, Connecticut had left by mistake and a shirt that Avi Shoes had brought from Japan and which looked like a dress. I gave her some milk, she drank the whole bottle, and then I carried her to the bed.

She was all skin and bones and as light as a baby. She fell onto the bed and slept for two whole days. She didn't move. I took her clothes to the Chinese laundry and the guy there said, What's this? What's this? I was given a dirty present, I said, I don't know why. He washed and ironed them and on Broadway I bought a bra according to the almost illegible size number I'd seen on the one I'd thrown out. I bought cheese, meat, eggs, bread, butter, sardines, vegetables—I made a salad. As she slept I saw on her face an expression of absolute helplessness, she was lost and adrift. I typed on an Olivetti typewriter with a Hebrew keyboard that I'd bought from an Israeli who had come to New York. I waited. Arthur called to ask about her and I said that everything was fine. She woke up after two days. She looked like she didn't have the faintest idea of where she was and who I was and what she was doing in bed. She stared at me and asked, a little frightened but without embarrassment, Was I okay? I told her my name and that I hadn't been with her the way she meant and she asked, You a faggot? No, I replied, and she asked, Aren't I pretty? You are, I said. She asked how long she'd been asleep and I told her. She started hobbling to the bathroom. I helped her sit down on the bowl. She still couldn't move her hands. When she finished I wiped her. I dressed her and she said, almost pleading, I want to eat. I served her the food I'd prepared and she didn't look at me. She drank three or four glasses of water, ate voraciously without raising her head from the plate, she wanted to talk but she choked and I told her not to rush and not to worry and she gave me a look that was now lit up with a kind of wild fire that made her beautiful. When she'd finished eating she sank into the armchair I'd found outside a building on Eighty-eighth Street and asked, Now, after all that, maybe you'll tell me, mister, who you are? What. Where I am. I told her. She said she had a faint recollection of being drunk in the railroad station and had married somebody, she didn't remember who he was, an old lady had dragged her off and a cop had come and she thought she'd said she was from the Galante family and he'd crossed himself, they'd ridden in a police car with flashing lights, there was a beautiful building near Lexington, she didn't remember the street, a brownstone, and there'd been a shingle, Dr. Something and the cop said, that's good, and dropped her off and raced away and she went up, the door was open, there was a bed there, she was so tired that she didn't notice the man sleeping in it, suddenly a blonde woman had shown up and yelled at her and the man yelled at the woman and then, she didn't remember but it was morning, the man said he had to go, that he'd had a fight with the woman and they'd hit each other, she thought he'd given her coffee and said, We'll talk later, she said he'd gone downstairs with her, outside lay the cop who'd brought her, wounded, and there was a paper near him and the paper said: This is what happens when you mess with the Galante family. The cop mumbled something and an ambulance came, she said, They excommunicated me, they threw me out of the family, my father wouldn't let my grandfather murder me, and then the doctor came down and brought me to his friend who's you I suppose, and that's where I suppose I am. I liked the way she said, "I suppose" and said, You put it all beautifully. She said thank you.

She asked what I did and where I was from and I gave her a five-minute lecture on what I did and what I'd done and where I was from, and then Arthur called, upset, and said he was sorry for causing me all this trouble, he'd heard that a policeman had been badly beaten outside his building and that I should be careful. In the clothes I bought her later, Carole Galante looked good, but there was still a hint of the old emptiness in her dress. She was in her own world and only occasionally brushed against the outside one. She understood things like murder and betrayal but not what you do the day after you've woken up from a two-day sleep and when somebody's not shouting at you or kissing you or talking to somebody who's brought in money from the numbers, from hookers, from drugs. Right from the beginning I was scared to get too close to her. An intimacy had begun between us that didn't need closer contact. Carole understood that she didn't have to fall in love with me and that she didn't even have to like me. It was easier for her and she said that for the first time in her life, apart from her family, she didn't have to be anyone's slave. She felt dizzy from not having any obligations. We slept in the same bed because there wasn't a couch but I didn't touch her. She'd sometimes wrap her arms around me and cry as she slept. I told her about Angelina from Naples who'd said she was my dog and barked at me not to leave her and Carole sat enthralled and said that her parents came from a village near Naples, she didn't know which one, and that now that they'd ostracized her they'd never take her back but that they wouldn't do me any harm, They said I could live with somebody and be what I want but I just shouldn't go near policemen or detectives and that's why they beat up the policeman but they won't touch you because you don't look like a detective and I confirmed that I wasn't. The secret of Carole's charm for me was in her dangerous naïveté. She said she was a dancer. That she'd slept with guys her brothers had brought for her and afterward they'd killed one of them. I fed her. I bought her things I'd never bought for Lee, but there was still this barrier of fantasy between us that we nurtured out of the desire not to ruin a relationship that was so complex and layered by turning it into something resembling love or schmaltz. Arthur came and talked to her. She thanked him for bringing her to me.

I was walking on Broadway towards Seventy-second Street to buy some typewriter paper and bumped into Mira. We went into the lobby of the shabby Broadway Hotel and sat there. She looked beautiful of course, but a kind of gloomy defeat emanated from her face. Stripped of her absolute malevolence, she looked naked. She told me that Avi Shoes had offended her. That he said he'd had enough of her. That she was too capricious and that he'd wasted years on her. And I thought, she added, that I'd given him the joy of being rich and yet knowing I could never be bought. We talked a bit more and I invited her to my apartment. Sandy arrived and I had to go upstairs to help Steve defend himself; Sandy punched her hand through the window and her hand was torn and blood poured out and we smeared her with iodine and cognac and dressed her wounds. I went back to my apartment. Mira and Carole were talking like old friends. I tried to figure out what Mira had been up to. Where she had been all this time and who had she been hanging out with. She said she'd heard that Avi Shoes and I had had Pat committed to a psychiatric hospital and she'd gone to see her and that Pat lay there so peacefully that Mira herself wanted to lose her mind in order to be able to lie there so peacefully too. I told her she had already lost her mind when she decided she had been born to her father without first going through her mother, and she said, You bastard, why didn't you love me? I said, A sexy spy once asked me the same question and she didn't like me any more than you do. And I asked, Why is it so important for you to know why I didn't

want you, and she said that all the men who knew her wanted her
and I didn't want her and that I was one of the only men she knew
and still hadn't slept with. I told her that I'd been married to her
best friend and she said, Lee forgave me in advance because she was
sure that you and I had an affair, and I'll tell you something, I didn't
deny it and she wasn't angry. What do you miss most, I asked and
Mira said, The convent, it was peaceful there, like Pat. There was
this nun there, Sister Camilla, who believed in God, and was pure
and chaste, which I never was, and we talked quite a bit. She said
to me, Sister Matilda—that was my name—you have no business
being here, you're rebelling against yourself, and here you have to
practice absolute obedience and repentance. Constant repentance.
And there's no compassion in you. I told her that there was no love
in me either. I'm scared and lonely because I'm not a child anymore
and what's going to become of me in a few years' time? Then she
stood up and kissed me on the lips and left.

Avi Shoes arrived an hour after Mira left. Carole Galante said it
reminded her of a railway station, only no one gets married or fucks
here. Avi Shoes knew that Mira had been here. He was following
her, apparently. I said perhaps she was lonely enough for him now
and he said, I want her but I want to want her more than to have her.
She's jealous. You were taken in thousands of times with all kinds of
idiots and missed out on her, he told me, she should have been your
wife, not Lee. I introduced Carole to Avi and said that she wasn't for
sale. I said it to earn brownie points with Carole but I knew that she
didn't stand a chance with Avi Shoes in any case. Avi Shoes drank
the coffee I poured for him and said, I've been to Israel since we
last saw each other. Warm regards from home. I asked him how it
had been. I remembered that that morning when I read the Bible,

as I was inclined to do every few days, I had come to the phrase in Jeremiah: O Lord, Thou hast enticed me, and I was enticed; and I felt a kind of shock, I smelled myself as I was but I could also smell the beach in Tel Aviv. I could smell the fields at Ein Harod after the rain, walking in the mud. I could smell Café Atara in Jerusalem, the Whitman ice cream stand on Allenby Street, a mélange of smells of carob and spices on Levinsky Street, the smell of sea salt in front of our house on Ben-Yehuda Strasse, and the sight of a ship sailing toward Tel Aviv Port, and I drank a glass of brandy and offered one to Avi Shoes. I said, I think I might go back some day because where in America would anyone understand: Thou hast enticed me, and I was enticed. Avi Shoes said: I went to Florentin, Emek Izrael Street. That's where I grew up. We used to be poor, do you remember? There's hardly anyone there from the old days. I stopped off at Itzik's grocery and he recognized me. The sign says "Itzik Grocery Wholesale." I asked him, Why wholesale? He said that when they made the sign he didn't know what "wholesale" meant but had seen lots of stores with "Ltd" and "Wholesale" and liked the sound of it, and Dr. Shapiro who used to live there and now lives in Haifa later explained to him what it meant, but it was already a done deal. I looked around, Avi said, and felt like my childhood was gagging me, the barrel of pickled herring in his store, the sacks of rice and flour and beans and the shelf of white and black breads and how he'd cut margarine to measure and weigh it on the scales. How he'd arrange the weights that were lined up, shining bronze, from the smallest to the largest, and how he sliced his cheese. He had sheets of dried apricot, he had carob, and there were bottles of pure olive oil in cans that looked like JNF charity boxes, and Meged oil and Yitzhar oil, and a woman came in and asked for buttermilk and he gave it to her in a jar, and also some toothpaste and sardines. And I asked him to grind me some coffee and he took some Atara coffee and ground it and mixed it with lots of chicory, and the salt was kept in sacks and the rice too, and the blend was strong and Itzik offered me figs and dates and we talked. It was hot, but in the shady store with the ceiling fan, it was nice. And I asked Itzik about the apartment my family used to live in. He told me that some Bulgarians lived there now. Two women. A mother and daughter. You're very highly spoken of here and every week at the synagogue they set up a match for you with a young woman, but then time passes and when she gets married to someone else here they set up a match with another, but there's still hope. The Bulgarians are all right. Clean. Polite. Quiet. The daughter's an actress. At Habima Theater. The mother is a translator for the Ministry of Defense. Later I went up to the apartment and the mother came to the door. It's not like in America where if you want to talk to your neighbor you call a week in advance and arrange to visit. I told her who I was and she got very excited and said she'd be happy to show me the apartment. I'm not a sentimentalist, as you no doubt know, but I had tears in my eyes. The shutter I had over my bed, though the bed is gone now, the same green shutter, the same slats, with Yehezkel the blacksmith's house out the window, the same lemon tree in the yard, the same carpenter's workshop with the half-naked shouting Polish guy, and the cobbler across the way, nails sticking out of his mouth that he spits out in an arc and then hammers them into a sole, and the steeple of the Abu Kabir church. The mother said her name was Irinia and gave me some strong tea. We talked. The daughter came in. She took my breath away. Her name's Miriam, and you'll say I was hallucinating, but she's the spitting image of Mira.

Miriam took me to see a performance of *Three Sisters* that she was appearing in and we went to Café Kassit where people were shouting and drinking their fancy instant coffee and eating hot dogs with *Kartoffelsalat*. I came back the next day, I can't explain what came over me, I put on overalls and brought paint and brushes and all the rest and I painted their apartment for them. They didn't know who I was apart from the fact that I used to live there. And after I painted the place, and I didn't even know that I knew how to paint because you're the painter who paints for the whores from Texas, not me, I repaired the shutters and bought a new bathtub and sink and faucets and lamps and closets, and they sat there and cried. And I'm carrying wood and hammering nails, I'd never done anything like that before, and it was great to work, and I drank coffee that the mother made, Turkish, and for two weeks we hardly talked. I just came and worked and in the evening went back to the Dan Hotel. One day I realized that I was running late and I came with the car and driver I'd hired and they saw me and said, Who's that? And Itzik shouted, That's him, the Brazilian ambassador, because that's as far as that "wholesale" guy's imagination could go, and they asked questions and I got confused and there was Mira's beauty on the face of a sweet Bulgarian. I arranged for them to have a telephone installed, it takes years in Israel, but I paid whoever had to be paid and now they've got a telephone and a Frigidaire and a radio and I call them and they tell me how much they miss me and no one has ever missed me before, except for you maybe. And Irina says that Miriam wants me and she sings a Bulgarian song to me over the phone, and I sit there and don't know what to do. The Hauser woman is still bugging me and I come to you and tell you all this, and I don't know why. Friendship, maybe, but perhaps too because I followed Mira and waited and watched until she came out of your house.

Carole gave me a pedicure because she said I needed it, and I discovered I'd run out of money. I thought about the no-money. Carole was a fatalist and so said there was no point worrying about it. We sat and drank beer and I remembered that six months ago I'd promised Gwen Verdon, a dancer who'd once seen one of my paintings, that I'd paint her. She was no longer married to Bob Fosse. She was a Broadway star and was appearing in *Damn Yankees* and singing a song that was then at the top of the charts, "Whatever Lola Wants, Lola Gets." Although I'd already decided to give up painting, now, in view of my difficult circumstances, I called Gwen and left a message with her answering service. Gwen called me back and suggested that I bring paints and canvas and everything to her dressing room at the theater and on Wednesday, between performances, I could paint, and apart from that she only had free time here and there because she was rehearsing for something else during the day. I went to the theater on Wednesday and started working. I'm a meticulous woman, she said. I'm calm. But she was actually very jumpy. You look miserable, she said, I'm also miserable and I want a painting without my or your misery in it, like the ancient queen you painted in your last exhibition, and don't make me prettier or uglier than I really am, and if you can get my dancing in, like the dancer you painted that I once saw, I'll pay you well. I told her that the truth was that I'd stopped painting and was now writing and that it was hard to make a living, But you're a woman who's inspiring, you're dancing even when you're just sitting here wondering, What can this guy do that all my photographs hanging here can't, but I promise I'll try my best. I hung my canvas on the wall with nails, as I had with most of the paintings I'd done in the last years of my painting days, and I worked with a large sheet spread beneath so as not to make a mess. I brought along the tools that had served me in my last painting years and told her she could do what she wanted, because I wanted to capture her in motion, not posed, and sooner or later there would be a moment in which I would capture her face the way her face wanted to be captured in the painting, so she didn't have to sit still like a model but I did need her next to me for at least part of the time. She liked the idea. She told stories about plays she'd appeared in and actors and dancers and her husband Bob Fosse and showed me movements he liked recently and tried to stretch her body into those movements and I saw that they were present in her even when she fell asleep in the middle of her rest period, which was in fact my work period. A frustrating intimacy developed between us; I didn't give up, I knew this was the last painting I'd be doing as an artist and not as a writer who paints just because he feels like playing around with paints, and I hated myself for going back and doing something that had departed from me and I from it and I felt that I was cheating her and myself and doing everything just for the money and I told her so and didn't deny it. She said she would rather be fishing in Maine, but instead of sitting in a beautiful wooden house on the magnificent coast of Maine she had to come to the heat of New York, somehow get refreshed at seven o'clock in the evening, put on her makeup, get dressed, dance and sing from eight-thirty in the evening until twenty after eleven just because someone from New Jersey and his little bourgeois wife had bought tickets. And paid a lot of money. And waited six months. And hired a babysitter for their kids and drove for an hour in heavy traffic and parked in a distant parking lot or traveled for an hour on the

train, and came to the Forty-sixth Street Theatre. They come especially to see and hear me and I don't even know them. I cost them a
fortune and I wouldn't pay five cents to hear me or see myself dance
nowhere near as good as I really can, because maybe today of all
days I have a headache, maybe I'm having my period, maybe my
husband nagged me about something, maybe a neighbor bugged
me, but I have to think of the poor idiot who paid a fortune for two
tickets for him and his wife, and waited six months, and there's the
cost of gas, and the depreciating value of his car, and his new tires
wearing out, the price of motor oil, a sandwich before the show, a
glass of soda, maybe a small whiskey, and everything wears out, she
said, but it's also appealing and somehow hypnotic to perform for
five years straight, six nights a week and once a week twice on the
same day, always the same role, singing the same song at fourteen
minutes after nine, dancing the same dance at ten after ten. She
laughed and then became serious and thought about what she'd said
and added that she always—and that was the trouble—spoke before
thinking; and meanwhile I painted, I tried to paint like an ex-painter.
I didn't care whether I was doing a good painting. As long as it came
from within me. Was I putting on a show for myself? I was a whore.
Nothing was expected of me. I expected nothing. I didn't have to
think about gallery owners, curators, friends, about Gandy Brodie.
I wasn't making anything new. I wasn't making something secret or
mysterious. I just had to please one woman, a woman who would
always love herself more than a painting someone painted of her,
but perhaps a certain aura would remain in the painting, or a moment's untruth would stay on the canvas, only on the canvas, and so
become a part of her lasting image, part of her immortality. Perhaps
she would think: I may not—or certainly won't—be around forever,

but at least this painting of me will remain. And that's different than some old photograph. In old photos the passing of time is evident. But paintings don't die, they don't get sick, they preserve a perpetual present. A woman painted by Rembrandt is alive. I painted as if the Flood was coming tomorrow. I watched her with ten eyes. I saw her from every possible angle and combined the angles and their contradictions, I wanted a painting of motion but I also wanted the face in the painting to really resemble her, so she would recognize herself even though no person really knows himself or realizes what he looks like, he walks around without ever seeing his head, just looking and seeing other heads all around. I worked for about ten days, perhaps more, and spoke little if at all. She saw me looked at me like she would a wall or a pillar or a cab driver and dressed in front of me without being embarrassed that I was seeing her half-naked, and she occasionally giggled and posed like an Egyptian dancer, or like Martha Graham, movements from a tomb wall and her stomach always contracting because of the terrible constipation she had suffered in her youth. She danced in front of me like a vaudevillian and said everything that came into her head. She gossiped about herself, laughed at herself, pretended to be naïve, and wallowed a little in some charming kindness that she dredged out of somewhere so that it would also go into the painting. She didn't look at the work until I was done and asked that I cover the painting with cloth when I finished working. When I was done I covered it. I went back the next day. She brought a bottle of champagne. I unveiled the painting in slow motion, like in the movies.

She looked at it and wept and I knew that after my painting of Bird it was the best painting I'd ever done, and she hugged me. More people came, dancers kissed me, stage hands and actors asked for my telephone number, we drank champagne and some people got angry that I'd made a spectacle of her and in the end she also paid me a lot of money and we parted ways. I don't remember the painting apart from its discrete moments, not its entirety, not the finished product. She sent me a bunch of flowers, and that was that.

Oved called to tell me that he and Hanoch were coming from Los Angeles and asked where they could stay. I went up to see my sweet landlord who said he was angry at America for buying another country in South America just for its bananas and I asked whether there were any apartments for rent. He said that just this week two apartments had become available, one with one-and-a-half rooms and the other with two, and he asked who the tenants were, because he didn't want any reactionaries and on the other hand he didn't want any rich people even if they were left-wingers, but was looking for people he called "decent." If they had been beaten down by society, all the better. I didn't tell him about Hanoch's right-wing views but exaggerated his and Oved's poverty. They came and I told them there were apartments available and they asked how much and I said that the landlord was ideal and Millard Thomas lived upstairs and this was Carole, and Oved said that he had spent two and a half years in Mexico, Honduras, and Guatemala and soon he'd tell me things that would absolutely floor me but first he wanted to rest. There had been problems with the authorities. The FBI had intervened. He needed American papers. He had plans. He'd been in prison. He was interrogated. He'd discovered an unknown Mayan city. Hanoch had separated from his wife and wanted a bit of New York. We'll manage. And they moved into my building. We threw a party at my place and sang Israeli songs and Ilka and Aviva came too and Ilka sang the plaintive strains of Bialik's "Shelter Me Under

Your Wing" in his amazing bass voice and we drove to Harlem. Ilka took us to meet Paul Robeson. They both filled the basement of Robeson's house with their basses, and he even sang "Ol' Man River" for us.

Meanwhile, Carole's presence had become awkward. She barely walked around, occasionally jumped for no reason, bought candy, and didn't think about anything. A wild girl, said Hanoch who wanted to make a play for the plain one on the second floor who lived with the girl with the breasts who tap-danced and whom I had a thing for. Hanoch always maintained that no woman would love him for his looks because he was ugly, but he was smart and knew how to talk, and he always looked for girls who would be grateful for his company. The girl was indeed taken by him and started talking like him but there was nowhere to do stuff because Hanoch's apartment was unfurnished and too small and the plain one's apartment was shared and Carole lived in my place, so I brought Carole over to Oved, who was shy, quiet, and looked absolutely dreamy. I told him that she was a gift from me. He took her into his apartment and they stayed together for ten years. The next year, they got married—he got a green card and then citizenship. Now I could go up and occupy the one with the breasts—Carole still visited my place once in a while—but eventually I went back to being alone. Oved lived with Carole, Hanoch with the woman who became his wife for thirty years. They were both fatalists. Relationships didn't matter. They were simply inevitable.

In Guatemala, he said, Oved had discovered the world's biggest trove of Mayan art and soon, he promised, it would be the news of the century. At an altitude of two thousand feet above sea level, in vast caves leading into a subterranean labyrinth whose area was two square miles, he had found, he claimed, huge caves that had remained from some geological upheaval from thousands of years ago. In the caves were ancient urns painted in a huge variety of colors and also wood and clay statues and idols: There are, he told me, thousands of amazing sculptures in glass and greenish jade and there are big bas-reliefs on the limestone walls. And manuscripts too. That's where the Mayans—who were well-known as a people who had foretold their own extinction—had hidden their treasures, close to the God of their Hell, and it was Oved who had discovered this treasure trove and he explained that in the famous pyramid at Tikal only three painted urns had been found and to this day no original Mayan manuscripts had been found anywhere. In Dresden, Germany there was a traditional Mayan document describing the destruction of humankind by flood, but this was apparently a later copy of an unpreserved manuscript. Now Oved had discovered manuscripts inside his caves. He claimed he'd found scores of pages on Mayan culture written in hieroglyphs that foretold that life on our planet was nothing but a series of recurring destructions that were always followed by new rebirths. A perpetual and cyclic apocalypse in which human beings disappear in a catastrophe and later return in another form. In the Sun God's pyramid the number of stairs is the number of days of the year less one. How this all started was that Oved had acquired a number of limestone blocks carved with figures and gods that the local archeologists had insisted that they were fakes. Oved knew that they weren't, however. Guatemala had suffered an earthquake and following the disaster the U.S. Air Force had undertaken to map the earthquake area geologically and their work had shown that there were vast hall-like caverns deep in the earth. It came to Oved that somewhere there in these underground caves might be where his "fake" relics have come from.

Some guy named Jackie Vasquez kept coming up in conversation as an expert on all things Mayan. Oved went back to the Guatemalan government, whose experts had made fun of him and his theory earlier, but when he got back to the city there was a new regime in place and it was chaos everywhere. Marxist terrorists had risen up from nowhere and toppled the government in Nicaragua and then, said Oved, according to reliable witnesses, had attacked both Guatemala and San Salvador. Now, however, the people in power listened. They realized there was something in what Oved was saying. As a token of their thanks they granted him permission to look for the legendary Jackie Vasquez and make contact with him to find the entrance to the caves. Vasquez, who had fathered a hundred children over his lifetime, had never left the region. He knew the jungle like the back of his hand. When somebody needed a hundred parrots or two hundred monkeys or jaguars they'd send a messenger to him and he'd supply the goods. When Oved got permission he established an initial contact that became a friendship that lasted until the day Jackie died. Oved wanted knowledge, though Jackie was afraid to give it. But Oved's stubbornness paid off. Oved sold arms to both sides in the civil war, sold Israeli weapons to both the rebels and the government; he hired a helicopter and went into the jungle and found an Indian family and confirmed that they weren't fabricating the relics that had made their way back to civilization but simply digging valuable statues out of the ground. Jackie Vasquez was the first foreigner to obtain the secret of the Mayan manuscripts. He found twenty square miles of interconnected subterranean caves. The government gave him a license to purchase

three of the rare manuscripts, the deciphering of which might perhaps provide an answer to various questions about the Mayans that
had been awaiting a rational solution for hundreds of years. Still
missing, however, was governmental consent to bring American
scientists into the caves. Without their seal of approval there would
still be accusations of counterfeiting. All the things Oved had and
Jackie found were located in a place that nobody, including the gov-
ernments of the region, knew about. The Mayan Indians, he said,
had had slanted eyes and their babies had the gray-blue Mongolian
mark above the cleft of their buttocks that disappeared between the
third and sixth year of their life, and go figure how they came by
their mathematical knowledge and how they built their amazing
pyramids and how they dragged those huge stones and how they
lifted them. It's also interesting that they date the creation of the
world 645 years after when the Bible dates it. And Oved slept with
women there who thought it was against God's law for a man to live
alone. He met ministers and generals. He met presidents. He medi-
ated. Some of his friends are in jail or dead now. Oved had a basic innocence about him. His life was strange, cursed. The Mayans
were a surrogate family for him; the jungle was a sort of homeland
to him, though now he couldn't go back because he'd mistakenly
sold a few phony urns to some Israelis. And he sold Israeli Arava
airplanes to Honduras but to this day nobody knows what Oved
really did in the jungles for forty years. In the 1977 earthquake in
Guatemala the Dutchman's hotel was destroyed but Oved got out
alive. He was to live there with Carole for five years and she'd convert and they'd live in the jungle and then they separated. Carole
would live in the jungle for years afterward. She'd write. Even years
later Oved was sure that the manuscripts he'd found or been given

or bought or forged or were forged for him were the discovery of the century. In 1976, a year before the hotel was destroyed, a tall soft-spoken American guy was waiting for him there. He asked Oved if by any chance he knew what the week's Torah portion was. He said he'd converted to Judaism and married Carole who told him that Oved was her first husband and now he'd forgotten he was ever a goy. He said that he and Carole had built a synagogue in the jungle. Oved went with him and saw a building made of dried goat dung. He found Jewish scriptures. The husband who'd converted studied the Talmud. They had two children. The rabbi of Guatemala City taught the husband his Kabbala. He opened a school in the jungle and Oved went out into the jungle with him and they reached some godforsaken hole in the wilderness. Just tracks and dirt roads. From a distance in the middle of the jungle he saw a woman riding a bicycle and recognized Carole. Kisses, and they went inside. A tin roof. No running water. A big bottle of mineral water and a broken gas cooker. Not clean. They put him in a dilapidated room on the second floor, the toilet was in the yard. On the first floor was the master bedroom where there were religious books and a menorah and Carole would touch it wearing a yarmulke on her head. She had the Tablets of the Covenant carved by Indians and the Ten Commandments burned into them by Indians with the sun through a magnifying glass. Her husband wrote and taught English in a galvanized iron schoolhouse. Oved sold arms to Biafra, made friends with some African rebels, and reached Cameroon, and there were jungles there too.

My brief affair with the sweetie with the huge breasts was over. Hanoch was living with his angel. Oved and Carole had shut themselves away. We were all waiting for something to happen. Avi Shoes came along and we sat in the Blue Angel. Irwin Corey was funny and my sweet Anita Ellis sang. And her brother Larry Kert came. He said that Lee had changed and of course she hadn't married Robbins; she had become tough, irascible, ambitious; she wasn't nice like she once was. We were joined at our table by a girl with a nice face, not particularly beautiful with its sharp angles, and her eyes were green and she was in a Broadway show, A small role, she said, and that's not really right because there aren't any small roles but only small actors, I'm a good actress and it's a small role and nobody recognizes me. She said her boyfriend had left her. She'd come to have a laugh with Irwin Corey who could make a bronze sculpture laugh, and we drank, Larry went off with a guy older than him and I saw them kissing by the restroom door and Sharon, that was the girl's name, took me to an apartment on the top floor of an old building at One University Place. She shouted that she loved me and I thought God knows what. I called Carole to ask how the brothers Oved and Hanoch were getting on and to tell her I'd be along later and Sharon and I were together all night and for a whole day we only got out of bed to bring in food and take a shower. She talked about mysticism and I suddenly thought I loved her too and went home and worked on two paintings Carole had discovered behind the closet and which had been slightly damaged because I'd wanted to sell them and I called Sharon to ask when I should come back and her voice was icy and she said, Don't come back. What happened? I asked. Nothing, she said. I'm busy. I tried to talk sense into her. She said her boyfriend had come home and they'd made up, and like an idiot I said, But last night you said you loved me and she said that things said at night aren't always valid in daytime. I begged her again and she said, All men are children who don't like being left. Thank you, Frau Freud, I replied. She said, You've got a lot to learn. What happened yesterday is yesterday. Today is today. I said I was coming over to get my watch, I'd left it there by mistake. She let me in and was cold to me. Her father came with two glass tubes filled with quarters and kissed her and left and didn't even look at me and she explained that it was her daily allowance. The two tubes were glass containers from the Churchill cigars he smoked. She said, Look, my father comes from Jews. My mother was a beautiful Irishwoman. Not a nobody like him. I told him that the Jews of Palestine should be thrown into the sea and he told me that the Jews had learned to swim in Auschwitz. My awful father worked as a foreman in an oil company in New Mexico and one day even though he'd never even finished third grade he invented a special cap for oil barrels, registered a patent, and every oil barrel in the world is closed and opened with my father's cap and ever since he sits smoking Churchills and counting his dough. He doesn't want to give me any real money. Just quarters in the tubes. And then she looked at me with a kind of contemptuous compassion and said she had no feelings for me. She said that when her father was young he'd wandered all over America and worked. So what if I said I loved you, does that bind me to you now? We had a good night and day and that's it. What do you know about women at all? I said, but your body danced for me, and she said it danced for everybody. What didn't I say, what didn't I try, I actually had tears in my eyes. She enjoyed seeing me humiliated and said, You're leaving now. My boyfriend will be back any minute. I went downstairs and stood for a whole hour outside the building and saw people going inside, I went to the public phone outside the Arts Club on University Place and called her and she cursed at me and slammed the phone down.

I went in and had a drink with Robert De Niro Sr. who I hadn't seen for a long time. He took me to his studio and showed me some new work and his little son came to play and I drew a camel and palm trees for him and De Niro Sr. said that artists were saying about him that he was over-influenced by Matisse but that he didn't understand Matisse and I told him not to pay any attention, that he was one of the best artists in America and that *Moby-Dick* had sold fifty copies in forty-nine years or forty-nine copies in fifty years and look at where Melville is today and he said, Six feet under, and eternity didn't help Van Gogh either. We had ravioli at the little Italian restaurant, the same one we'd eaten at before, it was great, I passed Sharon's house, I called her on the house phone and she said, Yes? I mumbled something and she said, Really, enough already.

Back home Carole had cleaned my apartment. Beulah Weil, who'd bought my first painting at my first show, called me up. I'd liked her once and she liked me. I'd met her through Jerome Robbins who at the time had wanted to help me make some money. She ran a company that made produced painted cloth patterns. She was twenty years older than me. Before she'd gone back to the family business she'd wanted to be an actress. She'd taught Jerry Robbins acting and had been a member of the American Actors Company, and had also directed it. Beulah helped me and commissioned me to paint cloth for her and I did a few samples of which only one was bought and I brought Gandy in who was better than me and he did a few very good samples that I later saw on lots of dresses, and I hadn't seen her for two years now and she asked how I was and she said that Dick Zeisler had had dinner with her and had spoken warmly about my paintings and that he'd be coming to pick her up for dinner that evening and she told him she'd bring me along and he got angry but agreed and she wanted me to bring some paintings and then we'd see if he might buy any. I worked on the two paintings that Carole had found and fixed what needed fixing and so that the paint wouldn't be wet I used a gouache mix. I went to Beulah's house on Park Avenue and Zeisler's driver arrived and asked us to come downstairs. We went down and Zeisler was sitting in his Rolls-Royce and he said, Beulah sure knows how to make trouble. We drove to his house near the Frick Collection and went upstairs and I saw an art collection you don't see every day. Modigliani's *Nude Sdraiato*. Two early Chagalls. A dancing landscape by Soutine. Two Matisses, a Chardin, a rare Juan Gris, a Ryder, and a Reuven Rubin sketch. We went into the dining room. The food was fine. The butler who served it looked as old as the Cézanne hanging on the wall facing me. Zeisler said he was bored, that each morning he drove to his office and there was a secretary sitting there with nothing to do—he was making fun of himself and it was touching—and all day she just wrote his name on her typewriter. It's not nice to be considered a wealthy man and then have nothing to do. Beulah had told me earlier that Zeisler had converted to Christianity in his youth and had been a monk and traveled to Palestine and Syria, but after the war, after what he'd heard about the Holocaust, he'd returned to Judaism and had been married for three days, meaning that he'd left his wife after three days but continued to receive wedding gifts and never returned them. I took out the paintings I'd brought and Zeisler looked at them for a long time and said that when one of my paintings was worth fifty thousand dollars I should come and see him and he'd buy it. Since he knew I was poor he said he'd give me a present. He left the room for five minutes with the aged butler at his heels and then came back and gave me a package. When we got out of the Rolls-Royce that had taken me and Beulah back to her home, I opened the package and found twenty used shirts and a necktie.

My writing was floundering, it wasn't good, from the play I'd written I moved on to the story of Hughie and the dog but that was too big for me and so I began another book. I decided I needed a change. Avi Shoes lent me a few hundred dollars and I packed a big bag and went to the Greyhound station at Penn and for seventy-five dollars I bought a pass that would let me travel on any of the company's buses for thirty days. The idea that had popped into my head was to learn from Oved's trip, when he had gone to Mexico City just because there wasn't a bus to Las Vegas. I decided to go wherever there was bus service. The first bus was going out to Illinois. I sat looking at the wide-open spaces in the silence. Every now and then we'd stop for some air and food. At one of the stops, in a small town whose name I've forgotten, I got off. I rented a car, checked into a motel, and ate at the local diner. In the evening the streets were empty and I could hear music. A guy was playing the guitar and people were singing country songs with him. I had a drink and the guy looked at me and invited me to join in a song about a lost cowboy. I reached Chicago, walked around the city, it was cold, snow was falling, the lake was vast and a strong wind was blowing in off it, from there I traveled south and passed through states I'd never visited, Kansas, Missouri, I went up to South Dakota, went down to Utah, I'd get off the bus, check into a motel, rent a car, and climb the mountains or drive through the deserts. The vast beauty of nothingness. The power of this big country. The people who didn't live in the cities I knew—stronger people. Repairing trailer rigs. Milking cows. Fertilizing fields. Hunting. Building log cabins. Stone houses. And there were girls. I was young and so were they. Everything was different and I was amazed that we even spoke a common language. I got off and got on buses and three weeks passed and I wasn't satisfied, sitting in buses, devouring the distance, the Rockies I climbed were desolation refined into scenery. I'd curl up at the bus stops, drink Coca-Cola or coffee, and just listen. Strangers stuck to one another and talked like brothers though they would never see one another again. There was something magical in all that detachment. In that journey to nowhere. In the absence of contact with everything you once were. I visited a ranch and helped a woman get her car out of the mud and spent a weekend with her near the endless cornfields of Idaho, and it was quiet and warm in the house and the woman, whose name was Cathy, asked what I did and I said I was a tie salesman from New York and she was a teacher, on her own, her husband had gone away and never come back, she was gentle and hungry for love and I gave her as much as I could invent on the spot and finally said I was going and she said sadly that I wouldn't come back, like her husband, and I said no, that I would come back, and I got on the bus. A few days later I reached the Grand Canyon and from there I went to Louisiana, and then, very slowly, by bus, after lots more heart-to-heart talks with my lost brothers, I got back to New York. Carole and Oved had looked after my apartment and Hanoch and Oved and me and Carole sat down to think about what we were going to do and Hanoch started talking about Israelis, what they're looking for, how they stick together in a city like New York, and he got the idea of a café. An Israeli café slowly took shape, hummus and tahini, falafel, and the Israelis would come, they'd have a home, and the idea sounded good and we needed five thousand dollars to start up. Avi Shoes said no. Falafel would never fly in America. Israelis should wake up and be where they were or else go back home. I'd known an Israeli woman in Paris who'd studied automotive engineering, a friend of a friend whose name I've forgotten. We met by chance on Fifth Avenue and she said that everything was okay now, not long ago she'd married a Jewish businessman called Bernie Cohen. She promised to find out if he'd agree to invest in our café. He agreed, and that should have aroused our suspicions at once, but at the time we didn't feel like trying to understand his motives. He signed a contract with us. Gave us the money. According to the contract we'd split everything down the middle, half for him and half for us. The checks needed two signatures, his and one of ours. He brought along a huge businessman's checkbook and asked us to sign about two hundred checks so he could transfer money to us as we needed it. We found a basement on Ninety-first and Broadway. A big filthy basement that had been standing empty for years. For two months we worked day and night on decorating it. We stripped the paint, repainted, and I even did a few small paintings for the walls that we framed. Hanoch built a beautiful mahogany-covered bar. We found tables and chairs like those in European cafés, things that weren't yet popular in New York, and we bought an espresso machine that was also quite a rarity in town. We built a kitchen, a storeroom, we experimented with the kind of coffee we'd use, where in the Arab neighborhood in Brooklyn we should buy beans and oil and tahini and pita bread, and about three months later, when we were almost dropping, everything was ready. We brought in the furniture. We put the espresso machine in its place. For a few days we experimented with making tasty falafel and hummus. Hanoch invented a device that put eight falafel balls into the fryer at once, rather than one, as was the custom in Israel. We worked long and hard to find the right quantities of ingredients, the right frying time, mixing the hummus and tahini, spices, coriander, it was good to work, good not to think, to argue a bit about politics. We brought in some Israeli friends for taste tests, we listened attentively, added more pepper, less salt, more fresh lemon juice and "The Cellar," as we called it, was almost ready. We brought a record player and classical and Hebrew records together with American folk songs and lots of jazz records. We signed a contract with the Chinese laundry opposite us to wash our tablecloths and towels every night. And then, while we were still working on the final polish, three guys came in who looked like our good friends from downtown Las Vegas. They talked with a Brooklyn accent and asked how's it going boychiks and said how nice that you're opening a Jewish café and we said thank you and invited them to have a cup of coffee and they drank it and one of them said, There are a few things you need to know. One, you need protection. We asked who from. There are all kinds, they said. Fifty dollars a month just because you're one of us. Out of the question, we said. That night our three apartments were broken into and some stuff was broken, they smashed a window and came back next day and ordered coffee. We gave it to them. Okay, we said, fifty. You've got a deal, they said, but there's a couple more things. No record player. We'll bring you a jukebox with our records. Who's we? Better you don't ask, sweeties. And laundry, no crappy Chinese is doing your laundry, we are. We do the laundry for most of the restaurants in town, and we'll discriminate against Jews from Eretz Yisroel? We said fine and continued as planned. We still hadn't let the public in but had done a dry run with a few Israeli friends. The second night all the windows were smashed. The third night the espresso machine was ripped out, but it didn't get broken. They came again and said they'd heard we'd had some trouble with the windows and the coffee machine and that they could fix everything, including sending the Chinese laundryman to hospital because when it all happened the poor guy had been hurt and he was lying injured in his laundry now and there was nobody to help him. We ran over. We helped him. He whispered, Don't bring any more laundry and you don't know me, eh? We said yes. We took him to the hospital. In an old phone book I had I found the number of my relative the policeman Braverman who had been promoted. I asked him over. I gave him some superior Colombian coffee we'd found in a store in Brooklyn. Man to man I told him what had happened and that we were going to file a complaint with the police and right away we thought of him. He looked at us in amazement, rubbed his hands, frowned, and said, No cops, you hear? Do you want to die for nothing instead of in some important war? We were surprised and he explained, Look, I can't help you with this. But if you do this alone it won't help either. You've got a license for an Italian coffee machine? We said we hadn't but we did have a café license and he said, You can't serve alcoholic beverages. We said we didn't. He got up, looked around, and took a bottle of rye from behind the bar and said, And what's this? We didn't know what to say. He said, There are rules here, unwritten rules, these Jews are gentler than the Italians or the Irish who don't have a Jewish soul, so you'd do well to listen to them, the others would have smashed up the whole place, you'd better learn to get along with them. After he'd gone the beat cop we'd seen from time to time in the neighborhood came in and asked to talk to us. He sat down. He had a cup of Colombian coffee too, said it was great, and said he understood we were new to the business so he was sorry he had to state the obvious. I'll come in every week and in a brown bag left over from the coffee beans you buy and grind you'll accidentally leave ten dollars. Next day my sergeant will come in and you'll also forget ten dollars in a bag for him. And then, that evening, before the place fills up—if the place ever even opens, because look you've got two sinks instead of three and that's against the law and you have no emergency exit which is even more against the law, and on the wall over there I see an obscene painting (I'd painted a dancer in the Canaanite style), and your entrance is only five feet wide instead of six and we found whiskey here when you don't have a liquor license—well, that evening an officer will come along and he'll also get a bag with ten dollars in it.

We told him about the jukebox and the laundry. He said that they, those nice guys, were none of his business. Next day a few tables were smashed and a sink was broken and the Jews with the cigars came and wanted our autographs in Hebrew on their Yom Kippur prayer books and they brought in a huge jukebox. We argued for a long time. They called somebody and there were raised voices and we reached an agreement: We would pay for the jukebox. We would pay for the license for the jukebox. We would pay for the records we wouldn't use. In exchange, we would be allowed to put our own records into the jukebox, and pay only a token sum for maintaining the original records and a not particularly high user's fee. Then people came from City Hall to check out the sanitation and saw the two sinks and we were a citation by the sergeant who was sitting waiting for his money, and they got only twenty dollars for a permit to open our kitchen with only two sinks but then another twenty for the small chimney we'd run up outside to get rid of the smell of frying oil. And Braverman brought me a sticker from the "Shomer," the Jewish policemen's association, to stick on the windshield of the car I didn't yet have, but surely would, and it's free, he said. The tussle continued for about another week. The sweet Jews forgot that we hadn't bought tables and towels from them. The windows were broken again and there happened to be a torrential rainstorm and so we paid more. We wanted two loudspeakers, which brought the City Hall inspectors in again, and which cost us another fifty dollars a week. And after all that we opened.

We invited Pete Seeger from the Weavers who played and sang. Harry Belafonte sang. Hordes of Israelis hungry for hummus, tahini, and falafel came, they brought the Tel Aviv Falafel King who was visiting America and they waited to hear what he'd say and he pronounced it good. The place was packed. Americans came too, and everyone sang songs together; the atmosphere was great, the food tasty, we worked very hard and had two helpers, one was an Israeli who was down and out and so we let him wash dishes and it cost us ten broken plates an hour and the same number of cups and sadly we had to let him go but he came back as a customer and ate and didn't pay and that was fine and he sat sadly in a corner and thought about the precision and beauty of Descartes. The place's reputation spread. The policemen kept on coming. Our nice Jewish "friends" didn't come any more but kept their distance and only sometimes, at two or three in the morning, after everybody had gone and only our beautiful waitresses were still hanging around, the cops came, and my relative, and then those kind Jewish souls as well, and we drank whiskey from a bottle we kept hidden so it didn't get reported to anyone. When I asked the police officer why we were paying him when we were also supposed to be paying the people he was supposed to be protecting us from, he said there were all kinds of foreigners who thought they knew about America. They wrote in the papers. Among them were also numerous Americans who never got fined for anything and who only knew New York through taxi windows. Do you know how much a cop earns? How do you think America was made? The English came and killed the Indians and then they had a country. The Irish, Italians, and Jews came. Now the blacks and Puerto Ricans have come. And people are crying about what was done to the Indians. I tried to protest and tell him that it wasn't just, but he said I was an idealist and that it wouldn't be to my benefit in later life. I told him that H. L. Mencken had said that an idealist was someone who believed that because roses smell better than cabbage you can make better soup out of them. My cousin asked if Mencken was Jewish and I said I didn't think so. Carole helped us out quite a bit. She saw who was stealing and who was trying not to pay and she'd point them out surreptitiously and that way we were in control, because the work was hard. Preparing hundreds of portions of hummus. Two hundred portions of tahini. Lots of falafel and salads and warm pita bread and espresso and cappuccino and Turkish coffee, it was all hard and we sometimes slept as we worked.

One day a nice girl came in dragging with her a young woman who for me was the fairest of the fair. Like a goddess in a composite painting by Fra Angelico and Botticelli. She was a little scared, looked spacey, she couldn't find her body in the place and wouldn't let her skin brush up against anything. The friend who'd brought her, Libby, had brought her along as a cover, since she was really there out of love for Oved, who didn't understand a lot about love. Libby's friend, who as it turned out had never been on the West Side except for when she passed through from the mainland once on her way to the harbor to visit Europe, was named Miranda. One of the waitresses with whom I'd had an affair and who sang Irish and American folk songs said she thought she was pregnant with my child, so I could only steal glances at my love every moment I was able and maybe sit down at her table once in a while. Miranda and Libby came in a few times. Distinguished guests too. The place was a success. But every week we got a statement from the bank that indicated we were losing money. We'd been so busy with building the place up that we'd paid no attention to how much of our money was left. There were the visits by the beat cop, the sergeant, the officer, the representatives of American Jewry with the guns under their coats, and again and again the City Sanitation Department sent emissaries about our two sinks and they said they'd been running a deficit and so needed us to contribute a little more. And the Chinese laundryman got out of hospital but wouldn't look at us. A friend of mine, Jack Rollins, who after discovering Belafonte and making a career for him was fired in favor of Belafonte's psychiatrist's husband, and who became one of the two producers who produced almost all of Woody Allen's films, discovered a comic duo from Chicago, Mike Nichols and Elaine May, and we became friends. They were appearing at the Blue Angel and they appeared at our place too and Mike's wife began studying Hebrew with me. Elaine May told Yiddish jokes for us and then we found time to visit the bank. We went into the office of the manager of the Chase Manhattan Bank on Ninety-second and Broadway and he offered us cigars and we said no thanks, and he showed us our balance and it turned out that in the three months since the Cellar's opening our income had indeed been high but our expenses had been higher. It seemed that we owed the bank the sum of ten thousand two hundred and fifty-one dollars, and when we scrutinized our cancelled checks closely it appeared that our friend Bernie—who had even shown up for our opening and cried and sung an old Polish song he'd learned from his mother—had simply been using the Cellar as his own personal checkbook, which the lawyer we hired right away told us was how crooks who'd had their own checkbooks taken away usually operated. They find suckers like you and pay their bills with your money—and that's what he did, we'd covered his meals in restaurants and clubs like the Hickory House, frequented by people who come from Texas to eat Texas-sized steaks and then pay off Texas-sized tabs, we'd covered his expenses with other crooks, covered his gambling debts, and, all in all, over the past three months, with our two signatures and his, he'd spent thirty thousand dollars, and now we were left with egg on our faces.

That night Miranda could see I was sad and asked why and I told her and her girlfriend and they sat in silence and wanted to help us but couldn't. At the time I'd already bought an old Studebaker from Anna-May, one of our beautiful waitresses—I paid sixty dollars for it. I'd stuck the "Shomer" sticker on the windshield and every Irish cop and his mother wrote me a ticket, whether I had it coming or not. So that night I asked the two girls to come for a drive with me—I was scared of being alone with Miranda—and drove as fast as I sometimes did along the road that ran around the city and that late at night you could get away with speeding on because there almost no cars on it. I talked to them—that is, to her—and was close to tears but I held back. The next day, Hanoch, Oved, and I met Bernie and his lawyer at the bank manager's office. Bernie appeared to be in high spirits. He congratulated us on the place's success and if it hadn't been for Oved and me restraining him Hanoch would have made falafel out of Bernie there and then. Hanoch calmed down, Oved sat there like a bereaved bear, Bernie smoked a cigar and tried making us laugh with Jewish jokes. The lawyer spoke. The bank manager spoke. I got up to speak on behalf of the Israeli trio. I raked Bernie over the coals, I said some choice words on the subject of morality and justice and everything I'd learned in my youth in the youth movement, but Bernie went on smiling though I saw tears in his eyes when I talked about his inhumanity. He didn't reply right away. Oved hissed a few quiet words of hatred. Hanoch sat with his fists clenched. The bank manager was quiet but it was evident that he felt for us. The lawyer tried to maintain objectivity—that is, to give us a definite maybe. Bernie started talking. In velvet tones, with tears now flowing from his eyes, he said he was sorry, but before you take five thousand dollars from a stranger you should check him out. His history was replete with what the police termed fraud and he called business acumen. Nobody has ever said, he said, that I'm an honest man. If I was, I wouldn't have had five thousand dollars to give to three foreigners so they could open a kiosk for selling *Araber* patties. To this day they haven't ever managed to arrest me for what I do, because what I do isn't always clear to the police, though they did manage, thanks to a dirty judge who got a lot of money from someone, to take away my right to have a checkbook. As clever Israelis who are heroes and the new hope of the Jewish people with Jewish muscles and guns and planes, you should have learned something maybe from the regular Jews who for two thousand years never won a single war, and be a little suspicious when a stranger gives you money in cash and not with a check. Look, I'm terribly sorry that you're the suckers. You deserve better. You built a nice café with your *Arabers*. People all over the city are talking about you. Entertainers who get five hundred or a thousand bucks a show appear for free at your place and even the NYPD is proud of you, even Braverman, the vice-chairman of the Jewish Policemen's Association, claims that you're really good guys and know how to play by the rules. But—when you needed the money, you found me. And I found you. I had to pay off my debts, so what could I do? You handed over this big checkbook and you handed it over of your own free will without me threatening you. You, the wise guys, the new Jews, what my wife calls "the Sabras," you signed a hundred and seventy checks up front, so did you think I'd do? Make a donation to local orphanages? Invite you to the 21 Club? Everybody does what he knows how to do best. You know how to do *Arabers* evenings and coffee, and me, I take, especially if I'm given. I'm a guy who's got big expenses. You didn't ask why I wanted signatures on the checks in advance and so, out of respect for your bleeding hearts, I didn't say why, and look, I've got nothing against you, and I can see you're angry and I even cried earlier when I heard Yoram talking about morals and friends, I don't have any friends and I don't believe in friends, I heard that one of your generals said that the only friends he knows are in the Egged bus company, and I've been to Israel so for the benefit of my attorney I'll explain that Egged is a bus drivers' cooperative, and nobody asked my father what he thought about morals when they killed him at Treblinka. Precisely what morals are you talking about? After the Americans did everything so we'd die over there I had to sneak into this country and marry an American because even after what went on over there they still didn't want Jews to come over, not only Jews like me but like you as well. Hanoch raised his voice then and told Bernie exactly what he thought of him, but the lawyer stopped him and Bernie looked lovingly at Hanoch and said, I understand you, cupcake. And then there was silence. The lawyer explained that the law was on Bernie's side. We couldn't do a thing. He could always claim that he gave you the five thousand dollars in exchange for the checkbook and didn't know that you didn't know it was illegal. In the meantime, due to the fact that you gave him your checkbook, the law can't take it from him unless he tries to obtain a new one without your signatures. And he can't. So you've no choice but to reach an agreement and close the matter. The bank manager started weeping and touched Oved's hand and swallowed his own tears and said, This is no way to treat people who've worked so hard and haven't taken a cent, and Bernie said that he certainly agreed with him and with Hanoch and with all of us and that he wanted to make us a generous offer.

We looked at him in silence and he ransacked his devious brain for the words and said, In any other case, if you were other people and not the people who've built a national home for the Jews, I'd demand twenty-five thousand dollars for the return of the checkbook. But—and here his voice became tough, low, slightly disgusted with himself, he looked at us with the eyes of a thief who wouldn't let anyone steal from him, and he went on quietly—I'll only take ten thousand, in payments over a year, without interest, but that's my last word, it was nice knowing you and doing business with you, I'll leave the checkbook with the bank manager so I won't be able to withdraw any more money. The quicker you pay, the better, because who knows what might happen if my wife Sophie needs an operation or has to have her teeth straightened or if anything else unforeseen happens, and look, I, out of genuine concern, I even donated money to the Defense Fund in 1947 at the beginning of the war with the Arabs, so I suggest you pay as quickly as possible, and be healthy and strong and may the Good Lord protect you. And he gave a little bow and left.

We were stunned. We sat there looking at one another. We went back to the café where the waitresses had started setting up for the evening, we prepared the food and went back to work to pay for Bernie's expensive tastes. Something had broken. Oved said, We've beaten a table, not the house. I still had an old newspaper from Pat's apartment on Division and Canal with an article by Karl Marx that I'd kept for some reason. There was an advertisement from Laconia, Indiana on one of the pages and I thought about Bernie and brought it out and read aloud: A Wonderful Opportunity to Get Rich! We're going to set up a cat farm in Laconia. We'll start with a hundred thousand cats. Each female cat has twelve kittens a year. Cat pelts sell at thirty cents each. A hundred people can skin five thousand cats a day. We can expect a daily profit of ten thousand dollars. Now, what do we feed the cats? We'll set up a mouse farm and start with a million mice. The mice reproduce twelve times more than cats, so we'll have four mice a day to feed each cat. And what do we feed the mice? The mice will eat the skinned cat meat. This way, the mice eat the cats and the cats eat the mice, and we'll get the pelts at no cost. Enthusiasm for the Cellar began to die down, although toward the end things started to pick up again and it got more and more popular and there were even people who came to eat an Israeli breakfast: eggs and a finely diced vegetable salad. And local men of Italian extraction came to advise us that they had replaced the Jews, whose numbers were diminishing, and they joked that only dead Jews were real citizens, and said that the mighty Jewish blood had become pudding in the veins of college boys who didn't want to follow in the footsteps of their forefathers, and from now on they would be our friends, under the same terms but for an extra twenty dollars a week due to the absence of Italian songs in our jukebox. Hanoch said he'd bring some Caruso records. They said, Okay, we'll check it out. They came back and we played some Caruso for them. They wept and sang along and said it was wonderful, but twenty bucks is twenty bucks.

Miranda came again, I looked at her, it wasn't easy. That waitress still thought she was pregnant, the parking tickets for my car cost a fortune, and one night I returned to my apartment from a drive to unwind and had to look for a parking spot for almost an hour. I was tired, I found a piece of paper and wrote on it: I've had it. Take the car. Be my guest. I shoved it under the wipers and they took the car and it probably ended up dead in some junkyard, may it rest in peace. Some time after that Libby stopped loving Oved, who was becoming more and more attached to Carole, and I was drunk and called Doctor Brandt and asked him whether it was okay that I'd given Carole Galante to Oved and he said that I could do what I liked with her. My call made him remember old times and so he came by the Cellar and fell for a waitress who looked like a gentle tiger with the eyes of a housecat and was about as elusive as a cat, and he started talking to her about psychological disorders because men and women are always interested in diseases, he said, though women are more interested in what's above and men in what's below. They started living together but she went on working because she said she had experience with men and wasn't taking any chances, which proved wise on her part. Libby stopped coming to the Cellar, but spacey and skittish Miranda still showed up once in a while and gave me her home phone number. Then we sat down for a chat, we three Bernie patsies, and I told my partners that Mr.

Ben-Zion who wrote for the *Bizron* magazine had asked me to write a children's story for them and said he'd heard that we'd worked with Bernie Cohen and I said we had, and he asked whether he'd told us about his father in Treblinka and I said he had, and he said that Bernie was born in the Bronx and that his father had never been in Treblinka or any other camp. This didn't help our cause, however, because when I called Bernie to yell at him about it, he explained that everyone knew he was a liar so it made no difference to him whether or not we knew it as well.

Hanoch and Oved and I were always thinking about falafel and finally Hanoch came up with an idea—after which there was a heated argument about whose idea it was, but today I have no doubt that it was Hanoch's. The idea was, Why don't we make frozen falafel like the frozen vegetables they sell at A&P, and sell it as a snack to be served in America as an hors d'oeuvre to guests before a meal or at an event like an art opening. We consulted with my cousin who was a food engineer in Pittsburgh, and he gave it some thought and gave us some advice, Tahini can't be frozen, he said, but falafel can. We rented a nearby bomb shelter and under Hanoch's leadership we started setting up a factory where we would manufacture packets of frozen falafel that would only need to be heated in an oven for two minutes and that's it. We stopped living off of the Cellar and invested in falafels. Oved and Hanoch worked out exactly how long the falafels had to be fried before being removed from the oil and then frozen so that they'd be ready after two minutes or a minute and a half of baking at home. But how would we freeze them? We tracked down someone who agreed to come up with an attractive mold for frozen falafel. In his honor we decided to name the product Chuck Puffs. The packaging, after several failures and adjustments and modifications, looked appealing. Oved and I continued working at the Cellar and hired a girl to help us. Hanoch was busy setting up the factory. Pots and ladles and ovens and attempts to construct a machine that would drop fifteen falafel balls into oil in one go. And what do you do with the used oil, and how many falafel balls can be fried in the same oil before you change the oil, and how do you freeze the balls rapidly—experiment after experiment. We helped with the ingredients and suggested a bit more falafel and a little less coriander, different types of beans, and we argued whether we should use Egyptian hummus or Lebanese and what kind of tahini we should buy in bulk. And the Cellar went on working for Bernie, and Miranda stopped coming, and Jo the singer-waitress stopped talking about her pregnancy, and I couldn't sleep and I just thought about Miranda. Late at night I'd go with Jo to bars and she'd sing folk songs and there was an Irish bar, or a huge saloon to be more precise, where a girl I once knew also sang, and I was too embarrassed to ask her if we'd had an affair or not, but she and Jo sang together, and Irishmen sat around the tables, waiters brought huge pitchers of beer to each table and they poured it into glasses and Jo sang Irish songs with the girl with whom I either did or did not have an affair, and when they got to "Danny Boy" everyone would sing along in their beery voices, and cops would come and join in and firefighters and students and they'd all cry, and in the end Jo would do the Weavers' song Pete Seeger was always singing, "Kisses Sweeter than Wine."

Avi Shoes, who had sold his entire chain of factories and was laying low, called occasionally and sounded mysterious and said he was working for Mossad and didn't want to tell me who he was with. Some said he was living somewhere with Rita Hauser. Others said he was living with Mira. Still others said he was with the Bulgarian woman from Israel. They said he was living in the desert in Israel. Or they said he was dead. Or they said he'd become a prophet in Alaska. In the meantime Hanoch finished setting up falafel factory. We decided to start production. We drank a toast to the rich life it would bring us and to what Oved always called getting onto the list, and we figured that this time—albeit without using the Las Vegas system and without using Oved's Mayan tablets—we would finally succeed. We enlisted about twenty pretty-to-beautiful Israeli students, and they went out to the supermarkets to demonstrate our product and hand out free samples. We bought small electric ovens that cost a fortune, and the girls stood in the stores and showed customers how the packages were opened and how you put the falafel in the oven for two minutes, and the customers tasted and some were impressed, falafel wasn't very well known in New York in those days, people said it tasted excellent, but after a good three weeks during which we began getting orders from the chains, everything came to a standstill. The stores all returned their stock. Despite their beauty, our students were thrown out of the supermarkets, and my relative, Lieutenant Braverman, came to us in our devastation and told us that we'd always been suckers. You can't penetrate the market just like that, he said, without capital or connections. The giants don't like little people who come in small and have the potential to grow and become big. They kill them while they're still small. And he added that the big guys, next to whom we were not even midgets, didn't want to wait and see whether we would remain small, they couldn't wait, they'd imposed a boycott and informed the stores far more elegantly and persuasively than I can tell you that they wouldn't ship them any more merchandise until they got rid of our girls. I searched high and low for Avi Shoes then because he had experience with being a small fry trying to penetrate into the big leaguers' market, but he'd vanished, and we sat humiliated, thousands of packages of frozen falafel in freezers we'd obtained at great expense. We sold some of our "collection" to Israelis who smelled blood and bought our stock for peanuts. We were now in even more debt than before. The Cellar continued to operate. Some kindhearted Israelis saw that things were good for us and opened a Café Kassit on Broadway, not far from the Cellar, and learned all the industry secrets from waitresses who had left us, and that was that, the damage was done. We weathered the competition, but barely, and then a pleasant American who had worked with us opened a café in the Village and called it Finjan and sang Israeli songs in an American accent and sold pretty disgusting hummus, and we struggled on, worked day and night, and then Jo said she wasn't pregnant and I called Miranda.

She came next day and I asked her out to a movie. She walked like a gazelle. Tall. Elegant. Gentle. We walked to Forty-second Street and the first show was Ingmar Bergman's *The Seventh Seal*, and I don't remember the name of the second feature. Between movies I told her that she would be the mother of my daughter and how I'd had to restrain myself until Jo told me she wasn't pregnant and I told her that we would get married soon, and she replied, All right, and smiled and asked when were we planning to do it and I said, In the spring. She said, Fine, and we walked for hours, I told her about myself and she, in a dozen words, summarized herself and gave herself to me and she was naïve but somehow also wise. In all the days of my two lives I'd never before had the honor and pleasure of knowing an angel, though now that I'd met one, I saw that angels weren't exactly angels. Although she was rare and blessed with qualities that for lack of a better word might be called "angelic," Miranda was all too human. And soon she would conceive and give birth.

She had a body, and therefore cast a shadow. She honored her father and her mother. She had not stolen. She had not committed adultery. She had not sworn falsely. She had not worshiped other gods. She had not killed. She had not borne false witness against her neighbor. She had not coveted her neighbor's house. She had not coveted her neighbor's husband. Nor his ox nor his maidservant nor his ass nor anything that was his. She was known as someone who never said no, but found a way nonetheless to be obstinate and always stand on her principles. She lived an autonomous existence. Her skin was transparent to the world. A donkey-foal would die in her house, years later. Its mother abandons it in a field in Ramat HaSharon after giving birth to it and turning away to feed. The foal waits. A factory worker passes through the field. The foal thinks the worker is its mother and hobbles after her. She gets to the factory where she works, pets him for a moment, and the foal, who knows that she's its mother, stands and waits for her. At the end of the shift, because she's having an affair, the factory worker exits the factory through the rear, and a married man—married, that is, to another woman—comes to pick her up in his car. The foal remains where it stands. It doesn't eat and doesn't drink. In the morning, a man on a delivery bike rides by and tries to load it onto his bike. Because he can't quite manage, he leaves it in the field. Then Miranda passes through the field and sees it and draws near to talk to it, to stroke it, and it dances after her with nimble skips. After inquiries that take at least two days, the owner of the donkey, the foal's mother, is located. It transpires however that the donkey will not take back her offspring, because there is a law with donkeys that stipulates the following: in the event that three days shall pass from the day of birth during which a foal is lost to its mother, when that mother sees her young again, she will kill it. So the beautiful foal, whose coat was soft as down, sleeps in Miranda's bed, and because it's never suckled on its mother's milk (and hence was never immunized), only survives with the assistance of an old veterinarian and the aid of plenty of milk bottles with teats attached to them, but the poor thing gets sick nonetheless and dies. Miranda sits with it on the floor. A summer's night. The children of the neighborhood are hanging in clusters from the windows of her house. They stare in amazement at the vision within. Relentlessly, for seven hours straight, Miranda gives the foal mouth-to-mouth resuscitation, until she turns blue and practically faints. The earth trembles in the presence of the Lord, who waits patiently, and with a certain admiration, but also with an unyielding determination, until He finally draws near to complete His task. The foal—whose eyes were the most beautiful ever seen, its coat the softest, the gleam of sorrow in its gaze as deep as a pool—will never be forgotten. Before being buried, it would even be given a name. The children would give it a beautiful funeral and a girl, whose father was a Marine at the American Embassy, would sing the Marine Corps hymn.

But, back in New York, 1958, Miranda and I went back to my place after work in the Cellar. The idea was that I'd speak to her parents. Before I could do so, Tony Scott called and said that Mike Nichols's ex-wife, to whom I still taught Hebrew once in a while and who'd forget what she'd learned soon enough, had given him my number. I asked how he was and he replied whatever it was that he replied and said that Lady Day was going to give a performance, she was in bad shape, with seventy-five dollars in the bank, and she was sick, and this would possibly be her last concert and she could hardly hold herself up and that I should come and help. I went to Tony's house and Billie smiled a broken smile at me and said, Hey, Yo! and put her head down on her hands that were crossed on the table. Percy Heath came and Prez and Oscar Peterson, but Lester looked bad too, gaunt and tired, his days numbered, and we decided what and where. I don't remember whether the concert was at Carnegie Hall or in some other place.

Billie could barely sing, but even in her devastation she was a palace. There were some critics back then who said that she couldn't sing anymore at all, but Tony and I and Prez and Mulligan who also came loved this tone of hers, the sad ironic whisper that could be heard in her voice. The rumor that she was doing a show spread like wildfire. There was no money for an ad in the paper. We brought her onto the stage. There was a microphone there, we fixed it to the floor with nails, we brought her in leaning on our arms and literally stuck her to the microphone stand which she clutched in her hands and then she stuck her mouth to the tip of the microphone as if in a kiss. A big crowd stood outside, mostly blacks, and several hundred were inside. I knew some of them. Everyone from the Minton Playhouse days who was still alive was there. Two whores that I recognized. Musicians. The bartender. Singers' accompanists and tap dancers, Ben Webster and Percy Heath, and she started singing. Her voice sounded as if it had passed through a filter, she even sang a newer song, "Fine and Mellow," and I remember Prez, who had come from Europe where he'd been living for several years now, and Coleman Hawkins, and Roy Eldridge joined in. She whispered, but forcefully, in the sweetness of her unique voice: a tender, miraculous scalpel. The audience sang with her in a whisper, and even outside, so I was told, the crowd sang along. She whispered the songs and the audience sang quietly and didn't make a sound otherwise, and outside buses stopped and people got down and listened. She'd never had such a loving, enthusiastic, and devoted audience in her entire life. She sang for about an hour. Her arms ached and you could see it. We went on stage and brought her down and she sobbed. A few months later she found out that Prez had died. She used more and more heroin, her health deteriorated, and she was hospitalized in serious condition. From the depths of her weeping she managed to organize a delivery of drugs even there, I heard, smuggled in by means of a rock hurled through the window of her hospital room, and she was remanded on her deathbed by the police for possession of drugs. A few weeks later she died at forty-four years of age. In the Cellar we only played her songs that night. It was sad that Lady died.

Miranda thought it was time for a talk with her parents. I went to their apartment in a building on the East Side, near the Park, and I sat facing two attractive, tall people, just like their daughter. I could see a younger brother and sister in the back of the apartment who watched me inquisitively, then disappeared. The table was laden with bottles of Dewar's and Cutty Sark, glasses, cookies, and Alfred Thornton Baker III, Miranda's handsome father, was smoking a pipe which he filled with a tobacco I didn't recognize called Walnut, and which I later went on to smoke for many years. The family's good looks, the gentility and aristocracy that emanated from them, made me feel like a crook. We talked. Miranda's mother remained silent most of the time and looked pained, but got over her anger with the help of the whiskey. Miranda's father, who was a senior editor at

Time magazine, did the talking. He was a warmhearted man and he liked me and said that Miranda was a big girl, older than her years, who knew what she wanted, and if she wanted to marry me, he'd give his blessing on condition that we waited eight months, until she turned eighteen. I sat facing them and said that I was Israeli. Jewish. Divorced. Twenty-eight years old. Trying to make a living from frozen falafel and a partnership with one of my friends—Hanoch had left by this time because of a falling out with his brother—in an Israeli café that owed all its profits to a crook by the name of Bernie. I said that I was writing my first book but it wasn't finished yet. I said I knew I wasn't a great catch and what I brought with me wasn't much, but I loved their daughter. It took time. Miranda's mother was badly shaken but tried not to let on. Things changed slowly. Miranda persisted. Gradually they accepted, they had no choice, the fact of our forthcoming marriage, and Miranda's mother said that her mother, Miranda's grandmother, had already demanded that our marriage be annulled, though she had no real authority in this matter, no more than did Miranda's uncle, the giant Moose Morehead who was vice president of Gulf Oil, and had said that he ate "kummus" with Saudi sheiks and how would he explain that his niece was getting married to an Israeli, but, Miranda's mother said, if I wanted I could go with Miranda to her grandmother's because her grandmother loved Miranda very much and at least I'd be able to get some insight into a problem I was getting as a wedding present.

The grandmother lived in Sea Bright, New Jersey, in a not-too-large house between the ocean and the river. Whenever the river rose and flooded this strip of land, she'd be evacuated by helicopter. Sea Bright is a summer resort town, but the old lady lived there throughout the year. She was about five nine, a real beauty with violet eyes. Her hair was tinted blue and she had meticulously trained her three poodles to bark like German shepherds. They were small, irritable, and well groomed. She made a habit of spraying them with fine French eau de cologne. She called her house *Malgré Tout*, which in French means "in spite of it all." Her last husband, or perhaps it was the one before last, had been a peacetime general who like most of the generals of the time didn't know how to shoot and had lived with her for a few years in an American camp in the south of France. She was renowned for her escapades in her youth: for instance, a famous duel was fought because of her between a betrayed lover and a cuckolded husband and had been the talk of the town in Philadelphia, once upon a time. She had had several love affairs in her lifetime and had been ostracized by Philadelphia's high society. And despite the fact that there was a Scots nobleman in her own family tree—Mary Queen of Scots's right-hand man, in fact—she called the Puritans who fled to America in the seventeenth century "riffraff," because her own ancestors, when they came, came as noblemen—not to seek refuge but to reign over the land. When Miranda's mother and aunts got married, the old lady hadn't been allowed to attend the weddings. She was obliged to hide outside the church windows and peek in. Her blend of arrogant nobility and ignorance seemed to be a legacy from several generations' worth of relatives who did nothing but live lives of self-indulgence and alcoholism and tennis and cricket, and then the crash of 1929 pulled the rug out from under them. Her somber cuckolded husband, who owned a distinguished bank, lost everything in a single day, then climbed up his favorite oak tree and shot himself with a gun gripped in white-gloved hands. She kept the ancient pennant of a savage Scottish clan to which she felt kinship in her house in

Sea Bright. She had a French companion living with her, an orphan named Nina, whose huge eyes blinked through the fog in her brain at the woman she worshipped and with whom she lived and of whom she was absolutely terrified. During an angry phone conversation the old woman told Miranda's mother that it was inconceivable for Miranda to marry a Jew. She said—so Miranda's mother told me—that she had never met a Jew in her entire life, and Miranda's mother added that there was no need for me to go out to see her, but I wanted to and someone let us borrow their car so we drove to see the old lady. The windshield wipers struggled heroically against a heavy rain, the road was virtually empty, Miranda sat beside me in silence. I thought about Penn, after whom the state of Pennsylvania is named—Pennsylvania meaning, more or less, "the woods of Penn"—who was one of her ancestors, likewise one of Theodore Roosevelt's wives, who was herself the descendent of Jonathan Edwards, who had been an important philosopher and theologian and had been one of the first presidents of Princeton University, and whose grandson Aaron Burr had been Washington's Vice President, who in turn dueled with and shot dead America's first Secretary of the Treasury, Alexander Hamilton, who was in fact one of Miranda's father's forebears.

The flouncy dogs started barking as we approached and the rain was still beating down. The fog was thick and through its festoons materialized Nina, flickering in the mist, adorned as ever with her beautiful eyes and her perpetual sadness, which stood between us like a second shroud of fog. She waited at the door and asked who we were. Miranda kissed her on the cheek and said, This is Yoram, and Nina who had been reaching to shake my hand pulled hers back in fright and said, So, is that you Miranda? as if she'd never

seen her before, and she felt obliged to ignore me with a coolness
that was quite difficult for her, but her anxiety overwhelmed her
politeness. I was wearing a suit for the second time in my life. I had
borrowed it from Miranda's younger brother, and I wore a tie at the
advice of Miranda's mother. We were shown in and stood shivering
and wet in front of a blazing fireplace. Nina brought a tray with
drinks while the old lady lurked upstairs. We could hear the rustling of her dress up there. She was waiting for the right moment
to make her entrance. Nina was nervous and stared at me in alarm
from the staircase. She apparently knew that she was supposed to
ignore me, but the water dripping from me was the same water that
was dripping from Miranda. The sound of the ocean intensified
outside, becoming a roar and then abating, and at last the old lady
started coming down the stairs. Her enormous conceit was perfectly encapsulated in her staged descent down those stairs, in perfect confidence. Even with her blue hair, she looked like an ancient
Greek goddess of vengeance. Even from the topmost stair, she had
already done everything she could to show me her scorn. Her every
step was angry. Her height was emphasized by a light that shone
directly down upon her. When she reached the bottom step, she
didn't even glance in my direction; she opened her arms and waited
for Miranda to fall into them. She embraced her granddaughter as
you might embrace a recently widowed woman. And after this embrace, she simply stared at Nina who was standing and trembling
and shooting frightened glances at me and the old lady said aloud:
You!—she used a quite correct tone of voice, she must have practiced for hours—you can see how difficult this is for me because
of you. Please wait for me in the morning room, and Nina led me
into a small room overlooking the ocean. Attractive old paintings.

Books bought by the yard. Large windows that seemed to tame the storm. A cabinet and several old armchairs, and a large table with a huge jigsaw puzzle on it. She let me wait for a while and I heard the barking of the dogs outside the door and then she entered. She sat with her better side facing me. She asked me what time it was and I told her that it was twelve noon. And she waited a moment. Then she picked up a small silver bell and tinkled it gently. Nina came in carrying a tray with a bottle of bourbon, a small pitcher of water, and a glass with ice cubes. The old lady mumbled, poured a little water into a glass that she filled with bourbon, and swirled the glass gently so the ice cubes clinked. I looked at her glass and smiled. The great lady turned toward me and looked at me directly for the first time since we arrived. Something in my appearance disturbed her and I could see the furrows on her forehead deepen uncomfortably. She said, But you people don't drink, do you? I said, If you people drink then sometimes we drink too. She gestured with her hand and Nina ran out of the room and I could hear weeping. Nina returned with another glass that had apparently been prepared in advance and mixed bourbon with water without asking me how I liked it. Then the old lady, who had apparently forgotten what she'd said before, grumbled that Jews probably drink first thing in the morning. Silence fell because I didn't respond. She allowed Nina to leave and suddenly rose from her chair, went over to the table with the puzzle, picked up a piece, looked, found a place for it in the appropriate space, looked at me with a sense of triumph, and sat down again. She waited for the right moment and said: I don't understand why a Jew wants to force himself into our family. There's never been a Catholic in the family, let alone a Jew. You're the first Jew I've ever met. She sounded angry and afraid as she said it. Something about me didn't sit well with her expectations. She looked disappointed and drank her bourbon. She leveled a glance at me, an almost personal glance I'd say, and said, You don't look like you should. I told her that perhaps her education as to Jews was lacking and she didn't respond. She began trying to make it obvious that she wasn't listening to me. She began naming the presidents and generals and distinguished people and inventors that her family had been blessed with. She said she was proud of her pedigree. That that sort of thing couldn't be bought with sycophancy or new money. She talked about the ear-locks of ultra-Orthodox Jews and their crooked noses and all the thieves and cheats who were my people and I couldn't believe what I was hearing. She said nothing would help, we'd never be really respectable, that we had no brains or honor or heroes or leaders and now, she said, you're pushing yourselves where you're not wanted. She called Jews "Hebrews" and spoke to me only in the second-person plural. However, there was something off about her performance. I was getting a bit of a kick out of being referred to as "you people," straight out of *The Protocols of the Elders of Zion*, but at the same time she sounded a little embarrassed and wonderstruck. She kept asking if "you people," namely me, if we weren't by any chance French, if we weren't perhaps Frenchmen impersonating Jews? She didn't want me to marry her granddaughter, but if I were French, even a Catholic, she would reconsider, and since I looked French to her, But why are you people trying to infiltrate us, pretending to be Jews? I told her I had to be excused for a moment. She asked me where I thought I was going. I asked her if her bathroom had running water and toilet paper because otherwise I'd have to ask Miranda for some tissues. She tried to get angry, restrained herself, and said of course there was. She was serious. She wasn't going to rise to my banter. In the bathroom I made an effort not to make a sound. I tried to make sure that not a single drop dripped onto the floor. With the tips of my fingers I took some of her soft pink toilet paper and then worried that maybe she'd prefer that I use some other paper just in case she or Miranda had to go in eventually and powder their noses.

When I returned she seemed to be deep in thought. The storm out the windows had intensified and it was raining in sheets. She said that even the Oxford English Dictionary defines the word Jew as thief. You're all thieves. Your Talmud is packed with lies and malice. What would happen if you wanted to drink Miranda's blood on your Jewish Easter? She looked at me again. She couldn't understand where the nose from the illustrations in the Dickens books and the newspapers she had seen all her life had disappeared to. I was supposed to have a dirty straggly beard, a crooked nose all the way to my mouth, but I didn't. At last she said, And where's the nose? She said, Your Talmud is packed with agitation against Christians. She said that her best friend, Mr. Freedley, who produced the *Ziegfeld Follies* and was an aristocrat and an honest man, was going to send his Rolls-Royce for her to take her to New York to buy clothes, but not in the New York of the Jews; not the New York where Miranda's parents lived with the Communists and the Jews. She'd spend a few days with Freedley, he always knew how to make a woman feel like a lady. The last of the great cavaliers in America is courting me and yet here you people come wanting to marry my rare flower, my Miranda. I sensed her defeat long before she herself sensed it. She was already actually looking at me every time she addressed me. She admitted sadly that she liked me. That was why she suddenly told me about Mr. Freedley, because he was supposed to protect her from the truth she saw on my face with her own eyes that wanted to be strong and had now become weak. She no longer spoke so passionately about her hatred of "you people." Hatred was apparently the only intellectual virtue she had been blessed with. She waited for me to say something. I decided not to speak, not yet. I wanted to hear more from her. She asked how I intended to support Miranda and I told her that I was a partner in a factory for frozen falafel. I wanted to help her and told her that I was twenty-eight and divorced, that I was a man of no means, but like all Jews I was sure to get a windfall from one shady business or another. I thought that the frozen falafel would be sufficiently rare and mysterious for her. It was apparent that she was trying to understand what frozen falafel was without revealing her curiosity. She said, You know very well how to cheat the innocent. I saw the contempt oozing out of her eyes, you could have seen it from miles away. She didn't want to waste any emotion on me, but she was legitimately concerned. She suffered in silence and drank more bourbon and again forgot to offer me some. When I started talking about my future as an author I saw that she viewed this in much the same way as she would smallpox or tuberculosis. She sounded concerned over the fate of her family's chromosomes; that I had come, so she said, to pollute them. She used the most dreadful words in a kind of tranquility coupled with disinterest. She looked at me and wondered, I could tell by the furrows on her forehead, which she wanted so badly to keep smooth, that she knew—just knew—that I was misleading her. She looked as though she were singlehandedly trying to foil a Jewish conspiracy aimed at her family, and even hinted that that heathen and rapacious Rothschild might be involved.

I was surprised at how little she annoyed me. She didn't get any-where near the place inside me where I'm an angry Jew, my grand-father's grandson. I was having fun. I was young. I could see that, unwillingly, and despite her meticulous planning, she was liking me more and more. She went on drinking and her look softened. We stood up and went to the bell room where we joined Miranda and where Nina was nervously waiting for us next to the gong to call us in for lunch. What the grandmother actually wanted was for me to fall in love with her like all the men in her life. All her dread-ful words about the inferior Jewish race, those Jews who trample over decent people and drink all the time and take revenge against good Christians and then run back to their ghettos, about how the Jewish character was irrevocably twisted—despite these words, or perhaps because of them, she wanted to steal me away from her granddaughter. It was all she knew how to do. Throughout her life she had stolen men's hearts left and right and then stranded her suitors at the starting line; they seldom if ever really caught her. What she had learned in the enormous house on Chestnut Hill in Philadelphia up to the age of seventeen was all she had at her dis-posal for the rest of her life. That was it. She'd learned nothing since. The loathing she felt toward me was too abstract for it to touch me. I had to leave revenge to luck. I thought, "Luck be a Lady Tonight." I wasn't sufficiently angry to know so early on how to get her back. She fought with a pathetic, ancient enthusiasm, like seltzer that had lost its bubbles. The bourbon also did its part to slow her down. She waited for the gong and Nina rang it and then we went into another room to eat lunch. She looked tired and sleepy as we started eating. Nina served eagerly. After making a huge effort to finish the meal Miranda's grandmother stood up and went upstairs, saying that she had to rest. Miranda and I went out into the storm and were swallowed up into it. At dinner, for which she changed her dress, she drank coffee and wanted to know about my family. There was a seductive tone in her voice now. Her eyes were veiled. After a few more words about the inferior Jewish race, I said I was a descendant of Joseph. She asked who Joseph was. I told her he was Jesus's father. She stifled a shriek of alarm and said, Yes, yes, and added that due to the distress I was causing her she would have to watch some television. I don't watch television very much but this evening it's important, she said in a bracing voice. I already knew before we came, from Miranda's mother, that the old lady was addicted to Scrabble and television. I told her that Miranda and I would join her. She yielded with disinterested dignity. She went upstairs with restrained enthusiasm. She switched on the television and watched her first program. She stole a glance toward Miranda and suddenly appeared childlike. It was the *Jack Benny Show*. She immediately laughed because she remembered what had happened at the end of the show the previous week, and told us all about it. And then she stared at me in contempt. The program gave her strength. Benny was a real person, not like me. Shedding all the Jewish problems she'd been having that day, she said, I'm crazy about him, just wait until he plays the violin. I waited a moment and said, Yes, he really is a wonderful Jew. Her face caved in a kind of twitch and she wanted to protest, but I could see that she was running out of weapons to use against me—though her anger reinvigorated her. She waited for the next program. This one was with Danny Kaye, who was her favorite, so she said, and then on another channel they were showing *The Postman Always Rings Twice*, with the magnificent John Garfield, as she called him, and then we went on to watch a program about the man she called her genius, Gershwin, and then a short movie with Tony Curtis, something with Lauren Bacall, an old Josef von Sternberg film, and then a late-night conversation with Irving Berlin, as she flicked from channel to channel (though there were only three in those days); hours passed, she gradually wilted like a flower in the hot sun, and I didn't show her any mercy: a Jewish God had gone into battle this night to destroy a poor woman. It hurt me and it hurt Miranda, but I was caught up in the battle: it wasn't me who was fighting, the Good Lord spared me that, no, it was Melvyn Douglas and Phil Silvers and Sid Caesar, and she drank one glass after another. She reeled again and again from the impact of my words, "Also a Jew." Kirk Douglas was beneath the belt, as was Eddie Fisher. She sat defeated and stunned. And then, late at night, in her defeat, she suddenly looked cheerful—though the bourbon made her cheerfulness somewhat melancholy. I knew what she was waiting for. I had looked through the *TV Guide* while she waited to ambush me. There was a sad smile on her face. She smoked one cigarette after another, her blue hair speckled with light from the wall lamp, and Miranda fell asleep. Nina also fell asleep. Three of us remained—Miranda's grandmother, me, and the God of Israel. We sat tensely. Waiting for the last movie of the night. Then, at one o'clock in the morning, hours past the time she was accustomed to retiring, the movie she was waiting for was finally shown: *The Scarlet Pimpernel* with Leslie Howard. She wanted Leslie Howard on her side, you see, more English than the English, more British than the British, she needed him for one victory over my loathsome race, she needed him in order to vanquish me. She said, Look at the funny Englishman. Charming. Witty. Astute. Elegant. Athletic. He was her lifeline. Her last chance. And she said in a tone saturated with compassion, Now you can't possibly tell me that *he* . . . but I silenced her with a laugh. The blow had to be a painful one. I waited for the right moment, I didn't want her smile to vanish at once, I wanted to see blood, and then I drew out the words, Leslie Howard *Steiner*, that's right, his mother's English, but Jewish, and his father's a Jew from Hungary. And then the old lady burst out laughing too and Nina woke up and rushed out to fetch a glass of cold water. She switched off the television. I told her that the name Leslie comes from Laszlo and he was a distant relative of my mother's. He wasn't really, but I wanted to have a personal stake in the old woman's defeat. Now, her deep sorrow was without anger. She stood up, stretched her body, and slowly and proudly went to her room. All her beloveds were Jews. One cold night the God of the Jews who hadn't defeated Hitler managed to defeat Mrs. Anderson Elliott Brooke in Sea Bright, New Jersey. Now she is sitting in Heaven with all her beloved Jews, singing all the songs she loved so much and that were written for her by Jews. With her ancient ignorance, where else could she have gone? God probably treats her like an honored prisoner of war.

For our wedding she sent the most expensive gifts. We went to visit her. She invited us to her swimming club that refused entrance, so she said, to Grace Kelly because she was Catholic, and I swam with people who all had green-blue eyes and straw-colored hair and looked alike. She was happy that her Jew had sullied the water. Miranda swam deep in the nearby ocean and a shark came near and I yelled and she didn't hear me and then she saw the fin and like a fish she darted to the shore. Some time later the old lady decided to go and visit one of her daughters in Switzerland. She asked us to come and see her off. She was sitting in a huge first-class cabin on the *United States* when we arrived. She was drinking whiskey and on one side of the room there were piles of toilet paper, hundreds of rolls, and bourbon whiskey and paper towels. She was going to visit her daughter, the sister of my wife's mother, who had married a Swiss nobleman and lived in an eighteenth-century palace with forty rooms and a huge garden. The Swiss nobleman owned Novartis, I heard, who manufactured Ovaltine and drugs. Miranda's grandmother told me she didn't trust those "foreigners." And when we moved to Israel in 1961 she sent us kerosene lamps and dozens of rolls of toilet paper and bars of soap. She wrote to Miranda that one should be careful when riding on a camel because someone had told her that camels could be dangerous.

Miranda and I got to know one another and it was cold but in the apartment it was nice and warm. Marzani came over and was sad because Stalin, the Sun of the Nations, was dead. Like a baby, he tried once again to explain how wonderful it would be in the world of the future, and I said some nasty things about the peace movement supporting the great murderer and he smiled at me in pity and forgave my impatience and we toasted him with vodka. And things were sad at the Cellar. People still came. They celebrated Purim and yelled. But the money went to Bernie. There was nothing left. The frozen falafel had died. I wanted us to sell the place but Oved insisted on going on until we'd finished paying back our debt and so I left. Before that, at Christmas, I was drinking there on my own. Oved and Hanoch were off drinking in some club.

I called Miranda and told her I was sad on my own. She came at one o'clock in the morning. I drank beer and we talked and looked at one another and it was only later, after spending Christmas Eve with her family, that I found out that she had been compelled that night to practice a deception for the first and last time in her life.

She had left a doll in her bed, under the covers, and her sister had promised to cover for her, and since she didn't have money for a bus she walked across Central Park in the cold in the middle of the night. In my mind's eye I saw a young woman walking in the dark among drunks and criminals and not knowing it. That part of life passes right over her, perhaps her senses understood but it didn't get inside her, and I was touched but didn't know how to say it right. Perhaps I was testing her. And then the betting started. Everyone knew that we would be getting married soon and so our friends tried to make some money off it. Our best friends said that we'd last a month to six weeks. Some went up to three months. The bets ranged between ten dollars and twenty. One guy, an amusing and assertive redhead from Rishon LeZion, collected all the money and handed out receipts. Two people went as far as four months, but even for the closest of our friends it was hard to imagine us lasting as long as six. Oved gave in and was planning to sell the Cellar. The wedding drew near and when it took place it was a simple affair. We got married in a charming room at a family friend's, surrounded by a respectable collection of Wyeth and O'Keeffe paintings and a painting of a boat at sea by Ryder and above us a dome-shaped ceiling that had been painted by an Italian painter whose name I wasn't familiar with. I wore a suit and tie. Miranda wore the wedding dress her mother had worn when she got married and together we wrote additional lines to append to the formal New York City ceremony, we quoted from the Book of Ruth, chapter one, verses sixteen and seventeen: "For whither thou goest, I will go; and where thou lodgest, I will lodge; thy people shall be my people, and thy God my God; where thou diest, will I die, and there will I be buried; the Lord do so to me, and more also, if aught but death part thee and me." After the short ceremony we all posed for a family photograph. Miranda and I stood in front and she was only half a head taller than me. Her twelve-year-old brother stood next to her, a little less than a head above me. And of the elegant grandmothers, one was slightly taller than me, while the other, adorned with her blue hair—the one with all her Jews—towered above me. And then there were the father and mother and several uncles, the shortest of whom was five eleven, and Uncle Moose Morehead of Gulf Oil—who didn't know what he'd say to his sheiks in Saudi Arabia when he ate "kummus" with them—over six feet tall. The photograph looks like a badly planned city. All the proportions are off. Oved, who was my best man, is almost six feet tall, and only Miranda's sister, who was fifteen at the time, was more-or-less my height, but stood far away from me and so gave me no support. Afterward there was a party and there was lots of laughing and singing and lots of drinking and then Miranda and her father danced the waltz. They danced together like the notes from some heavy sonata. Their arms courted each other. They touched yet didn't touch, they hovered, everyone stopped dancing and watched them, and a silent circle formed, and only the music could be heard and they watched a father and daughter in a final moment of ceremonial ownership celebrated in absolute blindness to its significance. He didn't lose her and she didn't lose him, but the ceremony demanded attention to something that was not only in the blood but also in their emotions. The only person who really understood this woman was him, her father, and I, after forty-three years together, have yet to attain anything close to his understanding. Father and daughter danced as though they were blind to all who were staring at them and they sometimes deviated from the beat and the steps had to search for them, but I remembered the prayer for the Jewish New Year: "The stone which the builders rejected is become the chief cornerstone." Their cornerstone and mine would be used to build a tower that would become a building of healing, fear, meaning: "God loves you," as Miranda's devoutly Christian brother would later say to me. Here there were two gods: this handsome, tall man, a little hesitant and drunk, with the strapping body of an officer who served two years on a warship in the Pacific, dancing like a Native Indian who'd studied Mozart, and Miranda, who went to her parents' house for an hour in the evening, though I guess it was already night and not evening, I sat and read the Bible and realized that I wanted a daughter, that I wanted to plant a tree and die.

Next day somebody lent us a car, we left on our honeymoon, we heard police sirens, we pulled over. They dragged us out of the car. They were rough. They wouldn't listen to us. They shoved us against the car and handcuffed us and Miranda tried to raise her head and they pushed her back against the hood. They switched off the engine. They began firing questions at us in harsh voices. Now and again they roughed me up a bit more and laughed and laughed again. I started shouting that she was the daughter of one of *Time* magazine's editors and they didn't listen, and in the end they shouted into their radio, or at us, or at the pines along that beautiful road, and the officer with them came over and said, *Time* magazine? What's the name? I told him. He asked who died yesterday. I said we'd been married yesterday. More shouting: If it's *Time* magazine then who died yesterday? We didn't know. In the end, their hands got tired, they were worn out from shouting and they radioed to someplace and from there they contacted Miranda's father and we were released without explanation. Take off, they said, and we did. We called Miranda's father who said that, yes, Ed Cerf, a dear friend of his had died. He had committed suicide on the morning of our wedding and Miranda's father hadn't wanted to spoil Miranda's day.

And around then a photographer named Bezalel turned up. He wanted to work in New York. I found another painting of mine at a friend's who didn't want it any longer and I sold it to a stubborn collector who believed I'd go back to painting and with the money I bought a Hasselblad camera. We rented a studio on Fourteenth Street. We decorated it. As I knew nothing about photography we decided that I'd be the second cameraman and artistic director and he'd be the photographer. We made phone calls all over. Two or three people came along to see our portfolios, somebody commissioned a photograph for a Manischewitz wine ad. We did a publicity photograph for a hernia truss. A heavily bearded Jew asked for a nice poster of the Lubavitcher Rebbe's maxims. A girl came along who wanted to get—cheap—a model portfolio. There were a few more customers, but there was no real money in it. Expenses were high. I dreamed of an artistic and commercial photography studio, I wrote letters, but zilch. Then Miranda's father wanted a piece on the architectural standards of New England. He said that there were basically a limited number of building archetypes. He wanted to do an article for *Life*. We were given an advance and off we went, Miranda, Bezalel, and me. Two or three weeks in New England. It was June. The trees were in full leaf. The air was heady and astonishing. We drove through Massachusetts along side roads until we came to typical-looking wooden buildings and Bezalel photographed them. We reached a small town in New Hampshire. We stopped at a diner. We had lamb chops and people in hats and checked shirts came in and said hi to everyone and sat down. Somebody came over and talked to us. Another played an Eddie Fisher record on the jukebox and a hundred-year-old waitress danced with a man who had arrived on a green John Deere tractor and asked us amiably what we were looking for and said maybe he could help us. We told him. Leave your car here, he said, and come with me. He brought over a pickup truck with huge wheels and we drove along dirt roads and passed farms and silos until we reached a line of hills and a long avenue of margosa trees that ended in a kind of flower-bedecked crater: an old cemetery and a winding road that went up a hill. Facing us, on the green hill divided by a line of oaks, we saw a secluded house. We stood about seventy yards from this beautiful, classical building and the man yelled and a tall pale man in a rumpled suit came out. Our man had brought a flashlight and he took it out now. He flashed a signal at the man in the doorway and the man on the hill returned the signal with a flashlight of his own. They communicated in this way for about ten minutes. Our guy said that the man had said we could come up and take photographs but had asked us not to talk to him. I asked why and he said that the guy's name was Stanley Webb and once he'd been driving too fast in his car and had seen two children and he'd yelled to them to get out of the way and they'd panicked and run in the wrong direction and he'd tried to stop but he ran them down and killed them and it had happened twenty years ago and since then he hadn't spoken to anyone and didn't want to hear anyone speak. We went into the house and without a word he offered us fruit juice. The house was empty of pictures and there were antique furnishings and a mahogany staircase and we took photographs from every angle and tried to say thank you and the man pointed to the wall on which was written: "Love! Go!" We went back to town and stayed at a motel and then continued through that land of rivers and forests and isolated houses and small old towns in which nothing had changed in centuries except for power lines and TV antennas. We enjoyed the simple monotonous New England food. Butter that was almost red. Cheese from heifers and cream that you could stick a spoon into and the spoon would stand upright, and sharp Cheddar cheese, and we saw deer, and at night we saw foxes and we drove to Vermont and then Maine along the coastline dotted with bays and fishing boats and my friend took photographs, I found the houses, Miranda knew exactly what her father was looking for, we did a catalogue of New England's wooden houses. We were invited to stay at farmhouses and we found small hotels near colleges with huge gardens, wooden buildings everywhere, white and a few yellow ones too. Porches. Varicolored roofs.

We went back to New York and found that Sandy and Steve had disappeared. I'd tried to find Gandy in Vermont but without success. Avi Shoes had vanished and so had Mira. Oved had gone to Los Angeles with Carole to get married and travel for forty years between Mexico, Los Angeles, Guatemala, Honduras, what was later called Belize that I once visited before it became Belize, and even Peru. Hanoch had gone back to Israel. There was no money. I wrote a new version of the book that wasn't to be, *Hughie and the Dog*, and I ran into Jerry Tallmer who invited me to a small party and I met a lawyer there who was representing somebody who'd opened a restaurant and bar and was looking for a bartender and I said I'd worked for a year in the Cellar and I had experience and he didn't ask if I was a certified bartender but his mother was an devoted Zionist and next day I was introduced to one of the two owners who was one of the last people around who really believed in Israel and

Israelis and he took me on to work the bar on Madison Avenue, and I started work as though I really knew all about it. For a few days at home I'd studied books on how to make drinks and when I got there they wondered how I knew so much, and I said I was a pro and after a few days of experience that I came through with flying colors thanks entirely to luck, I went to take the test to get my bartending license, and found myself facing four Irishmen. They were sitting with their hands folded on their vast bellies and said, Kid, make a martini. I was surprised, because I'd got myself ready for all the usual crazy crap, all the weird names like "Moscow Mule." But one of the Irishmen, who barely spoke at all—the rest didn't say a single word, with what appeared to be moral fortitude—asked, Has the young gentleman ever been to Paris? Yes, I replied. Paris, France? Yes. Does Paris, France have the most important restaurants in the world? Yes. And who prepares the food? Chefs. And how do they test a chef there? I didn't know. The Irishman said, You were in Paris and you don't know? I'm sorry, I said, but no. He said, They don't test them on all the dishes you can learn from books. They test them on an omelet. If you can make a good omelet, with soul, you'll be a good chef. Now mix a martini. I mixed a martini. They said I had an innate talent and embraced me and gave me a license to be a professional bartender in the City of New York in the State of New York in the United States of America. I went back to the restaurant and apparently I knew how to mix a superior martini. There were two of us, me behind the bar and Big Charles in the kitchen.

He was very black and thought about me for two days and finally came to the conclusion that I was a real crook and a man after his own heart. He said he'd learned to cook in the navy. He said he'd served on an aircraft carrier as the assistant cook's assistant. The chief cook had taken ill. The assistant was drunk and there were hundreds of hungry sailors, they were at sea and trying out new anti-aircraft guns, and he was told that there was no alternative and he'd have to do it and he should just work out of the ship's cookbook. So what was for dinner on Tuesdays? He read: One thousand ounces of red meat. Two thousand onions. A barrel of cooking oil. Five hundred ounces of peas. Make gravy with the roast meat. With his assistants he peeled one thousand five hundred potatoes. He took fifty bottles of gravy with the picture of the naked woman on them, mixed it in with the meat, and then read: Add a pinch of salt. Five hundred sailors and two hundred technicians and another hundred and fifty men sat down. The pilots ate in their own mess. The officers in theirs. And they ate hundreds of pounds of well-cooked food with one pinch of salt for everybody. It was almost the end of Big Charles. But he had magical hands and was a quick study and he began cooking from his soul, where a good cook keeps his food, and he was forgiven and after the Korean War he came home and wanted to work in a restaurant and he had certificates but he was black and how could a black cook white food, and he met the restaurant's two owners, one a wannabe author and the other a wannabe politician, and they hired him and now everybody knew where to find the best hamburgers in town. From the word go he knew I was the sucker he'd been waiting for and maybe I'd passed a test but you also have to know something about a pinch of salt. For the price of a shot of bourbon or Kentucky sour mash he would teach me how to mix every cocktail in the world. The customer would order something, I'd lean over toward Big Charles, he'd tell me what and how and I'd serve the drink and give Big Charles a shot of bourbon.

In the kitchen next to the bar there was a huge stove. On it was an enormous iron skillet and underneath some knobs that Big Charles had invented and installed. On the left-hand side the heat was slightly lower than in the middle or on the right, where the heat was fierce, and Charles twiddled the knobs like an artist, raising and lowering the heat and at any given moment about a dozen steaks were sizzling simultaneously in varying stages of broiling. Charles spread his wonderful sauce all over and caressed fifteen hamburgers with a brush dipped in egg white and he'd have ten omelets going too. He'd shove bacon over the low flame and at his side was a metal basket he filled with chipped potatoes frying over a low flame, and he bent over and looked at them and refilled and his sauce was top secret and he guarded it with his life. He'd spread his spices by touch and knew each of the hamburgers and steaks and bacon strips by their size. They all danced to his baton, leaping, landing, that one's thin, that's well done, that's medium, that's rare, each one needed its own time, its own treatment, a fried filet steak needed to get this much time while being flipped over and over and hamburgers without cheese needed to get that much time, and if cheese was needed he'd add it, and everything happened at the same time, the potatoes hissing quietly, he was focused, smiling as he worked, he loved every hamburger he cooked and each perfect omelet and every steak and they all came out just right. Big Charles had a real craving for beauty, he noticed if a hamburger was changing shape and he'd flatten it, straighten it, add more egg white, move it left of right, he danced his creations around like a puppeteer maneuvers his creations and he'd produce broiled and fried masterpieces. He knows every order personally, said Verity the beautiful waitress, he remembers every detail, and sometimes he'd throw a steak up into the air and before it came down would flip a frying egg to get a perfect over easy. One of his greatest talents was making triangular omelets. There was no chef like him in town. As the meats danced he'd fold an omelet into a perfect equilateral triangle and study it, correct it, while the rest of his children jumped and sizzled. He didn't look as if he was working. He smiled his lovely smile, give me a recipe for a cocktail, quickly gulp his drink, his shirt and apron as white as the driven snow. He looked like the conductor of an orchestra whose musicians were constantly changing, and he went on conducting, orchestra after orchestra, with the greatest respect for each and every member. I called him the Toscanini of the grill. And the best waitress we had was Pat Bosworth who was a professional and worked with total seriousness though sometimes joined our table when we sat drinking after closing time. She was an actress who'd recently played a leading role on Broadway, the show had closed, she had to make a living so she became a waitress. Together with her twin sister Kate she'd been in a movie, *A Stolen Life*, in which she played Bette Davis . . . unless I have that backward. She later wrote biographies of Montgomery Clift and Marlon Brando. It was a surprise to me that such an important actress was willing to wait on tables, because in Israel such a thing would have been unthinkable. One night we were particularly busy. We both worked very hard. There were college students trying to impress their girl-friends with their knowledge of drinks and they'd gotten some dazzling, long-forgotten cocktail names from their grandfathers—or books by O'Hara or Fitzgerald or the Algonquin Round Table gossips—long-forgotten, but which a professional bartender had to know, and despite the rush Big Charles shouted: Rye with lemon, a drop of Granier, the purple one, not the pink, and a pinch of sugar.

A dash of raspberry cordial and orange zest. I did it. In the mean-time I'd learned a lot. I'd hear somebody order a Black Label. Black Label was expensive. As in every bar the owner kept a case of cheap whiskey under the bar. You would use it if the guy who'd ordered didn't look like he really knew what he was doing—which was most of them. Then you'd pour the whiskey below bar level and say it was Black Label and the young man would smile at his girlfriend and I could see how excited she was that he knew exactly what Black Label was and she would put her hand on his. Actually, we did it with most name whiskeys. And I almost never heard anyone say, for example, Hey, this isn't Beefeater. But once there was one guy, an older man I didn't know, he was on his own, annoyed. He asked for a J&B, I gave him the cheap stuff, he rolled it round his mouth, pulled a face, and said, Come on, throw that shit away and give me the real stuff. I pulled out the bottle of J&B so he could see it, apolo-gized, and poured him a shot, and he said, Don't apologize, you've got to do it. I was a bartender in a whorehouse, I know whores and bartenders, they're are the same thing really, and thanks. There were some guys that even from across the room I knew would order Jack Daniels or Chivas Regal or Johnny Walker, which I'd taught Big Charles to call *Johnny Ha'Mehalech* in Hebrew and he pronounced it perfectly just like everything else he did. Then another waitress by the name of Melinda told me that it seemed to her that I'd found my vocation, found myself, the meaning of my existence; at the time she was taking courses on self-realization and said, It's like you have no yesterday and no today and no tomorrow and no death and no life, everything flows, she said, your eyes are fixed on the drink and you're flying into it as though it's a sculpture but your flight has turned it into a sculpture and not the other way round. I was happy.

The usual drinkers sat hunched over the bar and told jokes about me. Or cried. Or grumbled. There was nowhere to run from or to. The place was a sealed off universe. Most or the customers were regulars. They were looking for warmth. Looking for a home. We gave it to them. Big Charles and his skills and the skills I'd acquired were the core of their lives. It was an eternal moment. The farthest thing from the cemetery. Winter had already come. It was cold. Snow fell. Miranda announced she was pregnant. I waited for a daughter I'd call Chamoutal. Miranda said that was fine. I didn't have a name for a son. In the daytime we'd walk after I'd slept. We had visitors. We went visiting. I missed my old friends, but they had gone. Each to his or her own remote corner. There was one cold evening and snow had started to fall. Big Charles and I were getting the restaurant ready. I did the bar, sliced lemons and limes, cleaned the shakers, wiped glasses, cleaned the countertop, put out plates of snacks and appetizers, made jugs of orange juice and tomato juice, and Charles cleaned the kitchen thoroughly, the Puerto Rican busboy had finished and we helped him arrange the tables and chairs. As he did every evening, Charles locked the kitchen door and prepared his secret sauce, and then opened the door with his usual apologetic look. It's okay Charles, I said, have a drink. The waitresses hadn't arrived yet and Dick Haven the crook, who played Gangster C or D in movies, and who came in every evening, called as usual to say he'd be coming and we should save him a seat, as if he didn't know that his seat was as safe as Fort Knox, and through the window we could see a thin layer of snow spreading over the street.

A big white Lincoln pulled up outside the restaurant. A tall broad-shouldered black guy got out. He stopped to look up and down the street and his upper body was inclined forward with a gentle carelessness. He was wearing a white suit and a bow tie. He looked a little heavy but he sailed inside. He sat at the bar I'd just finished cleaning and looked at me with a smile. I looked back. White boy, he said, give me a boilermaker, I asked him what whiskey he'd like and he said, Old Crow. Right, I said. White boy, he said, you know of course that it's a double? I said I'd worked at Minton's Playhouse. He asked, Did you know Art Blakey? I said I'd heard him but I didn't know him personally. Pity, he said, a great musician. The man had a little gray in his sideburns and his smile was that of a young boy. He wanted me to lean closer to him. Charles was busy preparing hamburgers and slicing steaks in the kitchen. The man asked me to move up very close to him and whispered, That's far enough, not too close. I began pouring his double bourbon and opened a can of beer and was about to serve it to him and he said, No. I want it here, I want it here at this crappy bar, I want thirteen doubles in line like fucking soldiers. And thirteen cans of Tuborg beer even if they get warm, and you just open each one the moment I finish the last. I said I was worried because it was an awful lot, and he said, Listen, cute Minton's boy, you just worry about your mama, I'm the customer here. You think you're a wise-guy but you're not. You do exactly what I tell you and leave the prophecies to Walter Cronkite or Moondog. I asked whatever happened to Moondog who used to walk the Village like a prehistoric seer, and he said he wasn't an information desk and asked if I understood him or not. Not eleven, he said, not twelve, thirteen doubles and thirteen beers, *capice*? So I stood the doubles in a line. Altogether there were twenty-six shots: that equaled a fifth, which is a standard bottle. The man sipped with a kind of blithe indifference and took the beer I served him and chased the whiskey down his throat and his Adam's apple jiggled slightly but he didn't move a muscle and didn't make a sound, he just smiled at me in a friendly way, he realized I was watching him and gestured for another. At the fifth, Charles, who had been watching with no real interest, came out of the kitchen and stood in the doorway. At the sixth I could see a look of disbelief on Charles's face, He whispered, The guy's cheating. He sounded threatened and angry. After the ninth—the guy was putting them down one after another at intervals of less than a couple of minutes—I could see an expression of admiration being etched on Big Charles's face. He whispered, This motherfucker's a king, he's sticking it to all the white boys. The guy didn't move. He didn't turn his head. He didn't wipe the moisture from his mouth because there was no moisture on his mouth. His lips even dried the tiny tears of a foaming beer after it had been standing open for a few minutes. He almost swallowed the big glasses. He drank to a certain rhythm, a rhythm I'd heard about from Charlie Parker, the syncopation, the phrasing, and when I gave him a beer he poured it into a big glass, shook it, and downed it in one. Never in two swallows. I saw how he kept a little whiskey in his mouth for the next beer and then how the swish of beer down his throat must have blazed its trail. His Adam's apple always bobbed up and down at the same pace, but gently. I'd be waiting with the next beer in my hand. He'd roll the whiskey in, take the beer, smile his thanks, and drink. And something cracked in Big Charles. The guy facing me didn't get up from his stool, didn't chew potato chips, didn't chew the thin carrot sticks I'd prepared earlier. He didn't swallow almonds or peanuts from the dishes on the bar. He didn't get up to go to the bathroom, not even after the ninth beer. Not even after the tenth. Not even after the eleventh. He drank thirteen boilermakers as if he'd been walking through the desert for a week. By this time Charles was in love, but also anxious. But mainly he was happy. I'd never seen him so happy. His face glowed. His tongue was hanging out. The guy finished his twelfth and picked his last one, stopped for a moment, drank, smiled at me, asked me to show him the bottle, I showed it to him, empty, he saw it and said, The bottle's gone. And how it's gone, I replied. Charles growled. The guy gave him a friendly glance, like a king to a loyal subject, and said, Stick your nigger tongue back in your mouth. A nigger doesn't stand with his tongue hanging out it front of white trash. He got up as if nothing had happened. He asked for his tab, paid, gave me a big tip, and I said, No! No! Shut up, he said, when a nigger gives you a tip, you take it. He started to leave. There were three steps at the entrance and he climbed them with a strong, steady gait. He stood at the door. He looked like a statue. The snow was now falling heavily. It was windy. He put on the heavy coat he'd kept on his knee while he was drinking and stepped lightly into the white Lincoln that was covered with snow. He yelled: Hey! White on white! You were an artist, weren't you? I asked, How did you know? I was told, he said. He started the engine and Charles said, He drank like it was a commandment, or a punishment. I could hear boundless loyalty in his voice. We looked at the man in the car. He drove straight through the thin slippery snow without skidding. Charles prayed that everything would be okay. Now he'd found a hero, he didn't want him to fail. He said, Just as long as he drives like he hasn't been drinking. I understood him, and complimented the guy—he'd stopped at the first red light. We waited. The light changed and he took off without skidding. When he was out of sight we went back inside. Charles looked depressed and happy at the same time. He checked the empty glasses. He bent down, picked up the beer cans, and counted them. He tipped them up to see if there were a few drops left, but there weren't any. He even checked the cash register to see whether the guy had really paid for thirteen "Killers," as he called them. Even then he didn't really believe it. He tried to find a flaw. A trick. Are you sure he didn't go to the bathroom? I said I was sure. He didn't move? I asked how he'd known to ask about the painting in the museum, the white on white, and how he'd known I'd been an artist. Charles said that anybody who can drink thirteen boilermakers knows everything. Just think, a guy sits here for maybe an hour, it's snowing outside, he's got a white Lincoln, a Brooks Brothers suit that costs thousands of dollars, the hands of a boxer and a mama's sweet face, a bottle of Old Crow, thirteen beers, thirteen strong Tuborgs, and then the king gets in his car as if nothing's happened.

I'd hear later that Charles had married a Danish girl and opened a bar in Copenhagen called Thirteen Boilermakers. I met him by chance in the Queen's Bar in the King Frederik Hotel in Copenhagen and he was glad to see me, and the first thing he asked was, Do you remember that sonofabitch?

We sat down, the waitress brought a Polish vodka for me and bourbon for him, and Tuborg beers—we were in their motherland—and draft too, and Charles downed the draft beer, talking about the great hero of our time, the hero of his life with his thirteen boilermakers and he drank another and I sat there silently, enthralled, and Charles lauded that black king and went on drinking and talking about his wife, a beautiful Dane, he said his children were like half-and-half cream. Big Charles had become an important man in Copenhagen. But he hadn't forgotten that guy. All around there were blonde Danish girls, it was snowing outside and dark in the middle of the day. We were both in a strange city. People were licking the sidewalk to clean their tongues. Everything was aesthetic and sad. A country that was a kiss without lips, and when he talked about his hero his eyes lit up. I suddenly noticed something and then I said to him—though in mid-sentence knew I shouldn't have said it, but I'd already started—You've just drunk thirteen boilermakers, Charles. He looked at me maliciously for a long moment. He got up. He called the waitress over and asked how much he'd drunk. Tell him. His face was burning with rage. The waitress wasn't surprised at any of this, because the last time anybody was surprised in Denmark was in the sixteenth century when the Swedes had staged a sneak attack from the sea. Big Charles looked miserable. Defeated. He had lost the hero of his life. He ordered another, drank it, got up, gave me an angry, pained look and said, You people like to kill heroes, Jesus, the Son of God, you didn't want Him so you killed Him. What exactly did you want? He waved and left. I could see tears in his eyes. From the doorway he said, Don't try coming to see me again, don't even run into me by accident. After that I never saw Big Charles again.

But in the meantime I was still working the bar and Charles was with me, and I was writing my book and found Ziva Shapiro and gave it to her for translation and with Miranda we met Norman Mailer who I'd once known, an angry and funny man, who when he'd asked me to read him a chapter of *The Naked and the Dead* in Hebrew—I'd asked for it to be sent from Israel, and the book arrived, and I read for him—he wept and said, A book about those things you read in the language of prayers? At the time he had a tall black poodle bitch that had had two black pups whose tails he refused to dock on principle. The bitch pup was big. He asked if we wanted it but only on condition that we wouldn't dock its tail. I think it was then that his wars with the world and his wife Adele began, his wife who he stabbed but she hadn't died, and I loved the dog at first sight. She didn't behave like a poodle, she didn't know she *was* a poodle. She was independent, determined, stubborn but soft as butter when she was treated with love. And she was loved and she loved back. I walked her in the park at the end of Eighty-seventh Street by the river and let her run free. She took her place in our life. She sometimes slept with us. She'd express herself force-fully and gently and was a member of the family. One night heavy snow began to fall. It fell quickly and in thirty minutes the streets were covered. The restaurant was full. People were afraid to go out into the freezing cold. We all had a drink together, the beautiful waitresses and Big Charles and me and one of the owners, the wan-nabe author. Snowdrifts began forming. All the regulars lived in the neighborhood. There was a moment when driving was still possible and they ran to catch buses and jump into their cars and left. The wannabe author lived opposite and asked us to close up and make sure everything was locked. Suddenly there were only six of us left, three waitresses and three drinkers. Big Charles managed to catch the last subway. To get home I had to cross to the West Side through the Park. Forget it. No vehicles could get through. Madison Avenue looked like a vast cemetery of snowed-in cars and buses. A horse-drawn carriage appeared from the Plaza Hotel. Kitschy. The horse walked slowly and a cloud of heat emanated from it and the driver offered to take us home for a decent price. It was a big day for car-riages; they covered the entire city to remind its denizens of the difference between a horse and a car. We got in and drove off. The snow was so deep that the horses struggled, but they managed to get through. It was cold but it was nice to drive through a city whose modes of transportation had all died and in a horse-drawn carriage with its tinkling bells. Cars were stuck and locked. Here and there we saw someone trying to drive and getting stuck deeper in the incessant snow. Buses stood silent and the driver brought me home and Delilah the dog who'd been named by Norman Mailer—he asked us to keep the name, not just the tail—barked joyfully when she smelled me from the street. She had become part of our life. In a dream she'd lie at my side and I'd kiss her eyes, which studied me intently. I talked to her. She loved us and would smile showing her back gums. She was absolutely loyal and on numerous occasions she slept between Miranda and me and I remembered how Oved used to kiss cows, there was warmth and sweetness in her but also a capricious stubbornness and she loved a challenge.

The winter passed and I went over the translation I'd paid for and today I haven't the faintest idea where I got the money from. Sam P. Shaw, a friend of Miranda's parents, gave us his summer home in Fairfield, Connecticut for a month. He lent us a car. The house was an eighteenth-century wooden building. In the middle of the house was a stove that heated all three stories. The floorboards weren't fixed with nails but wooden beams. Although the house had electricity and a modern kitchen, it remained more or less as it had always been. It stood in four hundred acres of woodland, streams, a small lake, no houses could be seen from the windows, the remoteness of Maine and Vermont, but there in Connecticut. Horses grazing. Deer skipping past the windows. I'd go into the village that was fifteen minutes away and buy groceries. Delilah loved the place and romped on the soft lawn. Miranda's parents and some relatives and friends came and we sat on the vast lawn like in a British movie eating and drinking and lolling in hammocks strung between trees. At night you could hear the frightening silence of the bears that weren't there. An Israeli friend came to visit me from Yale in New Haven and asked if we had a gun. It was wonderful in the vastness of nature and the damp scent of morning dew and the neighing of the horses, and after ten days I went back to New York to look for a publisher for my book. I asked who the biggest publisher around was and was told Doubleday. I went to the bar and heard from Big Charles that my stand-in was useless and they were looking forward to my return and it was nice to hear that they were waiting for me and all the drinkers were saying that if I didn't come back soon they'd move out. I asked the wannabe author where Doubleday was and he told me and I went along. I carried the translated manuscript in a small bag. In the lobby there was a secretary at a desk with some phones. I told her I'd come to see the editor-in-chief. Mr. Seldes? she asked. Yes, I replied. She asked if I had an appointment and I said no but that he would be glad to see me. On her face I saw the expression shared by every unsympathetic secretary one meets in this life and I saw too that she felt entirely in control and she said that Mr. Seldes didn't receive callers just like that, I had to make an appointment through an agent or find a way of arranging it through his personal secretary and she had to tell me that as far as she knew he would only be free for a meeting—if he would be free at all—after the Frankfurt Book Fair at the end of October. I looked at her and smiled. What are you smiling at? she asked. I told her to pick up the phone right away and tell Mr. Seldes that Yoram Kaniuk from Israel had to see him right away about a certain bit of dirty business and to tell him that I wouldn't wait long. She asked what it was all about and I told her it was better she didn't know but

Mr. Seldes certainly would and he'd be angry if she didn't inform him right away. Now she seemed helpless. Americans aren't very good at improvising. And something in my appearance scared her. I put on the look of a desperate man à la James Cagney and Humphrey Bogart movies: shifted my hat slightly forward, leaned over, and could almost feel the gun I didn't have. Since I'd anticipated something like this happening, I'd brought along the document I'd been given on my discharge from the army that said in Hebrew that in 1948 I'd served in the Fourth Battalion of the Palmach and on the reverse side I'd stuck a stamp in English I'd found at the consulate at an Independence Day party I'd stopped by for a few moments and during which I'd wandered around the building because I was so bored and wound up finding a bunch of stamps that said "Consular Service." The secretary deliberated and apparently decided that you don't question your superiors and led me to the elevator and said she'd call Mr. Seldes and that I should go up to the fourteenth floor. When the elevator doors opened again I saw lots of people working at typewriters and talking loudly into phones and at the end of the room, which was partitioned into working areas, was an elderly secretary who looked quite suspicious of me. She was sitting by a door bearing the legend, Seldes, with no Christian name. She started interrogating me and I glared at her and raised my voice.

Silence fell in the huge room; the assistant editors, the editors, the secretaries and the stenographers were all looking at me and I said, Let me see Mr. Seldes because he'll be very angry if he doesn't see me immediately. The old woman reconsidered and showed me in to see Mr. Seldes, who was sitting at the far end of his office, the walls covered with photographs, books in glass-fronted bookcases, framed book covers everywhere, photographs of authors on one high wall, and he glanced at me questioningly and asked, What exactly do you want and who are you exactly? I heard more curiosity than anger in his voice. I realized I'd hooked him in the sense of gaining his confidence in the way you sometimes trust people precisely because you have no reason to trust them, so I moved closer, introduced myself, I said I was an Israeli living in New York and I'd written a book and wanted Doubleday to publish it. He looked at me for a long time and asked, What about the dirty secrets and all that stuff you said downstairs, what was that? He was angry but also somehow intrigued by my chutzpah. For a moment he saw himself in a book that someone had brought him to read. He asked, Are you sure this isn't about information that might benefit our house? It seemed he was awaiting some kind of revelation. Then he thought a while and smiled and said, Do you mean to tell me that you've come to see me just because you've written a book? Do you know how many people write books? More people than there are authors, let me tell you. Don't you know that first you go to an agent and the agent tries to get your manuscript in to me, and then there are quite a few editors under me who read a book before it reaches my desk? I said I'd swum here from Tel Aviv. But what's this "dirty business," he asked, what's this certificate of yours? How did you manage to sucker everybody here? Then he got up and shook my hand, asked me to sit down, he seemed amazed at the sheer magnitude of my chutzpah and offered me a cigar that I declined. I explained that I had painted and I had a friend, Gandy Brodie, who'd taught me that there are no closed doors in New York; that anybody can get inside anywhere if he's daring enough in taking advantage of people's blindness. I haven't deceived anybody, I said. The certificate I showed you states that I served in the Palmach. I come here, write, pay a lot of money I don't have for a translation, I have no contacts, no agent, so how could I get to see you? If I'm the new Faulkner, who'd know about it? And Seldes, who was staring at me with growing amazement, got up and came over to me, he was shorter than me, dragged me to the middle of the room, shook my hand and said, Is that how you won the war? We sat there for two hours. Every few minutes his secretary called to say that so-and-so wanted to speak to him, and he told her to hold his calls and asked me about Israel, the Bible, the rebirth of the Hebrew language, about Eliezer Ben-Yehuda, Gandy Brodie whose colored scarf and wolfish dancing in the basement I described as picturesquely as I could, we talked about literature, art, our mothers; he said that the secret of the Jewish mother was that she understood that in life love is a fleeting thing, that's why she doesn't base her relationship with her children on love but on guilt, because guilt lasts forever. He told me about his father, Gilbert Seldes, a playwright, author, and critic who had written a book on the so-called "low" arts, like musicals, folk tales, pop, jazz, and had defended them as legitimate arts; Seldes talked about his family, said how much he wanted to visit Israel, and we concluded our meeting with me leaving him the manuscript and my number and he said, I'll tell you what everybody says, don't call us, we'll call you! But in your case, because of the guilt I'll feel and because you're such a cheeky bastard, I promise I'll call.

I went back to Fairfield, the scenery dropped on me as though it wanted to squash me. The rivers. The fields. The morning mist. The clouds that touched the treetops. The avenues of trees. The horses quietly grazing, far from the real world, and I told Miranda's family, who had come to visit for the weekend, about my meeting and they looked at me as if I'd just landed from the moon. One of the relatives hung Japanese lanterns on the trees. A grill was brought out and Miranda's father cooked hot dogs. People sang. We were drunk, but not Miranda. She sat in a chair and somebody gave her a screwdriver, which is vodka and orange juice. She emptied the glass, then looked straight ahead and fell flat on her face unconscious and slept for ten hours. Bobby, Miranda's father and I began telling stories about our military pasts and I wanted to beat him by sounding as though I'd had the harder time, even though he'd been under fire, in a sea of fire, in fact, for two years in the Far East, so I talked about our training and suddenly invented a story about how we had to do one-handed pushups. Show me, he said. It seemed that my entire reputation was on the line. I looked at him and smiled. I lay down on the ground. Face downward. And I raised myself on one hand, and despite my fears—if for no other reason than that two thousand years of Judaism were at stake, or that's what I thought, like an idiot, as if Miranda would be less mine if I didn't succeed—I succeeded. I tried it again a few months later and failed. They all sang and danced around a bonfire like Boy Scouts, like I'd done in my youth, and then we returned to the city and our apartment.

Miranda was in her fifth month. A call from Seldes. He wanted to meet with me. I went to see him. I went up to his office and this time the secretaries smiled at me. He was sitting at the far end of his office and said something positive about the book but, as we say in Israel, that it "wasn't for his school." He said it was too different, but added, I'll suggest something: Hiram Haydn, the legendary editor, and Mike Bessie, editor-in-chief at Harper and Row, and Knopf's son, are founding a new publishing house to be called Atheneum Publishers, and this book is just what they're looking for. We said good-bye. I went to Thirty-eighth Street. The place was humming with workmen putting in finishing touches. I was taken into Hiram Haydn's office. He was a tall Yankee with beautiful clear eyes and a furrowed forehead, when he spoke you could hear ancient music, he was both strong and gentle, he said he'd read my book and I left, and a few days later he called and I went back and he said they'd publish it as the fifth book on their list, and that he and his friends had all left big publishing houses to bring about change in the industry, but in his opinion the third chapter needed more work because it was missing something. Miranda and I looked for an apartment with a room for a baby girl, although Miranda didn't know the baby would be a girl, but I did. Sandy and Steve's apartment in the building next door became vacant. We rented it and furnished it and people brought us gifts. A crib. A baby bath. And all the other things we needed, even diapers. Miranda wanted us to sign up for an experiment in natural childbirth that was being conducted at the New York Hospital. In return Miranda would be able to have the baby there and not at whatever hospital my financial status would have forced her to use. I remembered how Lee's mother, so Lee had told me once, wanted to have Lee not at Bellevue but at a good hospital, and throughout her last month of pregnancy she'd walked freezing cold outside the hospital of her choice so she could give birth there because once her labor pains began they'd have to admit her. I gave Ziva Shapiro the translator the revisions I'd made and took the manuscript back to Haydn. It was okay and we talked and the book was signed on. I met Mike Bessie, the second partner, who wanted to drink a toast and said that Atheneum would be a different press, loyal to literature, and he said he was happy that my book would be among their first titles, and I went home and a few days later I got a call from Mr. Ford, Atheneum's graphic designer, who said that he'd given the manuscript to the Robert Lowell grant committee, unless it was some other grant committee, and I'd won, and that together with the advance I'd be getting the following week I'd also have a nice sum of money to continue working. To participate in the hospital experiment we had to go there with our wives, in light clothing, for three consecutive meetings. We were taken into a small hall. There were mattresses on the floor and we were fifteen husbands and fifteen wives. We were all laid out on the mattresses and a stern-faced woman inspected us, asked us to lie down and she got up onto a stool. In a commanding voice she explained that we had to learn the natural childbirth process so that we'd be able to cooperate with our wives and then the births would be natural ones. We all lay down, quite embarrassed, and in a drill sergeant's voice she ordered us to raise our legs and blow hard and breathe deeply, to strain and push the infant out and for the men to understand every shout, experience them, and we shouted, we learned to hurt, we screamed, we learned to imagine pain and try and bring the baby forward into the vagina which for women is natural but we men needed the guidance of the SS officer on the stool. We learned how to understand our wives and move together with them, we learned in which directions our legs should be pointing when pretending to be our wives struggling to give birth, and we raised our legs that were trembling more than a little and from our empty bellies expelled children, and she shouted: Harder! Push! Push! And I was overtaken by the feeling that I was indeed giving birth and during the break we all started to make friends with each other and tried to understand what exactly adults like us were doing there, but we knew we were doing it for the use of that excellent hospital and so that our wives could give birth in a nice room and we moaned as ordered, and the women filled with their real babies rehearsed and we tried to imitate them, the SS officer yelling at us: Imagine you're giving birth! And we did. She said groan—we groaned. She said push—we pushed. We'd all seen movies and so knew how to give a performance. Hardest of all was the bit about pushing the baby the rest of the way out after our waters had broken and it had left the womb. The SS officer said we were doing well and that if the experiment was a success, this new method would be used all over New York. Then one morning, September 27, 1960, I'd just come home from the restaurant, Miranda whispered to me that she thought that perhaps, but no, surely not, but then again maybe she was about to have the baby. Her case was already packed. Miranda was completely calm, but I became hysterical. I ran downstairs to stop a taxi. I didn't succeed and ran back upstairs and then remembered that I hadn't finished what I'd meant to do downstairs and I ran down again and then I realized that when I'd gone back upstairs I'd left the case there, and the next time I went back up to get it, I forgot Miranda. Miranda saw I was shaking and she took the case from me. The taxi she'd stopped was waiting downstairs. We got in and Miranda did so quite gracefully despite the pregnancy but I fell and got up and the driver helped me and Miranda was concerned about me and I explained to the driver that I was having a baby. We finally drove to the hospital, which was on the East Side. We went into the ward and the doctor, who knew us, examined Miranda and said that she was indeed having contractions but it would be a few hours before they started coming closer together and perhaps we should go for a walk. I asked him whether a taxi ride to Thirty-eighth Street was a reasonable request. He replied that being in motion in a taxi sounded good. We took a taxi to Atheneum Publishers so I could pick up the proofs of my book. I was nervous and wanted to hold the proofs in my hand but Miranda's contractions confused me. We got to Atheneum and Mike Bessie gave me the proofs and Miranda suddenly turned pale and didn't say a word and groaned quietly and Mike said, Get a taxi right now, it's close. I called a taxi. We got in and went. Suddenly the street was blocked. There were sirens. Black limousines sped by. Miranda was swaying and choking back her groans. This was the only day in the twentieth century on which the majority of the world's leaders assembled at one time at the United Nations, which was only a few blocks from the hospital. Miranda was climbing the backseat and mumbling to herself and Nehru drove by. Nasser drove by. Khrushchev, who would later take off his shoe and bang the table with it, drove by. Eisenhower drove by. Ben-Gurion drove by. The British drove by. The French. The Greeks. The Italians. And each and every one of them blocked the street and I was trying to keep Miranda together and the driver said he'd once delivered a baby in his taxi and could help, and I was trying to remember what I'd learned in the birthing course and began breathing and blowing like Miranda and thinking about pain but I had no pain and she did, and she was fighting it, climbing over the back of the seat, contorting, and the driver got us there at the last minute, her water broke, she was in pain, nurses were running and taking her away and I followed them, looking for doctors, she was taken inside, I was standing and looking at her spread legs and the blood and my head was spinning and the entire class was a blank in my mind now and a nurse led me to a bench to contemplate that SS officer and then the pain suddenly came to me, the proofs were in my hand, I glanced at the first page, the title and my name on the first page, it excited me and I felt like a monster because what was preoccupying me then was that maybe the title wasn't so good and a nurse came out and said, Congratulations, you have a daughter, and I was breathless and asked, What's she like? Beautiful? And she replied, Beautiful, and I went inside to Miranda. She was still drained but she smiled to fortify me. In the hall, I asked them to show me the baby through the big window, they did, and I went back to Miranda and her parents came and we sat with her and then the nurses asked us to leave so Miranda could rest. The three of us went into a nearby bar. We had a drink in honor of the big event. Then Miranda's father, the new grandfather, asked me what we were going to call her. I said, Chamoutal. Her mother asked if I'd consulted my wife. I said I'd told her. She asked me to repeat the name and I did: Chamoutal. They had another couple of J&Bs without water or ice and began trying to pronounce their first granddaughter's name. The new grandfather said, Jamoutal? And his wife said, No, Bobby, not Jamoutal, Camoutal. And he, Gamoutal? She tried very hard: Amoutal? I tried again: Cha-mou-tal. They said it was a lovely name, Jamoutach, and said it again, Jamoutal, they tried, their mouths open, their lips searching for the correct angle, I looked at them in despair and said, Aya.

Miranda came home. Aya was breast-fed. I went back to work at the restaurant. My book was published. The regulars together with Big Charles and the waitresses threw a party in honor of my book. Humorous speeches were made and at home Elizabeth Love came to help Miranda. She was a silent black woman who had helped Miranda's mother when Miranda was born. She belonged to the sect of Father Divine, who was a messiah whose followers had to lead lives of abstinence and live in communes they called Heavens but without partners and without alcohol and they worked hard to get their just deserts from their God. The sect came into being in the early twenties and the Father was a charismatic man who tried to get black women to stand on their own two feet. Elizabeth, who wasn't allowed to talk about her life before she became addicted to the great Father, and who therefore had to erase everything that had happened to her previously, was a gentle woman. Strict when necessary. Loyal. Serious. She knew how to work without sweating. She loved every baby she was given to raise. She looked at Aya and Aya was Miranda for her. She had diapered both of them. She stayed with us for about two weeks and then vanished once she realized that there was no further need of her.

The author Davis Grubb came into the bar. He had a girlfriend, maybe his wife, she didn't say a word, she was as quiet as a character who's erased herself from a book. Davis wore an earring because he'd survived the sinking of a submarine. Everybody who'd been saved from a submarine that sank wore an earring so they could recognize one another. Davis had written one book, *The Night of the Hunter*, which was a huge bestseller. He lived off the royalties and the film and television royalties from that one book all his life. He'd drink with me late at night. He liked quoting Mae West who among other things had made movies with the great W. C. Fields and said, "When choosing between two evils, I always like to try the one I've never tried before." And about his book he said that he'd faked the freshness of the language, minced the English, falsified life, he said that everything was shit, but when he said these things there was an expression of kindness on his face and he was a good friend and waited all his life for his second big hit, which perhaps came and perhaps didn't.

Libby, the woman who'd brought Miranda into my life, asked Miranda if we could join her for dinner at her lover's, the ambassador of India, though their relationship was still a secret. She was afraid of being there alone with the ambassador's daughter, who was her close friend, and accidentally revealing the big secret. We took Aya to Miranda's parents and drove to a magnificent apartment on Fifth Avenue. We went into a big room, on one side there was a long table laden with food and behind it waiters in white. Everybody was Indian. Most of the guests were wearing Indian dress and the women had a mark on their foreheads. Indian music was playing. Libby was happy and stuck to Miranda who was worried all the time about Aya being at her mother's. The food was colorful. Roast chicken under gold covers. Dishes in every imaginable color. Pungent aromas that mingled with delicate perfume. Water flowed into a small pond. Slender chairs and delicate paintings on the walls. I ate a tasty portion of duck covered with a layer of gold speckles, I poured myself a Dewar's whiskey and sat down by the fireplace. Next to me sat a very beautiful young Indian woman who didn't eat or drink. After some time I asked her if I could get her something to eat or drink and she said, Thank you, but not at the moment. She sat there, there was a tiny smile in her eyes when she glanced at me, and I felt uncomfortable and got up, joined Miranda and Libby who were chatting with the ambassador, who behaved like a lovesick boy, and I got another drink and went back to the fireplace and the beautiful Indian woman was still sitting there with her legs crossed beneath her fine silk sari. I again asked if I could help her and finally, after about an hour during which I saw how an Indian minister who was visiting New York came over to talk to her and other distinguished personalities sat down with her to whisper a few words I didn't hear, and Libby on her way back to the bar told me that the woman was number one at the embassy,

I sat down again and again made my offer and again she declined and I told her my name and who I was and she told me her name but not who she was and I asked why she wasn't eating and she said that today was *Erev* Yom Kippur. I clammed up. I felt uncomfortable and said, I read that if you drip a drop of alcohol onto a scorpion it immediately goes crazy and stings itself to death. She smiled and said this wasn't quite as bad as that and added in Hebrew, Atonement isn't stinging yourself to death. A hot wind blew. We had lunch at a German restaurant. We looked for somewhere to live. Steve and Sandy's apartment had been restored to them. We moved into an apartment that was noisy and then into one on York Avenue. It looked like a boat. The first room was the kitchen, and the bath was under the draining board, and behind it was a smaller room for Aya and behind that a tiny room for us and a kind of small arrowhead at the end for storage. I wanted something better. There was a house around Seventieth Street that had once been used as a home for Tammany Hall mistresses. We found an apartment on the fifth floor. There were hundreds of small apartments in the building. They were made up of individual rooms that had simply been apportioned out in groups as apartments. Every room had its own door, we had an apartment of four rooms that had been joined together but all the doors leading out had been locked so you could only get in or out by the main one. In the middle of the building there was a huge courtyard that was overlooked by all the inner windows. The floors creaked and downstairs lived an Irishman who played "If You Knew Susie like I Know Susie" on his player piano day and night and nearly drove me crazy. It didn't bother Miranda but I couldn't stand it. Miranda understood me now and knew what to expect, since over a period of three months we had lived in three apartments—and some of that time included moving, storage, unloading, and so forth—but then another apartment became free in the building on Eighty-seventh Street where Steve and Sandy lived occasionally and that's where we ended up staying until we left America.

On one of the moves from apartment to apartment I lost my phonebook. I was looking for Jerry Tallmer's number and in the corner of a page of a *TV Guide* I found a handwritten note: Boris. Funeral. November 2. 4 P.M. I don't know what made me do it and maybe I hallucinated the note, but I went to the cemetery in Brooklyn. I walked along the path and tried to let my feet lead me and I came to the two graves, the graves of Boris and Zhenya. I saw Mira facing me. She was standing and crying. She looked at me wonderingly and asked, How did you remember? I said I'd found something I'd written down as a reminder and felt a longing for them, for you, for our lives, for Marilyn, Lee, Al Brown, the city we were part of, and Mira whispered, Thank you for coming. Then she placed two wreaths on the graves and we left. We were both ten years older than we'd been when we first met. She looked good, she looked withdrawn, and for the first time I could remember, she looked restless. It was as though all the energy that had been in her like the Niagara Falls, in all her speeches, her adventures, had evaporated. She said, I miss them. Boris. Mama. It wasn't Mama's fault that Boris was a character torn from a Dostoyevsky novel. Not far from the cemetery we found a bar that was almost empty at that time of day. We ordered drinks and Mira started crying. It was strange to see her crying and I looked at her in astonishment. She stretched out her hand, touched mine, and said, Lee's turned into a monster. Calls herself Mrs. Theodore. She doesn't want anything to do with any of us. I've given up. Given up. I'm twenty-eight, I've had it with everything, I've done some terrible things. All of a sudden I'm a person with grief and a conscience, I'm going to marry an academic, a good man, he writes books, studies. He doesn't know anything about me. In fifteen years I've lived ten chapters of a life. I'm tired of adventure and a life of searching for myself and for excitement. As Emerson says, the mass of men lead lives of quiet desperation. But I'm desperate for a life like that. In the movies, in books, they tell the bitter truth: little frightened people love crooked and uninhibited heroes who shatter all conventions. I could have been a movie heroine, but I no longer want to live in that movie. I want a man like a toaster. At my side. Who'll tell me I'm beautiful even when I'm old and even if he cheats on me, but who doesn't, because I want him to have the conscience of a good petit bourgeois. And the most awful thing is that Yuri is still after me. Remember that pitiful violinist I was married to for what, two days? Three? He chased me to Spain, actually he's chased me everywhere. I despised him. In my next, quiet life I don't want to despise anyone like him. He never even forgave me for leaving the church. Mira drank some coffee and concentrated on her hand lifting the cup. I had a beer that wasn't cold enough and she fixed me with a miserable stare. It was a wound of a look, she said she'd read my book and she didn't know what to say. She said, I know where every line comes from. But listen, Yuri is threatening me. He yells at me on the phone. I don't know. Boris really was a genius of a chemist. He really did flee Russia and we really did live in Los Alamos and I remember a phone call from Stalin who asked me to call my father to the phone and he didn't only announce that he was Stalin, he sounded like Stalin, I'll never forget the sound of his voice, it was a part of my earlier childhood, I'd apparently heard it more than once, and what Lee always said was absolutely right, Boris wanted to marry me off to Stalin and he even sacrificed his brother, who I never knew, to Stalin. My uncle's name was Leonid. That's all I know. And Mira said, Avi Shoes's in the hospital. He doesn't speak. Pat vanished again and somebody said he saw her wearing a fine, tailored suit, walking down Fifty-seventh Street by the Russian Tea Room. Maybe it's true and maybe it isn't. For you New York could have been a new homeland, but you missed out on it. I thought about you when I found the Hebrew manuscripts in the convent in Spain. But I was a bitch and I sold them.

We parted without kissing, I went to the hospital, I saw Avi Shoes, the Hauser woman was sitting there and she looked at me and cried. She said, I'll wait for him, the idiot never knew how much I've loved him all these years. I went home. I had a daughter at home. But Delilah didn't like Aya. She was jealous and didn't want the baby in the house. We tried. We even went to a canine psychologist. Meanwhile, Aya was at risk. With great sorrow we put an ad in the *Village Voice*, a woman came along and I told her that the dog was wonderful but she was jealous of my daughter and I had to get rid of her; I didn't want any money, just a promise, because this dog was the sister of the son of Norman Mailer's dog—I just had one demand, that her tail must not be docked. The woman smiled, stroked Delilah and took her. Delilah cried on the way out and I looked at her lovingly but we had no choice, she had bitten Aya, had jumped into her crib and tried to stop her nursing.

One evening my friend Arthur who I hadn't seen for a long time came over with a beautiful young girl and asked us to go with them to a very special place. He said he had left and been left by several wives. I asked Big Charles to say I was taking the evening off and that Patricia should stand in for me and we drove north by the park near the Hudson above 230th Street, an area I'd never been to on my own, I'd just passed through in the car on my way somewhere else. He took us to a restaurant near Henry Hudson Parkway and there was a beautiful garden that went down to the river. After he parked the car we approached a white building with green windows and he said we had to do what we were told. We went into a waiting room that was locked from the inside and a tall young woman was sitting there wearing a purple dress, and Arthur said something to her, she checked in a big book on the table in front of her and said, Welcome. There's no talking in the restaurant. Quiet is the key word. If you can't manage it, come out and talk to me. There is only one option for each course on the menu. To call the waiter, press the red button on the silent bell in the middle of the table. Have an enjoyable evening. She pressed a button, a door opened, for a moment we were between two doors, and when the outer door closed the inner one opened and a young waiter in white indicated with a crooked finger that we should follow him. He sat us at a round table by one of the windows, smiled, and left. We sat down. There was deep silence in the restaurant. Music could be clearly heard from very far away. Almost all the tables were occupied. Nobody spoke. We were served wine and a pitcher of cold water and we looked at one another in a kind of amazement and the waiter came over carrying a small green blackboard on which he wrote with chalk: Welcome. Make your silence the most intricate conversation possible. Say in silence what you do not want to say. The first course is cream of lobster soup. The entrée is roast veal with pumpkin and cucumber purée and *pommes de terres de la maison.* Green salad with capers and Gorgonzola gratin. Courgettes stuffed

414

with dates cooked in wine and if you have any problems with this please write them on the board and I'll do what I can. He watched us and waited for a response but took care to appear that he wasn't. We wrote that everything looked fine and we thanked him. The thank you was an addendum by Miranda. The meal was served and each course was better than the last. Through the window we could see the entire length of the Washington Bridge, and the quiet was a friendly quiet, not a burden. Something in the room's precisely gauged acoustics gave the space the impression of being a vacuum. One didn't so much feel the quiet, more the absence of noise. I heard clothing rustling against chairs, the sounds of people breathing, chewing, there was a tranquility to it all, Miranda smiled and looked so beautiful, our daughter was like a wondrous toy, and Arthur smiled, he wanted to say good-bye to us without saying a word. We could feel things, the walls moving in the wind that was blowing, the chalk scratching on the small blackboards held by the waiters. In the middle of our table was a small plastic square with a red hat on top, and when I pressed it the waiter came, leaned over, and I wrote that I'd like another roll. We sat there for about two hours. The quiet wasn't oppressive. It was easy to learn how to speak without making noise. Every now and again the light changed and we didn't exactly understand where it was coming from and I thought of Vermeer and his illusive light and Hopper's gentle toying with light and we parted in silence, it was hard to talk even after we left, it was the first time I'd experienced love entirely through looks and gestures. Arthur said afterward that it was sexy, refined, and exciting. Maybe Arthur had a reason for taking me there. Perhaps he wanted to show me a form of subtle, conditional freedom that was nonviolent and strong at the same time.

A few days later I met Al Brown to say good-bye. He had been one of the first people I'd known in New York. He sat in the restaurant with me, I worked and he sat facing me, all the waitresses working that night and those who weren't came to say good-bye. Al said, If you come back sometime, for a visit or for good, which is what I expect you to do because you belong in this city, but if you go and come back after some time, you'll be a map of the city that once was. I'll be seeing the city changing every day and lose the profound sense of what it was, but you've been family here and you'll carry away a city that won't exist in your head!

We packed everything, said good-bye to all kinds of people and family, Aya was a year and two months old and we boarded the *SS Zion* and I discovered that the chief engineer was Bambi who'd worked with me years ago on board the *Pan York*. I looked at New York as it moved away. The sea remained. There was a storm that lasted five days. I was occasionally seasick and Aya's right thumb was crushed by the heavy cabin door. A doctor treated her but forbade her to walk lest she fall. Miranda and sometimes me, but mainly Miranda, carried her for five days as the ship rocked. Miranda carried her and walked the decks for at least four and a half days, hundreds of times a day, and the passengers looked on in disbelief. We reached Madeira, the sea was calm, there were flowers there and we disembarked and walked. We stopped in Gibraltar, there were apes there, we sailed on and reached Haifa after two weeks at sea. My parents came and we went to their house in Tel Aviv. They rented an apartment for us in Kiryat Sefer Street. In the evening a friend who had visited us in New York took us to Café California on Frishman Street. There were all kinds of artists and poets there, it was noisy, there was cigarette smoke, shouting, a huge table to the right, and there were people there who remembered and shouted *Shalom*, and a man I didn't know got up, smiled at me and said he was Yossl Bergner, I knew the name, he was a good painter and he asked if I was Yoram Kaniuk and I said yes and he said in Yiddish-accented English: I've read your book. In English. A very bad book. I looked at him for a long moment and understood that I'd come home.

HEBREW LITERATURE SERIES

The Hebrew Literature Series at Dalkey Archive Press makes available major works of Hebrew-language literature in English translation. Featuring exceptional authors at the forefront of Hebrew letters, the series aims to introduce the rich intellectual and aesthetic diversity of contemporary Hebrew writing and culture to English-language readers.

This series is published in collaboration with the Institute for the Translation of Hebrew Literature, at www.ithl.org.il. Thanks are also due to the Office of Cultural Affairs at the Consulate General of Israel, NY, for their support.

YORAM KANIUK was born in Tel Aviv in 1930. A novelist, painter, and journalist, Kaniuk has published more than thirty books of fiction and cultural commentary, including the novel *The Last Jew*, which appeared in English translation in 2006. A feature film based on his novel *Adam Resurrected* was released in 2009 to great critical acclaim.

ANTHONY BERRIS was born in the United Kingdom and has lived in Israel for most of his life, working as a teacher and freelance translator.

SELECTED DALKEY ARCHIVE PAPERBACKS

PETROS ABATZOGLOU, *What Does Mrs. Freeman Want?*
MICHAL AJVAZ, *The Golden Age.*
The Other City.
PIERRE ALBERT-BIROT, *Grabinoulor.*
YUZ ALESHKOVSKY, *Kangaroo.*
FELIPE ALFAU, *Chromos.*
Locos.
IVAN ÂNGELO, *The Celebration.*
The Tower of Glass.
DAVID ANTIN, *Talking.*
ANTÓNIO LOBO ANTUNES, *Knowledge of Hell.*
ALAIN ARIAS-MISSON, *Theatre of Incest.*
IFTIKHAR ARIF AND WAQAS KHWAJA, EDS., *Modern Poetry of Pakistan.*
JOHN ASHBERY AND JAMES SCHUYLER, *A Nest of Ninnies.*
HEIMRAD BÄCKER, *transcript.*
DJUNA BARNES, *Ladies Almanack.*
Ryder.
JOHN BARTH, *LETTERS.*
Sabbatical.
DONALD BARTHELME, *The King.*
Paradise.
SVETISLAV BASARA, *Chinese Letter.*
RENÉ BELLETTO, *Dying.*
MARK BINELLI, *Sacco and Vanzetti Must Die!*
ANDREI BITOV, *Pushkin House.*
ANDREJ BLATNIK, *You Do Understand.*
LOUIS PAUL BOON, *Chapel Road.*
My Little War.
Summer in Termuren.
ROGER BOYLAN, *Killoyle.*
IGNÁCIO DE LOYOLA BRANDÃO, *Anonymous Celebrity.*
The Good-Bye Angel.
Teeth under the Sun.
Zero.
BONNIE BREMSER, *Troia: Mexican Memoirs.*
CHRISTINE BROOKE-ROSE, *Amalgamemnon.*
BRIGID BROPHY, *In Transit.*
MEREDITH BROSNAN, *Mr. Dynamite.*
GERALD L. BRUNS, *Modern Poetry and the Idea of Language.*
EVGENY BUNIMOVICH AND J. KATES, EDS., *Contemporary Russian Poetry: An Anthology.*
GABRIELLE BURTON, *Heartbreak Hotel.*
MICHEL BUTOR, *Degrees.*
Mobile.
Portrait of the Artist as a Young Ape.
G. CABRERA INFANTE, *Infante's Inferno.*
Three Trapped Tigers.
JULIETA CAMPOS, *The Fear of Losing Eurydice.*
ANNE CARSON, *Eros the Bittersweet.*
ORLY CASTEL-BLOOM, *Dolly City.*
CAMILO JOSÉ CELA, *Christ versus Arizona.*
The Family of Pascual Duarte.
The Hive.
LOUIS-FERDINAND CÉLINE, *Castle to Castle.*
Conversations with Professor Y.
London Bridge.

Normance.
North.
Rigadoon.
HUGO CHARTERIS, *The Tide Is Right.*
JEROME CHARYN, *The Tar Baby.*
MARC CHOLODENKO, *Mordechai Schamz.*
JOSHUA COHEN, *Witz.*
EMILY HOLMES COLEMAN, *The Shutter of Snow.*
ROBERT COOVER, *A Night at the Movies.*
STANLEY CRAWFORD, *Log of the S.S. The Mrs Unguentine.*
Some Instructions to My Wife.
ROBERT CREELEY, *Collected Prose.*
RENÉ CREVEL, *Putting My Foot in It.*
RALPH CUSACK, *Cadenza.*
SUSAN DAITCH, *L.C.*
Storytown.
NICHOLAS DELBANCO, *The Count of Concord.*
NIGEL DENNIS, *Cards of Identity.*
PETER DIMOCK, *A Short Rhetoric for Leaving the Family.*
ARIEL DORFMAN, *Konfidenz.*
COLEMAN DOWELL, *The Houses of Children.*
Island People.
Too Much Flesh and Jabez.
ARKADII DRAGOMOSHCHENKO, *Dust.*
RIKKI DUCORNET, *The Complete Butcher's Tales.*
The Fountains of Neptune.
The Jade Cabinet.
The One Marvelous Thing.
Phosphor in Dreamland.
The Stain.
The Word "Desire."
WILLIAM EASTLAKE, *The Bamboo Bed.*
Castle Keep.
Lyric of the Circle Heart.
JEAN ECHENOZ, *Chopin's Move.*
STANLEY ELKIN, *A Bad Man.*
Boswell: A Modern Comedy.
Criers and Kibitzers, Kibitzers and Criers.
The Dick Gibson Show.
The Franchiser.
George Mills.
The Living End.
The MacGuffin.
The Magic Kingdom.
Mrs. Ted Bliss.
The Rabbi of Lud.
Van Gogh's Room at Arles.
ANNIE ERNAUX, *Cleaned Out.*
LAUREN FAIRBANKS, *Muzzle Thyself.*
Sister Carrie.
LESLIE A. FIEDLER, *Love and Death in the American Novel.*
JUAN FILLOY, *Op Oloop.*
GUSTAVE FLAUBERT, *Bouvard and Pécuchet.*
KASS FLEISHER, *Talking out of School.*
FORD MADOX FORD, *The March of Literature.*
JON FOSSE, *Aliss at the Fire.*
Melancholy.

FOR A FULL LIST OF PUBLICATIONS, VISIT:
www.dalkeyarchive.com

SELECTED DALKEY ARCHIVE PAPERBACKS

CHRISTINE SCHUTT, *Nightwork*.
GAIL SCOTT, *My Paris*.
DAMION SEARLS, *What We Were Doing
and Where We Were Going*.
JUNE AKERS SEESE,
Is This What Other Women Feel Too?
What Waiting Really Means.
BERNARD SHARE, *Inish*.
Transit.
AURELIE SHEEHAN,
Jack Kerouac Is Pregnant.
VIKTOR SHKLOVSKY, *Knight's Move*.
*A Sentimental Journey:
Memoirs 1917–1922*.
Energy of Delusion: A Book on Plot.
Literature and Cinematography.
Theory of Prose.
Third Factory.
Zoo, or Letters Not about Love.
CLAUDE SIMON, *The Invitation*.
PIERRE SINIAC, *The Collaborators*.
JOSEF ŠKVORECKÝ, *The Engineer of
Human Souls*.
GILBERT SORRENTINO,
Aberration of Starlight.
Blue Pastoral.
Crystal Vision.
*Imaginative Qualities of Actual
Things*.
Mulligan Stew.
Pack of Lies.
Red the Fiend.
The Sky Changes.
Something Said.
Splendide-Hôtel.
Steelwork.
Under the Shadow.
W. M. SPACKMAN,
The Complete Fiction.
ANDRZEJ STASIUK, *Fado*.
GERTRUDE STEIN,
Lucy Church Amiably.
The Making of Americans.
A Novel of Thank You.
LARS SVENDSEN, *A Philosophy of Evil*.
PIOTR SZEWC, *Annihilation*.
GONÇALO M. TAVARES, *Jerusalem*.
LUCIAN DAN TEODOROVICI,
Our Circus Presents . . .
STEFAN THEMERSON, *Hobson's Island*.
The Mystery of the Sardine.
Tom Harris.
JOHN TOOMEY, *Sleepwalker*.
JEAN-PHILIPPE TOUSSAINT,
The Bathroom.
Camera.
Monsieur.
Running Away.
Self-Portrait Abroad.
Television.
DUMITRU TSEPENEAG,
Hotel Europa.
The Necessary Marriage.
Pigeon Post.
Vain Art of the Fugue.
ESTHER TUSQUETS, *Stranded*.

DUBRAVKA UGRESIC,
Lend Me Your Character.
Thank You for Not Reading.
MATI UNT, *Brecht at Night*.
Diary of a Blood Donor.
Things in the Night.
ÁLVARO URIBE AND OLIVIA SEARS, EDS.,
*Best of Contemporary Mexican
Fiction*.
ELOY URROZ, *Friction*.
The Obstacles.
LUISA VALENZUELA, *He Who Searches*.
MARJA-LIISA VARTIO,
The Parson's Widow.
PAUL VERHAEGHEN, *Omega Minor*.
BORIS VIAN, *Heartsnatcher*.
LLORENÇ VILLALONGA, *The Dolls' Room*.
ORNELA VORPSI, *The Country Where No
One Ever Dies*.
AUSTRYN WAINHOUSE, *Hedyphagetica*.
PAUL WEST,
Words for a Deaf Daughter & Gala.
CURTIS WHITE,
America's Magic Mountain.
The Idea of Home.
Memories of My Father Watching TV.
*Monstrous Possibility: An Invitation
to Literary Politics*.
Requiem.
DIANE WILLIAMS, *Excitability:
Selected Stories*.
Romancer Erector.
DOUGLAS WOOLF, *Wall to Wall*.
Ya! & John-Juan.
JAY WRIGHT, *Polynomials and Pollen*.
*The Presentable Art of Reading
Absence*.
PHILIP WYLIE, *Generation of Vipers*.
MARGUERITE YOUNG,
Angel in the Forest.
Miss MacIntosh, My Darling.
REYOUNG, *Unbabbling*.
VLADO ŽABOT, *The Succubus*.
ZORAN ŽIVKOVIĆ, *Hidden Camera*.
LOUIS ZUKOFSKY, *Collected Fiction*.
SCOTT ZWIREN, *God Head*.
